BASSAM

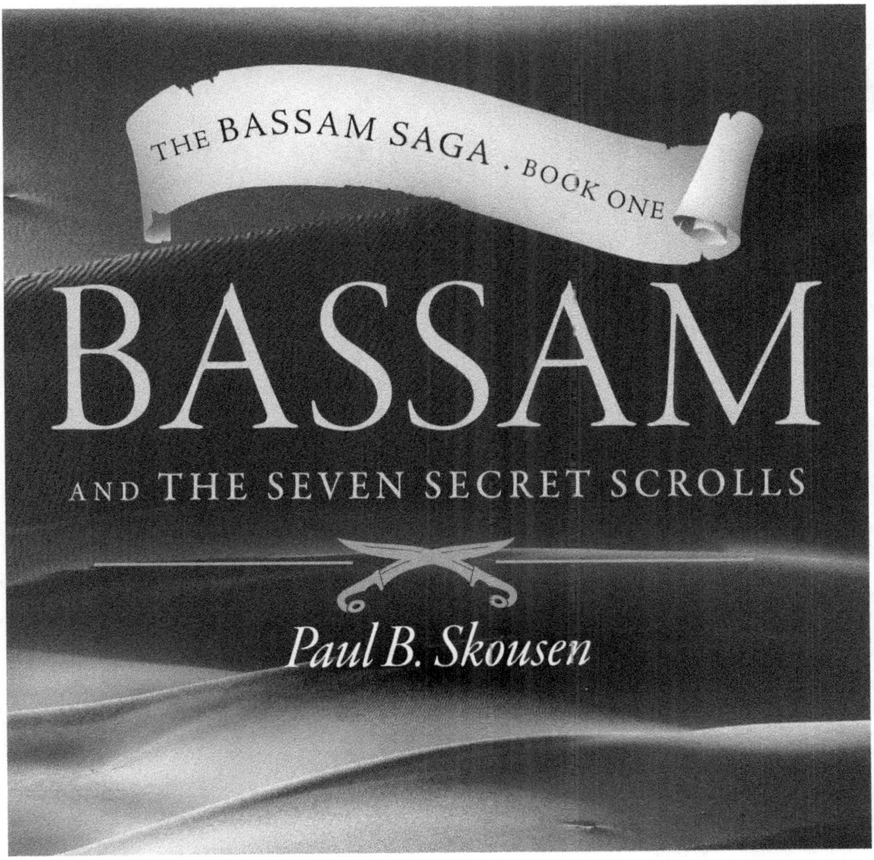

THE BASSAM SAGA . BOOK ONE

BASSAM

AND THE SEVEN SECRET SCROLLS

Paul B. Skousen

OTHER BOOKS BY PAUL B. SKOUSEN

Bassam Saga, Book II: Zafir and the Seventh Scroll

Bassam Saga, Book III: The Search for Rasha

How to Read the Constitution and the Declaration of Independence

The Naked Socialist

Comrade Paul's Socialist Bathroom Reader

Treasures from the Journal of Discourses

Contact Paul B. Skousen at info@paulskousen.com.

Published by:
Izzard Ink
PO BOX 522251
Salt Lake City, UT 84152

Bassam Saga, Book I: Bassam and the Seven Secret Scrolls, 2014
Bassam Saga, Book II: Zafir and the Seventh Scroll, 2016
Bassam Saga, Book III: The Search for Rasha, 2017

Softback ISBN: 978-1630728991
Hardback ISBN: 978-0910558815
eBook ISBN: 978-1630720568

Narrated by Mark Deakins, winner of "Best Voice of 2010," "Best Audiobook of 2010," and six "AudioFile Earphones Awards."

"BASSAM" IS PRONOUNCED "BAH-SAWM"

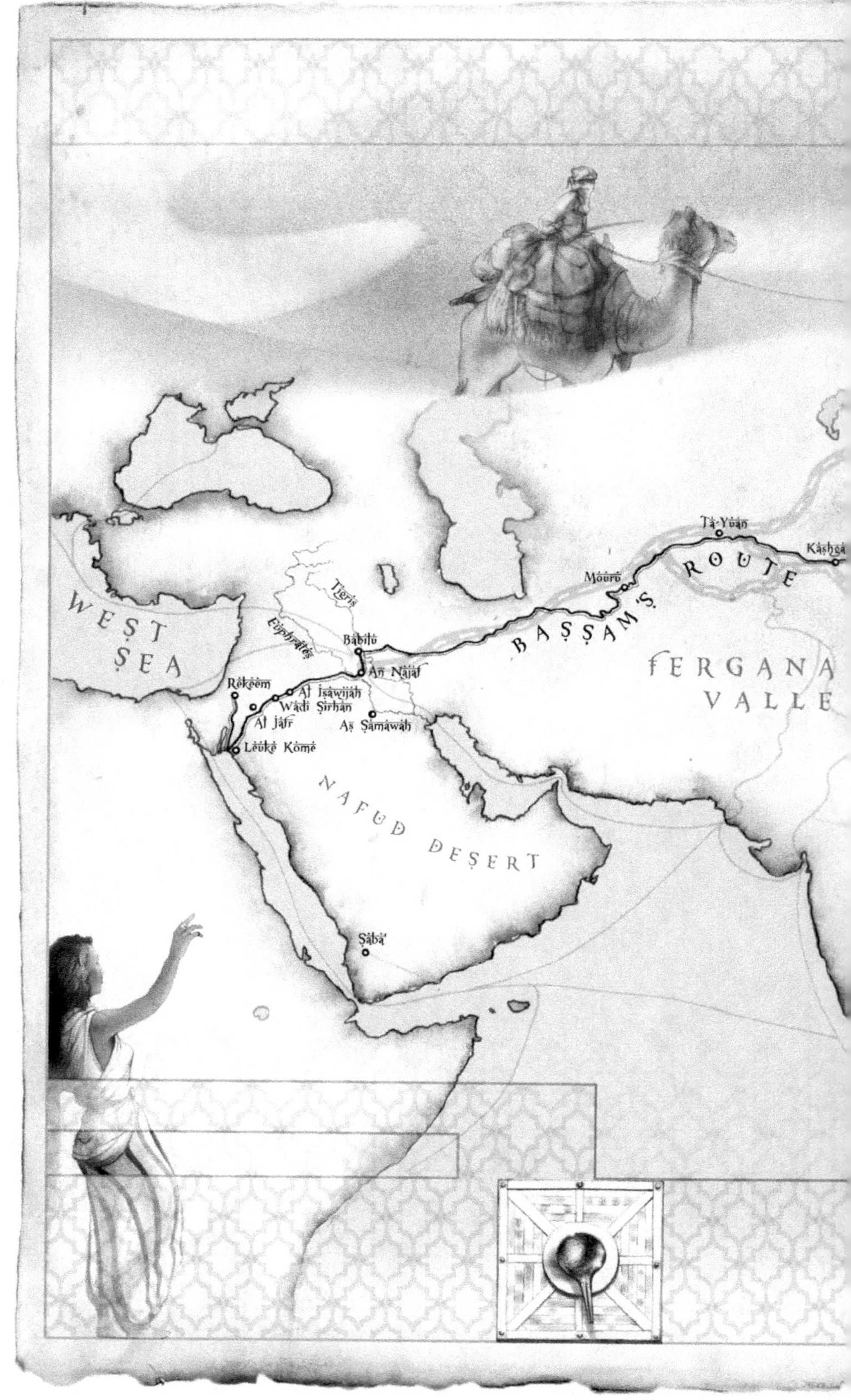

WEST SEA
Tigris
Euphrates
Babilu
An Najaf
Rekeem
Al Isawijah
Wadi Sirhan
Al Jafr
As Samawah
Leuke Kome
NAFUD DESERT
Saba'
BASSAM'S ROUTE
Mouru
Ta-Yuan
Kashga
FERGANA
VALLE

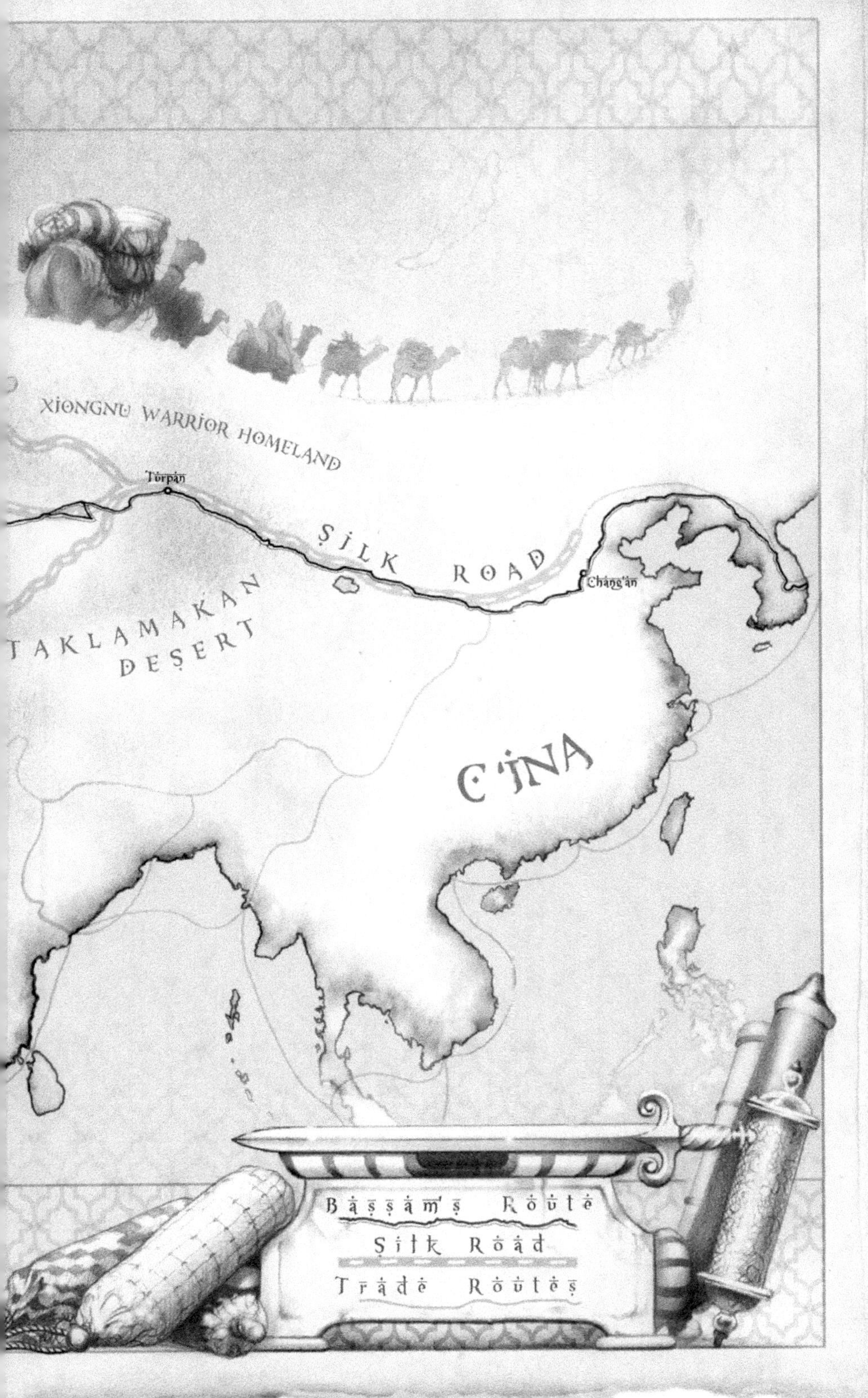
XIONGNU WARRIOR HOMELAND
Turpan
SILK ROAD
TAKLAMAKAN DESERT
Chang'an
Bassam's Route
Silk Road
Trade Routes

1

HENRI

Henri Hiram Smuilen was a puzzle—not like the usual sort of puzzling people everyone knows, but an odd combination of misfit parts, secrets, and mystery. The people who knew him well said he was a perfectly confusing conundrum.

Henri was 77, an age when most men should be dead, but his name was nowhere near the Grim Reaper's "to-do" list.

He was, in fact, quite the opposite.

Henri was vibrant, with a balding head of white hair, lively blue eyes, a wiry frame, broad shoulders, and stronger than men half his age.

Everybody knew Henri. He was that old familiar fixture around the museum that everybody came to know over the past 50 years—the old man who warmly stopped his sweeping to greet random adults, people he had first met when they were children. The marbled chamber halls of the old Museum of Natural History had witnessed his familiar shadow plying past the windows night after night as he faithfully cleaned and polished his way through that regal monument to knowledge, a permanent part of the old section of downtown since 1892.

Henri loved his job, never missed a shift, and took great pride in all the tasks given him.

The museum directors enjoyed the old man's resilience and work ethic, but oddly enough, nobody could discover much else about him.

On the one hand he was a good janitor—efficient, dependable, very particular about the smallest details. On the other hand, he carried the most enigmatic wealth of knowledge about history and antiquities than even the best of their curators could muster. From everyone's best guess it was a brilliance Henri kept tightly masked for reasons none could fathom, and he was careful never let others see it except on the most rare of occasions.

One secret already known about Henri, but rarely spoken of, had become legend among the museum staff. It was a secret he mistakenly let loose many years before. It didn't serve to answer anything about the old man. In fact, it heaped astonished mystery on top of utter admiration. Somehow, somewhere, for some reason, the old janitor knew languages. Indeed, he was surprisingly fluent in an assortment of languages. But the curiosity of it all was that these were languages without much value in the modern world—they were long past their utility for any of the scholarly literature or university classrooms. When his linguistic genius became known, most people watched behind Henri's back to scratch their heads and wonder, of what value is the old man's fluency in ancient forms of Arabic, Hindi, and Chinese? Pre-Dynastic Egyptian, Akkadian, Hittite, Sumerian, Gaulish, or extinct languages of Italy?

Henri knew, of course—but he wasn't talking.

Indeed, Henri was a curious puzzle.

Putting these facts to the side for a moment, there was something else about Henri that was disturbing. And if not disturbing, at least a source of speculation and wonder.

More than once during his decades of labor the old man was caught fixing things he shouldn't. For example, museum staffers had seen him quietly correcting a date or a name on a placard for an exhibit dating back two, three, sometimes four thousand years. Or, he was seen passing a note to a guest speaker, a message that was later reported to be a correction of an error given in some scholarly presentation on an ancient *this* or a prehistoric *that*.

Even the visiting researchers who passed through on the lecture circuit found themselves stopping the man who pushed his way around with a broad sweep-broom. They'd pull him to the side to engage him in conversation about the richer context of some ancient discovery. After a minute or two of friendly chatter they could always find a surprisingly deep well of knowledge hiding inside Henri—knowledge that lent color, understanding and context to any curiosity they might wish to discuss. They could be seen listening to him patiently—and upon returning to their homelands or universities or excavations or studies, they inevitably discovered that Henri's contribution checked out correctly, or even more amazing, helped open doors previously unseen.

Yet the old man allowed no inquiry into his personal background or fantastic depth of knowledge. To those who dared broach the informal protocol by asking about it, Henri waved them away with a smile, turned his back, and returned to sweeping.

Perhaps this natural humility and disdain for public accolade can explain the remarkable change to Henri's life that suddenly unfolded on that particular and most unforgettable night.

It was a night when inexplicable events cascaded to his favor—events that for some odd happenstance were denied others whom history might otherwise honor as more worthy or deserving.

One might say that what happened to old Henri carried all the telltale trappings of an intentional gift from forces unknown and powers unseen. As if the kindly hand of history's immortal and gentle way had come to rest upon the old man—to reward him for his profound respect for things past, things ancient, and things long lost and forgotten.

And so it happened, long after closing, when the regular staff had counted their tills, restocked the souvenir shelves, and vacated the building for home, that Henri hurried about his anxious task.

He quickly swept through the floors, locking doors, windows, security offices and supplies, and then disappeared into a darkened wing of the museum. What he had seen earlier that week had been gnawing at him for days.

Over the years Henri had seen dozens of sarcophagi come and go, put on display, or otherwise held for restoration. But never before did he see an old crypt bearing the markings of the *Combination of the Crescent.*

The *Crescent* was ancient—the culmination of art, manufacture, and numbers that were cleverly used to shelter hidden secrets—secrets stashed away in false chambers, hollow bottoms, disguised panels, or any number of tricks to hide away in the old clay coffins the worldly wealth of the deceased. Such wealth was treasure for the dead and was hidden on board to help them bargain their way across the river of death. It was their worldly fare for passage into immortality.

When this particular sarcophagus first arrived, it rested on a thick wooden pallet and was moved by a forklift to a heavy-duty wheeled cart. Henri was there when they removed the packing, and instantly recognized the patterns decorating the casket—the rare and lightly studied art of the *Crescent.*

The pattern was inscribed in ribbons of gold leaf, carved into the clay in groups of sevens—seven interlacing thorny vines, seven lions, seven diamonds, seven bunches of grapes, seven sculpted blooms, seven pointed petals, and seven curling ribbons, all of it beautifully pressed in gold.

What excited Henri about this particular find was a mistake, a flaw, an unexpected revelation brought on by time itself. Had those of the *Crescent* known of it, they might have repaired it. But time is such a fog for matters as these.

It was, simply enough, the unexpected shrinkage of clay.

Back in the day, thousands of years earlier, and shortly after the dead one's secret stash was first installed in a sarcophagus, the workmen routinely covered the openings to the little vaults with a thick clay panel held in place by moveable wooden pegs.

If they needed to open the little vault for any reason before the coffin was sealed and put in its tomb, the wooden pegs made that easy. However, the correct pegs had to be depressed in the right order for the crude combination lock to open. And what was the combination? It was hidden in the gold leaf filigree, carvings and emblems spread across the surface of the ancient casket. Without the code, nothing short of a heavy sledge hammer beating at the rock-hard clay could open the thick panel.

The workmen's final chore was to hide the little pegs with wet clay. After drying, the places were smoothed and painted over, and then marked with whatever emblem was called for by their *Combination of the Crescent.*

And that was the flaw.

As the clay cured for years, then for centuries, it shrank. The location of the secret pegs could be found by the indentations—thumb-sized dimples neatly spaced across the glossy, smooth surface. Thus were they made easy to find and easy to open.

Henri was well versed in the ways of the *Crescent* and had come prepared for the examination that night. Feeling with his hands across the surface, he found the expected dimples on the underside of the coffin. Shining his light, he saw each dimple beautifully centered beneath one of seventeen gold-leaf roses.

"Roses," he mused. "Most likely a woman resting here."

Henri seated himself on the cold cement floor and drew out a fine-pointed dental tool. With gentle strokes, he carefully peeled away the gold and scraped out the thin clay plugs. In the yellow beam of his light, there they were, as real as life—finely polished wooden pegs as new and fresh as the day they were sealed.

And then came the test. Did Henri have the correct sequence to press the right pegs in the right order?

Using the code he deciphered from the patterns of seven, he stood at the foot of the sarcophagus and reached underneath to place his fingers into the little holes and atop the pegs—four pegs touched with his left hand, three with his right—seven pegs in all, typical of the *Crescent* combinations, he observed.

With steady strength he pressed firmly—and waited. Nothing moved. Pressing again, suddenly, all of them give way and sank softly inwards beneath his touch.

Now what?

Henri held his breath, expecting something to spring out or jump or fall or somehow surprise him.

But there was nothing.

He waited a moment more. Dare he move his fingers away? Should he press the pegs again? What was going on under there?

And then he heard a hissing sound—soft—barely audible.

No, it wasn't so much a hissing—it was more like ... more like someone quietly hushing him.

And then—*what is this*?

Henri felt a slight pressure on the top of his foot. Startled, he reached for his light and splashed a beam to the floor. What he saw made his face break out in a broad smile. There, in the flicker of the light, he saw a small stream of sand pouring onto his shoe.

VOICES

It wasn't a spider bite, a nest of scorpions or the squirming spaghetti of newly hatched vipers that worried Henri the most. No, it was nothing living that he feared hiding inside that tiny, dark vault that hung open—it was the very likely possibility that inside the black emptiness he might find something very dead.

The sarcophagus was on its back, and that was the first problem. If those museum staffers had placed it only six more inches across the pallet, the panel underneath might have opened all the way. As such, it made a very tight reach, especially for a hand so strong as Henri's. Could he move the clay monolith just a little?

Standing at the foot of the coffin he wrapped his arms around, linked fingers for a strong grip, bent his knees, and heaved with all his strength to lift the end of it.

It didn't budge, not even a hair's width.

"Must be a thousand pounds," he panted. "We'll need a small crane to move this thing, *if* it will move at all!"

But that meant summoning help which was the last thing Henri wanted.

He squatted down again, shining his flashlight underneath at the panel. The black void was just too tempting. Grinding his teeth to work the problem, he decided it was now or never. Reaching with his right hand, he gingerly tested the opening, and spread his fingers in the void, feeling around blindly.

Something was in there, he could feel it with the tips of his fingers—something solid, roundish. It moved when he pushed—then fell back in place. He pulled his hand out, startled and excited at the same time. *Was that a big bone*?

"No, Henri," he said aloud, scolding again. "No curse, no trap, no spiders. Just get it."

Taking a deep breath he reached again, pushing his hand as far as he could. The object was round, curved, shaped like a cylinder. He scratched at it, rolling it closer, and finally pulled it near enough to the opening to wrap a couple of fingers around. The object was soft on the outside and it compressed slightly in his grip—it felt heavy.

Like working a temperamental puzzle, he cautiously turned it one way, then another, twice more, once more, and found that magic position that cleared the narrow opening. The object was free.

Henri's eyes widened with anticipation as he brought the object in front of him and reached for his flashlight to reveal its mystery.

Of course, he breathed. *A scroll!*

The scroll was about 14 inches long, as round as a rolling pin, and wound on a single olive-wood spindle. It was bound by an old leather covering held with three ties. It felt solid and heavy, like a short roll of quality wallpaper.

"Leather that lasts the ages!" he whispered almost breathless, turning it over in his hands to feel the softness of the covering. "It's still supple, pliable. They must have known something about leather—a way to treat it for *time*."

Laying the scroll on the floor, he propped up his flashlight. Holding the dental tool he paused to weigh his choice. *Do I dare open it here, right here?* It was an easy calculation, and the temptation being so great for just such an excavation too long delayed. *Yes!* he decided, *right here*.

Henri picked at the knots gently—one by one, until finally, they loosened.

The leather wrap limply fell open revealing the yellowed parchment of an ancient papyrus that remained neatly coiled about itself.

Feeling along carefully for the leading edge he slowly lifted back the parchment—just far enough to see if the fragile fiber paper might crumble in his hands. Gently sliding his fingers underneath, he lifted a portion that to his relief withstood the action.

It's a heavy, sturdy papyrus, highest quality, he noticed. *Maybe I can see just enough of it to ....*

Ever so slowly, Henri let the scroll unwind in his hand until about six inches were exposed, one gentle turn, just enough to see if it could open without splitting or crumbling—and most important, to look for ancient paintings or lettering.

Oh, yes! Henri's eyes sparkled as he adjusted his light. Rows of neatly penned characters—small, artistic, deliberate—opened to him, inscribed in a flat black ink as dark as pitch. He shook his head in disbelief and a smile of adventure curled across his face as he squinted more closely at the swirls and lines.

Suddenly he stopped. "Could it be? *Could it*? I think I *know* this writing!" he whispered.

Outlining the vague flowing cursive loops of the first characters stirred a memory and his heart danced with anticipation.

Reaching to his pocket, Henri pulled out his old spidery spectacles and wove them over his ears.

"An ancient text, I believe I know this text!" he gasped. "Probably early Roman—a dialect. Yes ... yes, reformed, an old one, a rare one, the southern region, Arabia, at least—some Egyptian influence, a rare form, expressed for what? A couple of centuries? Can I read it? Can I read these words?"

His lips trembled in excitement at the small characters as he moved his mouth as if practicing.

Taking a breath he allowed the first words to crowd into his mind with halting execution, until finally, he let them whisper forth through a gravelly voice that delivered an eloquence of locution as crisp as the day they were written.

They began simply enough, "My dearest Rasha ...."

REKEEM

Before the pyramids—*there was Rekeem.*

My Dearest Rasha,
As I promised, here is the record. It is for you and whomever else you might give it. If something happens to me, you know what to do. I don't know where this labor will take me. If it takes me far from you for a very long time, these words will give you comfort. Here is my treasure.—Bassam

I am Bassam.

The chronicles tell of an ancient and powerful sheik in Arabia who carved the first caves in the canyon city Rekeem. Before dying, he put there among the caves, somewhere in hiding, his secrets to wealth, to power and to prosperity, written onto seven scrolls.

For three centuries—a long time for gossip to create giants—men came looking for the secrets and found nothing but rumors—tall promises that the scrolls had escaped the caves, and went forth to serve those who held them, granting them untold powers and riches.

Thus, every camel caravan and tracer passing between the high deserts was always suspect for their good fortunes—and were watched closely with greed as hushed voices wondered aloud, "do they bear the burden of the scrolls?"

The mythical bond between the scrolls and the caves gave Rekeem a reputation of good and bad, safe and dangerous, secret and legendary. Travelers thought that the village was both a place of destiny as well as a curiosity, and so they came—to wander and to wonder.

Rekeem is my home. It is at the crossroads of the caravan trade routes on the western end of the great barren deserts of Arabia. It is a sunken city, settled at the bottom of a wind-swept canyon, a long narrow crack in the earth where tall walls of red sandstone cliffs rise above to either side, towering into the sky.

There is one entrance into the canyon—a narrow fissure in the rock at the south end. It was hidden for a thousand generations.

Until its discovery, travelers steered clear of the canyon crack for fear that in the blindness of a sandstorm or the dark of night they might stumble over the cliffs and fall to their deaths on the wash below.

When local beggars found the entrance, they marked the way and sought refuge between the safety of the stone walls. The earliest of them learned that the sandstone gave way easily to their crude tools—hammers, picks, chisels—to cut small caves into the base of the cliffs, rooms and chambers cleanly carved with patience and precision, directly into the solid rock walls. These became shelters from the hot sun and the blowing sands.

Over time, others staked claims in the canyon city, and the number of little caves grew from dozens to hundreds—large rooms that could serve many people with their belongings and beddings and material possessions, or simply as small crypts to bury their dead. The strange and haphazard growth of the settlements became a symbol of endurance in the heat of the sands, a place of repose for those who ventured near.

Thus Rekeem grew into an important way-station, attracting the trade from the King's Highway for the relative peace and calm within its sheltered embrace. It was the most important trading place for caravans on their journeys through the western desert lands.

Over time a community to serve such visitors was established. The caves became inns and dining rooms, guard houses and animal pens, storage rooms and finally, permanent homes—homes that became an inheritance and then a tradition that was passed from one generation to the next.

As decades grew into centuries, the visiting caravans knew it by memory, stopping by with wealth and business, and finally with the passage of a millennium our curious home of caves had become a permanent part of desert prosperity and lore.

The residents worked many years to improve their canyon village. They cut channels into the cliff walls to collect the infrequent rain water and guide it to their cisterns. They crafted wide stairways part way up the cliffs leading to new caverns higher up the rock. In these large, cool chambers a host of various governments of ruling chieftains and elders met to moderate the trade, manage the inhabitants, and fend off marauders.

From the eye of an artist, these caves became well-anticipated excavations attracting a great deal of attention. Cutting them was an artistic act of discovery, exposing a beauty that lay hidden in the very rock itself. Nature was the creator—painting the walls inside with murals of colored stone—sweeping, swirling rusty reds and creamy brown twists of marbled layers, rolling like great waves of sand dunes in assorted colors of a hundred hues and contrast.

The workmen were careful to grind the walls smooth and flat, letting the natural colors circle about in shapes and varieties too elegant and spontaneous to predict—beginning on one wall, spreading from corner to corner, then climbing to contorted perspectives across the ceilings, and resuming their fullest bloom down an opposite wall.

The natural murals delighted all who visited the caves, and each new chamber just started brought excitement for what dazzling colors and designs might reveal themselves as the work progressed.

After several long centuries the unusual caves melted into local legend, branding our home a place of mystery, often spoken of in hushed tones by those who traded along the routes. Nearby herders warned strangers away, but if an approach had to be made, they told travellers enter with caution because Rekeem was a city with ten-thousand eyes watching in the dark, holding secrets that strangers unannounced might come to steal.

Then one day, very much by accident—or more likely by sinister embezzlement, *it happened*—a secret escaped the sheltered confines of our city.

Truth masked as rumor escaped as a careless phrase or more likely, an unkempt communication—no one knows where such things begin—and lit upon the tongues of merchants and beggars. For a coin they swore to anyone so curious, an oath that the very scrolls themselves, the secrets from the ancients, were not lost at all! They were *at home* somewhere among the caves and shadowy cut-outs of Rekeem.

Men circulating among the market-place gossip swore upon pain of death that the scrolls had been seen—*even read*. And the words revealed the life of a mighty dynasty—a network of caravan traders that controlled all the major trade routes and commodities that exchanged across the vast distances between civilizations. The men of this dynasty, the rumors purported, drew their power *not* from swords and not from armies, nor by coercion or fear, but from the cryptic messages in these most mysterious and carefully guarded scrolls—*The Seven Scrolls of Wealth*.

THREE MEN

The secret of the Seven Scrolls promised treasure and wealth so fantastic that no man could behold it, no village could contain it, and no nation could exhaust it—and this stirred darkness in some men's hearts. To gain possession of such scrolls, there were many who would break their most sacred vow to just read them.

Thus the strangers who came to our Rekeem that night aroused suspicion for the very fact that they chose the cloak of darkness to conceal their numbers.

In the pitch of black they arrived in the canyon and circled a camping place near the heart of the village, beyond the market. There they knelt the camels tightly around their tents—like a wall—and posted a watch to ensure their peace.

My friend Faris was awakened by their arrival and watched them from a distance, mystified by their strange acts of secrecy. From this he guessed at once the visitors had to be carrying secrets—perhaps the very *scrolls* themselves.

Whether true or not did not matter. The mere possibility was news—exciting news that no boy could keep to himself. He hurried to the homes of his friends to awaken us, to come with him to see—to lie in wait and spy.

It was a moonless night when the four of us scurried barefoot through the darkened streets of the ancient city, sneaking our way toward the camping place. Racing down black narrow paths past slumbering homes, beneath clusters of tired date palms, tiptoeing over stone pavers and around pathways of compacted sand, we searched in the cool desert night for places we could hide, places along the routes where the obscurity of night could mask our ultimate goal.

We were dressed only in our night clothes, flowing in the wake of our diminutive forms sweeping through the darkened city in perfect stillness, youthful apparitions haunting every corner we could discover for refuge—behind old donkey carts, empty booths, and shuttered shops, running then dodging, stopping and listening, hushing then whispering toward the campfires in the center of town.

Our hearts beat fast—but not from the running. Rumor had spread that a caravan carrying the seven scrolls was headed toward our city—people claimed it was already laden with golden treasures—and seven scrolls that helped them find such riches. We hurried along hoping this was *that* train, and we planned to lay in the shadows to overhear, listen, or perhaps discover from a single misplaced word or the soft whispers through tent walls the mystery of the scrolls and their secret treasures.

All men suspected the keeper of the scrolls was the great trading dynasty known everywhere as Abdali-ud-din ("Awb-dolly-ew-din").

Abdali-ud-din is the largest trading dynasty in the world. They maintain secret routes, trade stations, harbors and villages, informants, spies and laborers at every village and port from Egypt to the C'ina coast. How could such wealth be accumulated by any other lest they had the secret scrolls?

As the story goes, rumor of the scrolls and Abdali-ud-din fell into the hands of the *bedawi*, a nomadic desert tribe.

The bedawi are wandering scavengers, friendly with malice toward no one. They had no place to call home and were always willing, if not desperate enough, to sell anything for the right price. They were the great gossips along the trade routes, the idle tale tellers who, for a coin, would announce truth or lies—it mattered not. For them, there was brisk business for news among the dunes and oases of the high deserts.

I have heard it with my own ears that a visitor enquiring after the secret scrolls need only stop a bedawi at his camel pen or in the market place selling his stolen chickens to ask where these scrolls were kept. For a silver coin the visitor could buy a hundred different answers.

Ask what words were written on the scrolls and for a gold coin he could buy a thousand answers.

But ask for the meaning of the words that were written, and one answer *only* was said to exist—and for that, no coin or king's ransom could pry it from the safety of its chain of passage. Since the day of their creation, the scrolls were passed from father to son, and son to grandson—and always with tests of loyalty and oaths that kept their meaning securely separate from the scrolls themselves.

Such talk of the scrolls and their treasures ignited interest of another kind—a lust among the unscrupulous who began their blood hunt, wherever it might lead. And because such wealth was worth the life of a man or of many men, and they could kill to obtain it—indeed, men *had* killed—the exorbitant labors to protect the scrolls from theft had become as clever as they were vigilant.

Thus were we spurred from our sleeping mats to slink past our slumbering parents, squeeze through windows to meet at the usual place, and go hurrying and then creeping toward the strangers.

It was our good fortune that night to happen upon a small cook-fire around which there lounged three well-dressed men, perhaps the age of our own grandfathers. They rested on blue- and golden-silk pillows spread across low-cut wicker day beds.

Beneath the black canopy of night, the flickering, yellow flames of the exhausted fire illuminated the details of the men and their successes—we couldn't believe our eyes and whispered to each other that truly, these must be kings. They wore expensive, light-colored robes hemmed with golden threads and tied with braided belts; soft-leather brown sandals laced comfortably around their feet, and headdresses hung loosely about their heads—not of the common type, but of fine fabric, richly framing their bearded faces. Their every detail showed the rugged desert wear that comes from many labors among the trade routes.

From a nearby hiding place we whispered excitedly back and forth, amazed that anyone could accumulate so much wealth that he could dress in such a princely manner—especially after the long trip to Rekeem. We decided there was only one possible answer for these extravagances—they must be carriers of the scrolls and they had found treasure!

Just then, appearing at the fireside, came two others who bore trays—servants or someone thus hired—to present the kings with large, steaming rice bowls and meat, served with a plate of fruit with bread and drink. They put the food on a squat table within reach, and the bearded men scooped into it with pieces of bread and ate as they talked. It made us swallow—we could smell it from where we hid.

The elders' conversation turned to a recent encounter with thieves in the high desert—and a sword fight that followed, and how one of them whipped his camel to death and the poor thing collapsed right beneath him, throwing him to the ground. And how his escape from the barbaric trap set before his band nearly cost him everything, including his life.

The enticing tale drew us closer. We crept directly behind a squat wall of crumbling clay bricks to listen, each of us pressing hard against it as if to draw the words to our ears through the very bricks themselves. The men's soft speech and hearty chuckles stirred magic into our curiosity.

Just then, a large shadowy figure loomed up behind us and bellowed, "SPIES! What do ye do HERE?" We jumped a fathom and turned to see towering over us a huge man in black robes with a thick black turban holding high a broad-bladed sword ready to behead all of us at once. "WHAT do ye do HERE?" he repeated.

We gasped in unison, drawing the attention of the kingly men who suddenly looked over in mild surprise. Seeing the catch they broke into smiles. It was, after all, only young boys doing what young boys do. By all appearances, we didn't look a day over 10—but *I* was 11.

"Let the boys come," the yellow-bearded man said, gesturing us to the fire. He wore a gold finger ring that flashed yellow in the glow of the flames as he motioned us.

We breathed gratitude that we were not to be scolded, or worse, and hesitantly stood, revealing our hiding places, and slowly approached the lounging men with caution.

"You, my young friends, you have come to listen, have you?" the yellow-bearded one said. "You have chosen a dangerous telling this evening, and so we must keep you, our captive spies!" The man smiled beneath his beard and the others chuckled softly. "You must tell me, you have come to listen, haven't you?"

I nodded nervously.

"Then you must hear about the treasures of gold that we have found, and our fight with bandits who came to steal it with their knives. Come, sit. Yes, come sit now, before our guard slices you for the fire! Come, sit!"

We nervously obeyed, taking a place near the fire for warmth, crouching in curious fear of these strangers and their seemingly brash ways. The three men smiled down at us, a serene expression of perfect contentedness spread warmly across their faces, as if remembering the antics of boys, of themselves, whenever they as youths had caught wind of strangers coming to visit.

These old travelers seemed comfortably glad to be in Rekeem.

"That cunning sense of his, for the ambush, is a legend in these parts," the brown-bearded man said, resuming the discussion from the interruption. He leaned over from his mat to poke the coals with a long stick, stirring a swarm of tiny sparks that danced up the curling fume.

"More than just these parts," said the black-bearded man. "Strangers trusted him from Luxor to Chang'an. I heard it so myself, all the way to the sea. That story has spread far, there is no doubt."

"Rightly so," said yellow-beard, "and that must explain the widespread respect at such an age to carry the sword."

"*The sword*?" I asked. My friends shushed me lest we be ordered away.

"Oh yes, and a great honor, too," said yellow-beard, catching my eye with his. "To be so young and trusted, why, it is unheard of. No one had carried the sword at so young an age."

"Who?" I asked.

"Oh! You wonder about this famous man, do you?" asked yellow-beard. "I will tell you, but you must first know this is a very important story from not long ago. You should know him because he brought respect and honor to all who called him friend. He was a warrior of Al Murrah, and a carrier of the sword."

"Then what *did* happen?" my friend asked.

Yellow-beard smiled. It seemed this was a story the man loved to share, and from the tired look on the faces of his friends, they knew it too—perhaps too well. They settled back on their pillows and comfortably stretched on their mats, arranging their blankets to cover their feet, apparently knowing that what followed could take some time.

"His name was Suoud ("Sue-ewd")," yellow-beard began, "a fighter for the great band of desert trackers and swordsmen called Al Murrah. The warriors of Al Murrah were the hired escorts who kept the great caravans safe during their travels. But first, before we begin—here—where are my manners! Don't crouch like that you'll cramp your legs—please, seat yourselves there," he said pointing. "There, right across from me, on the mats. And I will tell you all about Suoud."

That's when brown-beard picked up the clay jug of wine and offered us a drink. "This is a man's story, young friends," he said. "You must take it with a man's drink."

I looked down at the offering and smelled the biting fermentation wafting from its narrow mouth, and shook my head. I wasn't going to drink any of *that*. My friends just froze, not knowing what to say. Brown-beard smiled and winked over at yellow-beard, and set the jug in front of black-beard. Then he passed the fruit platter over to me. "All right then, something for boys—take all you want, you look hungry," he said. The tease was gone from his smile and kindness took its place. We took gladly.

We sat cross-legged, close to the comfort of the fire and looked into the pleasant warm face of yellow-beard and his sparkling eyes as he unfolded the story of Suoud—

THE STORY OF SUOUD

Far to the east of Rekeem a long caravan was nearing the end of a three-month trek through the great dune desert. Young Suoud rode at the front of the 300-camel train, dressed in his white riding robes and a brown headdress covering his forehead that came down to his shoulders, protection from the sun.

His boyish looks were chapped from the dry air for lack of a little goat fat smeared to protect him. But the real trial was the many hours each day atop his camel. Suoud's gangly frame squirmed with impatience at the slow lope of his beast. He regretted she was not one of the tall, slender war camels, but bore the burden of carrying trade items in large woven bags that hung to either side. And the saddle he sat upon was wrong from the start. That hard wooden curve was too narrow for his frame, covered only with a thin blanket that wasn't near thick enough for such a trek. Suoud improvised with a thick-woven rug he bought many weeks back, and since then his camel rode a little better, but not enough.

Suoud's impatience was forced upon him, having been born into life without the guiding hand of a father. He was a warrior at heart, or had always imagined it, having survived numerous flights for safety in the clutches of his mother or uncles, always fighting for a place to sleep and a morsel to eat. Joining the caravan of the revered Zafir ("zah-FEAR") was an honor rarely bestowed, but he received it in appreciation of Zafir's great wisdom and expectations. Even so, Suoud's childhood dreams sometimes caught the better of him, even on the trail, and he wondered why he was on a baggage beast and not driving a war camel as were the real warriors.

Hanging off both sides of his camel were two heavy, sagging baskets of seed, secured to a wide leather belt that wrapped under the beast's stomach, with another belt secured around the hind quarters. Suoud didn't know the kind of seeds these carried and he didn't bother to ask—only that the baskets weighed heavy and hobbled her gait.

The steady, rhythmic footfalls of his camel had long ago become hypnotic through the hush of the sand beneath them. But after these many months on the road, Suoud was at patience's end. He looked about desperately for something to ease his churning mind, an entertainment, a distraction, discussion, humming, anything to pass the time more quickly.

He tapped his riding stick on the camel's shoulder and urged her forward. Each strike stirred a small cloud of dusty smell.

"You need a vinegar bath, old girl," he said, pulling lightly on the leather rein tied to a stick through her nose.

The camel snorted, complaining as usual.

On that hot day such grunting and snorting attracted the tired curiosity from the other riders who plodded along more slowly.

"These are dangerous passes, bakra ("baw-kraw"=camel)," Suoud said whispering to his camel. He eyed with suspicion the towering sand dunes that slowly passed to either side. "This hot miserable place is not good. I think we are already somebody's broiled meal—but you should know old girl, they will eat *you* first."

His bakra snorted and shook her reins, ringing the small silver bell.

"Yes, you are right for once. We should be riding up there, up high on the dune ridges, not down in this hot pass. I don't like it."

Suoud hurried his beast to the front of the caravan and pulled alongside the lead guard, adjusting his headdress and pulling his skirts to protect his legs exposed to the burn. He intended to ride there for a while to beg stories from the warriors of Al Murrah who led the long train through those dangerous lands.

Passing slowly at a camel's pace between the white slopes of two massive dunes, the glare from the broad sweep to either side concentrated the heat directly to the road, and the temperatures suddenly grew stifling. Even the sky's own pale blue struggled to rise on waves of rippled heat. Riders drew out their light-colored cloths for a make-shift tent over their heads, holding them in place with their riding sticks. Most of the men dressed in light-colored robes in anticipation of the travel through these dunes. It prevented the glare, but the camels had to endure without.

The road to Zaranj was an ancient route, compacted by centuries of caravans that had come before. A half day's ride farther and they would arrive at the walled city before dark. It had been a long stretch, and all the men longed to rest beneath palms and drink the cool spring water that awaited them there.

Suoud took a deep breath and turned his view to the tops of the sandy heights, tracing with his eye their rounded ridges that cut against the sky with a distinct brown line.

"The trap these slopes make for those on this road leaves few options," he said aloud. "Between you and me, bakra, I don't like this—it feels too much like a trap in the making." His bakra growled.

Suoud had been feeling uneasy all morning, a sense that something was wrong, unsettled, but maybe it was just his imagination. He put his hand to the hilt of the sword that was tucked under his saddle, and turned his head to see if others were at all bothered by their trespass through the giant dunes.

Then he caught sight of a slight distraction of movement far in front of them where he knew that movement should not be.

Far to the distant left, two thousand paces beyond at the top of the largest dune, stood three small specks against the white of the sand. He gave them little attention at first. But then one of them moved, stirring impatiently, showing a side view and turned again.

What were horsemen doing perched so high, Suoud wondered, and here, in the middle of nowhere? Parting his headdress for a clearer view, he saw one of them raise an arm and a brief flash of midday sun betrayed a sword held high. Suoud wondered at the sign—could it be a greeting, a signal, or perhaps a command? Regardless, it wasn't gestured toward him so he just watched.

A moment later a dozen more specks rose up from their hiding places behind the dune and appeared along the ridge, standing atop, almost invisible against the faded sky.

The gathering specks of movement suddenly made sense and Suoud's worst fears came to life. "Bandits!" he shouted.

A CARVING

The story paused and brown-beard stood to stretch his back and retrieve another bundle of sticks for the fire. I was impatient and couldn't stand the suspense. "So what happened?" I asked yellow-beard. "Did they make it to Zaranj? Is this where Suoud earned the sword?"

"No, not yet," yellow-beard said.

"Who decides it," asked my friend, "about the sword?"

Yellow-beard scratched at his chin and smiled with his eyes. "You ask a good question that is not easily answered, my young friends. You first must know about the man who brought him on this long trek, to be a defender of the caravan."

"What man?" I wondered aloud.

"His name was Zafir. Have you heard of him?"

Zafir! *Of course* I had heard of him, I had met him, I was friends with his family, I grew up with them!

"Oh yes!" my friend blurted out before I could say a word. "His image is carved in the wall of the Siq, we pass by it all the time!"

"Oh no!" laughed yellow-beard, his eyes suddenly wide in surprise and looking over to his friends with a worried grin. "That is not a carving of Zafir! Oh no!"

I saw the other old beards draw the hem of their headdresses to hide their laughter but could not quiet themselves well enough for us to hear. *What was so funny,* I wondered. Yellow-beard glared at his friends a moment and then clearing his throat he turned back again to us.

"No, you must hear the real story of that carving. It is not of Zafir, but it is *because of* Zafir and his many kindnesses that the image is there. It is precious to us for reasons I will tell you."

I sat there astonished. Here I was knowing Zafir as a great friend of my parents, and here was a total stranger speaking about him as if Zafir was a great chieftain or legend. I was tempted to raise my hand and declare my friendship but decided to keep it for the time being, to hear what else Yellow-beard might say about my father's friend.

As the new load of sticks caught fire and the circle of warmth enlarged, we rearranged our seating for the continuation of the story. Every eye was bright and focused with curiosity for what Yellow-beard planned to say next—about Suoud and the sword.

ب هبعه 7 محبوب

SUOUD'S STORY

Seeing the bandits amassing atop the ridges of the great dunes, Suoud turned in his saddle and shouted an alarm, pointing. Others looked in surprise and quickly shouted back their warnings to the 300 riders that followed.

Then, as if by that very signal, there appeared more specks standing up across the tops of the great dunes, followed by others, then dozens, tens of dozens, more of them, many hundreds rising up from hiding places to line up all along the tops, packed shoulder to shoulder, side to side, a vast army spread out impatiently along the full length of the ridges, pushing against each other like the undulations of a living black rope that stretched for a thousand paces.

Before Suoud could even take a breath to shout, the distant riders thrust their swords skyward and let out a great roar that rolled down the broad sandy slopes to shake the very ground beneath the caravan.

The shout startled our long line of labor, and the camels snorted in reaction.

When a second great shout rumbled down from the dune tops, the menacing mass of anger suddenly began their descent, pouring down the sandy slopes in numbers too large to estimate. The vast army was like brown mud flowing toward Suoud and the caravan, each bandit braking his descent through loose sands that dusted the sky with their numbers. Solid ground met the riders at the base of the dunes where they quickly grouped.

Gathering strength for a full-on assault, the lead warriors in their dark brown robes and black turbans waved their swords and galloped directly toward us, crossing the vast desert flat in a growing cloud of yellow dust with hundreds more falling in behind. They shouted threats and bristled their weapons in a flurry of fanaticism.

The warriors of Al Murrah quickly assembled and broke ranks, charging past Suoud with a great shout, swords drawn, rising up as one to engage the attackers.

Suoud refused to be left behind and reached back with his knife to free his camel of her burden—the leather strap cut easily and the baskets fell to the ground with a heavy thud. He whipped his bakra to speed, pulling his sword from its sheath, and shouted his own oath into the deafening roar of the thundering hooves.

A great plume of dust quickly rose from the onrushing hordes that choked and blinded the charge on both sides. Their pursuits did not slow as the war camels spread out across the desert in a smoking cloud of sandy rage, with men shouting their mortal intents toward the swift-footed attackers.

Some thousand paces away in a level plain between the massive dunes, the camels and horses collided with a loud clash of clanging swords, shouting men and the screaming wounded as blood quickly ran hot on every side.

Suoud caught up without stopping, galloping full force into the fray, swinging his sword to either side—finding an arm, a leg, a shoulder, clashing sword to sword, and blood to blood. Horses and riders fell, camels threw their defenders to the ground, and the dusty melee ignited in desperate hand to hand.

Suoud gritted his teeth and swept his sword at foreign flesh that came upon him almost faster than he could meet it and was pushed back as men and animals collapsed under the onslaught of cruel knives. The spilled human life quickly mired the hooves and the footed men who frantically fought their way through the chaos of crimson carnage.

The horsemen had the advantage, swifter on the hoof, more maneuverable to out-flank the war camels to deliver the sword more directly. But these were gradually pressed back to a position of collapsing retreat by the superior swords of Al Murrah—their longer, heavier swords were unstoppable in a swipe or lunge. Under such heavy blows the lesser skilled bandits fell by the dozens and then more, and the flow of their blood and flesh quickly soaked red into the desert sands.

Suoud drove his camel after a fleeing swordsman only to have his bakra suddenly cut out from beneath him, throwing him off his saddle headlong into the ground, knocking his breath away. He came to with his head throbbing amidst shouting and screaming of the fighters. Lying there a moment he recovered enough to find his sword just beyond and gathered his feet beneath him.

At the very moment he stood, another horseman emerged from the dust and galloped hard directly at him, the rider grinning behind wild eyes and leaning out over his saddle to swing at Suoud's head. But Suoud met the attacker with a hard sweep of his sword, ducking at the right time, and took the man's forearm still clutching his sword, knocking the rider from his saddle. Suoud finished him quickly.

Challenging the attackers on foot, Suoud joined the hand-to-hand that crackled and clanged in a high pitched fever. The warriors of Al Murrah delivered their specialized skills, but the bandits' vast numbers pressed them to their limits. The horror of the vicious standoff stalemated for many long minutes until those of great numbers began to succumb to those better trained and equipped.

The bandits started backing off, splintering away into pockets, daring to corner Al Murrah's own, but paid for it quickly as others converged with flashing steel and skilled practice. For the better part of a quarter hour, such work of death burned fiercely—swinging swords and thrusting knives, bandits leaping from horseback to pull Al Murrah from his camel. Despite pushing and shoving, ducking and running, with new blood and flesh littering the desert with each passing heartbeat, bodies began to amass, too many in some quarters, stifling the movement of battle. As the fray passed to another quarter, the bodies of the hewn glistened red in the hot desert sun, silent proof of their misguided demise.

It came at last that the exhausted enemy finally admitted by their retreat they had fought beyond their strength. They began a chaotic and frayed escape, whipping their horses into a desperate sprint toward the sandy canyon passes in the direction from whence they had come. Al Murrah warriors who were still mounted broke free after them, galloping in hot pursuit. They gained on some but fell behind to the speed of the swifter horses.

When the last of their numbers retreated into a mask of distant dust, the pursuers returned to the battle ground where they joined those on foot to finish the grisly work. And work it was because the unwritten law of the desert demanded that in such warfare there could be no prisoners.

As the last of the shouting ended and the battle scene became eerily silent, Suoud stood a moment to catch his breath.

Scanning the slaughter field for alien movements, he cleaned his sword and sheathed it, noticing suddenly the ache of fatigue spreading to his muscles. He wiped his brow and cast his gaze at the wickedness that lay strewn over a large area where the brunt of unbridled anger was so heavily spent. Wounded animals struggled to stand amidst the crushed and slain. Lying among the carnage, many of the fallen were calling for help—others for mercy.

Walking to the edge of the battlefield, Suoud found an abandoned saddle and sat atop it to attend his wounds. A deep gash across the blade of his back required treatment—perhaps binding it up. Other wounds less severe burned with pain but the bleeding had stopped already. He reached to his head and gently felt about for the big knot from his bump on the ground—it was tender and bleeding, a sure sign he'd suffer because of it for days to come.

Hawks circling the sky numbered a few, but that hungry host of scavengers would soon grow to a horde when the lusty smell of recent death called to them on the desert breeze. In a week, nothing but the picked bones of the dead would remain to testify of the failed assault that took place here.

These were Suoud's first tokens of battle.

But wounds and scars were not his greatest concern at the moment. Young Suoud licked his parched lips and felt the stinging splits that had cracked open in the dryness of the desert heat. His throat burned for water, and the sands already began to cake over where spilled life once pooled. He watched his associates pick through the litter of the fight to corral their loose camels, and that became his new concern—where was she? The palm trees and fresh-water spring of Zaranj was still half a day away—he could not make such a journey on foot.

Raising his hand to shade his eyes, Suoud squinted into the distance. "Bakra?" he called hoarsely. "Bakra? Where did you go, girl?"

بهجه 8 محبوب

AL KHAZNA

I was young and impatient, anxious at the suspense. "Did he get away?" I interrupted. "Was Suoud all right?" I asked. "Is this when he won the sword?"

Yellow-beard smiled. "Suoud found his bakra, yes, he found her safe and sound. She had fled to a herd of other lost camels not far away. And they made it to the city, but they lost several of their men in the fighting. The *Battle of Zaranj* certainly proved the integrity of Suoud's loyalty and stamina, but no—the honor of the sword was his not yet."

"Then tell us the rest," my friend said.

Yellow-beard smiled. "For the next part of our story, we begin with Rekeem. Do you know the great library at the head of our city?"

"Library?" asked my friend.

"Donkey Brain!" chided my other friend. "Have you never heard of Al Khazna?"

"The treasury?" the first asked, puzzled.

"*Treasury*? Ha! Don't you know anything?" the friend scolded.

Yellow beard put up his hand to calm. "It is all right," he said. "I will tell it briefly because for a long time there was but one entrance into this canyon—this walled-in place we call our city. The old entrance is that narrow winding path, you know it well, or one day will. It is a crack in the towering rocky cliffs, at the very bottom many cubits deep to the sand, a cavernous split in the rock, grown over by leaning sandstone, almost shaded by day, and cool in the heat. A passerby walks its very bottom, seeing glimpses of sky at certain turns, otherwise in constant shadow. The path snakes its way into our canyon city at the south end, carved by nature and by chance," he said, pointing into the night. "These cliffs that surround our village stand apart these hundreds of cubits, moved by the same forces to give room enough to move about and create a city—but the entrance, it is almost a tunnel, leaving no other way in or out of this place except by rope. There is no rope strong enough to hold a man from the top of these cliffs, it is too far."

A rope, I thought to myself. *Could someone really descend such cliffs with just a rope?*

"No one knew about the deep cleft for a long time," yellow-beard said. "It is legend that young boys—probably about your same age—went chasing after their goats and followed them into a passageway that opens

"No one really knows the beginning of Al Khazna," Yellowbeard said. "It is the first sight that visitors see as they step out of the Siq and into the full sunshine of our canyon city. The great Al Khazna is very old, carved from the very cliff itself.

some distance to the east of our city, not too far beyond the small dunes. If you haven't traveled it, you will one day. Most everyone travels it all the time—they must.

"But these boys chasing their goats into the hidden cleft discovered that the passageway was an easy descent into our canyon city, surrounded by cliffs, and always in shadow. Even at mid-day the sun refuses her warmth. But the boys could hear the bleating of their herd, and gave chase until they grew weary and had to walk.

"After a long while calling and skipping rocks to scare the goats from the shadows, they noticed the gorge growing lighter ahead. They started running again and came upon the very cleft I told you about, a tall, slender crack leading into this very canyon.

"At the opening the boys found it wide enough for three camels abreast, and 20 cubits high. When they stumbled into the sun-lit plaza they found themselves standing on soft sands blown down from the cliffs above, therefore its name, the *plaza*.

"And there stood their goats, across to the far side some 40 paces away, chewing grasses in the shade at the base of the great red rock walls.

"When the boys brought their fathers to see what they had found, these men named their newly-discovered passageway a word in Badawi that means 'shaft,' and that's why today we call it the Siq ("seek")."

Yellow-beard paused to pluck a meat from the platter and chewed, staring blankly into the fire with a slight smile as if suddenly living in a far distant time and place.

I was curious. A lot of building and cave carving stood in our city, and I wanted to know their beginnings. "What about Al Khazna?" I asked.

"Al Khazna came many centuries later. Yes, Al Khazna is the great library that stands right across the plaza from the Siq. Some say the goats were prophets, marking the place by clearing the grass where one day artisans and masons could chisel this great monument right from the cliff itself! No one really knows the beginning of Al Khazna, but it is the first sight that visitors see as they step out of the Siq and into the full sunshine of our canyon city. It is the first monument of many. The great Al Khazna is very old, a work of magnificence that stands a hundred cubits high. The builders set it back beneath the overhang of the cliff so the rains couldn't turn it into another ruin. The six pillars are fifty cubits high and each of them as wide as a man is tall."

"And what about that big stone urn on the top?" I asked. "Does it hold gold?"

Yellow-beard laughed. "I thought the same when I was a boy. I think most boys do." He smiled again. "No, the urn is solid rock, carved there to impress the caravans when they arrive. I climbed it, long ago, I know what it is, just a giant piece of rock carved from the cliff. It makes the caravans greedy to bargain. But you are right—because of that urn some see Al Khazna as our great treasury. That it is, but they built it first as a library, to show we are not pirates or vagabonds, but learned people, knowledgeable after the manner of the builders of Luxor and the scholars of Alexandria and the Greeks."

His words stirred a challenge inside of me. I decided right then that one day I will scale the cliff and see that stone box for myself.

"But no treasure?" I asked again.

"No treasure. Maybe one day your mothers will let me take you between the pillars and into the chambers and show you the ancient scrolls and tablets. Some of them are as old as the city."

We all fell silent, our imaginations alive with possibility.

"Most of you probably live in a cave-home, right?"

We nodded.

"This is what makes Rekeem so different than other villages. These sheer red cliffs made ideal shelters for the first settlers. They cut hundreds of small caves into the walls—some long, some deep, others tall, of all sizes. And that is why we have few houses in the plain of Rekeem, only the many shops and diners. They are hard to build and very hot in the sun. Our cutout homes have cool in the summer, warmth in the colder season, doesn't yours?"

We nodded, not realizing that our strange city was a destination of wonder to travelers from afar, a curious wonder because of our desert and rock world.

"It is really important," yellow-beard continued, "that you also know about the scribe who stands at the head of our story. There must always be a scribe to count the trade as it enters our city. He sits at the same place on the steps of Al Khazna, atop an old pillow to cushion the hours. From his station he watches the caravans come out of the Siq, turn right onto the sloping boulevard toward the center of Rekeem."

"I'd hate that job," my friend said.

"Me too," said another. "Just watching? And nothing to do?"

What my friends didn't realize was that *I had done* that kind of work. *I had apprenticed* with my father. He was Rekeem's senior scribe. I knew exactly what yellow-beard was talking about, but I kept my quiet.

"Scribe is an important work, but not for everyone," yellow-beard said. "If you go looking—and maybe I will show you myself—if you go looking along the steps of Al Khazna, you will find at the base of the second great pillar a smooth, worn place about the size of a stool cushion, a slight depression in the stone. It was worn into that hard rock by the faithfulness of our scribes who always sit there in that very same spot, year after year, to count the caravans."

As the fire dimmed, yellow-beard's stories and answers poured from his mouth with tantalizing precision and intrigue. The adventures, the brush with death, the far-away lands, the strange people, the labors on the trail, the exploration, the power of the sword, the *honor* of the sword—it put a fire in me that kept me awake all that night, and as it turned out, for years afterwards, *imagining*.

I often reflect back to that spell-binding cook-fire with my boyhood friends, that amazing telling of tales, and how that old traveler gave unexpected direction to my passions and plans. The flames of the fire burned long after the coals went cold and the old men had disappeared from my life. Yellow-beard had mentored me that night, knowing it or not, and in the quiet of my heart I began mapping during my idle times the places and preparations for such treks as he had told that night.

And then came my 13th year, and then 14th. Father gave me permission for short treks in the accompany of older friends, to experience caravan travel for a day or two beyond our canyon city. Father wanted my skills tested with events to challenge my endurance. As I grew taller and out of my clothes, much to mother's humored frustration, I grew braver. I began talking about longer caravan rides, to Egypt and Greece, to the southern coasts, to the far east. I could see these places in my mind's eye—I could smell and taste them having never known their wares. I was restless.

Then, coming into my 16th year, I was nearly a man—and just as tall. That was the year everything was nicely coming together in my life. I knew my past, my present, and my future. But then, quite suddenly, I was caught completely by surprise. It was a girl.

BASSAM

با هبعه 9 محبوب

KATEB

No one paid much attention to my father, and he preferred it that way. He dutifully performed his labors, and was careful with the integrity of his calling. Most people called him "old Kateb," a permanent fixture in Rekeem whom everybody knew. They said he was like a big rock in the road—not making a lot of noise, but certainly in everybody's way. He was always there at meetings or gatherings, faithfully, to merchandize or welcome the caravans when they arrived to greet and count their goods.

One day, an important day, I was supposed to help him do an accounting of a newly arrived caravan. But I was late.

The sun was high, almost midday, when Kateb hurried to his usual place. He wore that same faded, brown robe—frayed and worn—barely hanging by a few threads from his shoulders. His whole appearance made him very much the part of village scribe, and for most, an odd but local celebrity.

He brought his favorite walking stick that day, working it to keep away the dogs or a goat in his path. He gripped it with gnarled fingers that refused to be idle in the heat of the day.

Kateb's beard had long turned white, and he combed it smooth for special occasions, a perfectly shaped bushy tail for his slender leathered face now wrinkled with time.

His prominent, gnarled nose and silvery eyebrows became animated each time he brightened his brow in smile. Soft brown eyes conveyed the pain of patient experience through some of life's most difficult trials. It was the way he held his head that impressed others, showing his refusal to let life or the years get the better of him.

Kateb's sandals stirred a small cloud of dust as he hurried through the market toward his usual place on the smooth sandstone steps of the majestic Al Khazna. The only shade for that time of day was beneath the monument's towering pillars, and the old scribe climbed the steps to find his familiar spot in the shadows.

Sitting cross-legged on an old pillow, he had trouble catching his breath. The years were piling up for him. "I am too old for such bother," he always mumbled. "Where is my young apprentice? I am too spent for such routines...."

Not to delay, he sprinkled water on his clay, kneading it smooth and pressed it to his writing board. With his sharpened scrawl he neatly inscribed *sita*, the sixth day of *Rajab*, before noon. It was the hottest time of year.

My father had great instincts about the coming of the caravans, he knew before anyone else that another was already working its way through the Siq. He could smell it long before he could hear it.

The customary breeze at that time of day always washed through the Siq's snaking passages telling of the traffic that descended it. On this day the breeze revealed the heavy earthy odors of many sweating, hot animals, long on the trail.

Kateb's long years at his post made him an expert at foretelling the loads that such caravans carried.

He could discern from the breeze as clearly as one might feel the carvings on the wall that this was the caravan of an old friend. Drifting above the tired smells of camel and goats, he could sense the tell-tale traces of oiled perfumes, the heavy aroma of seethed myrrh and incense, the pungent sweet of pippali, ginger and cassia.

Such loads were brought by none other than the merchants of the mighty Abdali-ud-din returning from the east with their burdens of spice, incense, jade and gems. Abdali-ud-din had roots in Rekeem, and was always welcomed this time of year, and this return visit would be celebrated. Father told me he could know by simply looking into the sky if it was to be a busy day of accounting. To the east, hungry hawks circling through the bright blue told of scavenging that was already underway, a sure sign this was indeed a train of some size, perhaps 300 camels he guessed. A God-blessed day this was, indeed, an omen of good fortune for the merchants of Rekeem.

The Sheiks who reckoned from father's clay tablets could be both generous toward his services, and harshly vindictive for the least oversight. The record he made had to be true lest the transcribers refuse it for deposit within the dark library chambers of Al Khazna.

The great caravans descended slowly through the Siq due to the walls crowding so close that hardly two camels could ride abreast without pushing. Besides serving as the main passage into Rekeem, this twisting, narrow passage also brought water from Wadi Masu, and emptied the runoff through cut channels leading to cisterns in the middle of town.

As such, many traders stepping into the shade of the Siq oftentimes stopped to chant and sing their load-bearers to drink at a trough or find cud on some greens, thus blocking the descent of traffic. It could take a whole day to funnel a caravan of any significance through the passageway before the last of them could emerge from the shadowed entrance and file past Kateb's observation perch.

For my father, the lesson was long ago learned that the duty of scribe must always include the duty of patience.

Kateb enjoyed the life such visits injected into our canyon city. He knew it wouldn't be long before a hundred, and perhaps a hundred more of the wealthier travelers arrived to mix revelry and eating with business and negotiation.

Although Abdali-ud-din sent the largest caravans through Rekeem, others also came every few weeks, and with such desert trade there came many men hungry for a respite from the monotony of the slow crawl across vast sandy wastelands.

Our merchants of Rekeem were well rehearsed to the chores of arrival, and, as Kateb waited for the first of the camels to appear, farther down the boulevard the merchants were already a bustle of activity. They prepared at their booths, stoking their cook-fires for meat and rice, and dressing their tables with platters of fruit, dates, dried figs, almonds, balls of jamiid cheeses, clay pots of fresh water, reed-woven skeps heaped with vegetables, and fodder standing ready as offerings to the welcomed guests.

By noon, Kateb's patience paid off as the noise of distant jangling bells and the snorting, growling complaints of load-laden camels echoed from the Siq's shaded mouth.

As these lead camels appeared to make their grand entrance, their clopping, plodding footfalls suddenly muffled in the sand of the plaza, Rekeem's large welcome mat. It greeted visitors with an imposing view of the splendid majesty of the towering pillars of Al Khazna, and turned them toward many carved masterpieces including a massive amphitheater, a cathedral, a chamber for singing, and tombs for many of the royalty since passed.

Kateb told me that if a caravan's lead camels bore loads and great bundles of commodity, it meant there would be peace—peace because these were offerings to the generosity of the Sheiks of Rekeem. Full loads were tokens of trust that the long trek had paid well, that they came in benign fellowship, and gave assurance that the caravan was a success.

But if the lead camels were sword-bearing warriors with no trade to show, he warned me to be on my guard because that was the tell-tale sign it was a train of little success and a source of caution that such men could be looking to take rather than trade.

Kateb watched carefully that day as the first group made its exit from the Siq. Several camels emerged from the shadowed opening riding along as a group, and turned onto the grand avenue leading them into the heart of Rekeem.

Kateb smiled beneath his beard, and was glad to begin the accounting by scratching into the tablet a tally of seven ragged grey camels bearing loads, three riders, three walkers and four goats by rope. Immediately after came 21 sword bearers on war camels. Why the armed guard for cargo carriers, he wondered?

But then he noticed something unsettling with this first group. The cargo camels were not walking normally as camels do. Instead, they struggled in a belabored sashay as if under a difficult load. Camels don't normally walk like that, unless .... And then his experienced eye spotted the problem, if a problem one should call it.

Hung over the shoulders of these first camels were several black leather sacks, partly draped with the dusty shawls of the traveler, and slung with such strain that the animals struggled.

These burdens could not be seed or spice, nor the satchels of clay pots used to guard the precious frankincense or spices so typical of the Abdali-ud-din.

Something was different, wonderfully different. He smiled knowingly beneath his white beard as if a secret had accidentally revealed itself only to him.

Sprinkling water on his clay, he took his stylus in hand and noted in neat, careful etchings the fact that spices did not lead the Abdali-ud-din, nor did seeds or brass goods. There must be, he estimated, perhaps five maybe six talents of gold on each camel accompanying the lead party. The Abdali-ud-din had brought treasure.

ب هيعه 10 محبوب

ZAFIR

Rekeem at sunset is beautiful. As Kateb waited, the afternoon drifted away and the sinking sun cast long shadows that crept across the valley floor almost as quickly as the last ragged remains staggered into the plaza.

Kateb's tally had filled a third tablet and stood at 338 camels, 134 goats, 210 sheep, 204 riders, and 89 walkers. Their loads appeared to mimic those of past trips, except of course, for the treasure. The noise from the Siq, the controlled confusion and raucous crowding of the large train finally quieted down in the shortened light, a sure sign that the last of the camels must soon make their entrance.

Kateb stole a glance down the dusty boulevard that opened toward the canyon floor. He could see the excitement unfolding—the gatherings of newcomers intermingling among the merchantmen to share food, drink, money and stories. Many adventures would unwind over dozens of sleepy fires tonight, told in great detail and exaggeration, and the curious youth like me planned to escape their mothers to spy around the fire to hear of such tales. The sheiks and merchantmen would dip dark pita bread into the meat and rice, and speak of such things that make young eyes sparkle.

As the sun disappeared behind the ridge, the slender columns of smoke from small cook-fires mingled with the dust of animal traffic, turning from a haze of brown to one of misty grey. Kateb could see the camels kneeling within range of the tents of their masters while the goats and sheep were herded to pasture lands beyond. The bustle of the evening's excitement began to settle into a peaceful din of contented discussion, occasional laughter, hushed by the lilting sigh of a distant shepherd's flute.

And then came the long-anticipated entrance of the honored elders of Abdali-ud-din. Twenty-two large, well-mounted dromedaries proudly stepping single file from the mouth of the Siq, each led by several men on foot. The escorts guided the distinguished visitors down the boulevard to the activities beyond.

Kateb looked for familiar faces, and for a moment was worried until he spotted the distinct form of his dear friend who was lead camel among the elders—yes, there he was as big as life—the wise and revered Zafir heading the pageant. Even in the fading light he could see Zafir's white headdress parted in the evening breeze showing the face of a long-traveled merchant wonderfully sun-baked and fit considering a journey that had lasted longer than a year.

Zafir rode carefully with the deliberate majesty of an elder chieftain. He wore elegant white robes and was seated upon an elaborately adorned Tuareg saddle. Its forked horn was dignified with bells and ornaments collected from afar, of copper, brass and silver. Luxuriously designed trappings with large hanging tassels draped either side of the saddle in shades of rich orange and brilliant red. A beautifully woven headdress of gold, red and blue adorned the head of his camel, an honor rarely displayed except among friends.

Zafir's long beard had lost its lusty black since his last visit, and was now lightly streaked with grey. His classic Arabic face had a strong chiseled nose, alert brown eyes, thick eyebrows, and a strong jaw. He held his mouth straight, in serious gratitude for the safe return trip and the success he had brought to his home city. The years of travel had firmly etched their strain upon his old friend just as the years of solemn duty had bleached Kateb's own.

Kateb didn't call out or disturb the procession. That would insult the congenial ceremony of greeting that was yet to unfold among the waiting Sheiks. But in the shadowed dusk, Kateb placed hand to heart and bowed to give an unseen thanks to God for the safe return of his old friend.

He would wait until the new day to properly greet Zafir, and planned to bring something nice to honor his old friend—perhaps a morning feast of the finest foods and coffees, and hear of his travels.

The camels that followed after carried a curtained litter—the mahmil—of Zafir's wives.

The first mahmil was adorned in veils of light green with white and gold tassels, and was no doubt Rasheeda, the first wife. She was also a childhood friend of Kateb's. The second was veiled in dark red with white tassels—that would be Asiya, followed by two in brown with no tassels for Azhar and Nasira, newer wives about whom Kateb knew little.

Zafir's two daughters came next, seated upon ratted sheepskin saddles, regally, like grown women—modestly draped in their black, formal abayahs, and lightly veiled to their eyes. Unseen to Kateb was Rasha,

Zafir's youngest daughter who made that descent through the Siq, with her mother, within the veiled enclosure of the green mahmil.

The other elders of the Abdali-ud-din with their wives came next, dressed for the occasion of their return to Rekeem.

The last camels bringing up the rear were escorts, a guard of armed swordsmen mounted on the trim frames of 28 war camels. The men scanned the shadows for danger or surprise, with hands on swords.

Kateb made note of the rear-guard on his clay tablet and set it on the step to be delivered to the Sheiks.

Reaching for his walking staff, he pulled heavy to raise himself, rubbing the knots in his legs and stretching his back. "Four tablets. And treasure!" he smiled. "It is a good accounting. The Sheiks will be pleased."

Holding his skirts he stepped down the red-rock steps and waved to the guardsmen. "Send for the watch," he called, "they're all here."

The old patriarch walked more stiffly that evening—the long days had become more difficult in recent times but he dismissed the discomfort and walked onto the boulevard toward the central place.

Our home at the time was far from the luxury caverns of the wealthy. It was among the poorer class of those with modest means, and consisted of a single long room with two side rooms set in the middle of a row of lower-level dwellings. Two long windows in front and the cavity of a slender doorway gave the only relief to the midday heat. A great black tent draped across poles shading the windows served as a makeshift porch that gave protection from the sun. It could be dropped quickly in the event of sandy wind.

Night finally shrouded the canyon city when Kateb limped toward the narrow stone steps leading up to our home. He could see from the walkway that my mother, Dalal ("Dah-LAW-L"), had fallen asleep on her dais by the dying cook-fire. She would be pleased to learn that Zafir was home at last. He decided not to awaken her—such news could wait until morning. He dressed and stretched out on his bed, hoping not to disturb.

The dark falls quickly over our slumbering city and the sky above is swift to put on her adornment of jewels. In the shadows at the south end, the four guardsmen took their places at the mouth of the Siq. A small fire flashed to life as two of them spread out mats and curled up to sleep. Two others leaned against the warm red rock in quiet exchange, chewing strips of jerked goat meat while standing first watch.

ب هبعه 11 محبوب

THE BLESSING

"Kateb! My old friend, salaam alaikum," Zafir exclaimed as Kateb approached. Zafir's smiling countenance matched the brightness of the rising sun. "Peace be upon you my dear brother!" Zafir's outstretched arms opened wide. "You live, you live! And my eyes behold it, God be praised!"

Kateb hurried to meet the embrace. "*Wa-alaikum is-salaam*, and upon you God's peace my dear Zafir!"

The men kissed cheeks and clasped forearms in a firm grip.

"I saw your lead last night, once more you've been blessed of God," Kateb told him.

"Yes," Zafir laughed. "And I saw you at your usual place by the pillar of Al Khazna. Did I manage this time to make your hand cramp? I've returned with a caravan much larger than the last you saw me!"

"My hand, my back, my legs, I'll be a broken man before my gray hairs lay me down if your wealth continues like this!"

They laughed and Zafir motioned Kateb to join him at his tent where preparations were just being completed for the morning meal.

"Your Sheiks," Zafir said, "they haven't changed at all. I received more excitement for our treasure than to see old friends. They fondled for an exchange before my camel could even spit!"

"Let him spit. Those Sheiks know only one thing, and you, my friend, are the only gold that is true treasure. But you're many weeks late, and we worried that . . . ."

"No, I was delayed in the east. My train has never traveled so far, but I've opened a direct trade between Kerala and Chang'an. The Emperors of the Qin love the spices more than incense and the Hindu saints of Puri love the myrrh more than their gold. I was happy to arrange an exchange—with me in the middle."

"And what an exchange!" Kateb said. "I tallied for the Sheiks 28 talents of gold and more than 50 sacks of spice. If you plan to continue on to Leuke Kome, those sea merchants will make out like bandits—or should I call them pirates?"

He laughed. "Kateb, you're a wise old student of history! And your accounting true, my dear friend. The tally of gold isn't what you think, but it will trade well, and after all these years, give me wherewithal to rest from these long trips."

"*Rest*? You couldn't quit this work now, Zafir! Not now when it rewards you with such prosperity. How could you even think of it? Did the sun get through that turban of yours and boil your head?"

Zafir's smile turned tired. "I've one last trip in me, Kateb. I must be honest with you. I'm tired. I really want nothing more than the peace and rest of my friends, of my family, of Rekeem. I'm going to use the profits from this trip to buy back my father's lands, and then I want to settle here, among those I love."

"Well, of course, that's delightful news! Dalal will be thrilled to see you and hear of this plan of yours. You must come by, come visit us for midday meal. Will you stop by and see us today?"

"Most certainly," Zafir said. "I have some exchange with your Sheiks this morning and I'll be honored to be welcomed into your home. Oh yes, and I'll bring Rasheeda."

"And little Rasha, we haven't seen her for ... why she must be ..."

"Just turned 15 and not little!" Zafir said. "She is a young woman now, as lovely as her mother. And just as quick. It's like having five women telling me what to do! I'll have Rasheeda bring her along."

A white-robed servant disrupted the exchange, presenting a clay pot of water from which the men washed to their forearms and dried with a white cloth.

"Come," Zafir said, "let us save business for a business time. I have other things to discuss, important things, things that will interest you, things that include Bassam."

Kateb stopped suddenly and looked at Zafir, curious. *Bassam? My Bassam? What plans could this old caravan man possibly have that involve my only son?*

Zafir discerned the furrowing brow beneath Kateb's headdress. "Rest your thoughts, Kateb," he said smiling. "All is good. And if it be God's will, I want to bless the household of Kateb and Dalal. Here my friend, please sit and eat. And tell me of Bassam."

ب هبعه 12 محبوب

BASSAM

Where does the story of Bassam really begin, my father wondered. He suddenly found his memories climbing back through the dusty chapters of his fondest and most painful recollections, digging into long-ago forgotten details that really didn't begin only 17 years ago—no, the events leading to my arrival began a whole life-time before I was born.

Many years earlier when Kateb was a boy he first learned of the terrible camel troops of the Fukara and the frequent *ghrazzus*—those bloody raids against the sheikdoms of the upper deserts. From these raids came rapid changes in fortune all across the trade regions when bandits stole camels, cattle, spices and treasure in the fury of a lightning strike. The victims of these crimes organized counter-ghrazzus to win back their lost wealth, usually stealing more, and from such back and forth there developed a pattern of war and strife that proved for the nomads the easiest although bloodiest path to prosperity. Why barter and trade when stealing and killing was so much easier?

Kateb remembered from his childhood that the cost in life from such raids was horrific. Family and friends, women and children, so many taken as slaves—and the men, always the men, their throats slit—his elders of old among them. In defense, a kinship among the clans grew through necessity. But their quarreling about leadership and honor wasn't resolved before they came to standoffs at the tip of a sword—sheik against chief, family against clan, until at last united although divided, a bulwark of desert nomads could stand shoulder to shoulder against the Fukara.

Once formed, the fragile defense ultimately succeeded. However, it took many years of Kateb's childhood before peace returned and the mountain retreats could be cleansed of the robbers and invading pirates. The prosperity of a more agreeable form at last returned to the region.

After many seasons the mighty caravans resumed their trek south between the Syrian and Nafud deserts. They returned to the old routes that were safer now, the routes that led to the pleasant rest and provisions in the oasis canyon city of Rekeem.

While Kateb apprenticed with his father he learned the important skill of the scribe. He filled countless clay tablets that counted loads and bushels, skeps and jugs, containments overflowing with great slabs of salt, collections of sandalwood, gold, incense, cotton, wool, and spices, plus the hordes of slaves, camels, cattle, horses and herds marching past his post. The fantastic parades dazzled the young boy who imagined its wealth exceeding even the grandest wishes of the legendary princes of old.

The years piled up quickly in Kateb's life. He had become the most respected senior scribe in Rekeem, and could always be found seated on an old silk pillow at his usual post beneath the mighty red pillars of Al Khazna.

Then came that terrible dark day when suddenly there ran shouting two ragged messengers from the Siq to sound an alarm that a shattered caravan of injured survivors sought safety. Would the Sheiks of Rekeem oblige?

Of course they would, and dispatched horses immediately, rushing to and fro through the narrow gorge and returning to deposit into waiting care all of the injured, the dying, and the dead. The attack, they learned later, was after the manner of *Tauri of the Pontusl*, a vicious and wicked tribe of bandits who feasted on the vulnerability of the smaller, less guarded caravans of badawi. These badawi had been caught in an open pass and had raced for the safety of Rekeem, but too late.

By nightfall the human toll had mounted to some three dozen dead, twice that number wounded, and an unknown number missing at the hand of the *Tauri*.

For the badawi, the way of the desert was the way of their lives. Like many nomads, they had no home or village to carry their name, and from whence they came and to where they journeyed, only God knew, for no man had kin among the badawi. To the dwellers of Rekeem, the badawi came as welcomed guests. For the exchange of a night's stay and a meal, they brought news of the mighty desert tribes and told of coming caravans. They fulfilled the roll of messengers of good fortune, except on a day such as this when the message was one of terrible tragedy.

That evening as the sun fell behind the rocks and while the rescue work continued, Dalal found crying among the newly delivered of the wounded, a lone infant still cuddled in the embrace of his dead mother's arms—her body having shielded the boy from the swordsman's blow. The mother's limp arm was still wrapped around the child in a final, loving embrace.

Dalal's heart melted at the sorrowful scene and she knew the child could suffer, perhaps die if not rescued from the dampness and danger. Carefully lifting the mother's cold arm and laying it to her side softly, Dalal drew the frightened, hungry orphan gently to her breast, hushing soft words of comfort, and wondering how best to give care. She knew that the badawi had no means to give claim to their own, and even less to their dead. With none other to care or to claim, Dalal's first instinctive concern was for the nurture of this child. She carefully bundled him up in her apron, holding him warmly to her, and carried him from that terrible scene. Stepping lightly through the blackness of the streets of Rekeem, alert for danger or strangers, she stealthily hurried him to the warmth and security of her home. That infant with no name and no mother, was me.

It was long past dark when Kateb's help in the exhausting rescue work was complete. He had labored all the day long to retrieve the belongings, the stray camels and herds, and dress the wounds of the beleaguered strangers who rested safely within our city. The people gathered the bodies of those who perished and laid them in the cavity of a rock to be dealt with at first light.

Finally, Kateb could return to his home.

When he reached the stoop and pulled back the curtained doorway of their modest apartment, he found Dalal with her precious cargo asleep on her lap with the velvet nap of a brushed lambskin neatly wrapped to secure his warmth. She confessed in whispered delight the genesis of God's benevolence and how such a young child was brought to their childless home. She smiled that for the baby's nourishment she had employed an obliging she-goat, and there had been no complaint. "He knows goat milk," she said, and cuddled him close, humming softly the hymns of The Mothers.

Kateb leaned over Dalal and gently lifted the lambskin. The young one's contented countenance breathed steady in a peaceful sleep. "Hello, my son," he whispered. Suddenly, a tiny crease lifted the infant's soft little lips into a most rapturous smile that immediately brightened the astonishment of Kateb and Dalal. It lasted just a moment, but long enough.

"We will call him Bassam," Kateb said softly, caressing the boy's soft locks.

"The one who smiles," Dalal whispered. "His smile will bring joy to our house."

Kateb nodded. Returning the skin, he gave a loving touch to the shoulder of his wife. "He will be our son," he said kindly. "He will be my heir and bring honor to our household. You will tell no one, my wife, only that he is our son."

* * *

In the short years that followed, my parents tell me I quickly shed the tender charms of an infant and, growing independent, I became a frightfully clever boy who turned into the most mischievous challenge.

When I was big enough to hurry along a camel and fetch water from the village well, things became difficult for my parents. Hardly a week passed that Kateb wasn't visited by an elder or an animal tender about a she-camel dressed in the missing tent of a widow, or a goat wandering the boulevard in Sheik's robes, or a coffee stand turned upside down with tables and stools legs up, and pots and urns on their mouths.

After each such event, the same five young boys confessed when confronted, and it was usually me who admitted to being the creative spearhead behind such bother.

By age 12, my growth spurt slowed for a year so that nature could finish some of her work—fixing my complexion in a light olive-color skin tone, and gifting me with unusually fair sandy-brown hair. And despite my mother's best efforts, that hair couldn't stay in place no matter how much she tried to wet it down. Nature also granted me a gift of deep ocean-blue eyes—a color not unknown in Rekeem, but still, it was considered unusual. Mother had green eyes, father had brown, so no one questioned the chances brought about by genealogical happenstance. Friends simply complimented my parents on the boy with the beautiful blue eyes.

It was this same year that I started paying attention to the burdens of adulthood. Kateb and Dalal worked hard to fill my days until I began to take my studies more seriously. With declining complaint I shadowed after Kateb, learning the ways of the scribe. With the passage of time my rambunctious side began to mellow.

For my first caravan excursion outside of my rock-walled world, I learned to be attentive to the needs of the train. A brief ten-day journey to the sea and back gave me first hand knowledge of the rigors such travel entailed.

I learned how to slay a camel and strip its bones of meat.

I was drawn into the blind estimations of erecting the tent of a Sheik in the darkness of night. I mastered the dung fires and took my turn standing watch while others slept.

And good friend Ammar ("Ah-mar") took time to teach me the art of the *kamal* and the science of the sun and stars. He also introduced me to the burning mirror, a polished sheet of curved metal that captured the sun's energy for fire, a God-sent improvement over the sticks and shavings.

"It's another idea from the Greeks," Ammar told me, "probably stolen from the silk-makers of Chang'an, who knows?"

I could hold the burning mirror in one hand and gather the sun's rays to a single spot that could start a cook-fire more quickly than rubbing sticks.

Ammar also taught me the utility of using a drill bow to achieve the same. Before I returned home, I had mastered the fire-starting techniques and could improvise with any of them as needed.

God granted me a quick mind for one so young. I naturally possessed understanding beyond my years, and this got me into trouble plenty of times. But in short order I had learned to live off the desert with a confidence that matched any of the grizzled veterans.

Such experiences helped me grow toward the responsibilities of being an adult. My pranks became less costly and creative, and a degree of trust started to replace frustration among those who knew me.

But the best change of all didn't come from scolding or complaining, punishment or deprivation of privileges—the best change came into my young life because of a girl.

13

RASHA

With Kateb and Zafir on the porch in deep conversation, Dalal and Rasheeda chatted in the curtained back room, catching up on old times.

Young Rasha was perfectly at home in our house, and knelt on a mat at Dalal's feet to examine a soft woven shawl that remained unfinished. She stroked the dyed green and blue mesh and turned it over in her hands, holding its softness to her cheek. The smooth texture of hand-spun wool with its natural lanolin gloss was a puzzle to Rasha. How Dalal could turn mere threads of hair into such downy perfection was a curious mystery for Rasha. She longed to learn the art.

Rasha was a young woman now and already as tall as her mother. Long black hair fell all the way down her back, and the oppressive heat of Rekeem made her want to tie it back.

She had spent many of her childhood years in our house, and the last time Dalal and Kateb had seen her, she was shorter, had a round girlish face and figure, and her hands sported the chewed nails of carefree curiosity.

But she was different now. Her face was slender with soft, high cheek bones, beautiful lips, and a natural blush in her olive skin. Her graceful oval eyes were bright with intelligence and joy. And like her sisters, she stood with a statuesque elegance that belied her young age. When she smiled there was a streak of sly tease that she rarely let free lest she get "the look" from her mother. Even though people who didn't know her might say she must be 18 or 19 years old, she was still playful at heart at 15, and was always scolded for refusing proper lady-like behavior around the stifling *pretend* that the adult world insisted she emulate.

But she was not always this way.

Rasha was born into the Abdali-ud-din legacy of fame and wealth, the third daughter of Zafir and his first wife. Wanting a son for an heir, Zafir had taken other wives but they begat him daughters as well. He loved his girls very much, and they loved him back, and were always welcomed on the great treks to the east. But the little personality who best captured Zafir's heart was young Rasha. She laughed in a tickle fight, had a streak of tease about her, and hugged her father's neck so hard at each goodbye he felt the little handprints until he returned home again. And upon his arrival, she was the first to come running and throw herself into his arms and plant a tender little kiss on both cheeks, saying, "I love you baba." And never leaving out mother, "You too amma!"

Zafir named her after her mother Rasheeda, and she was born right at the time when Zafir's caravan work to the far east was just beginning to grow.

Though Zafir worked to let the family travel together in the caravans, the new ventures east were fraught with the unknown for a child so young. Zafir and Rasheeda were both raised in Rekeem, and remained close friends with Kateb and Dalal. One day they asked if my parents could care for their daughter during a three-month caravan. The young girl was delightfully welcomed into our home.

She was not one for traveling, even for the shorter trips to Leuke Kome. She whined and cried as young children do, longing for the familiar places back home. And so began the annual pilgrimage to Rekeem to leave Rasha in the care of Dalal while Zafir and the family were absent for three months on the long treks east. But with me always there to play with, the separations were not as difficult.

The first few weeks from home were the worst for Rasha. She wandered about our dwelling lost and confused. It took a good time before she was settled enough to sleep through the night and not awaken in sobbing tears.

Dalal was always there to give loving comfort to Rasha, and thus began a bonding sincerity of kindness and love that gave comfort and help to Rasha through difficult times.

That next year Rasha actually looked forward to her visit. She brought with her a few precious things from her home to show and share.

By the time Rasha was 8 years old, her visit to our home suddenly opened her eyes to life. She realized for the first time that not all families lived with the opulence to which she had grown accustomed.

"Where are the women to make the food?" she asked my mother one day.

"We have no such help here," Dalal smiled. "We make it ourselves."

"Can you do that?"

"Certainly! Here, stand on that stool and let me show you how."

"Me? You will let me learn? You want me to help?"

Rasha was thrilled. She loved learning the arts that seemed so foreign to her own abilities. It took a few days and the young girl discovered she could do a great deal on her own. Dalal took her to market, spoke of shopping for vegetables, how to pick and choose from among them, how to test for meat and eggs, and the proper use of her prized spices.

Rasha learned how to fetch water from the cistern, to keep the kitchen clean, and learned by her own shocking surprise that the least crumb left unattended always invited the mice or other desert creatures who ventured in during the heat of day or dark of night to scavenge about.

Cooking over a fire was completely new to Rasha, but she learned it well—from starting a fire from cold coals to controlling the flames for proper cooking speed for rice and breads.

Dalal shared the art of sewing and embroidery, of twisting threads in her fingers and weaving fabric. She showed Rasha the irrigated fields in which flax and cotton were grown and how these were turned to clothing or works of decoration and art.

The earthy feel of modesty, humility and hand-crafted care in our home fit Rasha's curiosity and satisfaction perfectly. She confided to Dalal that she wanted her home to be just as this—where each lovely drape or covering, the smell of the food at evening meal, the clothing and blankets that sheltered the family, all could come from the industry of patience that is the loving work of a mother.

"You have so many things," Dalal said. "And kind hands to make them for you."

"Yes, they are kind hands," Rasha replied. "But they are not my hands. I want to care for my family as you do yours. Will you teach me more?"

"Of course," she said.

Rasha also had no brother. She found in me a playful companion with excitement and industry that brought a security to her young insecurities.

I was only a year or two older, and as young children are wont to do, we became the best of friends. We played, talked and dreamed. Many sunny days began with the two of us outdoors chasing after a stray lynx or standing by the roadside as a caravan crossed through town. We wandered through the market place for fallen fruit, or stood gawking at the door of a merchant of brass or glass works, wondering how such artistry was made. Once in a while, Rasha cornered me into pretending with mud pies or straw dolls, but I just couldn't show any patience for that and wanted instead to take her by the hand to my friends to run about the streets of Rekeem, often finding our way to the market to beg a fruit from a vendor. We played and raced, explored and discovered, and built a camaraderie that lasted a full six years.

And then, one year, when Rasha was 10, everything we had learned to expect from each other suddenly changed—Rasha was different and I could not figure it out. She suddenly became a great puzzle to me.

I couldn't tell at first what was going on, only that she was not the same friend I bid goodbye to nine months earlier.

Her demeanor and behavior had changed. She was difficult to understand. She started looking and treating me like … well, like my mother. She pointed out things such as me acting too much like a boy, or that I needed to grow up, that I needed to stop making such a mess and causing such bother in the city, or that I needed to stop teasing and start treating her feelings with more care.

On top of that she cried a lot.

I did not understand it. I was the worst of teases, and always got a good reaction by dropping a large-clawed scorpion on her head. But now? Now she just burst into tears for no good reason, and cried more after that. It was just no fun anymore. I stood back so many times to scratch my chin and then my head, and wonder in complete astonishment, what's wrong with Rasha?

That next year Rasha's tug-of-war friendship with me had grown distant. Our time together became sparse and reserved. We avoided each other and spoke little except as required.

But all during that time there remained between us a curious fascination that kept the puzzle of change alive for the duration of her stay—me choosing other boys for recreation, and her looking for companionship among the girls her age—but each of us looking over our shoulder at the other—wondering.

When Rasha left for her home after three months, I thought little more on the subject, and dismissed her with a shrug. She was gone, and that was that. I turned my attention to tasks reserved for boys my age, and relished in proving my budding strengths and maturing stature. Strength was coming to my lanky frame and I wanted to prove my new powers to anyone I could entice to watch.

When Rasha returned at age 12, I tried to show how I was becoming a man with new muscles and abilities, but she just rolled her eyes unimpressed—it was clear to her that I was no man. She was right, but did she have to insult me so?

That was the year when Dalal became an important adult in Rasha's life. Tender changes came, and the responsibilities of becoming a woman manifested themselves. Dalal gave loving, motherly guidance, and the two of them exhausted the lamp's oil late into the night, whispering secrets and sharing things unspoken.

All of this was driving me crazy. In the mornings I tried to leave as soon as I could escape out the door and headed off to stir up trouble, kick some rocks around, bother a few animals, argue with myself, and find my friends to complain and complain—about girls. They are *so much work*, I kept telling the other boys, and they all nodded their agreement.

I tried not to interfere between Rasha and the care that Dalal was tending her. But I certainly noticed that she was growing up. Once in a while Rasha caught me looking at her, but I turned away quickly. If she caught me again she tried to smile, but such unspoken messages hit me like a rock right between the eyes.

Other times I did try and be polite, trying to build on our years as young friends, but for some reason I was no good at it and hurt her feelings. She had a lot to say about her feelings and that didn't help.

With the passage of two more years, the distance between us remained although she continued to spend the usual three-month stay with us in Rekeem. And like all boys before me, and all boys that followed, the beautiful changes in Rasha would forever remain a great mystery to me, an unfinished bother that gnawed at me with perplexed worry, like a spider hiding in my room at night.

Rasha responded to my reticence with patience—a natural and generous part of her personality—and turned her trust to Dalal. Between the two, Dalal helped Rasha build on her girlhood dreams to become a wife to the one in whom she could one day place her trust and love. My mother and she engaged in soft talking for hours on end.

Now that she was back in Rekeem again, and kneeling on the mat as Rasheeda and Dalal talked the same way, Rasha looked around at the familiar and musty trappings of our modest home and breathed it in. These walls had come to mean kind arms embracing her during a cold time in her life, and it was good to return to this place of safety once again. The dressings of colorful hangings and handcrafted creativity that hid the walls of stone were still there, standing unchanged as comforting landmarks of a place unmoved. She loved it here.

Rasha had not paid much attention to what the women were discussing. She shifted and leaned against Dalal's knee who then reached down and stroked the girl's dark hair. Rasha smiled and closed her eyes. It was home beneath that woman's touch.

14

THE PLAN

Out on the porch a worrisome storm was brewing, but it wasn't in the skies above them.

"I must pass the scrolls to someone, Kateb," Zafir said in frustration. "I need your blessing if it is to be Bassam." He leaned forward to take a coffee and bread from the small wooden table.

The noon-time breeze ruffled the black tent that shaded their repose and Kateb glanced up to estimate the strain on the poles.

"The words on the scrolls, they are sacred words, they are wise words," Zafir continued. "I know I tell you nothing new. My elders passed them from father to son since the first caravans left the cradles of Babylonia, Egypt and the Far East. Those are my fathers, Kateb! My fathers whose wealth you know is legendary. It was no accident, these scrolls."

Kateb sipped his cup and winced at the heat, but it wasn't the heat.

"And he is not my son, Kateb, nor will he be," Zafir assured. "Bassam is yours, a tall, strong young man—your flesh and blood, and an honor to your family. I have no heir. But you are my dearest friends, my closest family. I don't take him from the bosom of his family, I want to borrow him to secure this bridge of friendship between us, a bond of prosperity from my fathers to your sons. Do you hear me, my friend? Your sons!"

"My *son*," Kateb emphasized.

"Your son and your grandsons, for generations!" Zafir said. "It is the uniting of our families that I offer. And only for this short while, to teach him as they taught me, lest these ancient words pass to the dust when I am dust."

Kateb weighed the prospect by his silence, and sipped again. "I have no doubt, my dear Zafir, I have no doubt." And sipped once more.

"These scrolls of wealth have guided prosperity through many dozens of generations, Kateb! This plan, the transfer of this great knowledge is not casually done, I promise you. Bassam is the perfect age now. But more important, he has the spark, the maturity, the zest to use these words, to use them wisely as his years multiply. My giving them is a rite of passage that could end right here and now without your trust in me, do you see it?"

Kateb *could* see it, Zafir didn't need to explain it once more. He was deep in thought, working a calculation.

Zafir's plan for me was supposed to begin with a trek south to the sea, back again north then east to the Fergana Valley and then farther east for a long, long time to Chang'an with the many customary side trips. It meant a journey of at least two years before our return—two years among distant lands where camels become horses and horses become yaks and yaks become boats to bring home the dead.

The trade and the markets in the east dealt unkindly toward strangers, and Kateb worried for how many centuries had the bones of desert entrepreneurs been scattered upon dunes of a different sort? He knew when I left my mother I would leave as a growing boy and when I returned to my father, I would be a new man of experience, a man of my own life, but a patriarch to none.

Much could happen to the old and infirm during such a span. Dalal was long past the custom of women and her shoulders slouched as if beneath a burden that was no longer there. And the strength of Kateb was now in a staff and the helping arms of a passing stranger. He could no longer tend to the family as in recent years. It was the evening time of life for this warmly yoked pair—an old bull with his dear old cow. It was time for lowing in green pastures where the joy of fleeting sunsets could not be missed, and drawn inwards as the breath of another day peacefully ended together.

But this—this idea of Zafir's! Why, this could take the strength of their lives, the heir of his name. And two long and dangerous years, should it be done? More importantly, could it be done?

Kateb knew Zafir had invested both cunning and wisdom into his plan. The true strengths of the Abdali-ud-din were passed down through the centuries in this fashion—father to son—time-tested traits of his fathers that were etched line upon line into their family's culture, a powerful narrative from untold ages of life on the trade routes.

It was a dangerous trip and the risk of raid or capture was too great for any but the most faithful.

As for his Rasheeda, Zafir's plan was to leave his wife with her mother's family in the great southern city of Saba', with his two eldest daughters attending to her separation. But to fill the empty arms of a mother and the aching attentiveness of a caring father, Zafir proposed young Rasha become Dalal's young prentice for the duration, to learn the ways of a household. Rasha loved Dalal and Rekeem, and the life in that place that was hers for so many of her childhood years. Kateb knew that welcoming young Rasha should be no burden, but still, *she could be no Bassam.* "There was none other like Bassam," he said.

Kateb looked across to his friend seated there under the awning, waiting for an answer, and sighed with surrender. *Oh you clever man, Zafir. You are a clever musician with the strings of an old man's heart.*

That night Kateb and Dalal watched the moon crest over the distant ridge, splashing the quiet canyon city in a bath of silver hues. In the darkness of a cold fire, he reached out for her hand.

"The boy must become a man," Kateb finally said. "If he left because of Zafir or if he left simply on his own account, that day had to come. Perhaps it has come at last."

"But he is so young," Dalal sighed. "A boy who wants to be a man, well, then a man he must be. Is it so selfish to want the boy to become the man here in this home where family is what he makes of us?"

Kateb squeezed her hand. "Oh my bride! Your skin is as smooth as the day I took you to wife," he said. "Even if God had so willed it to send angels speaking the days that we have lived, I could take you again and live it with you, just the same."

She pulled his hand to her cheek and squeezed it against her face, a tear caught between.

"I rise every day with an ache in my heart for the mother who brought to us our Bassam," she said. "I've tried to be the mother that gave him life, and I've received the love that for his mother was meant."

"It was your face he first saw from the crib," Kateb whispered. "Your arms gave comfort and love. She gave him birth, Dalal, but you gave him life."

"Then, I must do it," she whispered back. "For the love of his mother who died in the sand so that her little one could be spared, I won't stand in the way of our boy becoming a man."

A desert breeze lifted the covering of the porch with a soft ripple. The old man and his aged wife reached out to each other in silence and gazed across the canyon as the moon gently climbed higher into the night sky.

ب هبعه 15 محبوب

SHE'S DIFFERENT NOW

It was past midday when I was excused from my duties at the quarry and started for home. Turning the corner at the boulevard I waved good bye to my friends and began the slight incline toward my house. I was anxious to check on my bakra. We calved her again, I was excited to see what new life she brought us.

As our home came into view I stopped suddenly.

There in front, standing by idly, right there at the front of our home was a donkey with a seated pull-cart, and three kneeling camels with a man standing by. I recognized him right away—Talib, a captain of ten from Zafir's caravan. He was concentrating with his knife, whittling on a stick that was nearly all carved away.

"Talib!" I called out waving. "Talib, it's me! What brings you here?"

Talib looked up and his long face brightened into a broad toothy smile, recognizing his young friend running up to him. The years had not changed the appearance of faithful Talib. He still matted down his thinning brown hair with water, and the stubble of his beard proved he was awakened too soon this morning, too soon to wash for the day's labors.

"Bassam!" he said, clasping my forearms in greeting. I stood a good two palms taller than him. He looked into my face and my eyes, recognizing my familiar smile, that same smile, beaming ear to ear. I knew my hair was disheveled, and saw him grin at that as he studied my face.

"Good to see you! Great to see you!" Talib said. "And, well, that hair of yours ...."

"Never mind my hair you old goat!"

We laughed.

"But you, *you*, my young friend," he said. "You are missing out on all the excitement!"

"Excitement?" I asked.

"Oh yes, they went in just a moment ago."

"Who?"

"Your father and Zafir, they were sitting out here for the longest time talking. Talking and more talking. I heard your name, I don't know what they were planning, I couldn't hear what it was all about, but your father did not seem happy about the idea."

"What idea?"

Talib just shrugged and shook his head.

"They just went inside?" I asked.

"Yes, a little while ago—for meal or something."

"Then I must go see him!" and turned to go past.

Talib caught me by the arm. "Bassam, there is somebody else in there."

"Oh? Who is that?"

"Rasha."

"Oh," I said. "Of course, I see—well, good then, I will say hello to her, too."

"I think you better know something," Talib said.

I stopped, suddenly concerned. "What is it, is she okay?"

"Oh yes," he said. "More than okay, my young friend. She has become quite the lovely young lady."

"A lady, is that all?"

"Well, yes, but she's …"

"Oh!" I said with a smile of relief. "I thought you were going to tell me she had been hurt or was ill, or something! A lady huh? Well, that's good, finally! I've been watching her grow up all these years, it's about time. I'm glad she has become a lady. Yes, very glad. Thanks, Talib!" And with that I turned to the house, whistling a tune as I skipped up the stone steps two at a time.

Talib watched me bound up the walkway and smiled. Turning to his stick he started whistling my tune, a smile locked to his face, and whittled some more.

Pulling back the sheer that covered the front entrance, I stepped inside pausing a moment to grow accustomed to the dark interior. "Hello?" I called out. And then I saw them, seated on the cushioned chairs of the great room, caught in conversation. Kateb looked up first.

"Bassam!" he said, rising and motioning me into the room. "Come in son, come in! You came at the right time, the perfect time. We have visitors."

Zafir smiled and he stood to greet me with an extended hand. "Bassam! Good to see you Bassam, so good to see you! My, you have grown into a young man, hasn't he Kateb? You're taller than your father! Yes, I could say you are, don't you see it, Kateb?" and turned with a smile.

Kateb smiled back. "Come join us son, we were just talking, come sit."

I saw mother seated at the far side, Rasheeda next to her, but who was this lovely young woman who sat closest, smiling at me?

I sort of stuttered into the room where they sat talking, squinting to see by shaded window light the stranger among them. And then I saw the soft, curved outline of a face, a face I had studied for years. It was as familiar to me as my own. Adjusting to the dark, I could see her—a stunning new vision of my young childhood friend.

"Rasha?" I almost whispered, my mouth hanging open. "I mean, Rasha?" I said again. The adults stopped talking, realizing one of them had neglected to make an introduction.

I could see Rasha blush, then smile at me. "Bassam, hello."

The adults were caught unprepared for the reunion and Rasheeda tried to squelch a smile of her own, seeing that the missed opportunity quickly turned awkward—and obviously uncomfortable.

"Uh, um, Bassam!" Dalal said. "You remember Rasha. She's here visiting with her parents again, and we were just, um, just talking and thought, wouldn't it be a perfect time if you could take her out of here for … uh, for a …"

"Yes," Kateb interrupted, "she's been bored with our talk. Could you do her a kindness and show her the new honeycomb treats they are selling at the market? It's been very stuffy in here, and I think she might like to see what's new around town."

"An excellent idea," Zafir chimed in, producing a coin purse from his pocket. "Here, take this, and buy some for all of us."

It was obvious what they were up to. I cleared my throat and looked at Rasha. She looked up, her face lit with hoped-for escape.

"Of course," I said, taking the purse. "We will go and see what they have. So, …the honeycomb, right?" *Oh my goodness, how obvious is this?*

"Right!" Zafir said. Kateb smiled his consent and nodded once.

"All right then," I stammered, and stood there like a skinny donkey in the middle of hungry lions, not quite knowing what to do next.

Then Rasha rose from her chair—a beautiful, slender young woman as tall as her mother, with feminine curves modestly draped with a simple honey-brown covering that scooped at her neck and draped to her mid-calf. She was *beautiful.* I just stared at her, fixated by her long black hair that fell softly over her shoulders and down to her waist. And then I gulped—I'm sure she heard me.

Rasha stood uncomfortably in the shadowed silence as no one was speaking or suggesting or … or anything. And then she locked eyes with mine, smiling with a nervous little twist of a tease that said, *please get me out of here!*

"So, um, we'll be right back," I said, and the parents all gushed their approval as I led the way to the doorway, and holding the shear aside for her to pass through first, we stepped into the bright of day.

"No hurry, son!" Dalal called after us.

As the shear closed behind us, I was quite positive I overheard sudden muffled talking and delighted chuckles from inside. I hurried her down the steps and away from their scheming ways.

HONEY

Talib looked up from his whittling just as Rasha and I appeared at the doorway of the house and started toward him. Not wanting to interrupt the delicate reunion that was underway Talib was crafty and kind. He knew what I was being cornered into, so he quickly bent down at the donkey, turning his back to us, pretending an emergency examination of the hoof was suddenly mandatory—picking it up, scratching at it with his knife, and mumbling something, anything, to create distance when we passed.

With Rasha at my side, we turned immediately past Talib and walked up the path. I was laughing inside and thanking Talib at the same time for his quick-thinking strategy, and headed for the familiar stone road leading to the market square.

Rasha breathed in the familiar scents and scenes, the warm blue sky above, the air soft with the distant sound of children chasing after a leather ball and a dog barking after them. Across the road a camel chewing her cud watched us walk by, and snorted her disinterest. The sweet of wild rose shrubs scented the air as we passed a garden of them in full bloom. It was the best time of spring, and she loved it here.

"So what was everyone talking about in there?" I asked, looking down at my feet as we stepped along worn pavers of smooth, red stone.

"Oh, some very elaborate plan of father's," she said, "another of his big trips."

"Big trips?"

"Oh yes, all the way east, no stops," she said.

"That will take some time."

"A long time."

She paused to steal a glance over at my face. I could feel her eyes on me. She seemed to be looking to see that it was still her friend's face, and I could tell she was measuring me up for how I was maturing—and I bet she was thinking she still needed to do something about that disheveled hair of mine. *I tried—all the time!*

My jaw was filling out, my shoulders broader, my blue eyes didn't change—I hoped she saw strength of character in me, the way I stood, the way I held myself, my smile—she always told me she loved my smile. The years had softened me toward her, and it was easy to give to her the kindness and patience that she always longed from me.

I couldn't help but notice the long silence and I looked up to find Rasha's beautiful eyes fixated on mine, locked in a moment that caught me completely off guard. In that blink of a glance I could see into her, into her heart and her very soul, and there passed between us a surprising and unspoken exchange of intimate communion, from my heart to hers, and back again—forgiveness, understanding, discomfort, safety and maybe some renewed trust—and then the moment passed.

I suddenly melted with a blush and quickly looked back to my feet again, stuttering around for something to say.

Rasha looked away smiling—as if she had received her answer and knew that all would be well with the two of us. By her sigh I sensed that her heart swelled with a quickened beat, and she was comfortable to be near me at last.

I couldn't stand the tension any longer. "Um, there was some plan you were saying?" I asked.

"Plan? Oh, the plan. Yes, a big plan!" she said. "My father, he is always thinking up these huge ideas and trips and things."

"I know, I have always admired him for that."

"You have?" She turned to look at me, surprised, actually taken aback by my interest. I had *always* admired her father, didn't she realize that?

"Well, yes," I said. "He understands the way of the markets and I've always wanted to learn them. He goes and comes, year after year, bringing treasure every time. That's a good plan at work, and my father admires him for that, too. I plan to learn it some day."

We walked in silence to the top of the incline and turned to follow the main road. Rasha pointed out a new sand-brick dwelling on a corner that had stood unfinished for such a long time. I was happy to tell her all about it, that it was a popular diner now, and a place I often visited. The smell of roasted chicken and spiced rice already in preparation drifted across the boulevard, a familiar smell that had trapped me many times before. It reminded me that I was hungry.

"So, what kind of plan does your father have now?" I asked.

"Well, I'm not sure if I should be the one to tell you these details, it's a little bit complicated and I'm not sure I understand it all."

"I'm okay with complicated," I smiled.

"We probably should have him explain it, I guess."

"Yes, when we return, but tell me, what have you been doing these past few months? Does your mother teach your schooling?"

Just like old times, we must have talked for an hour, maybe two. Sometime later we returned to my home—talking and laughing, kidding and sharing, just like before. I suddenly realized how happy I was to have her back by my side. We climbed the steps to the door and went inside.

"Did you get the honey treats?" Kateb asked as we stood inside, adjusting to the darkness.

Suddenly I remembered! We both looked at each other in surprise, and then I grinned sheepishly. We had *completely* forgotten the honey. Even so, I had suspected all along that the errand was really just a ruse to get us out of the house, and alone. I could play along with that, but I would make Kateb suffer for his sneaky trick.

"No father, no honey treats," I said. "And we checked everywhere, up and down the market place. They must have run out."

"Strange," my father said, looking off into space and avoiding eye contact. "I saw plenty of them just the other day …."

I returned the coin purse and Zafir tucked it away. "Maybe you should look again tomorrow," he suggested. "Now is the harvest of spring honey, the sweetest."

"Yes, good idea, I will," I said.

"And I will bring Rasha back to help you look," Zafir said. "She is good at such things."

My eyes grew big at the suggestion, and then I felt everyone look at me, triggering the heat of embarrassment rising in my face. Despite my efforts to hide it, everyone knew I was blushing.

Fortunately, for the sake of my embarrassment, Zafir suddenly announced it was time to return to their home.

"Well, it has been a pure delight, my good friends!" Zafir said. "We must get on the road to be back home by night fall. This was a lovely day and an excellent dinner, Dalal, thank you for your hospitality."

The adults extended hands, thanking one another, hugs among the women, and bidding farewell. They moved toward the door but Rasha stayed, not moving, and looked right at me.

"You are coming tomorrow?" I asked.

"I guess so, father says so," she said. And with that she reached out and took *my hand* in both of hers and squeezed it gently. "Goodbye," she said, letting me go and quickly turned out the door.

My heart was pounding, I didn't expect that. I just stood there electrified. She *touched my hand*—actually touched it. And with both of *hers*, and oh, they were so soft—the softest I had ever felt, and smooth, delicate, and a tender touch that was warm—and *soft*.

My parents had seen the quick exchange from the corner of their eyes and let the mild breach of decorum pass without comment. They followed their guests out the door and waved them goodbye. I wasn't sure what I was supposed to do, I was still stunned. So, I stood behind, watching over my parent's shoulders as Talib helped Rasheeda and Rasha climb on their kneeling camels. The beasts rose to their feet, and with the family securely seated, Zafir led the way, starting up the road with Talib following closely behind in his donkey cart.

After just a few steps Rasha turned in her saddle and looked back, catching me watching her. She smiled warmly, directly at *me* for just long enough, and then turned back and continued on with her parents.

Poor me. I was a complete wreck after that—I couldn't eat, I couldn't think, I didn't even touch my supper. As my father explained to me the journey I was about to take, far away from home for possibly two long years, and the significance of the scrolls that I could be learning, I simply wasn't listening. Kateb could see his son was truly smitten, and gave up trying to compete with the powerful and overwhelming forces of nature that had just had their say in my heart. He decided to try telling me again in the morning.

As for me, I laid awake for hours that night, thinking of nothing else but my Rasha.

با هبعه 17 محبوب

THE CARAVAN

Zafir strode strongly through the center market places of Rekeem, past the tents and kneeling camels of his train as it readied for departure the next morning. He acknowledged the greetings of his relatives and servants. More than 300 camels were lined up through the center of town awaiting loads and drivers who busied themselves with their personal packing.

Although I was already the stature of a full-grown man, I still had some surprising difficulty keeping up with the old chieftain who barked orders, queried the riders, and checked on supplies.

"Dressing a trade caravan has some important differences," Zafir explained. "Today we prepare for Leuke Kome, leave our families to travel to Saba' by dhow. Did you know that Rasha has asked to stay here with your parents?"

"So I've heard," I replied, feigning disinterest.

"Good. She will be here in the morning. And then at Leuke Kome we will take on more camels and prepare for the trip east. Do you know of Saba'?"

"Your other home, I've heard of it," I said. "A city not far from the coast that watches the sea trade?"

"Yes, and a wealthy place. By dhow it's three weeks south of here—twice that by land," Zafir said. "We'll talk more later. But watch closely and learn fast, we have a long trip in the front of us."

When Zafir stopped to engage a supplier in negotiations over his pack camels, I drifted from the conversation to mingle with some familiar faces. There I found Ammar dressed in his usual light brown robe and turban, sorting through his bag of navigation charts. His thin face and sagging jowls were prickly with black whiskers and there was a look of consternation in his grey eyes.

"Ammar!" I called. "Are you coming on this trip?"

"Bassam! I heard rumors that you will join us, and I knew if any young man was chosen for this honor it must be Bassam."

"Honor? Oh no, I'm here in the place of my father, he's too old for such journeys, you know Kateb!"

"Too old? That's not what I heard."

"Well, I don't mind. Zafir tells me I'll learn the secrets of the caravan. Do you know the secrets of the caravan?"

Ammar smiled behind his whiskers and closed his satchel of maps. "Oh no, not me," he sighed. "I'm just a part-time navigator and a full-time goat herder. I couldn't find any of those hidden wells even if my life depended on it."

Just then I spied the man's weathered kamal with its knotted string laid out on a black cloth beside his saddle. "Seems to me you could chart a location for every stop using this instrument of yours." I picked up the kamal to examine. "And if I know my friend Ammar, he's got those wells already marked on his maps if not in his head."

"Now you flatter me!" Ammar said. "Can I be a good navigator if I can't be trusted by my masters?"

I looked up just in time to catch the old man's wink.

So! The old star gazer did know of the desert! I made a mental note of it—such knowledge could prove useful some day.

The efficiency of the ancient caravan was an organizational marvel. A wealthy chieftain like Zafir had supplies and animals stationed all along the trade routes, some to pick up, others to drop off, all of this according to the loads being shipped, and the families and investors who participated.

And where the desert sands gave way to mountainous paths of greater hostility, there were donkeys and horses that awaited their arrival. It was unusual for a single train to carry its burdens so far east. Typically the caravans served as intermediaries to move loads short distances from one center to another.

This trip was different. Zafir was securing new trade, and planned to continue these long treks until there was a well-entrenched pattern of expectations and returns. Or, so he told me—a long trade route that could end up with Zafir finally able to rest.

The merchants of Rekeem profited handsomely from supplying these large caravans. With the chartered help of two additional herds, Zafir's final tally exceeded 480 camels. That represented a large and costly purchase of supplies.

Since this first leg of the journey was through populated places, the load of edibles could be reduced—a relief for Zafir's purse. The camels could serve many days without stopping, and had the added advantage of being free to sniff out the thorny khulla or other shrubbery along the way. For the others our merchants were happy to stock them with whatever was needed—at a great cost for each train assembled.

Everywhere I looked, all along the sides of the grand boulevard, there were bales of feed-grasses and sacks of grain stacked close by where Zafir's men were positioned for loading.

The men's personal items were carried in smaller woven sacks which also carried cheeses and dried dates, skins of water—everything needed to be carefully collected separately and reckoned according to the travel time between re-supply stops—each to his own on the desert.

Zafir told me that it was customary for the Abdali-ud-din to reward the faithfulness of their laborers with a feast each evening of fatted lambs or calves, and plenty to drink. This worked along trails where sheep and goats could be herded for just such a purpose.

I was most impressed with the source of the Abdali-ud-din's strength. It was in their knowledge of an intricate network of cisterns. These were scattered all along the trade routes, especially in the deep desert. I asked Zafir about that and he explained that traveling the deserts was dangerous enough, but staying in the deep wilderness, away from the settlements where bandits could launch an attack, made for a much safer trip. That was why Abdali-ud-din had dug cisterns many centuries earlier. Secret cisterns that only they knew about. That was their advantage.

"Why don't they follow you into the deep? Seems none of them could last very long."

"That is why we have supplies hidden from the casual traveler," Zafir said. "They ensure that none but the informed could make such haste from place to place. Raiders could not endure the vast stretches of the desert interior and are thus obliged to launch their attacks from the foothills near hideouts, or on the outskirts of large cities where escape offered many avenues. In this manner, the long caravans of the Abdali-ud-din may move into the wastelands and remain there for long periods of time and long distances—and not be followed."

Zafir's plan for the first leg of the trip was a cargo trip to Leuke Kome, and by that, he meant his family and the families of his brethren. The families' last stop was Saba' by the sea. From Leuke Kome, boats would finish the trip. The route he chose traveled close to settled lands, an effort to avoid danger where possible—but also out of sight to avoid the trespass taxes. The journey to Leuke Kome was well traveled, and at a caravan's pace, we could deliver Rasheeda and her daughters in about ten day's time.

As the afternoon wore on, I lingered behind Zafir's long gait. The strain of imminent departure began to show in the old chieftain's tone and approach. The train had to be ready so that we could be out of the Siq and on the trail before sunup the next morning.

I stopped at a cluster of war camels where their riders prepared their packs. These men of Al Murrah were legendary for their amazing desert tracking skills. They could read the nuances of a week's old path in moving sand, and could wield the sword in protection better than any other.

For dozens of decades these fiercely loyal guards of the Abdali-ud-din escorted the trade east and west across the vast wilderness. It was for each man a great honor to be hand-chosen by one so revered as Zafir, and they would give their lives to prove his trust in them.

Then I spotted Fawzi and Habib, and worked my way through the camels to stand at their side. "Did you hear, Fawzi, did you hear I'm coming on another trip with you?"

"Ah, my young Bassam," Fawzi said, smiling at me in his usual mocking grimace that made his eyes go half-shut as if to hide a tease. Beneath his turban his tanned forehead wrinkled with mischievousness and his thin eyebrows arched like the back of a spooked cat. "Of course I heard. In fact, I wanted to warn you. Have you not seen the warriors of Al Murrah who prepare? Each man has a price on his head, so you must unsheathe your knife and keep it near you when you sleep!"

Habib smirked as the conversation unfolded, tightening down some bundles to his camel's saddle while suppressing a laugh.

"Ha!" I said laughing. "You gave me sleepless nights with such tales all the way to Aila. I'm wise to your old tricks, Fawzi. And so is my father. He said the both of you are in the very likeness of your fathers, the bearers of tall tales!"

"Your father, will he join us?" Habib asked, looking at me for the first time. His brown eyes looked sincere and his rugged face showed neither greeting nor disapproval. It was, in fact, quite blank.

"No, and I go in his stead."

"Then I'll tell the cutthroats," Habib said breaking into a smile. "I'll tell them that there will be a young throat in our camp this night."

"Oh yes," Fawzi cut in. "And I'll tell them that they need to sharpen only their short knives."

I laughed as best I could and called them a camel's tail. But walking away, my vivid imagination conjured up a nasty image and I instinctively reached down to feel the security of my own sheathed knife that hung at my side. Seeing this from afar, Fawzi and Habib laughed out loud.

There is never time enough for a proper goodbye. Though night had long fallen. Dalal busied herself with last minute preparations to get me ready. It was her way of sending me with a mother's love that should last for the entire duration of the journey. Extra clothing, mending materials, ointments and salves, and food for that first week of travel. Even with no extra room aboard my camel, I'm sure had I not been watching, she could have packed even more.

My father and I spent the evening reclined on mats beneath the oil lamp to study his old maps of the region.

He turned the skin closer and traced the large boot of Arabia with his eye. "A trek to this northern arm of the sea will be the shortest stretch," he said rubbing his chin, "unless Zafir wishes once more to try those spiteful merchants of Aila."

"Spiteful?" I asked.

"The men of Aila guard the southern passages to the sea through these hills," Kateb said, drawing a line with his finger. "They exact a toll for the trespass and once long ago they guaranteed safe passage to everyone. In recent years the raiders of the Fukara have been active here.

Many caravans have fallen prey before they reached the safety of the sea, and the Aila do nothing."

"For this the caravans no longer stop?"

"Greed has corrupted the merchants of Aila. For a deben of silver they waive the restrictions, but the traders are on their own once they pass from the valleys of the city."

"Why don't the caravans follow the coast more south?"

"There is no road there, only rocky terrain and swampy marshes right down to the shore. The best routes, a route Zafir has taken before, is through the western plains, a trip peaceful enough, though if he must stray he will have to pay the sheiks for the right."

"And this makes the Aila angry? Because the caravans pass by and pay no toll?"

"This makes the Aila angry."

And then Dalal interrupted our discussion and plopped right on top of our maps a leather-wrapped bundle. Kateb was pleasantly surprised. "My old writing supplies," he said. He smiled at the memories, and turned it to loosen the tie. Spread before us was half a dozen pockets with reed and brush pens, a bundle of styli, a small knife, a sharpening tool, an empty ink pot, and a dozen sheets of yellowed animal parchment and papyrus that curled together like a scroll. I reached for a stylus that looked interesting and placed it in my fingers. Its worn tapering form fit perfectly the gentle hold of my fingers. *That's* the pen I will use on this trip, I decided.

"You will record this journey of yours, my son," Dalal said. "And when you return, I want you to read to us from these pages and tell us all about your adventure. Until then, we'll pray to God for his protection and your safety."

"I will write, mother, I will write everything." I said. "I will write you a letter, to you and father, and, um, I suppose, to Rasha also. I will tell you about our journey. We will enjoy it when I return."

Kateb pushed to his knees and sat upright. "You will need ink for the pot, let me teach you an old guarded family secret to make ink as black as Zafir's fortune that will last twice as long"

"Guarded recipe?"

"Oh yes, a mixture of gall-nuts, henna and gum from the tree. You will need to add the soot and water, but first we must find a thorn tree. Bring the lamp and follow me."

"You two be brief," Dalal called after us. "It will be a busy morning as Rasha will come and you must go, Bassam. Be brief, Kateb!" She stepped back inside knowing that her words had fallen on deaf ears.

ب هبعه 18 محبوب

THE VEIL

It was still dark when Zafir roused his men to load their camels, round up their herds of sheep and goats, and prepare for departure.

I was already at the boulevard in the flickering light of a cook-fire when Zafir's messengers passed by, greeting me with a wave.

I had dressed well for the departure—my durable riding robes, a headdress of thick weave, dark-brown pants, a sheet wrapped about my waist, and a woolen covering for warmth. Acknowledging the passers-by with a nod, I tended to last minute details and supplies for my kneeling camel, pushing another change of clothing into the back pouch, checking that my writing materials were secure and within reach behind my saddle.

Already a few pack animals and lead camels were moving in slow plods past me through the dim light of the small fires, finding their way toward the shadowed plaza.

I slung a water skin over the horn of the saddle and Dalal leaned over to put extra bread in the back pouch.

"Mother!" I said. "My bakra won't give milk in protest if you add any more weight, let her be. I'll be fine, I've done this before."

"Before? Then my son you must have it because you'll be hungry by midday! God be with you, and eat this bread to remember the hands that made it." And then she held out her closed fist.

"What is this?"

"Our young Rasha wanted to give you this gift for your journey," and she opened her hand to reveal a neatly folded white silk, a small veil with silver lace along its edges. I lifted it from my mother's hand and opened it. Across its center, embroidered in carefully stitched threads of gold, were the words, "Be safe and well. Peace. Joy. Courage."

"The blessing of the traveler," I said, smiling. "And she made this herself? She has learned a great deal from you, mother. But I have no gift for her."

"I shouldn't worry my son," Dalal said. "Your gift is your return to us. Let this blessing guide your courage in all of the days you're away from us."

I took her by the shoulders. "I will miss you the most, mother," I told her, looking her squarely in the eyes. "I will not forget, and remember you always." I kissed both of her checks and wrapped my arms around her, hugging her tight. "I love you, mother," I said. And then over her shoulder I saw Rasha in the shadows, watching us from behind the slats of an empty coffee booth.

Letting go of mother, I beckoned Rasha closer.

"Rasha! Please, come, join us by the fire!" I stretched my hand to her. "And thank you for this gift and your thoughtfulness—it carries your heart-felt message that means the world to me. I'll always keep it—keep it with me always. And when I get to Chang'an, I will find a gift to bring back to you."

Rasha took a few hesitant steps nearer, holding from the dust the hem of her skirts and a light-colored woolen for warmth that was open in the front. It draped from her shoulders to her feet.

My mother wisely sensed that a difficult goodbye for the two of us was about to unfold. Wanting to give us privacy she took Kateb's arm and pulled him a dozen steps away to my kneeling camel. "Dear, will you double check these writing supplies? Does he have enough ink in the pot?"

Standing apart from me in the shadows beyond the fire, Rasha stepped forward stopping a polite distance, just out of my reach. The shimmering light of the fire danced across her face and hands, casting light and shadows over the curves of her slender form. It gave sparkle to her brave smile and a shine to her eyes. Her beautiful oval face was steady with seriousness. "I really won't need a gift from Chang'an," she said soberly. "I will be here with your parents while you travel with father. Living here with them is gift enough for me."

"They will love you just as they love me," I told her. "And better care you will not find, in this city or anywhere." I took a step toward her, and, lowering my voice so that only she could hear, "For you, Rasha, I will make the time pass quickly. These will be short months, and that will be my gift to you."

She discreetly shuffled her right foot, putting it nearer to mine, almost touching sandals. Looking up into my face to find my eyes she asked, "I hope you will write in your journal everything you see. All of the details, every day, will you? I want to hear you read them to me when…" and then she looked down again, sliding her left foot forward in the darkness, touching her sandal to mine, "… when you return safely to us."

I felt the touch, and I couldn't free my gaze from her eyes—warm and inviting portals into her deepest thoughts and hopes. Without thinking I reached out and took her hands to close the gap between us, an act of sudden intimacy that caught both of us by surprise. She didn't resist.

Without speaking, I smiled kindly and studied her for a long moment—her hair, her lips, her eyes, as if to engrave an image I could not forget, to carve the whole of her into my remembrance. "Will you be here when I return, my Rasha?"

I saw her eyes glow with pondering wonder at the request. *Will I be here*? she seemed to be weighing in her heart. I could see the struggle in her emotions. Many months—two years at least, it is such a long time. *Will I be here*? Who could possibly guess, so many things could happen—so much has happened. Two years? *Will I be here*? The words brought deep feelings to the surface too fast to restrain, and suddenly, two large tears broke free, creasing down her cheeks on either side. I watched her tighten up her chin, trying not to lose control, to hold firm, determined not to look away, not now. She kept her gaze fixed on me, her lips trembling, fighting the longing that challenged her composure. "I will be here," she whispered. "Yes, I will wait for your return, and you may find me on the steps of Al Khazna, there, by your father, the very day you come back to us."

I reached gently to her face and wiped the tears with the lovingt caress of my hand, and then combed my fingers into the fullness of her silky hair. She closed her eyes a moment to let me inhale the rich sweetness of her fragrance of myrrh, and to feel the warmth of her body so close to mine.

"I will write you," I said softly, looking for her to open her eyes again. "And if there is a way, a passing caravan, a traveler, a boat, or some other way, I will send you my letters whenever I can, and then…"

Rasha suddenly leaned forward, pressing herself against my chest and wrapped her arms tightly around me, taking an easy, slow breath—a remembrance of the musky desert perfumes that permeated my clothing—lasting remnants of my travels beyond the city, those faded reminders of trips I had performed and must yet perform. She squeezed tight against me—willing herself into me, to be a part of me, infusing a measure of her deepest feeling directly to my heart, her spirit reaching into my thoughts and my memory of her. "Will you?" she whispered, and looked up at me, suddenly becoming lost in the intensity of the moment.

Her face was so close I could feel her breath on my mouth and taste the heat of her skin—her long black waves of hair crumpled against my neck and the amorous lotions of desire clouded my mind with an intoxicating, wonderful fog. My world slowly vanished except for her lips and her eyes—soft blue swirls of passion, numbing my senses and masking my caution as I reached with halting desire around the modesty of her shawl and soft-woven robe, pressing it to the curve of her waist—carefully—slowly—to the smooth of her back, and pulled her tenderly against me, warmly. And then softly, all things about us fell dark and silent—no sound but the throbbing of our hearts pounding in our ears—no vision but our faces drawing to each other in quiet surrender—no whispers but shallow breaths exchanging—no reality except dreamy eyes closing—no feeling but trembling lips drawing near, desiring, closing together in hot, moist—

"Ahem! Ahem!" Kateb suddenly said, shocking us apart with surprise. Dropping our hands quickly and stepping back, we both looked over at him, stunned, blinking in confused annoyance—*who is that rude intruder*?

Oh—it was only Kateb.

"They're leaving, my son," he said with a pained smile.

Suddenly the animal noise of the moving traffic became loud again, a cacophony of goats and camels and sheep and riders passing up the boulevard in the fire-lit darkness, cursing and shouting, greeting friends and laughing—a jangling, snorting, growling, noisy crowd.

My heart was still pounding in my throat, my mouth was dry, my head was buzzing, and I felt short of breath. I swallowed hoarsely. "Yes, of course, I will," was all I could say to Rasha's question.

I looked at her—her face had paled and she swallowed, trying to find her voice. Looking up at me she stopped a word in her mouth to catch her breath. I could see the pounding of her heart in the smoothness of her neck and gently put my hand to her cheek, cuddling her face and then caressing the slight throbbing in her throat. She closed her eyes, tilted her head to the side to squeeze my hand against the softness of her cheek—then reached up to gently push me away, to let me go. She whispered as best she could a choked, heartfelt but final goodbye.

I dropped my arm to my side and just stood there, unmoving and alone, like an exhausted rag hung out to dry. I watched her retreat into the loving arms of mother who came to her side in comfort.

I could not make words come from my throat and could only look at her with longing in my arms, my heart and my eyes, and then mouthed to her my own heartfelt "goodbye."

Kateb pulled me over to him in a strong embrace. "Learn well my son," he said with strength, locking eyes and looking deep, trying to help me stay focused on the task ahead. "Zafir has told me of the scrolls. These are the secrets, my son. Be patient in learning, it is the way of the Abdali-ud-din. It will prosper you."

He hugged me again and smiled. Putting an arm around my shoulder he raised his other skyward and looked to heaven. "Praise be to God, protect and guard my son through the wisdoms of this great journey." Looking back at me, "Return safe to us, my son. With honor, and no regrets."

I tried to smile. "Thank you, father," and looking over at Rasha, I said, "I will write to you each day Rasha, but you must promise me."

She looked at me quizzically. "Promise what?"

"You must also write about your life with mother and father, what you experience, every day. And when I return we will read your letters and mine—together. Do you promise?"

She nodded her head and smiled. "I will," she said.

I nodded back and then turned dutifully to my camel and climbed onto the saddle. Adjusting my place, I snapped my riding stick to the beast's shoulder, "Hut hut!" My bakra snorted and complained but obeyed, pushing out her hind legs thrusting the load forward and then standing upright, thrusting it back into place. I reached down and scratched her, behind the ears, to calm her. Bakra always liked that, and this morning was no different.

The dancing flames of the fire illuminated me high in the saddle as I took the hem of my headdress and drew it across my face leaving only my eyes showing. In the flickering light, my suave manner gave me the appearance of royal magnificence and bravery like the sheiks themselves. But known only to me and, I suspected, by my mother, the scarf masked the trembling chin and welling eyes of a boy leaving home, truly leaving the only real life and family I had ever known and ever loved, to be gone for a very long time. I looked longingly at them, standing there, bidding me goodbye.

The train was well in motion by this time so I steered my camel into the crowd, guiding her steps carefully past the small fire pots, and rode her a few paces in the direction of the plaza and the blackened mouth of the Siq.

Finding my place in the traffic, I turned in my saddle and lifted my hand high over my head and waved my stick.

Faded behind a dozen paces, by dim firelight, I saw Kateb and Dalal standing. They raised their hands in return.

Between them Rasha leaned within the embrace of mother whose gentle arm around her shoulders held the girl warmly to her side.

Rasha had a strange expression in the faintly-flickering firelight—a new expression on her face that caught my eye and I slowed my ride to look. At that very moment she reached down and brought up her shawl to veil her face after the manner of the newly betrothed! She locked her eyes to mine to ensure delivery of the silent promise.

My eyes must have bulged in astonished surprise and I sat up tall in my saddle. The subtle gesture went unseen by anyone but *me*. It took a moment of shock, and then joy, before I thought to raise my hand to acknowledge her covenant. But the crowding camels moved into the road, blocking the view.

Did she see me, did she? Did she see me waving my hand, did she see me answer the veil?

The riders and loads pushed me into the throng, shoving me forward amidst snorts and growls and the curses of scolding drivers.

I sat taller, waving my stick high over my head, stretching to look back through the thick chaos of the large shadowy shapes crowding in the darkness. I strained to locate her again but could no longer find her in the dusty dark. Suddenly the great mass of animals rounded a bend and the glow of the fires behind us disappeared and blackness shrouded the cliff walls of my beloved home. My chance was gone.

With a broadening smile and a new thrill pounding in my chest, I turned forward toward the mouth of the torch-lit Siq, a rush of bewilderment and confusing thoughts now burning hot through my head.

I snapped my stick to the camel's side and urged her into the black entrance, vowing in a whispered declaration, "I promise you Rasha, I promise you mother and father, *I will return with honor*."

ب هبعه 19 محبوب

RULES OF THE DESERT

"So, did you kiss her?" Fawzi asked, steering his camel alongside mine.

I didn't hear a word. My eyes were fixated on the pebble-strewn desert flat that stretched out in front of us—lost in a dream. The sun had risen high since our departure from Rekeem, and shined hot on my shoulders.

"What?" I said, looking up, confused.

"I said, did you kiss her? Come on Bassam! We all saw you."

"Saw me what?"

"Kissing her! The whole caravan rode by, didn't you hear us calling? And besides, aren't you just a little young for that?"

"We weren't kissing."

"Well, if that's not kissing, then—okay, then it was an *almost* kiss?"

I just ignored him.

"And she's so much older than you," Fawzi continued. "Must be like, what, 18, 19, 20? Does your father approve you courting older women?"

I felt the heat rising in my face, and it wasn't the desert sun. "No, she's not older than me, and no we didn't kiss."

"If you weren't kissing, then what was so interesting that you had to look so very, very close into her eyes?"

"You couldn't get any closer," said Habib pulling up just then to join the tease, the three of us now riding in a tight formation.

"I was just saying goodbye, and …"

"Oh, I get it," Fawzi interrupted. "She's deaf! Is that it? Her ears, not working, couldn't hear a word you were saying?"

"Yeah, that's got to be it," Habib said. "Couldn't hear a word. And it was so noisy, wasn't it noisy Fawzi? All those animals and riders…."

"Yes, very noisy," Fawzi said. "In fact, I was pointing you out to Zafir as we passed by, and that's exactly what he said—'Poor girl, she can't hear him,' he said. I swear it, that's what he said!"

"We did not kiss," I said, and dug my heels into my bakra's ribs, making her jump into a fast walk, pushing ahead to pass by the riders in front.

Fawzi and Habib laughed hard. "Does your bakra also have bad ears, Bassam?" Fawzi called after. "Have you tried telling her 'good morning'?"

"Is bakra's breath as sweet?" Habib laughed after.

I rode out of earshot and pulled up alongside other friends near the front of the caravan. I reached inside my robe for Rasha's small veil and found it tucked close to my heart for safe keeping.

* * *

It wasn't until the morning of the second day that Zafir guided his slender war camel through the dust and traffic and pulled up alongside mine. The man's streaked black beard shined in the sun, his eyes were big and alive, and his skin seemed smoother in the open weather as if he was born to be on the trail. His headdress parted in the slight breeze, and his travel-weary hands gripped his camel's leather reins and a riding stick.

"At last we can speak, my boy!" he said with a zestful smile. "See that?" he said, pointing his stick at the vast caravan spread out before us. "That is the finest builder of wealth the world has ever known .... a fine line of camels, horses and flocks, making a full day's ride with food and drink to spare. We move the riches of the world, in short trips or long, from the utter west to the utter east, north and south, it matters not. And for each we profit, and with profit we exchange for more. Indeed, the finest builders of wealth in the world are the caravans of the Abdali-ud-din. So, my young Bassam, did you eat?"

"Yes, I've eaten well. And slept well, too," I told him.

"And you wonder why I don't offer you my tent?"

"Not really, I'm content to bed among the others, and you have your family, I have my own covering."

"Content? You don't know content. I'll show you the way of the elders and then you will want a tent of the elders. But first you must learn the way of the caravan." With that he snapped at his camel and galloped to the head, beckoning me to follow.

A dozen war camels headed the caravan, their riders eyed me with distrust.

"These are Al Murrah," Zafir said. I smiled at Tamir but didn't recognize the others. "All my men carry the sword, but only Al Murrah are skilled with it," Zafir said. "They guard the train front and back, along the sides. You'll see them in bunches, riding in advance, standing watch as we pass, chasing down the rear to see if we are followed, and advancing the trail far beyond the horizon. You can know them only by their swords for they will dress as all men. For now they ride war camels but after the pass most of them will take horses."

Zafir suddenly turned his camel in the way of mine and both beasts stumbled to a snorting, dusty stop. Zafir raised his stick and stabbed it directly onto my chest. Locking eyes he lowered his voice and spoke slowly, "The first, the very first rule of the desert is this—always keep up your guard, young Bassam. Always keep up your guard. You must never forget it. Ever. Keep up your guard in all things, this is the first rule of the desert." He dropped his stick and turned. "Come, follow." He turned his camel and rode 300 paces toward the rear.

When I caught up Zafir pointed his stick at a single rider. "He is Sofian, a captain of a hundred. I have four such captains. Each captains a hundred riders and their camels and the loads they carry. They know what I know, Bassam. I trust them and so must you. If there is trouble, always follow one of them."

Sofian studied my face a moment as he rode by, then offered a polite salutation. I tipped my head in return.

Zafir pulled his camel far to the side and stopped to allow the train to pass, pointing again with his stick. "That man on the white saddle, that's Rakin, he is a captain of fifty." The man rode past laughing with another as if deep in telling a story about some great adventure. "I have eight such men, they don't know what I know, only what their captain tells them. If there is trouble, and no other rises to lead, you must follow a captain of fifty. You will come to know them as our journey proceeds."

He explained the captains of fifty had charge of the family members and the mahmils, their pack camels, their comfort. These were always protected in the center front of the caravan. "Less dust, more protection," Zafir said. The men positioned the food and water baskets directly behind to follow whatever riches Zafir was moving—in this case, myrrh, frankincense, spices from the Orient, and of course, treasure. "Come follow, one more time," he said.

He kicked his camel toward the back of the train where additional Al

Murrah rode, swords to their sides. Most of the baggage camels were here with loads of tents, supplies and trade items.

"Those in front of Al Murrah, they're captains of ten. I have 40 such men, they protect our rearward. They don't know anything but what their captains tell them, and in time of trouble, if no other rises, follow a captain of ten. Is that making sense how I organize? We'll speak again tomorrow," and snapped his stick to gallop to the head of the caravan.

After many more hours of riding, the sun reached the western horizon just as the caravan found a suitable place to camp. It was on a slight slope near some desert growth where the animals chewed while we set ourselves. Dead shrubs in a ravine provided fuel for that night's celebrated dinner.

As promised, several sheep were slaughtered and roasted, a deliciously satisfying end to a long, hard push. The feasting gave me strength. Afterwards, the veterans circled around small fires to exchange stories of trials on the trails.

I retired early to my sleeping place—it was nighttime but too early to sleep. Spreading out my mat by my saddle, I propped up a pillow for a backrest. Tucking the corners of my blanket in the wedges of the saddle I pulled the other end over my head, stretching it into a small tent; two sticks held up the corners in front of me.

Placing an old brass oil lamp burning bright, I opened my writings, spread out a sheet of papyrus, and inked my pen.

"Day 2—Dear Rasha, Did you see the sun rise this morning? It was spectacular. The sky was orange and pink with small clouds like balls of fire—just beautiful. We passed a dead man off the side of the trail, a badawi. He was there a long time, many months. Habib said we don't bury or burn the dead, it is the way of the desert. I am eating well. I bought fruit and good bread from a small stand near an orchard. We traveled 200 stadia today, 250 yesterday, a little slow for a train this size, but your father said things will get better as men learn their place. Zafir has loyal men. The lazy have no place here, all have work to do, no one rides free. I will help Ammar to navigate and he will teach me the science of the stars. We saw strangers watching us from afar, but we are safe. We

have 400 swords to protect the treasures of Zafir. Inside my belt I keep your veil. It smells of myrrh.—Bassam"

"Dear Bassam—I hope you are safe. Kateb took a small fall today, he didn't have his stick. He has a bruise on his knee, but he is stubborn. We scolded him for you. Dalal will take me to market tomorrow and we will look for new wool. It is quiet in Rekeem, many people miss their husbands and brothers and sons.—Rasha"

ب هبعه 20 محبوب

THE KAMAL

Halfway to Leuke Kome we passed through a place famous for the desert sand storms. Such storms churn quickly on the shoulders of the infrequent winds, and rise reluctantly from the vast barren stretches where no earthly formation dares interfere. Like a sleepy giant waking from slumber, they grow tall into thick, billowing mountains of rushing brown clouds, infusing intensity with every passing moment. Rolling high through the sky such storms smother the flatlands in wide wheels of formless, boiling barbarity, venting their energies against man and beast with furious eclipsing onslaught that darkens the sky, claps thunder and flashes sparks. For the caravan, they hit like a million stinging flies that feverishly cut and scrape against exposed flesh, pummel the clothing, grind at the goods, and steal away the very breath of life.

To survive such maelstroms the veterans showed me to put our camels to kneel and take shelter behind them. These large humped beasts are indeed kin to the desert—distant cousins to the dunes—cursed for their banality to carry men from here to there, but dressed for little concern in such storms. Nature equips them in perfect armor—mottled tufts of shaggy hair that sifts immunity from the bite of the stinging sands. Their engineered eyes close to mere slits in such storms, and patience is theirs through the darkness till duration's end.

The storm that blew past our men with such ferocity that day startled even the most experienced camels that snorted and jumped. Rising high amidst the blowing sands was a thick red dust that covered all things in rusty film. The fineness of it found its way into our ears and eyes, down our shirts, between our toes, and as grittiness between our teeth.

When the storm hit I followed the others and knelt my camel, dismounted and covered my face. The roar of the wind and the hissing of the sand cutting against our clothing kept the entire train pinned for most of half an hour. And then, just as suddenly, the wind stopped and the airborne menace drifted like gentle fabrics back to earth—a hazy sky gave way to stark blue and a hot sun.

As we stood to check on our fellows, each of us had become a ghostly phantom of pale red dust. Removing scarves, our faces suddenly gave life to the members—mouths, eyes, teeth grinning through masks of reddish powder, all the silly aftermath of unwilling participation in an accidental masquerade.

"You're a mess!" I laughed, slapping Fawzi on the shoulder. A blossoming plume of red dust clouded Fawzi's face.

Fawzi countered, rubbing his hand on my headdress, stirring a thick cloud about my face making me cough. "Magnificent," he said.

The road to Leuke Kome was well traveled with expansive stretches of flat, open terrain. From the slopes leading into these flats a traveler could see from a great distance the long snaking line of other caravans in the same region.

It was no threat when such strangers passed—it was a welcomed relief and often led to salutations and greetings—cheering each other on in their lonesome journeys, even if only for the long moments it required to pass by.

For this trip Zafir employed camels of two kinds. The stronger dromedaries packed the heaviest loads—large hanging baskets, or long boxes straddling to either side of the animal's humps. These did not carry riders but were linked with tied ropes, one to another, in lines of 4 or 5, sometimes 8 or 9. Leading them was a camel of much leaner athleticism—single-humped, tall—a war camel—bred for their speed, endurance and height. These carried swordsmen and laborers, the senior elders, the mahmils, and their families.

Zafir liked the pre-dawn darkness for his departures. He was a disciplined leader. If a man tarried at his cook-fire or the toilet, the train never waited.

Tardiness was not so severe a sin as it could be in the deep desert. But still, conspiring eyes could always be assumed to be watching for the stragglers—those who dallied behind. *They* made the best ambush because of their neglect.

The regular pace of a camel was at least twice that of a man. Casual banter passed the time as hours rolled past, but in inclement or difficult periods, every man kept to himself, following unspoken directions, holding tight the leather reins as securely as he did his life. And thus the caravan became a silent line of life-saving conveyances to cross lands that God meant to kill those less prepared. And so we respected our bakras for God's work that they performed, and withheld the stick unless it was a stubborn urgency. My bakra was different. She obeyed an ear scratch more than the stick.

Stopping or slowing only meant more difficulties farther along. Even in the thick of a sand storm or sudden rain, the train rarely stopped or sought shelter. It was the customary practice to continue riding so long as visibility permitted it.

Regardless of the season, if it was a caravan led by Zafir, he was *always* on the move.

I adjusted quickly to the daily routine of life on the road. The bread my mother made me lasted the first three days—I relied on the foods Zafir provided for the rest.

Each night I made from my blanket a little tent by my camel so I could be among my friends. There I sat to write in my journal, blocked from the evening desert breeze that otherwise could snuff out my lamp.

"Zafir," I asked one day as we rode along in relative quiet, "I look out at this large, living cooperative and I'm learning so many things I never realized before."

"Such as?" he asked.

"The manner whereby problems are solved," I offered. "If there's an argument or difficulty, it's not yours to handle, is it? It falls to one of your captains, right?"

"That's the lesson from Father Moses," Zafir said. "Father Jethro saw his son-in-law killing himself with Israel's children, and told him to share the judgment seat with others lest he exhaust his patience to the grave."

"If a dispute can't be settled," I said, "it looks to me as if it is elevated to the next higher captain, and the next above him—until, if needful, to you."

"Have you seen any disputes brought to me?"

"No, not any."

"And so that is how it works, my son! Father Jethro was wise—I order my men to handle their problems on the lowest possible level. You see it for yourself don't you?"

I nodded. It was an amazing satisfaction of human nature and caravan needs—working together to benefit the individual rider while benefitting the entire group.

"So, if your captains handle the problems among their assigned members, what is your role?"

"I make sure there is fairness," he said. "Sometimes my men, the newer ones, come to see me for solutions—and I happily refuse. Solutions must be made among their own groups where the details and personalities are best known."

"What if a man feels his captain has dealt with him wrongly?"

"Then he may bring it to me, but it isn't my responsibility except to see that the rules are followed. If his cause is just, then I step in to correct all of those who were involved, especially the captains. I won't let my men use me to get their way against the majority. I give all my men equal opportunity to excel, make profit, share or not share their food and water—I expect them to see their place as I see it. So when there is a dispute, I demand integrity from all involved."

"And how do you do that?"

"It's fundamental, Bassam. I teach them correct principles and I expect them to govern themselves."

The herds of goats and sheep moved more slowly than the pack, and always came up on the rear when camp was established. Fawzi told me this luxury of fresh meat had to stop when we arrived at Leuke Kome—the place where familiar territory ended and real desert began for the route north-east. He said the sheep cannot follow us into the deep desert, so enjoy the banquet.

To everyone's delight, Zafir had six sheep roasted once again, and spiced rice and drink for all. The roasting night was a good time with music and games, a happy change from the long hours under a hot sky. I thought I could get used to sitting trapped atop my plodding beast, but after a full day of it, the break was badly needed.

On the fifth night out, after we had eaten well and the men spread out to their fires for tea, I tracked down Ammar just as he was organizing his navigation supplies.

"Ammar! I've been looking for you," I said. "Could you teach me the kamal and the science of the stars?"

"What? You've forgotten already?" He looked at me with a frown. "You were my best student, and you don't remember?"

"Yes, but that was so long ago. Will you show me again? The rest of your kit?"

Ammar grumbled and shook his head. "All right my impatient friend. Let us get away from these fires."

The star gazer took his bag of charts and I followed him carrying a lamp beyond the camp to a gentle slope overlooking where the men had spread out.

It was quiet and dark. The stars overhead blanketed the sky from horizon to horizon, and there was no moon to disturb the lesson. Ammar reached into his bag and removed his kamal—a small square of wood about 2 digits per side with a hole in the center through which passed a string with knots. He let the string uncoil to the ground.

"Before we use the kamal," he said, "you must recite to me the science of the qiyas, ("key-ya's") and tell me the number of isba' ("iz-bah") according to your best calculation."

I studied the sky a moment and spotted the pole star. Exactly as he had taught me before, I stretched out my arms straight in front of me with four fingers together horizontally. Placing hand over hand, I measured the number of finger widths from the horizon to the pole star.

"I measure 14 fingers even," I said, smiling at Ammar in the dark, proud for having so quickly mastered the navigator's skill. *Can it be so hard?* I wondered.

"Good try, now let me do it with a man's hand," Ammar said. Holding his hands at arm's length, Ammar measured 11 fingers and a quarter. "That's eleven isba' and two zam, you're off by almost three isba'. Your sloppy measurements are so far off, you put us *north* of Rekeem by some 2,000 stadia. Do you understand it Bassam? We're going south. If you were in charge we'd be swimming in the West Sea! A fine navigator you are, Bassam! We are already that far *south* of Rekeem this night!"

"Okay, so my hands must grow and so must I," I scowled impatiently. "Will you show me the kamal?"

In trained hands, Ammar's kamal and its strings served as the most accurate navigation instrument available. It was so designed to compensate for the differences in finger widths among its users.

Ammar stood facing north and placed one end of the knotted string between his teeth.

He pulled the string taut in front of him, level with the ground. Sighting along the string he slid the small wooden kamal toward him until he could see that the bottom edge lined up with the distant horizon with the top edge barely touching the pole star.

"Count the knots, and you know how many isba' high stands the pole star. I count eleven and a quarter isba'. Indeed, a boy's hand will gain him nothing but lost!"

"Let me try that!" I took the kamal, put the string between my teeth, pulled it taut and level. Sliding the kamal into position, I counted the knots. "Eleven and a quarter, Ammar! My arms are as long as yours, and this string smells like camel breath."

"Not before I gave it to you, my rude friend! See here," he said, "there are other strings."

Ammar held his bag near the lamp and dug into it for several other strings—each with a unique pattern of knots carefully measured and marked. "This string I use on the sea," he said holding one for me to see. "The seven knots each represent a port. No matter where we are at sea—when I measure the pole star—if the kamal is on the knot, we know to travel no more north or south, we only need to travel east or west to find our port."

"So what is it, east or west? Choose wrong and you'd have to circle the earth to find your port."

"That's why a man must navigate and not a boy. A man knows and you don't. You'd be lost and we'd have to bait a hook to find your bones off the bottom of the sea, or just leave them."

Ammar produced other strings, each carefully copied from the patterns passed down through the generations of regular travel by Abdali-ud-din.

He explained how some of the strings required knowledge of the 15 stars, Sothos being the most important this time of year.

"My maps tell me about the wind in certain places, Bassam. The wind shapes the dunes that point to the sea, and with my kamal and charts and the strings, I can put you anywhere on the map that you please. But it must be *my* maps, not another's because *mine* can be trusted."

It was an amazing science. I took each string and gently pulled them between my fingers, feeling the patterns of knots, each tied at an interval that revealed the secret to traveling from one unknown place to another.

Before the night was out, I planned to sit by Ammar's fire and copy into my journal the patterns of the knots and an outline of the kamal.

"Such knowledge once lost could be costly to regain," Ammar said. "I trust you to keep your record from falling into the wrong hands. Don't write all of this, commit some to memory, Bassam. This is the art and the science of the Abdali-ud-din, the secrets of the desert that grant us the liberty to travel at will—while others are condemned to wandering about the dunes and flats, lost. So, guard them well."

I spent much of first watch trying to create some kind of secret code in my journal in the event it was stolen, so the science of the kamal could not be discovered.

21

LEUKE KOME

When our caravan climbed over the last rise toward Leuke Kome, I suddenly noticed the smell of the sea—light and salty in the afternoon breeze. The change in the air excited my imagination, and the adventure became alive. I wanted Zafir to hurry the train—I wanted to *see!*

Nearing the city we passed between rows of wattle and daub shacks. They were bleached white with age and leaned against each other like sleepy cows. I guessed more than 100 of them housing merchants and venders presenting for the trade. Zafir passed some camp grounds where other caravans were setting up. Many hundreds were there—making their fires, organizing their trade for the market place, settling down after long treks from all directions. They crowded this small place with strange and foreign dress and language. Compared to some, our large caravan suddenly seemed small.

My first view of Leuke Kome was disappointing—I expected a wealthy city where the sights and smells and textures of world-wide exchange could be seen combined in busy and noisy mercantilism. Instead it was quiet, too quiet—*lazy* quiet.

Zafir rode up to my side and noticed my expression as we passed more rows of the little hovels.

"The men of the caravan say that a house is a grave for the living," Zafir said.

"Yes," I said. "So I've heard ...."

"And what do you make of these?"

"I couldn't make my home here," I told him honestly.

Zafir studied me a moment as if calculating a judgment, and then pointed ahead. "The first man I seek at each of my trade stops is my steward who also serves as my agent. In Leuke Kome that man is Jamal al-Din. Jamal should meet us at our camping place on the east of town."

He slowed down to direct other riders who plodded behind looking for the camp. "We'll leave on the third day. I have trading to do and we must prepare for the long trek to the Babilu. Are you friends with Fawzi?"

"Oh yes, he is a good friend."

"Then he will watch over you. Be careful in this town, Bassam. There are many dangers here. It is small, but wicked also comes in small."

A few minutes later the caravan arrived in a large dirt field above the village, giving a good view of the sea that lay beyond. The waters sparkled in the low sun and reflected the distant rolling hills on the far shores where the horizon faded to a thin brown line.

The train circled about and riders dismounted to set camp. I found a place suitable for the night and set my camel to kneel.

I removed her saddle and supplies, then gave her grass for cud and stretched out on my sleeping mat. It was so good to have finally arrived. I took another deep breath of the salty air—delicious!

As darkness began to fall, Fawzi and Suoud found me and set their place next to me so we could talk. They were restless for good food and something to do. When it became dark, the town lit up with night-time celebrations and music. They invited me join them there.

Funny thing about Suoud, this living legend I had heard so much about all my life—he had a swaggering brag as if he knew all about the fishing village, like it was his childhood home. I wasn't sure what to think of him. Back home when I was a boy, yellow-beard told me that Suoud was some kind of hero, but he seemed to me just another rider, another good swordsman for Al Murrah, somebody who had no time for a boy like me.

"It's an ancient sea port but not for the larger boats," Suoud said as we walked through the darkness toward the flickering town. "Only the shallow keeled dhows can float into this harbor, the larger ships are in deep harbors and come no closer."

We made our way down a little cow path to the main dusty road leading to the market place.

This was not a walled city, and the small huts for homes that crowded the outskirts seemed vulnerable, standing so alone like that.

Suoud led us closer to the village center, between rows of shops and diners, and right into the middle of pushing, anxious crowds. The streets were filled with strangers in foreign robes—strolling, mingling with others at coffee stands. The streets were narrow, twisting between rows of white-washed brick structures, haphazardly allowing passageways through the noise of business that became louder as we approached the square.

When we passed the open entrance of a small diner, I looked in and saw it was already filled with customers sitting around little tables. A delicious aroma of roasted lamb and spice bread oozed seductively into our path, enticing us to stop. "Something's cooking in there," Fawzi said. "Are you two hungry?"

I had my hand up when Suoud injected a new plan. "You don't want to eat here, this is for *badawi.* Come to the wharf, there is fresh sea food, and better prices."

In a way the village of Leuke Kome was no different from other places I had visited closer to home. This harbor town was a maze of narrow, crooked streets of paving stones, crowded on either side with open shops, some with canopies, others without, all pushed together side to side. Its dark alleyways reminded me of the Siq, except more dangerous for its blind corners. At the entrance of each shop a merchant or two waited to catch someone's eye, beckoning him to stop and view his wares. Tables of goods and food of all sorts lined the shadowed alleys. I wanted to go exploring. A merchant of knives stood with his brother and called to me as we passed, announcing "A special deal! Just this once! Just for you!

Come now for extra good price." Suoud led us right past, shaking his head.

"The special deal is for the foreigner who knows no better," Suoud said with a scowl. "Pay twenty-five times the cost, and buy two at twice the price. Ha!"

Other merchants offered clothing of every color, hanging on ropes and folded in piles on tables. Others sold baskets and pots, camel whips and carvings, sandals and glassed Egyptian perfumes. And then we approached one shop that did catch my attention. It was a place poorly lit with a few small oil lamps, but it sold reed-pens, inks, paints, brushes and papyrus.

"Suoud," I called out, "wait just a moment." The merchantman rose to offer a greeting. "I need some writing material," I told him.

"This is the finest quality papyrus straight from Egypt on the last boat," the merchant said. With Suoud leading the negotiations, I wasn't sure what to pay, but pulled from my purse an eighth of a silver for 10 good sheets. I bid the man God speed. He thanked me and tucked the money away like it was the crowning achievement of a long but fruitless day.

"So, who's going to read this important writing of yours?" Fawzi asked as we continued down the main street.

"Nobody is going to read this," I said. "This is for Ra—… I mean, this is for my mother. She made me promise to write each day, and then read it to her on our return."

"Ah ha," Suoud smiled, "the old Promise of the Sphinx."

"What's that?"

"The pharaohs placed the Sphinx to guard the pyramids and commanded it to lie when there was peace but to stand up against robbers. They called it Abdul al-Hol, 'Father of Terror.'"

"But it is made of stone, the Sphinx can't move," I said.

"Exactly. It doesn't move and the pyramids still stand. So you see Bassam, the Sphinx has kept its promise."

"That doesn't make any sense."

"Here, let me put it this way," Suoud said. "It's the same thing my father used to say. The secret to living forever, he told me, was to drink a goat-beer every evening and a goat-beer the next morning, and that way you could never die in the night."

"So did he do that?"

"Oh yes! He drank goat-beer every evening and goat-beer the next morning, and it drove my mother to leave that drunken fool, and take me and my brothers with her."

"But did it work?"

"Yes, it worked perfectly."

"So he still lives?"

"Oh no, he died."

"Died? But then how ..."

"It's not contrary young Bassam. He died in the afternoon."

Fawzi could hold it no longer and both men started laughing and laughing. I just looked at them, a perfect picture of bewilderment spread across my face. It made no sense whatsoever.

"Come," Suoud said, "Here is a place to eat. Good fresh fish from today—rice, breads and drink. Let us sit and eat and explain to Bassam the Promise of the Sphinx."

We stayed there late until the beginning of second watch.

That second day was spent exploring the city and visiting the harbor. Zafir introduced me to his friends, the boat captains charged with taking his family to Saba'. Many supplies and pieces of luggage from the caravan were already being loaded for departure the next morning.

As the sun set on that second day, my two escorts invited me for a return visit into the twisting shadows of the village's market place. The excursion, they told me, was for "food and some recreation."

I guessed Suoud and Fawzi must have caught wind of something going on that night because the center of town was alive with the noisy activity of a spirited celebration. "It's to honor the second full moon," a passerby shouted above the noise.

Oil lamps and small fires in red clay pots lined the lanes of the shops, colorful banners hung as enticements for visitors to linger. To me the appearance of this place seemed too much like a trap, a clever scheme to make one final try to relieve the men of their last remaining coins before their departure the next day.

As we pushed our way into the tight crowds, I guessed that another ten caravans must have arrived to account for the streets now thick with strangers. The party-goers clogged the paths and alleyways, and with tipsy silly effort they pushed through one another to move from place to place for more drink and dance and laugh. The music and merriment played loudly at every corner, and the air was lethargic with the wafting smells of fermentation.

"Watch your purse and knife," Suoud warned. "This place is where the thieves make good on old promises." I felt for my belongings and found them intact.

We pushed shoulders and arms to avoid the women fraternizing with strange men who then paired off and staggered, giggling, into dark shadows. It made me shudder. This is *not* a good place, I thought.

I had heard of such places, and upon quick reflection, my curiosity became swallowed up with suspicion and fear. Indeed, the thought most prevalent in my mind at the time was the simple reality that this was no place for a boy my age.

I called out to the others. "Suoud, it's too busy tonight, let's come back in the morning, I'm not that hungry anyway."

Suoud couldn't hear above the raucous activities and ploughed onward toward a large crowd of drinking and laughter. The odd smelling fog of burning incense and fermented thrill was almost too heavy for me to breathe.

"Fawzi," I called out again, pulling on his sleeve. "Where are we going?"

"For food and fun!" Fawzi yelled back.

"For you, okay, but I want to go back."

"Go back? Are you crazy? We just got here, the party has just begun!"

"Yes, but go back, just me, I'm not hungry anyway."

"Don't you want food?"

"I had food back at camp, I've got things I'd rather get done back there tonight."

Fawzi shrugged and called out to Suoud. "Hey party man, I'm taking Bassam back, I'll catch up with you in a while."

Suoud looked back over his shoulder. "Bassam, I thought you were a man for such things! Are you telling me this isn't the life for the kin of Zafir?"

"I'm not his kin."

"No kin? That's not what I heard. In that case, you have no honor to shame. Come!"

"No thanks," I said, stopping in my place. "Fawzi will take me, and he will come back to you. I'll see you in the morning, Suoud."

"It's your last chance before the desert! You must try some of this," and he picked a clay mug of dark liquid from an open counter and offered it to me.

I put up my hand and shook my head. “That poison is for you, wild man! I should go.”

Suoud rolled his eyes and brushed me away. “Be gone with you and don’t wake me in the morning, I’ll be suffering for my fun tonight. You won’t know fun until you put on a headache and burning stomach like I will!”

Fawzi grabbed my arm and led me back into the pushing, shoving horde of strangers.

ORPHANED SWORD

I felt no shame when I awoke the next morning, although I wasn’t sure how best to admit my reluctance from the night before.

I sat up scratching my head and surveyed my belongings. My saddle was undisturbed, lying on the ground with my pillow from the night before. My writing pouch was tucked underneath, away from the ground should a sudden rain wash through. My bakra looked at me with disinterest.

As the fog of sleep left me, I glanced over at Suoud’s sleeping place—It was empty.

Fawzi was asleep when I shook him. “Fawzi! Fawzi, wake up. Tell me about last night.”

He squinted from behind a draped arm covering his eyes. His headdress was all askew, and he had not changed from his riding clothes of the day before.

“Uh? Last night?” he groaned. “What about last night?”

“Did you go back to Suoud? What happened?”

“Uh? No, I didn’t go back, why are you bothering me Bassam, go away.”

“No Fawzi, did you go back?”

“I found some friends and we ended up talking around the fire until the second watch. Now let me finish sleeping, go away.”

“But Suoud didn’t return. See? His mat is rolled up, he didn’t sleep here last night.”

Fawzi rolled over and looked toward Suoud's camel. "So? It's none of your concern that he didn't come back. He found another place, and you shouldn't ask about such things. He'll show up. Now go away."

I didn't like it. The way of Al Murrah was with the caravan. Suoud's place was *right here*, not in the darkness of that loud celebration.

Fawzi was no help, and for a moment I wondered if he was right, that it was none of my concern.

I stood and scanned the large encampment. It was waking time and a shroud of gray wisps of smoke drifted past with the aroma of morning breakfast fires. Bright shafts of rising sunshine cut through the camp calling those sleeping to awake. A few were stirring about but none I recognized. Oddly, something was gnawing at me, things didn't feel right.

I decided to report Suoud's failure to return when I spotted Zafir on the other side of camp, standing in discussion with Malik, a captain of 50. Old friend Talib was also standing by. They were clustered in a large circle with Jamal and three others from the town, deep in an anxious discussion that was too distant for me to hear. I watched their gestures and pointing, and surmised that something was amiss and the townsmen were there to address some concern with Zafir.

The exchange lasted a moment longer, then Zafir and the others followed the townsmen directly toward the market place. I cut across camp and hurried after.

Arriving at the town center they stopped in front of an inn. Zafir and Jamil stepped inside, Malik and Talib waited by the door.

The deserted market was much different in the daylight—the ground was littered—red shards of broken clay flasks, scraps of bones from chicken and lamb, spills and stains, articles of clothing, broken beads, a lost sandal. It was dirty, it was raw, hardly the exciting convergence of wanton celebration from the night before.

I saw others watching us, a dozen or so, standing about, some beneath the shade of awnings or in shadowed doorways, curious and speculating. A man leading his donkey brought an empty cart to Malik, and waited.

A moment later, Jamal gestured for Zafir's escorts to follow him inside.

Several moments and then Zafir appeared. His head was down, watching his step, the others who joined him appeared next, awkwardly shouldering a limp shrouded human body between them.

My throat tightened. *Could this be?* Surely not, my brain refused to see it. Was this prostrate form not shrouded in the sheet of Al Murrah.

It was. It could *not be.* Not this, no, this couldn't be—my friend? *My teacher*, my mentor, the great tease?

The body was laid on the donkey cart, more gesturing by the gathered men, and then the cart was led forlornly toward the path leading to the western outskirts of town. Half a dozen of Zafir's men fell in behind and escorted it away from town.

Zafir remained at the entrance of the inn, speaking softly with Jamal, all the while scanning with suspicion the faces of those watching. And then, spotting me, he dropped his conversation and headed directly across the plaza.

"Bassam! Do you know what happened here last night?" Zafir commanded.

I straightened up and faced him. "Is that Suoud?" is all I could say.

"Do you know what happened here last night?"

"I do not," I stammered. "I was with Fawzi and Suoud, and Fawzi took me home. Is that Suoud?"

"Suoud was foolish. What is the first rule of the caravan?"

"Be on your guard."

"When?"

"Always."

"Suoud was foolish and not on his guard last night."

"W-what happened?"

"He was found upstairs in that inn, beaten, stripped, robbed, his throat cut. He was foolish."

My heart stopped, I bit my lip and drew the hem across my face.

"Return to camp," Zafir ordered. "We leave today. We have much to do, and this tragedy has delayed us already."

The chieftain turned to leave. I was shocked and could hardly speak. "Zafir?" I almost whispered, the word caught in my throat like an oversized piece of bread.

"What is it?"

"How does this change things? I mean sir, how does this change the men?"

Zafir stopped and took a long breath, watching the distant conveyance of his trusted friend moving across a wash toward the low, rolling hills beyond. Stepping closer to me he put a calming hand on my shoulder and lowered his voice. "It's a loss that you might see repeated many times before our journey is through, my young Bassam. I am sorry for the loss,

I know he was your friend. We all respected Suoud. But we can't carry the dead with us, and we don't return home because of them."

"So, what do you ...."

"There are ways, my son. There are ways of the desert and ways of the Abdali-ud-din. When traveling across the sand, we never cast the bones, the custom of the badawi. In the deserts we bury a man and let time decide his final place. But in a city like this we don't buy a pauper's grave, either. We put him to flames and let God and His winds decide his final place."

I looked to the hills west, realizing the finality of a new column of smoke that soon would rise that morning. It was not yet, but already it stung at my eyes.

"And his things?"

"We trade away his belongings, the camel we keep. Every man carries his own, and we don't carry a dead man's memories."

I wasn't sure how to ask Zafir, and looked at the ground in thought.

"There is nothing else we can do, my young friend. It's always a difficult loss when one of our own dies on the trail. Suoud was my friend before he was yours. I'm sorry he let down his guard in Leuke Kome. And, I'm also sure of this—he is sorry for it, too," and turned to leave.

"Please, Zafir, one final thing," I said. "May I, sir, may I keep the sword of Suoud?"

Zafir stopped, his face open with surprise. He returned slowly to stand in front of me, putting a hand on my shoulder and looked me squarely in the eye. "Why do you want the sword of Al Murrah?"

I was not exactly sure how to answer—only that the sword couldn't just be left there, or sold.

"Because, sir, I'll learn to take the place of Suoud, and Al Murrah will not be short a man. I'll be a defender of the caravan."

Zafir's countenance softened. He tried to rub the tension of reluctance from his chin and soften the stern resolve that was etched in his tired face.

"When you take up a warrior's sword, Bassam, you take up the responsibility of that man. You take up his honor and his legacy. You must then be responsible for the lives of others, even at the cost of your own. And honor—pure honor—you must have to use such a sword, with strength and mercy, knowing when death is certain or life just the same. You must be able to decide."

I straightened myself, weighing the burden of trust that was offered and decided on my ability to win it true and sure. But was it in me? Could I take up the honor of Suoud? I wanted to. I hoped to. I had to try.

"Zafir, I can—I mean, I *will* learn it. I'll take upon me the true burden of the honor of Suoud and his sword if you will allow me."

Showing neither satisfaction nor distrust, Zafir nodded. "Then, for now, you may borrow his sword, but only under this sacred promise, that you must learn to use it properly as do all my men. Such swords are more than steel, my son. These are emblems of honor, the mace of justice in the hands of the loyal guard of Abdali-ud-din. The swords of Al Murrah are for men who understand that."

I nodded and the look in Zafir's eyes eased with a confidence in the promise just made.

Gripping me by the shoulder and squeezing his trust into me, the chieftain turned and crossed the plaza toward Jamal who was waiting beyond.

Walking back to camp I hardly felt the ground. The shock of loss had numbed me head to foot. It was a sad unfolding of events for my friend Suoud, and I reflected back on how my own heart had guided me from danger that night, even while following in the trust of two who were older and should have been wiser. "When I know in my heart what is correct," I wrote in my journal that night, "I must act on it without thinking lest I fall prey to doubt, temptation, a trap. It could save my life, and could have saved Suoud's."

When I arrived at my camping place, Fawzi and three others had already stripped Suoud's camel of everything but the saddle, lumping it all in a heap where Suoud had slept—discarded goods awaiting the beggars and scavengers. Near to his camel was his sleeping mat and personal items spread out—a short knife, a brown leather neck thong with a silver locket, a black pouch neatly laced closed, a headdress, and the sheathed sword of Al Murrah.

Without speaking or even seeking Fawzi's permission, I went right up to the sword and gently picked it up by the handle. I hefted its weight and ran my hand down the decorative draping of the sheath. Wrapping my fingers around the worn girth of its handle I drew it part way from the sheath. The sun sparkled off its razor-sharpened edge, revealing the intricate silver scrawl of decorative engravings that proved its birth from the forges of the ancient sword makers of the Nafud.

Satisfied this was indeed an instrument of honor for which I had to earn the right to engage its employ, I re-sheathed and carried it with both hands to my sleeping mat. Finding a place at my saddle beneath the pack bag, I tucked the sword behind my journal kit—its new home, hidden from the casual opportunity of sticky hands, but always in easy reach.

Zafir returned an hour later wrapped in deep thought. He gathered his captains to his tent.

"We carry our gold to Babilu, and send our families to Saba'. They will arrive in six days, we should arrive in 40. I'm taking the deep desert paths north and will not stop at Jauf, there are raiders there. Prepare your teams accordingly."

He left his men to secure their plan for a longer journey than first anticipated. The caravan's new route would move outside the reach of the sheiks who harass the trains for the trespass and extract a tax.

The supplies were being loaded when the women and their escorts returned from morning shopping. They were fitted into the cocoon confines of their mahmils for the ride to the dock and the dhows that awaited them.

Zafir walked through the camp and stopped by as I tightened my load on my camel.

"Bassam, my boy. For the next while we will travel some distance. This next leg of our journey will be difficult, I think it's time I give you the words on the First Scroll. Not tomorrow or the second night, but on the third, come to my tent at the beginning of first watch, and we will talk."

At last, I thought, some quiet time with Zafir. I mounted my saddle and urged Bakra to stand. She stammered to solid footing and fell in line with the others. I felt like I was leaving something behind and glanced behind at the matted grass and worn paths left from a three-day camp. There, near the dead fire, I saw Suoud's sleeping mat and a few items of discarded clothing. I knew these would be fiercely fought over by the hungry poor who hid themselves, watching, perhaps not even waiting for the last camel to disappear over the ridge before scrambling from their shadows to fight like scavenging vultures over the abandoned property.

The death of a member of a caravan always extracts twice the cost. The loss of a man meant one less sword to protect the whole, one less back and pair of arms to perform labor, and one fewer set of eyes to watch for danger. Each had a job, a duty, and when a member was taken, his duties had to be shouldered by others.

To the elders of Abdali-ud-din, life was the most precious commodity of all, and defended at all costs—even at the cost of losing treasure. "My men, the chosen members of my train," Zafir repeatedly said, "they are the true treasure. The only true asset I bring on the trail are my men, and such assets I do not trade. All else is expendable."

The news of Suoud's death could not be conveyed to his family, out of necessity, for months or longer until a messenger could tender it away. I thought of Suoud's widowed mother who unknowingly awaited the sorrowful duty of grieving mother when she heard of what had become of her son.

"Day 11—Dear Rasha, This is a dark day for our caravan. Do you remember Suoud? He was murdered last night. We don't know by who or why. Men in the camp say the thieves in this town wait in the dark to overpower and rob. It's a puzzle. Zafir is not telling me everything. I didn't know Suoud as well as others, but I counted him a friend. It is a great loss. I respected him as a strong guide and mentor. Zafir has let me keep the sword of Suoud and its sheath. It has seen much battle. Suoud was a defender of the honor of the Abdali-ud-din. He will be missed. I will miss him.—Bassam"

"Dear Bassam, We had a dinner party with the wives and mothers of the men on the caravan. I met many who know of you. They send their greetings. A friend who is your age, Faris ("Fair-eese"), sat by us and wishes you safe travel. He has taken your job at the quarry. We plan to have such gatherings with these friends once every month. Your mother helped me sew my first dress. It is made of new cotton that is dyed blue. It fits me well.—Rasha"

BASSAM

23

LEGACY

A caravan packed for long distance is dressed much differently than a train transporting goods from place to place.

Zafir's caravan to Leuke Kome carried that which was customary for short-distance hauls. Our stay was three days so the men could off load their supplies into storehouses, and pack the rest to accompany the families aboard the dhows.

For the trek east, this changed. Zafir adjusted to fewer pack camels and more war camels—protection was more important than durability for the places we would visit, he said. And so the heavier camels were traded for those sleeker, that were single backed, fleet of foot, steady in the turn, best suited for defense. Zafir loaded them with clay pots protecting the precious incense, skeps of spice, frankincense, seeds, and, of course, the gold.

Other camels carried endurance foods that were dried for the trail, plus cheeses, dates, nuts, water and personal items.

Efficiency is crucial, so the luxury of the elders' extravagant housing tents was abandoned. Except for Zafir's large tent, every man was limited to whatever his bakra could carry.

Herds of goats and sheep, and the swift-footed horses so important in defense could also not follow us. There were few grazing opportunities in the high desert wastelands.

Fawzi was telling me that horses and herds did not endure the long treks in the deep desert without frequent water and feed. Such animals had no sure footing on that shifty foundation of sand as did the camel. Jamal took charge of those animals to be sold or not, to earn their keep for the year or two we were gone.

I spent some hours with Ammar working the maps to Wadi Sirhan, guessing and calculating the time of travel to the deserts eastward. With lighter loads and no herds to slow us, I estimated six days. Ammar said it could be at least three days more, maybe longer if Zafir stopped at the desert oasis of Al Jafr to pay the trespass tax. Either way this was to be my first experience with the secrets of the Abdali-ud-din and their hidden water stops. I wondered how secret they actually were.

It was midday at the harbor when we bid farewell, then began our leave of Leuke Kome. Not far from the city's outskirts the terrain east drastically changed from coastal pleasantries to a stony wasteland. Broad flatlands to the north stood between us and the mighty deserts, with shifting dunes and stony washes directly in our path.

Zafir told me this desolation gave protection to the train because few others knew how to survive in such wilderness. The route was too barren for the riders to last three days without water. But we had the secret cisterns, something I began to realize brought safety from knowledge of the desert. I discussed it at length in my journal, citing Zafir's recent comment about the losses the company had suffered at Leuke Kome. "It is better to travel the long stretches of denied pleasures to achieve one's goal," Zafir said, "than to risk lasting failure with a haphazard investment in the allure of indulgence."

It was hard to find an indulgence in the desolation that presented itself the morning after the first night's camp. I had difficulty fighting the boredom of my camel's long loping strides through endless stretches of plains and sandy nothing. The monotony lasted hours at a time.

Rounded hills with plateaus of grey came into view and left, without a green growing thing to see. The vapid vision ahead stretched on into flat nothing far beyond the horizon.

I desperately wanted something to do and was tempted to dismount and walk just to distract me from the long, hard ride.

Fawzi could see my impatience and came up alongside to introduce a lesson for the day.

"That sword you've got there," he said. "It's a unique creation."

"Unique?"

"Certainly. It wasn't new for Suoud, it was earned by him—from Zafir."

"I thought each man brought his own sword to the caravan." That's what I had heard, anyway.

"Not Al Murrah. Such swords are tokens of honor, an honor sometimes passed down through many generations, but always earned on the fields of battle, or in a war or such, or in service of Abdali-ud-din."

"Then tell me, how did Suoud earn this sword?" I asked.

"A long time ago—12, 15 years—I don't remember, we were on a long trek north," he said. "It was green and watered, a much nicer place than these deserts. There was a city called Kutatisi where Zafir planned to meet buyers from the cold lakes."

"Kutatisi, I've heard of it," I said. "There's a famous river there…"

"The Phasis."

"Yes, yes, *Phasis*."

"Our route took us through three passes before the main gates of the city. Suoud had the most amazing knack for knowing danger, he sensed it before anybody else. I never could guess how but I distinctly remember hearing him tell Zafir there were no birds."

"Birds? What does that have to do with anything?"

"Exactly! That's what all the rest of us thought. But Suoud noticed right away—no birds meant their nesting places were disturbed—the birds had fled."

"I never would have thought of it."

"Neither did we. When the caravan approached the first pass, Suoud told Zafir about his suspicions."

"Did the train turn around?"

"No. Zafir put Al Murrah on either side, like a moving wall of swords on our left and right. Any attackers had to penetrate those blades to reach the caravan. The passes were short and Zafir had us run at full gallop, like the head of a spear."

"Were there bandits?"

"Oh yes, and a great fight after the second pass, just as Suoud had suspected."

"What happened?"

"It was a hard fight, they were on horses, very fast. We lost two men and some wounded, but we killed more than half of theirs and they fled before we reached the walls of the city."

"And that is how Suoud earned the sword?"

"After they arrived in the city, we set up camp, and Zafir came through looking for Suoud. He made a big show of it, bringing along an armed escort. The rest of us gathered in a tight circle while Zafir recited several of Suoud's great battles and championships, and then awarded him the sword, and welcomed him into the brotherhood of Al Murrah."

"These swords," I asked, "does Zafir keep a few for occasions like that, to hand out for bravery?"

"Oh Bassam, don't you know whose sword that is you're holding?"

"No, just a sword, I thought."

"That's Zafir's—Zafir gave Suoud his own personal sword—the very sword he received from his fathers when he was a boy."

"This is *Zafir's*?"

Fawzi nodded. "Al Murrah is equipped with the finest swords from the forges of the Nafud. Abdali-ud-din has them specially made heavy and strong so they can break other swords in a fight. His family has been using them for who knows how many years, and then they find their way to different leaders, passed from father to the most brave and valiant sons—always kept in the family. Take it out and look—each name is engraved under the handle, father to son for generations."

"But why did Zafir give this to Suoud? Zafir has no son."

"Exactly!"

"Oh ...." I suddenly realized what the gift really meant, and looked down at what lay across my lap with new respect.

I unsheathed it and turned it over—a streak of reflection flashed across my eyes. There, beneath the handle, were the etchings of eight names carefully engraved—the filigree caught the sun with thin silky lines, each representing feats that outlived the man behind the name, but remembered with honor to the last. And the last on this sword was Suoud ibn al-Haroun.

"Did Zafir say your name could be added to that legacy?" Fawzi asked.

"No, but he said I could have the sword."

"Then what he means is that you may *use* this sword, but to have it, no, not yet. That you must earn."

I pushed it carefully into its sheath. "Then Zafir gives his sword to honor Suoud, so he must find another?"

"Yes, something specially made. He doesn't give away his sword casually. That is why a sword from Zafir carries such honor—all of them have been in his hand at one time or another, for many years, defending the investments of Abdali-ud-din."

"So, what about this?" I asked, running my fingers over the smooth burnished skin of the hard leather sheath.

"Each man makes his own because they wear far quicker than the blade," Fawzi said. He lifted his own to show the abuse. "Each is different. Suoud patterned his after his grandfather's, made of the leather from the very camel slain beneath him in an ambush. Suoud gives honor to him with this sheath."

I looked more closely at the deliberate, evenly spaced double-stitching, the branding and dates of memorable encounters that covered both sides. "He marked it with many of his own battles."

"Yes, he was faithful at that," Fawzi said. "Many Al Murrah make a record of their service like that. Some don't—in fact, I don't. But others insist on it and pass it along as proof of their integrity."

"I should make a sheath one day, but for now, for Suoud, I'll carry his."

"And that, too, is honorable."

For the balance of the afternoon, Fawzi and I exchanged stories—his of war and survival, and mine of life among the riches and fantastic wealth brought by distant travelers to Rekeem.

When evening camp was set, the riders unburdened their animals and clustered around small fires, eating from their supplies and drinking teas. I sat cross-legged on my mat and entered the memories of the day into my journal. The pages filled quickly, and I knew more would soon be needed.

"Day 14—Dear Rasha, Tonight I learned about the loyalty of Suoud and how he earned his sword. I see that I stand in the shadow of a great fighter, but more than that—your father gave his very own sword to Suoud. Now I understand his anger. I have much to learn about honor. Your father taught me that the life of a man is more than the deeds he performs; it must include the ideas that made his life. He told me all men are born, and all men die, but those facts do not make the man. What makes a man is how he lived.

Hawks are following us. Ammar says we're leaving too much refuse in our path. They scavenge. This makes tracking us easier. Enemies can look for the birds and see from a long way away that a large train is moving.—Bassam"

"Dear Bassam, a small caravan visited Rekeem today, about 40 camels and 21 men. They did not stay long, but traded Egyptian cotton and papyrus. Your father insisted Dalal and I visit the market and purchase enough for us both. I have plenty for writing, and to maker another dress. We will begin cutting and sewing it in a day or two. At meal time, your safety is always remembered as we give thanks.—Rasha"

24

THE FIRST SCROLL

It was dark and Zafir was already standing outside the door of his tent when I approached.

"Is this a good time?"

"Yes, but not here, come with me," he said, picking up a leather bag that he slung over his shoulder. He handed me a pair of rolled mats and a clay oil lamp. "Carry these," he said. "Let's climb a short distance to that hill over there, so we can see the camp."

The darkness was young and the moon was behind the far horizon—its rising would signal the start of second watch. Zafir walked as if he had a lot to say and was anxious to get started.

He led me to a flat spot on the slope of a hard-baked hillside. Setting down the leather bag and spreading out the mats, he motioned me to sit. "Put the lamp there," he said, pointing to a large rock.

"This bag," Zafir began as he unlaced the top, "was my father's when he was a boy. It was new then but it shows wear today. I may have to replace it."

Reaching inside, he carefully lifted out a long bundled pair of spindles, one of them holding the parchment, a roll about the same girth as the handle of Suoud's sword, the other to receive it. These were protected with a soft leather covering that was tied around with three cords. A single leather tassel dangled from the top.

Zafir placed it on the mat in front of us. With an almost reverent respect he carefully untied the covering and laid it back, letting the scroll relax—untouched. Its yellowed papyrus clung curled to itself with edges visibly worn from use. The spindles were ornately carved from olive wood—their smooth artistry shined warmly with yellowed age in the lamp light.

"These scrolls are not eternal," Zafir said, "but the ideas in them are. They date back to the beginning, and no man knows when that was. Since the first they have been copied and re-copied—to skins, later, papyrus, back to skins. It has been different over the years, but now it's papyrus, no different than the sheets that make your journal. The father of my grandfather's grandfather last copied them, 160 years ago. Before then, it is as I told you."

160 years old? It was a relic from history. I shifted positions for a closer look.

"Most men hope to find in these scrolls some ancient and lost guide to riches," Zafir said, "or the answer to all of their troubles, or a treasure map that could lead them to wealth unimaginable. But far from that, these secrets are precisely the opposite. In the wisdom of my fathers these scrolls provide only the keys to such riches and a pathway through life for their attainment. But such a key is only for those who know what true riches are, and only for them will the words in these scrolls have meaning. You, Bassam, are wise in your young years, but you must learn for yourself the meaning of the words. And from them will come the meaning of true riches. Most men cannot read these words because their hearts are not ready—they cannot understand them. I think your heart is ready, Bassam. Do you understand?"

"I think so," I said.

"Then let us begin."

Zafir held the scroll by the spindle stems and carefully unrolled the writing. I could see a beautifully penned calligraphy that softly revealed itself in the glow of the flickering lamp.

He turned the scroll toward me. "You will do the reading and I will listen. If you have a question, you may ask me. But some things I will not tell you, it's part of the test."

The writing was in an old script, stylized, but not too different from what father used in Rekeem. It was laid out in straight, neat rows—small, efficient, and deliberate. It was something I could read aloud without difficulty.

I cleared my throat then stole a glance toward the blackness beyond. Here, under the twinkling shroud of night, surrounded by a thousand rolling dunes in all directions, I couldn't help but wonder—*who else might be listening?*

"The Song of the Man," I began. "To the prosperous, prosperity is never measured with gold, but gold is a pleasant fruit ripened and blessed on the tree of the industrious ...."

The words that followed for the next hour gave a history of the scrolls and the benefits that came to those who heeded their words. Words of wisdom poured from the writings, neatly presented with meaning and purpose and explanation.

"The child of the creator is not dressed as the raven or the lion or the fish," it said. "The prosperous must compensate for his lack of natural tools, for his nakedness, by using the one tool he does have in abundance—his mind."

The scroll taught that the mind is both a weapon and a tool, and knowing the difference was a sign of wisdom. "Man's best use of his mind is to cooperate with others. To balance his abilities and desires with those of others; to help without fighting to get what one wants. To get for others what they want as the way to achieve the same for one's own. Competition is keen but cooperation brings harmony."

I learned the important distinctions about the role of government on a great caravan such as Zafir's. "All men have freedom to do as they wish," the scroll continued, "but liberty sets boundaries to freedom so that there is no injury to one another. Only when all men obey freely one law may they then be free. That law is eternal, it is not made by men. No man may enforce laws on another without his permission because all men are equal. But when one violates moral law, then he becomes subject to justice, or the law has no power or meaning. All equal men must agree on what law to follow, and only then are all of them equal as well as free."

The words poured forth in phrases and axioms of principled truth and abstractions, addressing personal and social behavior. "A world where competing men may achieve their greatest abilities is possible only if they live under the conditions laid forth in the seven scrolls. ... All men have vices and the true channel for unprecedented growth is not to smother the root of such vices—but to control them, like fire in a furnace, to guide and nurture them, to encourage them toward pursuits of self interest and common benefit, for that is the great creative energy of human nature."

"Human nature," it said, "cannot be changed by any one man, by any group of men or by any use of force—ever. A man must change his own human nature, and that is his very purpose. He must change his own soul, his heart and mind, for the *good* because none other can, or force him to—world's without end."

I had to pause a moment to digest the abstract ideas to let the knowledge sink into my mind. And then I came across something that wasn't clear.

"This passage is difficult," I said after a long silence. "It's almost like a riddle."

"Read it aloud, slowly," Zafir said, "and tell me what you think it says."

I traced the words with my finger:

> "A virtue of wealth is this for thee, One branch one limb on the self same tree; The coin and palace all men may gain, But woe is life when spent in vain. For joy that lasts and doth not cease, Embrace the virtues thou Prince of Peace. One branch one limb on the self same tree, A virtue of wealth is this for thee."

The last words lingered. "'*A virtue of wealth*,'" I said thoughtfully.

"And?" Zafir asked.

"I can only guess where to start ... I suppose this tells me that wealth does not need to be a fat purse or a palace, does it?"

Zafir sat silent looking at me.

"Those riches, all men may gain, 'but *woe is life*' ... that sounds so true. Gaining the treasures of the world without an honorable use, is, well, a waste. I saw such waste, many times in the eyes of cankered men traveling through Rekeem."

Zafir nodded but kept his quiet. I searched the passage again.

"*A life spent in vain*," I said aloud, "is one that's without purpose, without a guiding value. That indeed would be a life of woe. But—what am I missing?"

"You are correct," Zafir said. "A life exhausted on vanity and vice is indeed a life of woe."

"So, vanity isn't reserved for only the rich, it can be had among the poor as well ..."

"Yes."

I puzzled over the meaning while the old chieftain held a composed smile.

"You will learn it soon enough my son," he said. "I'll tell you this much—wealth is not necessarily a fat purse, but that's not all. What else do you read here?"

"This next passage seems clear, that to have joy that doesn't fade, a man should embrace the virtues ... I guess it means to embrace these virtues of wealth ... but you must be a man of peace to do it ...."

"*Man* of peace?" asked Zafir.

"Yes, well, it says 'thou Prince of Peace ....'"

"A *man of peace* is not what it says."

"That sounds like an important difference, but I don't understand it ... I'll need some time, I guess."

"You've surprised me, young Bassam," Zafir said. "You've gained far more understanding of this first passage than I did at your age, and you don't even know it. It will come to you as we study more, and if you prepare yourself. Why don't you read the next passage, perhaps that will help."

I turned the scroll to better take the light:

> "Oh wisdom behold now The Song of the Man:
>
> "I stand as lord over the awful expanse, My foe is legion, takes daily his stance; With belligerent blows I wield my lance, My host conquers all before mine advance. What meaneth this The Song of the Man? Only one wise, shall he understand."

I read it again, a little slower.

"—I'm not sure," I said, looking at Zafir for help, but he sat there so much the stone sphinx, wanting *me* to figure it out.

"'The Song of the Man' talks about *one*—a person, an individual."

"Yes," Zafir nodded.

"This one man, he faces a great challenge, a terrible something that he calls 'awful.'"

"And what might that be?"

"It doesn't really say, does it? In the next line it says his foe rises up against him daily, every day. Every day the man must face this foe."

"Yes?"

"And before man can do anything, before he can take his 'advance,' he must conquer this foe...."

"And what foe does every man have, each and every day?"

I became quiet. "There is really only one foe that I can think of and that's ...."

Zafir started to smile in anticipation.

"The one foe, the challenge that all men face, anywhere, anytime..." I fell into silent thought. *What evil or difficulty must I face each and every day? Who is this speaking about?*

"Bassam," Zafir said, "the rule is, you must say aloud your thoughts."

"Yes, it's just that ... I was thinking ... for me, the foe I face each day is life, all of life ... or maybe of my own making."

"How is that?"

"Well, the things I have to do, worries, chores. Sometimes, it's just getting off the sleeping mat while it's still dark, and I'd rather keep sleeping ...."

"That's it, Bassam!" Zafir said.

"What's it?"

"What stands in the way of what you want to do? Tell me more about that."

I drummed my fingers on my leg. "That *expanse*, it must be what each man fears alone in his heart. It's not really another man he worries over, or an enemy who wants to break down the wall and come with his sword. It must be inside, his feelings of weakness and doubt. I suppose he fears himself the most, doesn't he?"

"Go on," Zafir said.

I was thinking about my own weaknesses. It was a very interesting idea. I had never considered it before, but it made sense because I had fought my weaknesses, fought them my whole life. Is that natural? It must be.

"If our own heart wars with us," I said aloud, "if it tell us to do right when we want to choose what is wrong, if we choose an evil path, when passions swallow up our good sense, when that speaks to us the loudest, why then—*that's* our foe, our greatest adversary. Am I right? To face our own awful expanse of weakness, is to face... well, to face ourselves?"

"You're almost there, Bassam!" Zafir said smiling.

"Well, that enemy, taking his stance daily, that means—that must mean he is with us all of the time—when we wake, when we eat, when we do *anything*. He is always there, daily ..."

"Yes?"

"This passage says that ... it says that ...." I suddenly grew quiet. Ideas were coming together. My mouth hung open as I stared blankly into Zafir's eyes that now twinkled with delight. "Zafir," I said in astonishment. "Haven't you already told me this? The first scroll of wealth, this song of the man, is to keep up my guard, always. But not my guard against *mine enemy* as I thought—but ... but against *me*."

Zafir burst out in a laugh and smiled ear to ear. "Bassam! That is precisely what it says! Good job my boy, you have found it!"

"Then it's *me*, I'm the enemy that daily takes his stance," I said.

"Yes!" Zafir said. "The first scroll of wealth speaks not to palaces and coins or desert bandits or wealthy merchants, it speaks to *you*."

"Me ...."—my thoughts trailed off a moment.

"So, my son, draw the ideas together. You read about virtue, a key to wealth. Now you read about this enemy each man must face every day all day. Do they connect?"

I furrowed my brow. The idea seemed so familiar. There was something here I couldn't quite understand. *Doing good* is a deliberate act for most men. *Doing good* is one of man's daily foes or challenges—to rise up and do what is right when a natural man wants to do otherwise and shrink. Doing good is a natural act for those who already have slain that daily foe. *It was starting to make sense.*

"I think I have it, Zafir. The Song of the Man is a virtue, a virtue of self control, of winning the war against your own self, is that it?"

"Exactly! In a word, self-governance, Bassam. It's control over yourself."

"That fits!" I said. "The man who governs himself must do so each and every day until it's a part of him—not an act one day and forgotten the next as if they add up to something at the end of my life. No, it's a daily war, new and fresh each morning. They may *advance* while others in defeat and struggling, do not."

Zafir nodded. "You think well in the abstract, my son," he said. "This will help you as we study the scrolls. These are the guiding principles, the virtues that lead men to lasting wealth of the most precious kind. When you have read all of them, made their messages your own, only then will the scrolls be yours."

I pulled my knees to my chest and rested my chin. My eyes felt bright, full of new knowledge. I looked into the black distance—my mind whirling like a fish caught splashing about in shallow waters, gasping for the depth. "Tell me more, Zafir," I asked.

Zafir sat silent, letting me ponder.

"All of these scrolls," he said, "will make more sense now that you understand the first. This first secret of wealth is to possess and become the virtue of self-governance—indeed it is the *most important* of all."

I had seen the opposite a thousand times—coarse men at the markets of Rekeem, unable to hold their coins the moment their masters paid them, and spent themselves captive to whatever the coins could buy.

Such men often purchased more trouble than if they had remained in their poverty—they would have been better off with no coins at all. That's why control had to be natural, a part of a man's *changed* nature, never doubted or questioned because it is always there, always the victor in the daily war against the vices—the pre-determined answer for when in doubt. Self-governance had to be a thriving virtue, a distinct and living part of me.

"You will learn," Zafir said, "how a great tapestry of virtue is woven by the words of these scrolls. A beautiful tapestry of the well-lived life. It has nothing to do with how many coins a man may gain. It's everything to know the correct treatment of what coins he has, be they few or many. And this tapestry becomes complete as a man nears the end of his life. It's an emblem of what he has achieved and accomplished, built and experienced. For most people it can be a lasting legacy to his descendents for many generations that follow. Such tapestries can be added upon because such fortitude and achievement carries honor down through the years. And this happens to a man without any defined place among the poor or the rich because life is *not about the coins*."

I had never thought it. It was a beautiful way to live life.

"But you must never forget, young Bassam. All it takes is *one moment* of slack, one forgetful instance of lowering your guard, just one hanging thread on your tapestry of integrity and virtue—be it forgotten or ignored, it is just the same—one thread caught on any of the most brazen or innocent vicissitudes of life, and your beautiful and difficult work can suddenly unravel in a single and terrible instant. I'm thinking now of Suoud."

Suoud. Yes, an instant. That was all.

Perched on the midnight slope I focused blankly on the stars above that stood like sentinels, steady in their place.

"There is no lasting good from great treasures, is there?" I asked. "Or chasing after treasure just for the sake of treasure."

"No, not to those who fail to yield to the teachings of the first scroll," Zafir explained. "Great treasure allows great works, but only when good self-government precedes them."

"So, a man finds a coin and he rejoices and tells his friends all about his good fortune," I surmised. "And most men spend that coin, and then it is gone."

"Well, Bassam, you talk like you have personal experience in this," Zafir said.

"More than my share," I confessed. "I brought little with me because I saved little. Any coins that come to me are short visitors."

"Then you didn't have the self-governance to put them to work for you, did you?" Zafir asked.

"No, most certainly not."

He straightened back his shoulders to ask me the last question of the night. "Do you see then, why self-governance is the gateway to the road of prosperity?"

"I'm not certain yet, but it makes sense—a man must be disciplined to keep his coins. But everybody knows that, don't they?"

"If all people knew that, this first scroll would not be needed and there would be no discontent and fighting among people—poor and rich alike. All of us are quick to recognize the right from the wrong, but few of us stop to consider *why* we fail to choose the right. We are blind to our own blindness, Bassam. We can't see what we haven't seen. And we suffer for it for most of our lives."

The reading for the night came to an end. Zafir returned the parchment to its original spindle, carefully covered it over and placed it in the scroll bag. He said we'd talk about it more, and that I should get some rest.

I went to my sleeping mat wanting to capture what I had learned while it was fresh.

"Day 16—Dear Rasha, Tonight I learned the first scroll. It is so clear to me. We are our own worst enemies. Unless we conquer ourselves each and every day, we are hindered in any progress we choose. That is why your father is so successful. He is a master of himself. And for such men does God grant blessings because they can be trusted to do what is right with the gifts that God gives him. Do you remember old man Khaleh'an ("k-LEE-on")? Zafir said he is a close relative and a man of the scrolls. He was an example of self-governance in all things, do you remember it? No wonder why we loved him so, and no wonder why he was so wise. I

miss him and his wisdom. This is my first time in the northern deserts. They are more vast than I had imagined. No wonder why visitors to our Rekeem look so spent and weary each time they come for a visit. —Bassam"

I grew tired of writing. Morning was coming—an end to the magical night. I needed to find some rest. I gathered up my materials, cleaned the pens, sealed the ink pot, returned them to their pouch, and tucked the bundle in its place next to the sword of Suoud. I pulled my blanket tight, it was cool in the desert night air.

"Dear Bassam, I went to a school today. There were other girls my age learning the art of writing and about the history of Rekeem. The teacher taught us how to make tablets. I wrote a message for you on a clay tablet that I made myself. I baked it in the fire. Teacher said the fired clay will last longer than the pyramids. I don't know if that can be, but the message I wrote to you will last even longer. —Rasha"

CONSEQUENCES

Zafir said nothing to me about the scrolls for several days. It left me wondering how much of the teachings were known by others. As the caravan continued its northerly trek I decided to start watching—I was curious, did others know?

One night while the train was camped between cisterns, the only water available was what the men had fetched at the last stop. A baggage man named Amin returned to his cook-fire and caught a thief stealing from his water skin—an older, skinny man named Bah'mak.

Amin's angry shouting drew a small crowd to see what the trouble was. "I've caught you thief, I've caught you!"

"I'm doing nothing wrong," Bah'mak countered.

"Stealing? I've seen my water disappear and wondered, who could be stealing Amin's water? It is Bah'mak *the thief*," he shouted for others to hear. "I don't appeal to our captain, you must answer to Zafir himself."

"You *accuse* me for finding water to drink or food to eat?" Bah'mak shouted back—gesturing as if to invite those nearest to come closer, to agree with him.

"You're lazy and now everyone knows it," Amin shouted.

"I am not lazy, you liar," Bah'mak roared, shaking a fist.

"You steal because you're lazy!" Amin said. "Get your own water—*thief*."

"You're the thief, always first to the well, draining it dry, so others have none." His eyes were white with fury, dancing about for support from others. "You're the thief because you make me *a desperate beggar* because of your selfishness."

Amin glared. "Thief—*Bah'mak the thief*. I wait, I always wait my turn. I take my turn with the others. You? You do nothing. You sit around and watch. You don't fetch your own. You are lazy—*you steal*."

"How dare you *Idi-uber*! You, the *offspring* of mule killers, the son of cattle stealers, *a pirate*. You Amin, your mother mated with scorpions—stealers of water. All of you," he shouted to the onlookers, "you agree with me, do you not?"

Bah'mak looked around but no one moved. They watched with disinterest wrinkled in their faces.

"Ha! *See*?" Amin said, pointing. "You're all alone, Bah'mak. I've caught you. The elders will judge you."

Bah'mak lowered his voice and stepped into Amin's face and growled, "You make me thirsty because of your greed—there is no honor in you, *badawi*. No honor when your selfishness makes men thirsty."

"This is not the first time, you lying dog," Amin said. "I've seen my water disappear each night on this journey, and wondered if it was you. Could it be my *trusted* friend Bah'mak? Now I know it *is* you—*thief*."

Bah'mak rolled his eyes and scoffed, "You'd let a man die rather than share your water? Can any man here trust one as you?"

The watch finally arrived to stand between the arguing men and ordered Bah'mak to follow.

"Zafir wants to see you," said one, taking Bah'mak by the arm.

As he was led away he shouted back, "If I were in charge I'd force all men to share—share equally so that the *whole* caravan drinks—*and eats*, not just the selfish few—like *you*, Amin, and all men like you. I'd make it all the same, always."

The skinny man was hauled away to the other side of camp.

With the disruption quieted, Amin returned to his cook-fire to check for other supplies that might have been pilfered, and the small group of observers melted back into the shadows of their own camps, speaking softly, shaking heads at the rudeness of Bah'mak.

I marveled at how quickly the rigors of hardship brought out the worst in the men. The veterans knew these difficult stretches could also bring out the very best. It was, in a way, a true test of what a man was made of. Those who were lazy exposed their vice under the duress of desert travel. Now that Bah'mak exposed his heart for others to see, everyone knew what kind of man he was beneath that smile and friendly demeanor—a man set on self-gratification with no consideration for the labors of others. In such a man's heart was hiding a nest of serpents, hatching their bite and venom when the cost for his laziness had to be paid.

I asked Zafir about the problem of dishonesty. He said that was the one thing for which he had no patience.

"Such men do not last through a full life," Zafir said. "At the next village I will sever ties with Bah'mak to go his own way, for reasons that are justified. And you watch him, Bassam. He will not change. In the end, he will wander his days looking to steal rather than work. I have seen such men—many men, and they never repent of their error unless those who feed their laziness finally stop. Only then do they learn that all men must carry their own. As he travels back to his home, he will have to fend for himself. Who knows if he will make it there alive? Perhaps then will a lesson be learned. But I don't think so, not in the case of Bah'mak, he is a lazy man. He believes others owe him. He appeals to their compassion. People who give to the lazy the same as they do to the needy, from a sense of compassion, are wrong because it furthers their laziness—and such charity will never serve the caravan until the lazy are compelled to work for their own survival."

I saw the teachings of the scroll and wrote about them in my journal. I decided that most certainly *no*, the words of the scrolls were not known by others. "Goodness is natural in all men," I wrote, "but few are strong enough to show true allegiance to principle when the gnawing desperation of thirst and want chews heavily upon them."

ب هبعه 26 محبوب

RIPE

That next day we resumed our journey east, and I saw no sign of Bah'mak. Someone said he remained with the caravan but forced to the back, under escort I supposed, I didn't bother to check. Sofian told me Bah'mak was to be dropped off at the next convenient place, but not tonight, it was too far removed from the regular trade routes.

By late afternoon we arrived at a nice watered village where fruit grew and the spring water was sweet. We circled about, set camp, and some of the men went to bargain for supplies for the next leg of our trip.

This is where Fawzi decided to pull another prank on me. He had been plaguing me with pranks since the day we first left Rekeem. As it turned out, this was also the last time he pranked me—and for a good reason.

After evening tea Fawzi invited me to take a walk to the market, but I declined. Instead, I sat by my fire to write in my journal. I had my supplies stacked on a small table I made atop my saddle bags, and was eating an apple when Fawzi came along.

"I shouldn't eat those apples if I were you—not if it's from around here," he said.

"Why not?"

"They grow from the blood of the dead," he told me.

"What? Another of your tall tales, is it?"

"You don't have to listen to me, Bassam. Go ahead and eat, but look around you. None of the other men are eating that fruit."

"And why is that?" I asked.

"The orchards here were grown from seeds that were lost in a great battle. A caravan transporting seeds was attacked by bandits, at this very spot. Many innocent people were slaughtered by the sword. Those who survived were rounded up to this very place, over there, where the orchard stands, and their heads were chopped off. Their blood spilled onto the ground and pooled around the baskets of seeds. The trees that grew from those stand here today—with the spirits of the dead inside of them. Their fruit falls from the tree trying to avenge an unjust death on any who dares eat it. I shouldn't touch those apples. They carry the blood of the dead in them."

"That's the most stupid thing I've ever heard," I told him.

"No, I'm not kidding. Do I need to show you, donkey brain?"

"Show me? I wouldn't believe you no matter what you did."

And with that, Fawzi reached into the bag he carried and pulled out an apple. He set it down on my little table. "Eat if you dare," he said. "It comes from the orchard of ghosts, raised on the blood of the dead," and then he turned about and walked into the shadows.

By then the sky was completely black, and only my small cook-fire illuminated my journal entries.

With Fawzi and his tall stories out of sight and out of mind, I just shook my head ignoring him and went back to my writing.

A few minutes later, it was the strangest thing—I thought I saw, from the corner of my eye, something move—was it that apple?

No, no, it couldn't be. I looked at it a moment ... had to be the dancing flames making shadows. Nothing changed, nothing moved, and so I returned to my journal.

Then, a minute later, there was slight motion—what? Did I see something move—and then stop? Or was it my eyes getting tired already?

By then my concentration was disrupted enough that I had to stop. My heart started to pound with suspicion and a little concern. *Is this some kind of trick?* I looked around to see if anyone was nearby watching, trying to fool me.

Setting down my writing materials I turned my focus to Fawzi's apple and watched. At that very moment—*it moved*! I saw it rock side to side, all by itself! It *had* been moving, only slightly, but it did!

I gasped and stood up, reaching for my knife with one hand and feeling around for my riding stick with the other.

Ghosts in the blood of the roots and the seeds and the fruit?

And then it moved *again*.

I took a step back and tripped on my saddle, sitting down hard. I stood up with my riding stick in hand and poked the apple, making it fall to the ground.

It hit hard onto the dirt and its top broke off. I watched in growing terror at what might happen next.

Just then, a very large and worried beetle scurried out of the apple and hurried across the dirt and under my saddle.

"What is this?" I said aloud. I picked up the apple and found it neatly hollowed out with a perfectly matching top carved to fit.

Then I heard laughter from the shadows. "What?" It was Fawzi and his conspirators. They emerged from the dark laughing and laughing—so hard in fact, there were tears on their cheeks. Others came to discover the excitement and Fawzi couldn't even explain what he had done, he just pointed. When they saw the apple they just smiled at me. "The Ghost Apple, it's an old trick, Bassam, I'm surprised you fell for it," and they'd walk away shaking their heads. And I was left embarrassed and determined to get back.

It was unfortunate for Fawzi to choose this very night to try his pranks. I had been planning one myself, but the Ghost Apple made me decide it was time to plot my revenge. But first, I unfortunately fell victim to one more of Fawzi's tricks.

It was about three days later and we were in a place with grapes ripening at large settlement. Zafir camped us for the evening, and that's when Fawzi tricked me with Wine Bread.

"They don't have grains around here," he said as we prepared evening meal. He held up a small loaf the size of two fists. "This is the bread they make around here. They use what they can because in these parts, there can't grow grain."

"No grain? What's *that* made of?"

"Grape seed," Fawzi said.

"Grape seed? Can you make flour with that?"

"Sure, easy. You have to let it dry, and then grind it up like your grains."

"Into flour?"

"What else?"

"So, what does it taste like?" I asked.

"It's funny, but it tastes just like wine. A very excellent wine, in fact. It's quite ingenious because once the seed dries, it ferments and that gives off the bubbles that causes the bread to rise. It's their specialized leaven. And the bread is actually quite soft."

"That's the most amazing thing I've ever heard."

"There's a lot of things you haven't heard, Bassam," Fawzi said. "But that's not all. They use it to make their wine," he said.

"Huh?"

"Here, let me show you. Where's your water skin?"

He asked for a mug and I filled it half way.

"Now watch this," and he broke off a piece of the little loaf and dropped it in the mug.

Fawzi swirled the bread around, then poured a few drops into his hand so I could see that the water had turned pink.

"We must add more," he said, dropping in several more pieces, and testing it in his hand. Gradually dark blue drops appeared, then with more bread, deep purple, almost black.

"Taste it," he said at last.

I sniffed it first. It sure smelled like wine. Then I took a sip from the mug. It *was* wine! Not very strong, but yes, the fruit of the vine.

"I wouldn't tell anybody about this," Fawzi said. "It's a nice little secret that you might want to try one day." He left the remains of the loaf with me and went on his way.

Later that night I brought the loaf with me to Zafir's tent.

"This is the most amazing thing, Zafir! Look at this," I said, holding up the loaf for him to examine. "Bread from grape seed that makes wine! It's actually quite fantastic."

Zafir listened to me unfold the whole story and his grin grew larger and larger. He shook his head, looked down at the rugs of his tent and outlined a pattern with the toe of his sandal, waiting for me to finish.

"Bassam, I think there's something you need to know about this bread," and then he explained how it was soaked in dark wine, allowed to dry in the sun, and when put into a little water, it unleashed its trick—a trick to fool people like *me*.

That did it. I was angry at Fawzi, angry I had fallen once more for one of his tricks. It was time to hatch a plan I had actually started several weeks earlier. A farmer at one of our earlier stops let me buy an egg. I kept it carefully protected in a clay mug, and put that in my camel bag where it shouldn't get broken. I knew that after a couple of weeks in the heat and sun, it would have turned ripe enough to extract a lasting revenge.

Well. With this latest trick of Fawzi's Ghost Apple and wine bread, I knew the time was right.

Before departing that next morning, Fawzi left his camel just long enough for me to plant the egg under the riding blanket of his saddle. It was hidden toward the back under the folds where he shouldn't notice it.

When he came to mount his bakra, I distracted him with a question about bathing, how a person is supposed to stay clean when there was no water for washing. He offered his best veteran's advice, and without noticing, climbed onto his saddle and ordered his camel to her feet. In that back-and-forth jostle, the egg broke but Fawzi didn't notice.

A few hours later we were long on the trail and it was hot. Somebody noticed a foul smell emanating from somewhere. Everyone in the proximity of Fawzi commented on it. No one knew exactly where or what, but Fawzi sure noticed. In fact, as the sun grew hotter, the smell grew worse.

After some sniffing around, Fawzi was sure it had to be his bakra, ill from foraging on something not fit for camels.

As people held their noses and moved as far from him as they could, Fawzi tried to explain it away.

"She got into something that doesn't agree with her," he'd tell others as they moved far to either side.

As the hours wore, the smell only got worse.

Fawzi spent all that day apologizing and joking and laughing it away. But no one wanted to ride anywhere near him, and frowned their disgust.

Toward late afternoon, he was all alone—at the very back of the caravan, pale and nauseous from the powerful wafting odors of rotten egg.

We couldn't stop the train for him, and he had to endure the stink until evening camp. Even then, not a single soul wanted to join him at his fire. He was left completely alone, and downwind of the others by unanimous demand.

That following morning, Fawzi looked a wreck. It was obvious he had not slept well, and at first light he was busy trying to discover the source of the smell.

When he removed his saddle blanket and found the dried remains of the egg shell, he stopped for a moment, realized it was a prank, and then looked around more angry than I'd ever seen him. When his eyes fell on me, I put my hands under my armpits, shrugged my shoulders and went "cluck, cluck cluck!"

He hasn't bothered me since, as I expect he knows I am capable of far greater evil than this.

ب هجعه 27 محبوب

BAH'MAK

At the next major supply stop Zafir used that place to dismiss Bah'mak. The skinny old man complained and begged, pleaded and threatened, but Zafir was unmovable. The lazy thief had pushed his abuses too far.

That whole exchange a few days back had stirred some questions in my mind. I wanted to ask how shortages were dealt with, especially out across the deserts. I caught up with Ammar one night to ask.

"Water is our fuel, foodstuff is our energy, and a sense of direction is our hope," Ammar said. "Men must consume from all three to survive, while the camels only need foliage for their chew-cud. For the rest, Bassam, it must be every man for himself—the caravan is not equipped, it could not be equipped, to support people like Bah'mak."

"Ammar," I asked, "how many of these trips have you taken with Zafir?"

"Many," he said. "I've been his navigator for more than 25 years."

"What does Zafir do with men like Bah'mak, men who think the caravan owes them for their laziness?"

"He does not allow men like that to ride—it turns others soft who see his behavior. It hurts the entire enterprise."

"How?"

"Some men believe others owe them their comfort—water, food, clothing, a place of security in the caravan."

"Why does Bah'mak think everybody must work but him, even for something so simple as fetching water?" I asked.

"That's just it, that's the problem. It's the nature of some men, and they haven't learned the lesson of survival, the lesson that all men must care for themselves as best as they can."

"I don't understand him," I said. "He's an old man, he should know better—to get water when water is there, when we're at the cistern taking turns, and …"

"But it's true—true for many," Ammar said. "Men such as Bah'mak believe it's the duty of the caravan to make up for their laziness—so they don't have to suffer. They prey on the compassion of others. They know there will always be one who will pity them and give of their substance when it is asked for. A man can go a long time with such charity. It becomes a way of life for him, a life with no suffering."

"Zafir told me that suffering *is* the lesson," I said. "Unless these lessons are severe, a man won't learn to change his nature—change himself to be more prepared, to work harder, to not be lazy. To *end* the suffering."

"Exactly. Bah'mak is no slow learner—worse, he's just a lazy man. He has been that way for as long as I've known him."

"Then why has Zafir let him be a part of his caravan this long?"

"One reason, really—he's the brother of Asiya."

"Asiya?"

"One of Zafir's wives," Ammar said.

"Oh! Yes, *Asiya*. So, Bah'mak is *her brother*?"

"Her oldest. And that makes things complicated and difficult. Bah'mak has benefitted handsomely from the trade for several years now. And by allowing this Zafir keeps peace in the family. But it looks like Zafir has had his fill—he is angry. Bah'mak will have to make it back to his home on his own, he is no longer invited."

Back home, I thought. *Maybe for a price I could ask Bah'mak to stop in Rekeem*. "Do you think if I sent my letters with him that …"

"No, don't trust him, Bassam. He could just as soon burn all of your letters to give him a little light at night while he slept than to carry that responsibility all the way to Rekeem."

"Yes, all right. So—I guess things won't be the same with Asiya when Zafir returns home," I said, smiling.

"Probably not," Ammar laughed.

We sat in silence for a few moments, looking at the rising stars to the east.

"Then tell me," I asked, "what is the right way for the caravan when a man has no water?"

"What you don't see, Bassam, is the kindness of Zafir's loyal men."

"Kindness? I see it all the time."

"I mean in ways not seen. Zafir has made it clear, the caravan is not responsible for the choices the individual makes. But when suffering comes—and it comes to us all—there is no scorn or punishment for a man to ask of his neighbor for some temporary help. And these are good men, Bassam. They help freely when asked by their friends."

"Shouldn't the caravan agree," I asked, "as a whole before they even set out on their trek to be prepared to help the suffering in their midst?"

"No. There is a trap in that," Ammar said. "Setting out to spend resources like that helps create ideas in the minds of the lazy. And in the middle of the deep desert, desperation changes a man—a man without water. He begins to think the caravan owes him the help. He stops helping himself. It is dangerous ground to force others to be generous. It creates men who won't work. It creates the lazy."

"What is our duty, then?" I wondered aloud.

"To do our best for ourselves, first. *All* of us. And should a brother in the group fall upon an accident or make a foolish choice, we can help. But only because we respect one another, not because Zafir orders it—which he never would."

"So, a wise man makes honest friends among all, and sees value in helping others when he can," I said. "To build trust, to have friends to whom he may turn—trusted friends who know him and he knows them."

"That really helps," Ammar said. "To become acquainted, to become a true team. We're in this together, but remember this, Bassam—we help each other to be strong, not to be lazy."

"I see," I said, scratching at my chin. "The principle, then … Zafir has been teaching me to look for principles …"

"Yes, it is the way of the scrolls," Ammar replied.

I suddenly stopped and looked at him. Ammar would not make eye contact and declined to comment. *Does the old star gazer know the scrolls*?

"Then wouldn't the principle be that Zafir gives each man the same opportunity to prepare and care for themselves. He doesn't force the most industrious to share so that everyone has the same water skins and food rations, is that it?"

"Exactly right, Bassam. Every man for himself, every man compassionate, every man free from coercion, every man self sufficient. It's the only way a caravan can survive out here in the middle of nowhere—the *only* way. And that, my young friend, is why the Abdali-ud-din have survived and grown strong for these many centuries."

"Give a man a water skin and he drinks for the day," I offered. "But leave him be to suffer and learn, to draw it on his own and he drinks for the entire trek."

"Very good, Bassam, you are becoming a Greek philosopher, now you must grow a beard so men will believe you."

The next morning I steered my ride off to the roadside to let the train pass by. I watched as the riders spread to the left and right, pushing away from each other to reduce the dust in their faces. In other deserts, they traveled single file, but not here.

The scrolls, I thought, they must teach correct principles, but some men, in fact all these good men I have come to know, seemed to know how goodness worked to their benefit. And this without being taught or told. Because their hearts are good, they are loyal to the honor of Zafir. And those looking for the free ride, the hand out, the welfare, they are quickly expelled. Individual hard work, united in purpose but separate in execution, is the key to prosperity for the whole. It is the first scroll. I hadn't thought of it that way.

I smiled at the large undulating carpet of men and camels in front of me, creeping across the expanse—it reminded me of an afternoon back at Leuke Kome, and I decided to put it in my journal that evening.

> *"Day 24—Dear Rasha, Today I was reminded of an evening at a diner with Fawzi and Suoud, one of those fresh fish eateries that Suoud was bragging about. The chef added a pot of water to the hot coals so it could boil. And then inviting the three of us to choose, he netted live fish from his barrel and dropped them into the pot. I was amazed as the fish stirred around and then settled down, flicking a fin, twitching a tail. 'Why don't they leap out of the cook pot?' I asked. 'Don't they know they're being cooked?' The old chef grinned at me and winked. 'The water is still cool—they don't know it's their cook pot. The warmth comes to the water ever so slowly, gradual, little by little. When it's too hot for them to jump,*

it's too late to escape, and your dinner is served.' Out here in the broiling heat of the mid-day sun on the rocky flats of the endless stretch of sand, I wonder if our great caravan is just like the fish, traveling at ease through a comfortable pot of desert that grows warmer with each passing day—and the growing distance from known settlements. I wonder if leaping to safety might already be too late for me. If it is, I take comfort in that I'm surrounded by men who may never have learned the first scroll, but they live its principles because they have good hearts.—Bassam"

"Dear Bassam, It was a small market today and we had trouble finding the fresh greens and fruits that should be abundant this time of year. There is water, and the farms are growing. Another small group of visitors came today, Egyptian by birth. I bought more writing materials from them, sheets of papyrus. An older man who called himself Amenemhet ("ah-men-EM-het") said he was a friend of father's. They did business years back. He wanted to say hello, sorry he missed father and you when he came.—Rasha."

با هبعه 28 محبوب

THE SWORD

"Bassam!" Fawzi said, pulling his camel alongside. "Four weeks on the trail and you're already sulking or scheming or angry like a little girl? What's on your mind, did Zafir scare you with his scrolls?"

I smiled. "He told me to beware of cutthroats like you, that you could sell your mother for a rice table for one!"

"I could sell you too, for dessert!" he said. "Get out that sword of yours and let's take a look."

I reached under my pack bag and produced the sheathed steel.

"Unsheathe it, and be careful of its edge," Fawzi said. "The sword of Al Murrah has a long history."

"I thought you said every sword came from Zafir?"

"There's more than that, camel brain. You look like you're bored out of your head. Let's get schooled in this. And pay attention, I don't want to repeat myself."

I sighed. I was in for a lecture by somebody more bored than me. "Okay, tell me about the swords."

"Bronze, as you might have noticed, was the first metal of choice. Very expensive, a mix of copper and tin, and copper is hard to find. Bronze is much easier to work. I carry a bronze knife," he said, pulling back his shirt to reveal a short, curved knife with a wide-tipped blade. "It's my family's, and more ornamental than useful, although it will do its job if needed."

"The early iron swords," he said, "ended up too brittle in battle, and often broke against other swords—or the ground, or an armored man or beast. Even so, plenty of them still exist among the nomads of the deserts. But not until trade with the far east did a more refined steel come to us. The sword makers of the Nafud became the center of the craft where the secrets of their forges continue to be under constant guard. Perhaps I will take you there one day. They keep skilled patrols who will challenge with death anyone making an approach. It's a very carefully guarded secret. But you can know if it's one of theirs by the unique signatures on each sword. It has intricate engravings that lace down the side and across the base of the blade where it enters the handle. It's the mark of excellence for the sword makers of Nafud."

I pulled out Suoud's sword, and there it was, beautiful engravings flowing from the hilt.

"But such a sword must be kept sharp or it will break in battle," Fawzi said.

"But steel is stronger than bronze," I countered.

"Yes, but steel against steel gives way to the man whose sword is the sharpest.

Fawzi showed me the art of sharpening. He told me that sharpening stones are not arbitrary rocks picked up just anywhere. Most Al Murrah carry their favorite stones with them, and that with time and practice I could work the edge until I could shave a camel. He said the stones worked best if wet, better with oils.

"Always keep it sheathed," he said, "unless you're going to sharpen it. Then it's always ready for battle."

Fawzi wouldn't let me try it. "I won't let you ruin the edge until you get some practice. Where's your knife?"

I had sharpened blades all my life, but never the way Fawzi showed me. I needed practice. I could tell just by looking that Suoud was an expert at it.

"Besides," Fawzi said, "you'll cut your fingers off, and then what good are you?"

When the caravan stopped for the evening, Fawzi started me on the basics of sword fighting.

"Most of your fighting will take place from the back of your camel," he said. "Sometimes we end up carrying two men on one camel, one to direct, the other to fight. It's a little slower, much less agile than the horse, but an effective fighting machine in battle."

Fawzi explained that the techniques for fighting came from ancient desert traditions. On foot, a soldier had seven major stances, each a collection of moves meant to attack or withstand an aggressor. He said I could learn these over time, and when I trained, I could know instinctively whether to employ a form showing aggression, moderation, ferocity, resilience or perseverance. The stances even served a man who had no sword. Fawzi taught that aggression wasn't always the wisest strategy, that oftentimes the skill of taunting and distracting could prove just as important.

Then Fawzi had me stand in front of him to learn the five strike zones.

"The advantage of the swordsman is his strength," he said, "but a weaker man with superior skill can make all of the difference. If you can learn the skill until that day when you have the strength, you will be the victor every time."

Fawzi stood in front of me and drew his sword high, dropping it slowly, directly over my head.

"Some men are helmeted. Dead center on top of the head is your first strike zone. It's the most exposed, the easiest to wield in battle, and the best in heavy combat."

Fawzi lowered his sword to either side of my neck, thankfully not touching my flesh. I froze at the nearness of so sharp an edge.

"Your second strike zone is either side of the head. This doesn't always kill a man, and it's a place more easily guarded with heavy leather, but the shock of a hard blow will take him out of the battle just the same."

Fawzi stood back again and holding his sword at his waist, he made a slow thrusting motion toward my throat.

"The third strike zone is to the throat, a move best saved for the foot soldier, but also effective on your camel when you're close enough because you can deliver it quickly, and you don't have to expose yourself by raising your sword high as with striking the head and neck."

Fawzi raised his sword again. "Now, you raise up your sword."

I did, as best I could, as if to strike. Fawzi let his drop slowly, showing me how a glance to my arm could be delivered.

"Al Murrah are merciful, Bassam. Death is not always the best outcome of battle. When defeat is certain, a conquered people of the dead is of no value to anyone. Your fourth strike zone is the arm of the swordsman. It doesn't kill but it stops, and it honors your opponent with the least physical damage. His striking arm is his power, strike him thus," and he demonstrated the technique.

"Your last strike zone is for the kill. You aim right here," he said, pointing to my right chest. "In battle, the sword arm of your assailant is raised and the other arm he will use to protect. Aim for the right chest for the least guarded place, and you will fell your man."

I stood back raising my sword, slashing at imaginary foes, directing a thrust, cutting across. The sword soon became heavy, the muscles in my arms burned, and I dropped my arms.

Fawzi shook his head. "Oh my donkey dung, you'll wear yourself out, Bassam, you're doing it all wrong."

"How can you keep this weapon raised for so long?" I asked. "My shoulders ache."

Fawzi stood in front again. "It's how you hold your feet and turn your body," he said. "Always stand one foot forward, the other back, like this." He took a stand and pointed to his feet. "You keep your body turned away, sideways, never expose your front to the sword, and in this way a glancing blow is usually the worst an enemy can make."

I gave it a try. I faced Fawzi and turned, putting a foot behind, twisting my body, but holding the sword awkwardly in front.

"No, no," Fawzi said. "The feet do you no good like this. Always raise your back elbow to your shoulder. This puts the power of your whole body behind the strike and you have balance that will preserve your strength."

I took a step back and raised the sword, my back elbow in the air, my face behind the blade.

"Perfect. That might scare my donkey in the dark, young Bassam. You keep practicing, I'm going for food."

"I'll join you in a while," I said, and taking my stance I took more thrusts at the air.

A band of conspirators can easily hide. It was dangerous work to carry gold and valuables between centers of trade, and the caravans watched for those who might sweep down on them to claim for their own what wasn't theirs. Much of the success of the Abdali-ud-din was in their selection of Al Murrah, men true to their legacy of loyalty as much as they kept faithful allegiance to their elder chieftain. But wealth has power among the unprincipled to sway an allegiance, and in the solitude of the desert, a rotten man can never hide for long. When conspirators are ultimately discovered, their fates of necessity come swift—and their bones are left for the hawks to finish.

For Al Murrah, those who waited in ambush just over the crest of dunes or near mountain passes did not pose their greatest concern—the enemy they feared the most was the traitor in their midst.

"Day 29—Dear Rasha, I'm learning the sword, to defend and to protect. Fawzi knows tricks and he is teaching me. Suoud's sword is heavy but strong. I must grow into it if I'm to be any good. We travel many days with only water from the hidden cisterns to drink and give to our animals. It is bitter so the men boil it for tea. There is little for the animals to eat in these long stretches. My bakra shows ribs, and so do I. But a new stopping place, an oasis with a good well and palms is not too far ahead. I think about you on these long, lonely rides. I hope you and mother and father are well. Crossing these deserts is a test. Zafir tells me this is a short hop through the sands. The real desert lays many months ahead of us. I hope to be accustomed to this saddle by then.—Bassam"

"Dear Bassam, Dalal is letting me take charge of one dinner each week. I enjoy it very much. I am learning to bake bread, make goat stew and fried sweetbread. Kateb says I'm a very good cook and he always cleans up the leftovers so there is nothing to throw away. Your mother and I have to laugh. He acts the tease sometimes, and eats like one too. We are

clearing a place in front to make a garden. I will need to carry water for it.—Rasha"

ب هبعه 29 محبوب

NIGHT SHADOWS

The moon rose brightly in the east and cast long, sharp shadows of Ammar and me as we stepped past sleeping travelers to the outskirts of camp.

"Bring the lamp anyway," Ammar said. "We could track scorpions in this moonlight, but you'll need it to read my maps." And then he stopped. "Why do you have that, young Bassam? Why do you bring the sword of Al Murrah? You don't plan to slay me tonight, for meat?"

"I keep it with me all the time," I said. "Fawzi has been teaching me. And it's night."

"Oh Bassam! That's a man's sword. You may be tall enough, but you aren't strong enough. Dragging that around will wear you thin before this trip is out." He shook his head and continued toward a slight rise at the base of a towering basalt formation. This perch put us far enough from the camp that no one could be disturbed by our talking.

"We'll set up here in the shadow," Ammar said, "so I can see the stars without that great light in my eyes."

I laid out the maps and found a small crevice where I pushed the oil lamp to hide its light until it was needed. In the shadowed dark we scanned the night sky.

"I still don't understand how we measure our travel west to the east," I said. "Zafir said the best measurement was a day's journey on a healthy camel. I asked him how far is a 'day's journey,' and he said 300 stadia."

"Or 35 Roman miles," Ammar corrected. "If you plan to travel the great caravan routes west, the Roman mile is your guide, and they mark their roads with mile stones so you can measure progress."

I shook my head. "Stadia works better," I said. I pointed toward the east at a bright rising star. "The wandering stars, like that one," I said. "Do they help with your maps?"

"Sometimes, and they tell me what part of a season we're in, that helps. But you're right, they move about so much."

"Then how far do we travel in a day?" I asked. "Can you tell how far we are from Wadi Sirhan?"

Ammar couldn't answer, he had his kamal in hand, the string in his teeth, taking a measurement.

"Not far," he said, coiling the string and returning it to the pouch. "At this rate, I estimate about 12 more days."

Twelve more days before an oasis stop. Twelve more days of buried cisterns and dried foods and dung fires.

"Tell me about Sothos, and the other stars, Ammar. I want to learn the art of the navigator."

Ammar stepped out of the shadow and crouched down to make markings on a parchment, turning to capture the moon's light. "I thought you gave up after our last lesson, you ignored me most of the time!"

"No, it was Zafir. He is teaching me his scrolls."

"And are you a better student with him than with me?"

"Naturally, he is a much better teacher, you old goat."

"Okay, stop being a girl and let us start with the pole star again...."

Almost an hour later, after multiple uses of the kamal, various strings, frequent reference to "my fathers," and "out on the sea," and "when I was your age," I yawned for the lesson to end.

"Remember the 15 stars and you can calculate what watch, what place and what season without needing your fingers or my kamal," Ammar said. He bent down to pack his maps. "After some experience, you'll get good at it."

Just then, I spotted movement on the far side of camp. I saw the tiny distant shape of a black figure moving stealthily against the silvery gray landscape, away from the camels and tents. "Who is that?" I asked.

Ammar stood up and squinted to look. "That's not the watch changing ... perhaps he goes to toilet."

"But so far from camp?"

"Did he eat from your pouch, Bassam? Would you poison your friends, too?"

We watched in silence as the figure continued west, too far west, and climbing a steep incline, he disappeared over the ridge of a hill. We watched and waited for several moments. He didn't return.

"That doesn't look right," I said, feeling an uneasiness growing inside. "Should we tell the watch?" I scanned the camp and spotted on the far opposite side the tiny fire of the watch and two men poking it with sticks.

Ammar slung his bag over his shoulder and estimated the possibilities. "Extinguish the lamp, lets take the long way back to camp," and led me west along the ridge leading toward the disappearance of the stranger. It was easy in the bright moonlight to step over rocks, hug the ridge past the silver-lighted rocks and stubby desert plants.

Several minutes later, after creeping through shadow and dark, Ammar reached out his arm to stop me. "Silence," he whispered, and pushed me into the black shadow of a formation. He pointed to the far slope of a hill below us, hidden from the camp but bathed in the full light of the moon. Some 200 paces below, I could see a small group of figures standing in a small circle, talking. I counted seven camels kneeling and five men standing. There was no fire or tent.

"Who is that?" I whispered.

"It's not good whoever it is," Ammar answered.

We watched a few moments longer as the figures conversed and one handed off something to another, while one pointed to the east with a broad sweep of his arm.

"Now listen carefully, Bassam," Ammar whispered. "If this is what I think it is, we must capture those men—all of them." He looked back to camp. "There is the watch. I want you to run carefully, leave your sword with me, and run carefully down this hill—but be careful, it's steep—and hurry as fast as you can to the watch. We don't want to scare them off into the dark, we'd never find them. Tell the watch what we've seen and that Ammar wants them to circle around. Hurry."

I obeyed and stood to free the sword from my belt. Handing it to Ammar, I turned to find the best way down the hill.

Suddenly from the corner of my eye, a moving shadow caught my attention and I turned to see. At that exact same moment, a black-shrouded figure stood up from his crouching place behind the formation and came around silently like a violent cloud directly at me. Ammar was three paces away and turned just in time to see the attacker leap. In my panic I saw only one thing: a long, sharp knife flashing in the moonlight and pointed directly at me.

"Ammar!" I screamed, turning in vain to avoid the shrouded shape, but the stranger fell into me, knocking me off my feet and the two of us went right down the slope. He was shouting, I was calling for Ammar as we tumbled and turned in a great blanket of black dust, head over heels, until we stopped with a heavy thud at the bottom in a heap of choking dust and pain.

I immediately rolled to my knees and tried to get up. I felt dizzy and dazed, and suddenly noticed a terrible searing pain spreading through my right shoulder—I could hardly breathe and couldn't move my arm. The attacker lay there close to me, slower in getting up.

All I could think to do was stagger in the direction of the camp, shouting, "Help! Help! Help Ammar, somebody, help!"

Fortunately, my alarm roused those nearest me, and the men of the watch stood quickly looking in our direction.

I could hardly take one step in front of the other as pain rushed through my shoulder and across my chest. I felt like I was going to pass out. I called again—limping and dragging myself toward camp—"Help! Help! Help Ammar!"

My attacker jumped to his feet and took a step toward me, but quickly stopped to feel about for his knife in the dark. Failing to find it, he turned and hurried to climb up the sliding sands of the rocky slope toward Ammar.

I could not see the brawl that took place up the hill in the silvery moonlight but I heard more shouting. Several dozen men with swords unsheathed raced past me, shouting, and attacking the hill to come to Ammar's aid.

I was just ready to turn around myself when the familiar voice of Malik ordered me to stop.

"Bassam! You're bleeding—sit here," Malik snapped. "On the ground. Lie down," he ordered.

"No, Ammar—he is up there—go help him—I'm all right."

Malik grabbed my arm and I cried out in pain. I took a few more steps and then quite suddenly, my world spun darkly into circles, and all went black. I collapsed into the arms of another.

ب هبعه 30 محبوب

THE WOUND

The first thing that came to me was a steady, relentless roar in my head, and pain over my entire body. As I became aware of awakening, the roar started to quiet, like the fading hiss of the receding tide on the beach. My eyes felt sealed shut and I tried to squint open one eye—the light hurt. It was morning and the blackness slowly opened to a thin slit of bright light—blue light. It was the sky above me. Though all was blurry, I could see that Zafir and Fawzi were crouched over me, smiling to see that I was stirring.

But with the pain of the bright morning sunlight came the sudden awareness of the shocking throb in my right arm. There was a wet cloth on my forehead. I tried to move my limbs and waves of fire radiated from my shoulder to my chest and deeply into my arm. I squinted down to see it was locked in a sling wrapped close to my body.

"What?" I said, trying to sit up. My head rushed with pain, and I laid back.

"Don't move, Bassam," Fawzi said. "You've lost a lot of blood, but you're going to be okay."

I tried again to open my eyes.

"Lie still a while," Zafir said. "Here, drink some of this," and he held my head up to give me a sip of a nasty-tasting tea.

I grimaced, sputtering. And then I remembered the attack of last night. "How is Ammar? What happened to Ammar?"

Zafir leaned over me again, putting his hand on my left arm. "Ammar is fine," he said smiling. "And do you know why he is fine?"

I just grunted a reply.

"Because he had the sword of Al Murrah. And I wonder, how did Ammar get the sword of Al Murrah?"

I could only look, trying to understand. My shoulder burned and my head pounded. Indeed, every muscle felt torn from its place. "What happened," I asked, closing my eyes again. "Those men attacked us ...."

Zafir stood to leave and I feebly reached to catch his sleeve. "Zafir,"

I said weakly. "The first—our talk—that's why I carried the sword last night."

Zafir smiled, clasped my hand and laid it back to my side. "I know, my young student. I know it, you didn't let down your guard with Ammar on that routine navigation lesson. And it saved your life—it saved the life of you both. We worried about you all night, but you're doing well and we'll speak of it more when you are better."

He rose, putting me into Fawzi's care who was more than happy to tell of the exciting event.

"Your shouting woke us and we raced to your aid," he began. "When we reached you, that Fukara was running back up the hill. Ammar had your sword and killed a second attacker who was hiding at the hilltop, and then fearing for you, he met the Fukara part way down the slope and made quick work of him, too."

"Did you find the others?" I asked.

"No, the alarm scared them off but we found their camp and a stray camel. They escaped into those hills. We found the knife—it is indeed Fukara. We mounted a search, but in the dark, even with the moon ...."

"What about ....?"

"The man you saw? He was from Leuke Kome, he was one of those who signed on with the camels that we added to our train. No one knew him well, but we know him now. Al Murrah are speaking with his associates this morning. But he has escaped. We have his things, but nothing that could betray him as a bandit."

I could only groan inside at the pain. "Then Ammar is safe, that is good. I'm proud of him. I thought he was just a star gazer." I shut my eyes a moment, the throbbing fire of my wound was burning with each breath. Weakness began to return.

"Fawzi?"

"Yes?"

"Thank you."

"Thank you? For what, you toothless camel breath!"

"Thank you for teaching me," I breathed. "When the Fukara was upon me—I turned—like you taught me—no time to think. I turned. And that knife, it hit my shoulder—not my chest."

Fawzi's eyes traced the entry point and shoulder position that met in the dark of the night, the damage now well buried beneath a heavy red bandage. It was a deep thrust, the knife was long. That same blow to the chest would have been fatal.

"You're welcome," Fawzi said. My breathing grew deep and I lapsed into sleep.

"Dear Bassam, The nights are beautiful now. I walked at sunset from the Siq toward the market and then to home. The air is sweet with perfumes of blossoms and the evening is best for families outdoors talking and children playing. I love Rekeem, it is a good place to make a home.—Rasha"

HEALING

The medical treatment for a deep wound had improved greatly among the nomads, and though painfully administered, the latest techniques had proven effective.

Several times that first day, my wound was opened—a terribly painful ritual that left me trembling. It was washed with salty brine until the old blood was cleansed from the gash. A poultice of dried leaves was applied with a new dressing, and I was bound up again. This was going to continue until the dressing showed no fresh bleeding.

It was expected that by the third day the bleeding should stop, however the washing and change of dressing had to continue another three or four days until the wound began to close with no inflammation. That was the plan, anyway.

Among Zafir's men was a scholar of the medical arts—wise and bearded Humam ("Who-mawm"). It was the second time he had come to clean my wound. Kneeling by my side I watched him knit his bushy eyebrows as he went about the chore, frowning with concern.

"Now—you're not going to let this wound get ugly, are you?" he asked. "We need to keep this immobilized, and dry."

Humam said he was looking for the signs of redness that could spell another danger, and he wanted to avoid stitching, an interesting idea he was learning from the medical practitioners from Chang'an.

"Bassam my friend," he always said each time he tended to the wound, "you'll live as long as your skin."

I closed my eyes tight as the washing commenced with a tear-biting, fiery sting.

"This will heal well enough, but it will leave you with a nice war scar. One day you will show it around a campfire with great bravado. Don't you go bragging about this narrow escape from the long knives of the Fukara. It almost killed you, young man."

I shook my head. "I'm not as eloquent at inflating my bravery as Fawzi and Suoud. I'm not sure I'll want to be bragging anyway. I should have seen the Fukara coming, I should have had my guard up, on the look-out before he struck."

Humam finished tying the last of the bindings with a 'harrumph,' and looked me over. "You're lucky, young man. Keep this dry and lie here for the day. I don't want you moving."

To allow my recovery, the caravan remained at the cistern another day while Al Murrah followed the prints to discern the escape route of the attackers. Even though Al Jafr was still a day or two distant, Al Murrah reported to Zafir that the prints indicated a retreat to that village, and was most likely their home base. The estimation prompted Zafir to amend his route. He directed us to turn from our northerly trek to a more eastern path directly toward the oasis Al Isawiyah in the Wadi Sirhan. That diversion would also put us north of the sand dunes, adding three days on the road—but a safer three days.

For the morning of the second day, I was obligated to travel. I was still terribly sore and required help climbing into my saddle. When my bakra rose to her feet, I almost passed out from the jarring motions. Just that simple thing was an exercise in painful endurance. I sat atop the saddle stiffly, grimacing at each step, trying to prevent fresh bleeding from oozing through the bandages. I dared not even try to scratch Bakra's ears, but she seemed contented, and walked carefully, as if knowing my pain.

Zafir put me near the front of the caravan under the watchful care of Humam and the lead guard. Zafir said none of them were ready to let the risks of the trade routes rob Rekeem of its valiant young son. I hurt too much to argue with him, and let it slide.

As for the two Fukara killed by Ammar, their bodies followed the train lashed to the poles of a travois dragged behind a camel. I asked

Fawzi why they didn't bury or burn them in the manner that Zafir had explained.

"It's the hawks," Fawzi said. "Up high. They signal to other travelers there is death here, and where there's death there once was life, in particular, at the secret place of the cistern."

"So we take them far away to bury?"

"Yes, but we won't bury them. The road to Wadi Sirhan is lined with the bones of the traders and traitors, and to that we'll add Fukara. It will be our warning to them."

After the seventh day the healing of my wound was well underway. The gash remained open, red and sore, the pain had turned to stiffness. For Fawzi, it meant the renewal of lessons, even if the caravan must remain on the move. He found me at the usual place toward the front of the train and urged his camel alongside.

"It's time to stop being a girl, Bassam," Fawzi said. "Take out the sword of Suoud."

"I can't," I said. "I can hardly lift my arm let alone the sword," and awkwardly attempted to unsheathe it with my left arm.

"You've got to exercise the wound, Bassam. Every day, exercise the wound and get your strength back. But today we exercise your left."

"My left?"

"And why not, you just showed me it works. If you had to defend yourself with your good arm is gone, what then, oh wise one?"

"All right then, my left."

"First of all—" Fawzi said as he eyed me for the best point of attack, "First of all, let me see what kind of strength you have in your left ... hold the sword above your head."

I obeyed and grabbed the sheath at its middle and held it up.

"No no no," Fawzi said. "By the grip, hold the sword the right way, vulture vomit. By the grip."

I took the sword by its handle and thrust it upwards.

"Now, that's the beginning," he said. "Keep your arm up, I'll be right back." And he turned, galloping toward the rear.

After several long minutes my arm began to ache with fatigue. I kept it up but the taut muscles began to pull across my chest to my sore shoulder. And when I could bear it no longer, I brought the sword to rest across my lap. At that moment Talib rode up and scolded.

"Bassam! You put that arm back skyward!"

I did. "Fawzi makes me the fool," I complained.

"Not Fawzi, you make yourself the fool," Talib answered. "Fawzi makes you a two-armed swordsman. There is great honor in that, Bassam. You do as he says because I'll be watching."

For a quarter hour longer, I kept the tip pointed high until finally Fawzi returned.

"What's this?" he asked, riding up next to me.

"My shoulder can't take this added pain, I've got to rest it," I said.

"Rest? Ha! There's not a man in this caravan who will seek rest before honor. You honor your life, you honor your health, you honor all those who hold you up by keeping that sword pointed skyward," Fawzi said, pointing up with his riding stick. "And when I say it is time, then you may bring it down."

I held the sword high until my arm began to tremble, beads of sweat broke out on my forehead and my eyes began to sting with tears beneath endurance—I refused to let him beat me, but my wound wasn't cooperating. Finding me near breaking point, Fawzi relented. "All right, Bassam. You may bring down your arm. But not to rest it, mind you—it's just that you look so silly riding along like that, it embarrasses me."

I didn't react —the pain across my chest was crushing.

"Day 35—Dear Rasha, I have not written you for several days because of an attack. I am all right but I received a wound from a Fukara bandit. He struck me with his knife but I shouted and woke the camp. Ammar killed him and another, but the rest of them got away. We are taking another path for fear a larger band of them might be waiting for us. I was very sore for a long time. People say I did a good thing, alerting the camp. I will show you the scar when I get home. We had bad meat two days ago. Many who ate it were ill. That slowed us down. I did not eat it and did not become ill. Now, I don't trust the cooks. The night sky has been filled with many falling stars these past days. Have you seen them?—Bassam"

"Dear Bassam—Your friend Faris came to dinner with his parents yesterday. We had fun talking. I planted seeds in our garden this last

week and I water them faithfully. So far, nothing has grown. There was a fire in a diner booth yesterday. It burned to the ground. No one was hurt. Kateb went to help but they didn't need him. He is restless. I think he misses you. —Rasha"

32

THE SECOND SCROLL

At the confluence of Wadi Al Abyad and Wadi Hadrai was an ancient cistern that predated all others. Zafir told us it might date back to the very first caravans, maybe a thousand years ago.

At first Zafir missed it and had to circle back for a couple of hours. By the time the caravan caught up for water, he decided it was too late to continue and we spent the night there.

"Doesn't it bother you, Zafir," I asked at evening meal. "That your men know all about the location of this hidden well? We're here now, and they're seeing it for themselves."

The old chieftain raised his eyes and looked about with a satisfied grin. "Yes, they know, and you can be assured that many of them are crafting their own map of its location, just as they have at every watering stop since we left Rekeem."

"And you don't mind sharing the secret so openly?"

"No, it's not open at all," Zafir said. "In two day's ride, these 400 men will have 400 different maps and 400 different recollections. It's not a map that leads us here. Nor is it Ammar's reckoning with his strings. We are here because I know the way, and that is all."

I thought it over. *How was this done?* Does Zafir possess a gift or a secret that he fails to share? The land looked all the same to me. I was left in a puzzle.

As night fell and the watch took their place, Zafir approached our cookfire where I was laughing with Fawzi over a story from Rakin.

"I didn't know the male camels ran so slow, but I was young," Rakin said. "I didn't know any better, but I stopped teasing my sister after that.

She was wise, I was not."

"The females in our lives," Zafir interrupted as he stepped to the fire, "compared to you, Rakin, all females are swifter, smarter, wiser and certainly better looking than you. But enough talk about she-camels ...." We all roared and Rakin just frowned.

Zafir reached out to me. "Will you walk with me a while?" I saw the bag of scrolls slung over his shoulder and two mats under his arm. I rose and stepped from the fire to retrieve my small journal-writing lamp and pulled the sword of Suoud from its place.

Fawzi called after us, "Not so late tonight, Bassam. You're always so grouchy in the morning!" I just glared, and then joined Zafir in the blackness that shrouded the sands beyond the edges of the camp.

Zafir found a place that was far enough away that prying ears couldn't hear, but close enough for safety. The men of the watch stood as we passed, scanning the blackened darkness for dangers in hiding.

"So, let us begin," Zafir said as we set things in place.

"This bag," he said, unlacing the top, "was my father's when he was a boy. It was new then but it shows wear today. I may have to replace it."

I looked up. *Was Zafir repeating himself?*

Reaching inside, he lifted out a long bundled pair of spindles, one of them holding the parchment and about the same girth as the handle of Suoud's sword. These were protected with a soft leather covering that was tied around them by three cords. Two leather tassels dangled from the top.

He placed the scroll on his mat, untied the covering and laid it back letting the spindles relax and the scroll rest—untouched. Its yellowed papyrus clung curled to itself with visible edges worn from use. The two slender spindles had been ornately carved in olive wood—their smooth artistry glowed with yellowed age, just as with the first.

"Most men hope to find in these scrolls some ancient and lost guide to riches, or the answer to all of their troubles, or a treasure map that could lead them to wealth unimaginable...."

They are the same words, I realized. *Is this some sort of a ceremony or ritual? Is there more to this passage of rites than just riding into the deep deserts?*

"... And from them will come the meaning of true riches. Most men cannot read these words because their hearts are not ready—they cannot understand them. I think your heart is ready, Bassam. Do you understand?"

I nodded.

"As before," Zafir continued, "you will read from the scroll and I will listen. When you have a question you may ask me, but I'll not answer them all, that is part of the test."

Yes, the very same words.

I took the scroll and turned toward the light.

> "The Song of the Soul. To the prosperous, prosperity is not in the possession of things, but in the knowledge of things. There is of this earth, for all, an abundance for possession, but a man who embraces scarcity in his mind, with doubt, lacking faith, consuming for the sake of consumption, never did a treasure create ...."

For the first half hour the words gave me a new set of thoughts that linked to the words of the first scroll. Philosophy, values, morality, economies, as if one stand of bricks was being placed atop another by master masons, understanding added to understanding, and truth to truth.

From the words I understood that most men exhaust their lives in fear of loss, constant fear that they will lose what they've worked so hard to obtain. They fail to understand that what they *are* is what makes them strong. Possessions signal many things to the worldly man, but the truth is that the thing of greatest value is the man himself.

I read that a proper exchange of goods must profit both the giver and the receiver. If either is unhappy, the exchange was not fair. Allowing a profit is how both parties magnify themselves. And from such are the fruits of the earth multiplied for the benefit of everyone else.

I read that of all creations in the earth, only one has intrinsic and natural self-created value, and that is man himself. This is because only man has the power to create more things than he consumes. All other forms of life must consume to sustain themselves—none other gives back as can man.

And then came another riddle.

"Read it to me aloud as before," Zafir said.

I cleared my throat and stumbled over the same passage repeated from the first scroll.

"The sayings of The Second Scroll, the Song of the Soul," I began.

> "A virtue of wealth is this for thee, One branch one limb on the self same tree; The coin and palace all men may gain, But woe is life when spent in vain. For joy that lasts and doth not cease, Embrace the virtues thou Prince of Peace. One branch one limb on the self same tree, A virtue of wealth can be for thee."

"Zafir," I asked, "This line about 'one branch one limb on the self same tree.'"

"Yes?"

"A tree has many branches, and would die without them."

Zafir nodded.

"Each branch adds strength, just like each virtue will add strength to the man."

"Very good," Zafir nodded. "You are beginning to understand. Read the rest, there's more that will help."

> "Oh wisdom, behold now The Song of the Soul:
> The blind that leads, he is cautious still, He feels his way past phantom and real; To climb a way he believes is pure, In chase of his wants, they act the lure; But reclined at last amidst his cache, The blind fool sits above the dash; He sits balanced high, a place that where, Eagles or lions never could dare; The plummet to death he cannot see, For blindly he went, a fool is he. What meaneth this The Song of the Soul?"

I fumbled around for some deep hidden meaning, but I honestly didn't know what it was trying to tell me.

"This talks about all of us," I decided. "He can't see far into his life. And he must feel his way along, testing things along the way to learn what is real and what is not?"

Zafir offered no guidance.

"So, to make progress, he must decide, he must make choices that are not always clear because he is blind ..."

I repeated the last phrase again, "'In chase of his wants, they act the lure.' This must mean that being blind, he still presses forward because he is trying to obtain what he needs."

"He needs?" Zafir asked.

"Well ... he wants."

"Is wants the same as needs?"

"I suppose, sometimes."

"And knowing the sometimes and the *sometimes not* makes all the difference," he said. "You need water in the desert, you want it, too. A man may want gold in the desert, but he doesn't need it."

Wants and needs, they are so different, but also the same. I fell into another stupor of thought. There was something hiding in the words, I could feel it.

> "He sits balanced high, a place that where Eagles or lions never could dare; The plummet to death he cannot see, For blindly he went, a fool is he."

For some reason I felt impatient. My shoulder hurt, we had been a long time on the trail, I didn't like my arm wrapped up for so long, and I wanted to get out and do something. I missed Rekeem, I missed mother and father, and what of Rasha? At that thought my heart suddenly beat faster. Looking toward the horizon I straightened from the mat with Zafir watching.

"Just a moment," I said, and stood up and took several paces away from the golden glow of the single lamp, searching for solitude in the darkness.

Overhead, the black arching canopy of glistening stars rolled over me in wonder and awe. God's handiwork sparkled reliably overhead on that peaceful night, there was no *plummet to death* for the things God put his hand to.

I cast my gaze across the motionless black lumps of the camels and the men, quietly resting in darkened shadows. Each of them was loyal to the caravan as an employee for the duration, devoted to Zafir and his enterprise. On such a night as this the wealth of the caravan seemed grand indeed. I guessed those golden treasures rested somewhere in the center of camp within the watchful care of Al Murrah and within sight of the watch. Such wealth could be a fantastic prize and set a man for life if he could obtain it. And how hard could that be, especially on a night as this? Why have the men not conspired to rise against Zafir and his captains and take it for themselves? From this very place a ride to any of the oasis villages stood only two or three days, and once there, victuals could be bought, a new train assembled, new men hired, and ....

Suddenly I froze, my brain clicking into a thousand places at once. "How could I be so foolish?" I thought, and hurried back to Zafir and the lamp.

"Let me look at that again ..." I said, seating cross-legged and pulling the scroll to read. "The blind that leads ... Zafir, maybe I'm wrong, but hear me out."

A cool breeze caught the lamp, flickering its flame in a few short puffs. I leaned over the scroll, my eyes focusing.

"The whole point of this riddle is that the man is blind. It doesn't really matter what danger he puts himself in by chasing his wants. The fact is, he's blind and that's why he sits satisfied with death just at his elbows, am I right?"

Zafir looked at me without speaking.

"The problem is not that the man is in a dangerous place," I said, "it's that he is *still* blind."

"Very good, Bassam," Zafir said.

"So the whole point of the riddle is that the man is blind ... or better, the man is *blinded* ... Oh! That's it," I said. "Men are blinded by their greed, and go chasing after things even to the point of foolishness, am I right?"

"Why do you think he is still blind?" Zafir asked.

"I'm not sure ... I had it a moment ago ...." I looked out again over the camp. *Why didn't the men rise up against Zafir? What was it that kept them in their place, to not take the caravan's treasure and ....*

"Zafir! I think I know it!"

He looked at me with patience.

"The blind that leads is like a man leading himself through his life."

"Yes?"

"But *this* man, the blind fool, has surrendered that job of leadership to his worldly wants, to treasure, to power, to anything that has tempted him. That's what leads him."

"Almost!" Zafir said.

"And that false leader has taken him to a dangerous place, and he doesn't even know that."

"Being blind, how could he know?"

"The man must learn to follow ...."

"Go on," Zafir said.

"The man must learn to follow the true leader. A leader who knows the way, a tested leader, one who always has the best interests of others at heart. And such a leader would be ..."

I went quiet and looked at the words to guide me. *To climb a way he believes is pure* ... that word, 'believes,' it's not the same as ....

"It makes sense, Zafir!" I said. "The scroll teaches that a man can't safely rely on himself and what he believes. Believing is not the same as *knowing*."

"And what leader knows, who daily takes his stance?" Zafir asked.

"Why ...." I sat up again and looked into Zafir's eyes. "Knowledge? It's knowledge! The great expanse that he must fight and fear each day, that enemy is his ignorance?"

"Exactly!"

"A wise man who knows he is vulnerable to being led by his greed," I said. "Such a man *knows* he is blind while nearly all of us do not. A wise man therefore seeks help with his ignorance, while the foolish man simply goes forward stubbornly and blindly believing his wants are what is best for him, and for that, he risks his all."

"That's it." Zafir was smiling at last. "Part of keeping up his guard always, a wise man never trusts his own ignorance, and certainly not the tempting lure of his own wants. A wise man waits to gain his sight on the matter before him. He never goes blindly."

"And gaining sight, that is like gaining knowledge, knowledge from others, those who could help him not be blind any longer?"

"The most severe form of ignorance is to not know you are ignorant," Zafir said.

"Then the wise man, the man of virtue, is willing to confess his ignorance?"

Zafir changed positions and began using his hands.

"Let me ask you something, Bassam," he said. "Does God answer your prayers?"

"Sometimes yes, sometimes no."

"What if I told you the answer is *always* yes. What do you say about those times when you thought he didn't answer you?"

I had weighed that very problem over in my mind many times. The story of the woman who gave me birth and her cruel death—was that God's will that she bleed to death in the sand with her child wrapped in her arms? What about my own mean-spirited teasing of Rasha, or animals, or the elderly—was that God's will that such a wicked heart be in a boy so young? And what about Suoud, did God wish him to die?

"I'm not sure, Zafir," I said. "I've struggled with this all of my life. Some say such things are written and no one can change the writing. I'm not sure anyone could count on that to be true. God does not stand in the way of our choices. That is how we learn."

Zafir stood and motioned me to join him. "Leave the lamp" he said. "Let us walk into the darkness a little to see if there is some light there."

He led me away a few dozen paces. The only noise was the gentle whispering of the desert breeze and the crunch of our sandals on the hard soil. Zafir stopped and gestured toward the vast iridescent emptiness of the desert lands that spread before us and ended abruptly at the starry horizon.

"We'll speak more of this later, Bassam," he said. "For now, let me teach you this. God does not wish tragedy on anyone. Tragedy is the work of imperfection. It is the deliberate work of evil. But God rarely stops such action. And why is that so?"

I wondered the same thing.

"God is the master teacher. He is *always* teaching, my son. He teaches his creations the laws and principles that govern his whole kingdom. Think about it. We'll spend a great deal more time in his world than ours, shall we not?" Zafir grinned at me. Even in the dark I could hear him smile. And then I realized the oddity of the statement.

"It makes sense then, Bassam, that God prepare his creations properly during their years on this earth. He gives us our choice and doesn't interfere. And whether we are a victim or the perpetrator, he doesn't let embarrassment, frustration, deprivation, poverty or even death stand in the way of the lessons he wants us to learn."

The idea penetrated deep into my heart. *God does not let the consequences of our choices prevent us from learning lessons.*

"God is the master teacher," he continued. "To him life continues beyond death, and for that next journey his creations must be prepared. And such lessons are brutal. Brutal because they must teach with such power that they are remembered forever. And what better place than this life, this desert, to give all ideas a try—good ideas, bad ideas, His ideas, your ideas. But in all, people will benefit or suffer from those choices, and God leaves us to learn it ourselves. To purify the impure, to polish the rough edges, to conquer ourselves, to gain understanding of why things happen as they do, to see as He sees—that is the lesson if people can live long enough to learn it."

"But it's confusing to me, Zafir. If blind obedience is foolish, and ignorance is worse, what am I supposed to do in the face of the unknown?"

"Don't miss the basic point of the second scroll," Zafir said. "Having self governance is not enough. It must have direction. The strongest man whose passions and wants are arrested is still not wise. He can thrust his strength behind the wrong army and not know it. Haven't you seen men put forth their greatest effort, their greatest strength, behind a cause that's evil?"

"Oh yes. Many times."

"And you wonder, 'why are men so cruel and selfish?'"

"Yes, I wonder that a great deal."

"Such men may not see themselves as cruel and selfish, but passionate about the cause they have chosen to support. That's why humility and being teachable in all things go hand in hand with self-governance. You think of the first scroll as a virtue directing your strength of *restraint.* What about your strength of *pursuit*?"

Suddenly I felt my brain catch hold of a new understanding. "Strength of pursuit .... I had not thought of that. Pursuit of what?"

"What does the second scroll tell you to pursue? Do you remember it? 'He feels his way past phantom and real.' What of those two is the most desired?"

"Past phantom and real...," I repeated softly. "The real, of course. Those things that he can rely on, the truth and not the falsehood."

"Then consider this. A man who relies on the word of another, about whom he knows little, has not *knowledge* but merely opinion, which may be true or false testimony. If he relies on that and nothing else he may suffer for his gamble."

"A man must know when he is being taught truth or fiction," I said. "He must know the source, am I correct?"

"More than that. He must know it himself."

Zafir stood silent a moment, giving me time to absorb what he was trying to teach.

Shouldn't we strive to learn all things—not as God does, that's not possible, but as much as we are able. Is that possible for *any* man? To know ALL things in this earth? No, that's impossible! What foolishness is this?

"Zafir, how is a man to know all things? That doesn't make sense to me."

"My young student, you have eyes but you still do not see," Zafir said. "You believe you have climbed to the precipice of knowledge, but it is me and this scroll who led you here. Do you see imminent death at your elbow?"

"No," I said. "The truth is I'm confused. Faith and blind faith, how can they be different?"

"Then tell me, my impatient young son, in whom may you place your ultimate humility?"

"In God, most certainly." And then it hit me. "In God!" I gasped. "Only in God! Only in God can I place true humility, all others I must question. Is that it, Zafir? All others I must question?"

"Now you're getting it," Zafir smiled. "A humble man is cautious, always asking, always looking, studying all that he can. He knows that ignorance is a cruel taskmaster whose lash leaves deep wounds that will place a scar into his memory, a tangible reminder of his folly. He fights ignorance. He goes out of his way to slay it, destroy it, put it as far from him as he can in all things, not just a few. That is how to reverse the blindness, to see with new eyes and know, to trust in knowledge and not greed and avarice for these are sure to lead you in a circle where no worldly gain can possibly satisfy all needs."

"Day 36—Dear Rasha, Your father is teaching me the second scroll. We spoke of Suoud who let down his guard. He was not humble to Zafir's council. I feel it is my fault for not being there, but then, I must confess that it isn't.

I am trying to become content that I did the best I knew how. We are entering desolation and few travelers can cross such deserts without knowledge of the cisterns. They are ancient—who knows when they were dug. More mystical than that is why did they dig them here? How does one know where water is to be found in this parched place? I must ask Zafir.—Bassam"

"Dear Bassam, Our garden place is lovely. It is penned in by split-wood rails to keep out the goats. The seeds have not yet sprouted. Rekeem has way too many rocks in its soil, and most of them were in our garden place. Did I tell you the three of us removed them to make a rock wall around our garden? It stands only knee high, the rails do the rest. Faris helped too. We talked. Another caravan is coming in a week or so. That is what the badawi told us. Kateb sends his best. His knee is healed.—Rasha"

WADI SIRHAN

Al Iswaiyah ("All Iz-Ah-wee-yaw") was a tidy village built around an oasis of palms and natural springs. The soil wasn't easily cultivated, but the water made up the difference. A large enough settlement had survived for ages in this desolate, distant place.

Zafir had no steward in Al Iswaiyah, but the residents knew well of the Abdali-ud-din, treating each visiting caravan as if royalty had come. It proved to me the irreplaceable value of an honorable and goodly reputation. This trust didn't require an army of swords to bear, it came from honest and fair dealings in business and to others.

The people of Al Iswaiyah were pleased with our arrival and hurried about to entice the hungry and tired. Sofian, a captain of 100, led the train to a suitable place for camp where the camels watered and we could prepare for a two-day stay.

With Zafir and the elders busy negotiating in town, I was taking inventory of my supplies for the coming trip. That's when Ziyad ("Zee-yawed"), a captain of 100, approached.

"Young Bassam!" he called.

I looked up to see a great, wide man, robed in the whites of a Sheik. "You and I have learning to do!"

He wore a great belt of braided camel hair that embraced a large and well-attended stomach. His headdress parted to reveal a broad and joyful face with jowls that lifted when he smiled. It made me smile because he looked very much the living image of a happy sphinx.

"Come!" he said, "Zafir told me to teach you the way of the caravan."

I scrambled to my feet and strapped the sword of Al Murrah to my side.

"That sword," Ziyad said, "it has become famous for you, no?"

"Not for me, but for Ammar."

"Maybe yes, but maybe for you, too. I'm glad to see you wearing it. My men should be such an example all the time."

He led me toward the center of the camp, past others who looked up curiously from their tea, while others slept or ignored us. Many of the men were gone for trade and supplies.

Stopping at a large cluster of kneeling camels, Ziyad gestured to them with his short stick. "The size of a camel train must be measured according to its route and its load."

"You mean large enough to safely carry gold?" I asked.

"No, but to safely carry a profit," Ziyad said. "Gold can be found in every land we visit. It's not the gold that makes us a successful band of beggars, it's our trade. See, look here," he said pointing to a stockpile of supplies watched over by two men. Lifting a large black tarp, he revealed two dozen skeps of straw that lay leaning against each other. Ziyad reached down and fished into the yellowed grass and pulled out a brown, rough-woven, two-handed pouch. Untying its drawstrings, he drew out a small handful of yellow translucent nodules of hardened resin.

"These are the finest tears of frankincense in all the world, Bassam. Known throughout the trade as the purist, most aromatic, and highly prized."

I took a chunk. It was lightweight with some sharp edges as if it had been broken from a larger piece. The light diffused warmly in shades of amber through its golden center—a solid piece worth a fortune to the right buyers. I hefted it in my hand, testing its aroma with my nose.

"Sprinkle that on your next cook-fire and even the she camels will be asking after your name," Ziyad laughed.

I returned the sample in amazement, realizing that each skep must carry a man's weight of the resin. And each camel carried at least two such skeps.

"Zafir bought this cache in Leuke Kome," Ziyad said. "And for a good price, too. It was shipping for Alexandria. Zafir is a good trader and he bargained it away from the Omani merchants for a fraction of what he could have paid the orchard owners."

"The *orchard* owners?"

"Yes, the trees of Levonah, the white oil, the hardened resin. You don't know this Bassam?"

No, I didn't. I hadn't thought about it. I just looked at him blankly.

"Oh, I have much to teach you," Ziyad said.

Returning the tears to the bag, he placed it back into the straw.

"We usually buy from the orchards directly, but not this time. It will save us a trip to the narrow sea. That's why we go north of the Nafud. Come, follow," he said.

As the tour continued, Ziyad revealed loads of beautifully crafted items of colorful glass, table items of brass, high quality papyrus from Egypt, hundreds of jars of various dyes, chunks of ebony, slabs of crystallized salt, heavy bags of cinnamon, and bolts of cotton cloth.

"Our profit is not in moving product all the way across Asia," Ziyad explained. "That journey is 6,000 Roman miles."

"Yes, I know," I said. "Ammar and I counted it on our maps—45,000 stadia."

"You should measure in Roman miles, young Bassam, if you want to trade to the west among the Roman buyers," Ziyad said.

"So I've heard."

"Our job is to carry goods from one trade center to another, and so forth, working our way to Chang'an and then back home. It's a long journey."

"Then tell me Ziyad, if it's such a long journey, why doesn't Zafir move a larger train?" I asked.

"Ah, yes! You don't ask about gold, copper, or brass. You ask about the *lead* caravan!"

"Lead?"

"It's an old desert joke. Gather a caravan of 50,000 camels and it is as lead. It's so heavy *it can't move*."

"Why not?"

"My young Bassam, how many skins of water do you draw from the cisterns for your she-camel?"

"Five or six, usually. Sometimes more," I said.

"How could you water 50,000 at such a well? Or 10,000? Or 10?" Ziyad asked. "They could all die and the well go dry before you could pull up that much water! A caravan of such magnitude has been done in ages of old, but always in companies of 500-1000 camels. They move ten days apart from each other so they don't overwhelm their hosts. Naturally, they each must pay the tax, but it is all one."

"So this is a small train?" I asked.

"Yes, compared to others. Maybe not small but average."

I looked at the hundreds of camels with a new respect—the hundreds of riders and walkers, surely this was enough to make profit at the end. Unless ....

"Ziyad," I asked, "tell me about the gold. Zafir arrived in Rekeem with bags of it hanging from the sides of several camels. I don't see any of that here."

He looked at me and smiled, making his headdress part. "The secret of the gold. You wish to know it?"

"Well, I didn't know it was a secret if that's what you mean. I just wondered, where is it? Surely we carry gold, don't we?"

He nodded and motioned me to follow. We found two Al Murrah leaning against their saddles, poking a cook-fire with sticks, talking between themselves.

"Nadim, Yazid!" Ziyad said. "I'm here with Bassam. I have instructions from Zafir to teach him the way of the caravan. This boy is taller than all of us, but he knows nothing about this business we're in. But his heart is good." And leaning over, he poked me in the ribs with his stick, "Your heart is still good, no?"

I jumped. "Yes!" The men laughed.

"Your student is standing better since we last saw him," Yazid said. "Fawzi has trained you well in your left arm. You're healthy again."

I rubbed my shoulder. Yes, it was strong but stiff—I had trouble extending it, and I carried a scar that could forever raise questions.

"Nadim," Ziyad said, "that's a nice coat you're wearing. Please slip it off and let Bassam try it on?"

Nadim stood and slipped it off, handing it over to me. I took it and the weight of it dropped it through my fingers to the ground. "This is heavy!" I said, stooping to pick it up.

"And there you have it, that's your gold," Ziyad said.

I picked it up, brushing off the dust and felt the hard nodules in the fabric. It must have carried more than 100 pieces sewn into its lining.

"And every Al Murrah carries the gold like this?" I asked.

Yazid smiled back, and sat down on his large saddle. "My saddle could buy you a dozen horses," he said. "And some dinner afterwards."

I eyed the curved, wooden saddle. I could see no obvious places where gold could be hidden. Watching me hunt, Yazid reached one hand under the saddle, the other along the edge. Silently, a small slat released and the golden edge of a coin rolled from a secret compartment underneath and into the waiting palm of Yazid. Its yellow wealth glimmered in the sun.

"There are many here," Yazid said. "More than you will ever need."

I bent down to see the device, but it was closed again before I could discover it. Yazid smiled like a magician who had successfully performed his trick.

"The gold is all over this camp," Ziyad said. "You might even be carrying some yourself, young Bassam! Did you think it? You, a treasure bearer for these many weeks?"

I wondered suddenly. Was it not *my own* saddle and camel?

"I don't understand," I said. "Zafir came to Rekeem carrying large leather sacks of gold, many talents hanging off the sides of his pack animals."

"Oh, *that was for show*," Ziyad said laughing. "The caravans don't keep their gold out for any bandit to seize. Zafir was making an entrance to impress your sheiks. He pulled out some of his gold to fill the sacks to make a good show, to parade his wealth for the merchants to see, to make them greedy before the bargaining began."

I remembered back, that long train that ended by sundown as the last camels with large sacks joined the first, a treasure of gold that bought their place, the victuals, more men and camels, and the esteem of the greedy sheiks.

"There is safety in this, Bassam," Ziyad said. "A wise caravan owner will spread his treasure among all. In that way, no one has enough gold worthy to steal, and no bandit knows where all the gold lies. Either he attacks and takes the whole train for all of the gold it carries, or he goes after another load, say a bundle of incense or spice. He too must be profitable, and a shaggy goat-hair coat with ten pieces could feed their families for a few weeks, but that's not enough. And the cost in blood—well, no single coat or saddle or groups of saddles are worth it, that's why we carry so many swords of Al Murrah."

We continued our stroll toward the back of the train and passed the tents of the elders.

"Don't assume those tent poles are solid wood," Ziyad said with a twinkle in his eye. I looked hard. *There could be gold everywhere.*

FRECKLES

The morning of departure was upon us sooner than I wanted. Ammar told me to enjoy the fresh water because we would have nothing but cistern water for the next several weeks.

"Here's the map," he said as we awaited the final call to mount up. "We have some 3,500 stadia to Babilu, how many Roman miles is that?"

I did the calculation in my head. "About 480?"

"That's correct. About two weeks on the trail and these mountain passes will slow us the most," he said, pointing. "We'll move a little faster now, the northern Nafud is not the place for man or beast."

"Are there hidden cisterns there?"

"For part of the trip, the other part we must carry our water. We carry now, the cisterns come later."

I saw a dozen new camels added to the train, but no riders or walkers—the new camels were pulled by rope, carrying loads of skins brimming with fresh water—four days' worth, someone said.

Ammar rolled up his maps and placed them in his pouch. And then as an afterthought, he called me to his side.

"I need to give you a trick," he said as he pulled a small pointed scrawl from his pouch. I knelt to the ground and watched. Ammar opened his pot of ink and dipped the tip of the scrawl.

"Give me your arm," he said.

I raised my eyebrows. "What?!"

"I said give me your arm."

"Now you're a skin artist? A spy from the Cult of the Bee?"

"No, just relax, I'm giving you a trick, you may need it."

Ammar opened his pouch of kamal strings and carefully sorted them. Finding the one he wanted, he uncoiled it.

"Hold this against your arm, palm down. Make it tight."

I bared my arm and put an end of the string between my fingers and pulled the other tight up to my shoulder.

"No, no, that's backwards. Put this end at your shoulder," Ammar said, taking the string and reversing it.

He carefully pressed it against my arm, and at each knot he firmly but gently poked the scrawl, injecting a tiny dot of ink into my flesh.

"Ouch!" I complained. "So now you're poisoning me? Ouch!"

He continued until 14 tiny black dots lined my arm. "There," he said. "That's the map. If you need it, these are the knots of the 14 large villages from here to Kashgar, and then some. You will learn their names tonight, I made a list for you. Memorize them, don't forget."

I peered down my arm at the little black freckles. "From this I make my own kamal string?"

"Right. Tie them exactly as the dots on your arm, or let your arm be that string, it's the same. Point at the horizon, slide two fingers for the kamal in the same manner. And don't worry, they won't wash off, they'll be gone in a few months—Maybe."

"*Maybe*?" I asked.

Ammar rolled up his sleeve to reveal a time-wearied arm sagging with age. "This dot here, here, and down here, my father made for me when I was your age."

"So now I'm a map? Wonderful!" I mumbled.

"Yes!" Ammar said. "You are a map, so no more sword fights with Fukara. You lose that arm and you lose your way."

"I'll lose more than my way," I said, pulling my sleeve back down.

DESERT BONES

On the fifth day out of Wadi Sirhan, I woke early. I didn't sleep well on my mat that night, staying up later than I should have, writing in my journals. When sleep came, it abruptly ended. The morning was overcast with a wind from the north when Humam shook me awake.

"How's my patient this morning?" the old medical magician asked.

"I'm fine, never felt better," I told him truthfully.

"That soreness in your shoulder—I told you a few weeks ago it should be gone. Is it?"

"Mostly. Fawzi has me scrimmage with him each evening, and I feel its strength returning."

"That's good," Humam said. "When we reach Chang'an, I'll introduce you to their art of the needles."

"Needles? *More* needles?"

"An ancient art, Bassam, dealing with the body humours for healing and pain—with needles."

"That sounds backwards to me," I said.

"Here, take this," he said, handing me a small leather pouch. "Keep this with you, always." Then opened another black pouch filled with a dark yellow fat. "The wind, you felt it?"

"Yes, it kept me awake all night."

"There's stormy weather coming," Humam said. "This is goat fat. I want you to take some and put it in that little pouch. Keep your lips moistened and place some into your nose, it will keep you from bleeding."

I dipped my fingers into the yellow sticky goo, scooped out two finger's worth, and scraped it into the little leather pouch.

Humam stood. "If the sand hits, you'll be ready," he said.

"A sand storm?"

"Probably. Ammar estimates the conditions are right. Not to worry though, the storms here are nothing like the Gobi." He gathered up his things to make his rounds, taking with him the bag of goat fat.

I tucked the little pouch in my robe, wiping the rest to my lips and nose. It gave no distinct smell and its moisturizing relief proved almost instantly just how dry the wind had made me. My lips felt normal again. I looked to my bakra wondering if she-camels need such care? *No, not so*, I decided. She sat on the ground nearby, content to close her eyes to narrow slits, probably wondering when I would come scratch behind her ears—with breakfast.

The steady northern blow did not abate the entire day. I was ultimately glad to have the goat fat, it soothed as promised. With veiled faces we tolerated the blowing sand, and light cotton draped over my hands stopped the stinging particles from chaffing. My bakra didn't seem to mind and just plodded along following the others.

The overcast sky was thick, hiding the time of day. We could tell when the late afternoon approached by the grey light falling toward the west.

Within an hour of reaching the camping spot I heard a murmur of concern passing among the riders. I sat straight, wondering what the problem was, and then saw it myself. The camels in front parted to the left and right as if avoiding something in the road. I leaned over for a view and then saw them.

And then, there they were, lying still on the ground as we passed by—the bodies of a man and a camel, long ago dead and long ago left to the elements. The threads of his clothing and saddle tugged by the wind, sifting the sand, hanging there like sagging drapery over desert-baked skeleton.

The man's body was clothed but the flesh was sanded clean to the bone—his bare skull with black holes staring, clenched teeth grinning mysteriously.

I winced at the sight and steered my bakra to avoid stepping anywhere near. But there was more. Another clump came upon us, a long-dead camel lying on her side, feet pushed out straight, and not far from that, another two men, face down, one curled with his arms to his chest. All of them, clothed skeletons.

More bodies and beasts, an entire train from what I could tell, lay stretched out in a swath. Maybe eight or ten dozen men and that many more camels. Between the subsiding crests of blowing sand, I could see off into the distance hundreds more pimpling the ground, a complete disaster now blown over by obscurity. As we passed, each was the same—a rider, his beast, two riders, four beasts, as if they had suddenly just curled up and dropped right in their footsteps, their loads stripped away, salvaged by strangers, the badawi, none could tell.

For the better part of an hour the tragic scene stretched in front of us. The puzzle made no sense to me. The scene of an attack should have left such death in a more terrible state than this. The tools of fighting, the trauma and damage to the victims, the scene should be much different. What curse of God could lay down so many at once? The answer came soon enough, and it wasn't what any of us wanted to hear.

A cluster of elders stood about the craggy mouth of the next cistern, the very well we had been traveling toward these five days. There stood Zafir, the captains and Al Murrah caught up in deep discussion. I thought it odd that no one was dismounting except those dozen who peered into the cistern. I ordered my bakra to kneel, and joined them to learn of the problem.

"It's the work of the Karduchi," Fawzi told me as I neared. "They work against the great caravans, killing to control the trade themselves north of here."

I made my way to the cistern's mouth. In the dim of evening light I could see some six cubits down the glint from the water's surface and the tell-tale rainbow reflection of something oily floating on it.

"That's it?" I asked, pointing.

Fawzi shrugged. "We always test the water before allowing the train to drink. The others are guessing that last group was careless."

I looked down the sides of the well and saw that the stones lining the shaft shined with wear. It was evidence of an unknown number of centuries of use with buckets and skins lowered by ropes and hauled up again, rendering it smooth.

"Can anything be done?" I asked.

"Not really," Fawzi said. "We can't drink here and we haven't the time or supplies to spend two days to empty the well and clean it of the poisons."

"How does the Karduchi find the wells of the Abdali-ud-din? Aren't they secret?" I asked.

"Yes, secret, but there are spies and there are traitors. Who knows, Bassam? Somewhere, someone betrayed his trust and his oath. We are so far into the desert—no one could stray and find this by accident. It's the work of evil."

Two others dropped ropes with weights. "They're looking to see if an animal was dropped in. That could make men ill, but it couldn't kill a whole train," Fawzi said. "The camels would smell it, they wouldn't drink."

"But how does it do such carnage so quickly? Those who waited should have seen the first fall ill."

"Good question," Fawzi replied. "Perhaps it was something other than the well ...."

The leadership returned to their camels and we resumed our trek eastward—there was nothing that could be done here.

It was another half hour before the last of the caravan passed the tainted cistern and the death that surrounded it. As for Ammar, he scrawled the mark of death on his map, a note to his memory that on this route, there is not a safe cistern at this precise place.

Zafir led the caravan another two hour's ride into the stormy dark before camping. He put distance between his camp and the poisoned cistern, wanting to remove us as much as possible from unseen dangers.

The blowing sand filled the night with blackness and caution. Most men found shelter behind their camels, using them as a windbreak, making a small camp on the leeward side of their large-humped beasts. In vain many of them tried to make cook-fires or burn their lamps. While others like me stacked our saddles and supplies near to us, hoping to do the same.

Finally, a damp chill settled on the camp. The hushing whine of blowing sand obligated us to our places, no one wandered. I managed to keep my lamp lit by sheltering it beneath my makeshift tent. I made it by tying my blanket to my saddle and pulling it over me. Two sticks held it over my head, with large stones holding its corners against the wind. It stopped the wind enough to write by flickering light.

It was then that Fawzi stopped by for a visit. He lifted a corner and cautiously peeked in.

"What are you doing, donkey brain?" Fawzi asked.

"I have to get caught up on events in my journal," I said. "I'll be only a moment."

"In that case, you must use this," and he pushed through the opening a goat hair covering. I was so glad and grateful. I pulled it over immediately and poked my head through the hole in the middle. Warmth against the cool damp immediately embraced me. I thanked Fawzi who winked and then lowered the covering and replaced a rock to hold it steady in the wind.

"Not late tonight, owl brain," he said, his voice fading in the wind. "I'll tell Zafir on you ...."

By flickering light I was able to write a few notes.

"Day 42—Dear Rasha, The work of death was spread out more than an hour's ride this afternoon, both animal and man. The elders think someone poisoned the water. This storm won't stop and drives the sand into our faces and dries our nose and skin. I used Humam's goat fat to prevent the dry bleeding. Without water many of us are becoming accustomed to camel milk. A calf was born three days ago, and its meat provided the meal. So long as Bakra fills her udder I will not go wanting. There is a

black bee that torments us. He can't bite Bakra, but he looks for moisture in our eyes and nose and ears. Our trip forward will not be impossible, just more difficult. — Bassam"

I returned my pens to their pouches and closed the ink pot, tucking them into their usual place. Suddenly, a voice called to me, a different voice, hardly audible above the whistling of the wind. "Bassam!"

"Who is it?"

A hand lifted the corner of my little tent and the lamp begin flickering wildly. "It's me, Habib." His bearded face appeared at my feet, his dark brown eyes shining and his white teeth gleaming in the yellow light.

"What is it?" I asked, wondering how he'd found me in the dark of a moonless night.

"It's your tent," Habib said. "Your lamp makes it a glowing red emerald on this black night, like a lantern in a cave. You're easy to find, Bassam. Are you finished?"

"Yes," I said. "Just putting my things away now."

"Zafir needs to speak with you."

"Zafir?"

"Just for a moment. He asked me to fetch you."

I hesitated. It was an unusual request, but Zafir wouldn't call for me unless it was something important. "All right, coming now," and I reached for Suoud's sword.

"Leave it," Habib said, "I'm carrying the sword, hurry."

I reached for it anyway but the wind caught the lamp and snuffed it to darkness, leaving me grasping for air. Then I realized how dark the storm had made the night. I could see nothing around me, not my hand, not Habib, no fire or glowing embers, not even the swirling blast of sand that stung my skin. It was pure blackness.

Then I felt Habib's hand grip my upper arm. "Come, I'll help you," he said, pulling me to my feet. The wind caught my blanket and wrapped it against my saddle, I would find it there later.

Habib took my wrist. "How will we see in this pitch?" I asked.

"I have a rope, a long rope," he said. "It leads to Zafir's tent. I'll lead you."

He pulled me quickly along, almost stumbling in haste. The blowing sand continued its work, and I drew my scarf to shield the sting. There was no sense of direction in this dark, and I could only take staggering steps to keep up with Habib. I thought it was the blind leading the blind, but the rope was a good idea—without it the trip could certainly be one-way until it was light again.

After a few moments of laboring through the wind the length was disorienting and seemed longer than I remembered. The direction, it was wrong also, too far.

"Habib, where are you taking me?" I shouted against the wind. "Zafir wasn't this far from me."

"Just a little more," Habib shouted back. "Just a little farther."

That familiar sense of suspicion started swelling inside. I started to doubt. Just then the ground began sloping upwards as if climbing the side of a dune. That wasn't right, I knew it! I pulled against Habib's grip, but he bore down more, tightening even harder.

"Where are we going," I shouted above the whining wind.

Suddenly on impulse I yanked free from Habib's grip, fumbling my way into the black, thinking to find my way back to camp. A second longer and a hand grabbed the back of my cloak and pulled me to the ground, a heavy body fell on top of me. I blindly lashed out shouting and kicking to push and free myself but the wailing wind drowned my call for help. Then the smothering crushing weight of a heavy panting man landed atop me shouting to someone, "He's a slippery fish, hold him still!" A mean hand gruffly shoved my head onto the cold sandy ground then a sharp, painful blow to the back of my head—all went quiet.

"Dear Bassam, your friend Faris came for evening meal today. We had fun talking about the things you and he used to do together. Is it true you once climbed the face of Al Khazna, to the secret urn? A caravan came this week with the honey bee. During their stay the bees found our garden. There are no blooms for them, but they looked. In other places it is fun to watch the bees move from blossom to blossom, bringing new life to our city. Faris is so funny, he makes us laugh. He took me to the shop where his father sells leathers—all kinds, for sandals, bags large and small, gloves, and coats. I tried on a beautiful jacket with white fur. He said I look pretty in white. What do you think?—Rasha"

BASSAM

36

PRISONER

When I came to, my head throbbed. I felt the heat of the sun on my neck and its warmth on my cheeks. The first thing I heard was arguing by men on camels in front of me. I opened my eyes and straightened up, finding myself seated on a camel that was moving at a brisk walk. I had no idea how long I was unconscious.

The terrain around me was shallow rolling hills of sand, tufts of grey grasses growing from the tops of the dunes, and the sky hazy blue. From the angle of the sun, I decided it was around mid-morning.

My head ached. How long was I out? It was confusing, those men, their arguing, at first I thought it was Al Murrah, but I recognized only Habib. Those others, seven in all, wore robes different from Zafir's chosen guard—dark turbans dyed in black, deep brown, shades of grey as if to hide—hide in the dark. And they were hurrying their camels along, pulling mine by a rope tied to the saddle of another. Just then I realized my hands were tied to the horn of my saddle.

"Ah, our friend, he awakes from his headache," a dark-bearded man said, eyeing me over his shoulder. "Did you sleep well, young Bassam?"

Habib turned, angry disdain written over his face. "Leave him be, Moluck," he said.

"What? What is it to you, my soon to be wealthy friend?" the bearded Moluck growled. "He's awake, that's all."

"And that's enough," Habib said. "Four days, he's yours, but for now, I watch him."

"You be careful, badawi," Moluck said. "I give orders, you obey, that's what we pay you for."

I turned to look behind. Our caravan was nowhere to be seen. The landscape stretched to distant horizons that gave little hope of being seen—this was not the desert our caravan was crossing last night. And those camels belonged to another, not Zafir's. My own mount was a skinny two-humped beast of little care or cleanliness—and the saddle to which my camel was roped was Moluck's.

"Where are you taking me?" I asked to no one in particular.

Moluck eyed me up and down. "You will fetch a good price, kin of Zafir. And the scrolls. A fair exchange, you for the scrolls."

"I'm not kin of Zafir," I said. "Whatever you're doing, he will find you and make you pay with your lives."

"Oh? Are you worth that much?" Moluck asked. "Then we'll ask a much higher price."

"Zafir will find me gone and send Al Murrah."

"Al Murrah is already here," Moluck laughed. Habib did not react. "And Zafir, the fool, he already knows you're gone, but we are too far away to find. The wind covers our tracks."

Another man, little with skinny hands, slowed his camel and pulled up to the side of me. "They call me Khan," he said, looking at me with a wide, friendly face covered in light sandy stubble. His eyes were bright but shallow—a friend-maker, but a man of weak will, a follower. "Khan is a nickname. But don't worry, you will be all right. We have a short trip to take and then you will be freed."

"A short trip where?" I asked.

"There is a place on the sea called Terdon."

"The sea? What sea?"

"The Pars, the ocean gulf. We are four days west of it right now."

"And what will you do with me there?" I asked.

"We'll find a boat at As-Samawah and sail to Terdon. It will be a pleasant journey on the Euphrates. Plenty of water unless you prefer your camel's milk?" The other men looked at each other and rolled their eyes.

"Zafir will find me," I said again.

"Remember, the caravan doesn't carry the memories of the dead," Moluck drawled.

"I wouldn't count on that," I said bravely.

The men huffed a smirk and resumed their quiet conversations.

Slavery was a common visitor to Rekeem—I had seen it many times. Some traders treated prisoners no better than the animals, while others marked them as bond servants—worth much. I compared my treatment to an animal—always tied, no freedom, dragged about with no concern for my needs or will.

We didn't stop for midday meal but carried on until Khan began to complain for a stop. We stopped at a small patch of grass under some date palms and rested beneath the shadows for Khan's sake. I was left tied to my camel.

We didn't stop again until after the sun was set and the orange haze was already fading. I was the last to be freed from my camel and stood off with my hands still tied. My back ached and I pressed back my shoulders to pop my spine and stretch my legs.

For that first night I was fed the same as the others—Habib had insisted on that. I drank from their water skins and the nourishment brought strength to my reasoning. I looked around to make an accounting of my options. I realized that in this darkness, with just one fire to illuminate the kidnappers, it was not a good time to attempt escape.

After the meals and tea had finished, the men laid down to sleep. Khan tied the rope to my wrists and the other end to his own wrist, and made himself comfortable on his mat under a blanket.

But not me. I stayed awake, watching.

At the end of the first watch, I quietly woke Khan and asked him to escort me beyond camp for toilet. Khan felt around for the knots, and seeing them secure, he agreed to escort, and led me through the darkness, yawning all the way.

It was clear that escape was nearly impossible. My camel was tied farthest from the others—it would be difficult to reach it unheard. If I could get my hands on a knife, or if my teeth were strong enough I could gnaw the ropes like a rat. But light sleepers could snare me within a step of going either way.

That next morning, Moluck woke the group early and they skipped breakfast to break camp and hurry along.

When the sun was high in the sky, the men became less jovial and started bickering about a proper ransom. The dangerous capture they had successfully carried out was worthy of much, one man said. Others agreed.

Another argued that simply selling me on the open slave market could fetch the quickest coin.

A quiet man suddenly spoke, dreaming to take his portion to buy a boat and enter the trade from the Indus Valley to the Romans and strike his fortune there.

Another declared he was finished with the bandit way of life, and was ready to marry the eldest daughter of a chieftain he knew, and start a farm.

As for Moluck, he was intent on Upper Egypt, the land of the pharaohs. It was through those deserts that Nubian gold and ivory was carried to the sea before being shipped north to Greece or east to the trade routes. He wanted to become a middleman with servants, wives, and treasure.

Unknown to the kidnappers, I had a stratagem that was already unfolding during their hurried pace over the desert sands. My brain whirled in tight circles, examining the varied weaknesses of my plan and its defects—looking for details overlooked that could ruin my ultimate escape.

I decided making an escape during the daylight was difficult, if not impossible. I was always tied to the horn of my saddle, it was roped to Moluck, and at resting stops I remained tethered to Khan.

By evening I was allowed off my bakra to stretch, but always with a rope. And as before, when we all laid down to sleep, my leash was tied to the wrist or foot of Khan. He made me sleep among the kidnappers, surrounded for safety.

Each evening by the fire, I pretended to listen with guarded interest to their bravado and threats and story telling. But when the fire died and the men drifted off to sleep, I perched myself facing northward, looking for the polestar. With my fingers I began calculating my place on the map, a map that stretched down my arm in tiny black dots. I calculated that we were only two days south of Zafir's route—only two days by swift camel.

Watching the first of the 15 stars to rise, I waited patiently for the start of second watch. When it was time I pulled on my rope and woke Khan just as I had done the first night.

"What is it, Bassam," Khan said disagreeably.

"I need to make toilet," I whispered. "Can you take me?"

Khan grumbled and stirred, and rose to escort me the 100 paces beyond camp. It was inky black during those nights, hardly a shape could be seen except for its place against the stars.

It made me so mad that the only thing keeping me from freedom was the rope and the stubborn little man who held it. I took my time, knowing delay and disruption was important. When Khan complained for the third time, I returned and we settled back to our sleeping mats.

At dawn we shared dried dates and nuts, some tea, and broke camp for another hard day at a fast pace.

It was late afternoon when Habib took the lead. From the discourses with his cohorts, it became obvious he was leading them somewhere that he alone knew and he alone understood.

The little caravan turned in detour toward some nearby hills and upon arriving, Habib circled them about for half an hour, finally dismounting near a stack of rocks.

"This must be it," Habib announced, and the other riders dismounted. I dug my heels into my beast to kneel, but couldn't move from the saddle.

Habib directed the others to help him remove the rocks and in short order, the small mouth of a water cistern was opened, a cistern owned by the Abdali-ud-din. The work of pulling the water skins began, and before long, men and animals were drinking.

I was disgusted, watching this traitor at work, wondering how many trips to this spot it took for Habib to map it out for a conspiracy such as this.

Khan returned to free me from the saddle and let me walk out the knots in my legs. "Drink well," he said, "the next two days are our last, and no water until then."

"Until when?" I asked.

"Until As-Samawah," Khan said. "And then our boat ride. Much better than this hot run through the rocks and parch, no?"

I ignored the question. "May I have water please?"

That night the men slept deeply, some snored even before the fire dwindled to embers. I stretched back on my mat to measure the stars. I calculated a half day longer north. By tomorrow, Zafir will be a full three days north and a part-day's ride west from the Euphrates at An Najaf. The caravan is slower, only 25 or 30 Roman miles a day. These kidnappers are farther from the river but travel faster, so they should arrive at As-Samawah the very same day Zafir does. If only I could get *on* that river.

Looking for the 15 stars, I estimated their change since the night before. I held up my fingers horizontal to the horizon and counted the number of Isab' to Sothos. From this I knew it was already the start of the second watch. I pulled on the rope of Khan to waken the strange fellow to again work my plan. He grumbled and obeyed as before.

That next morning I could see that we were nearing heavily traveled roads. The terrain was greener, more plants, an occasional grove of palms, desert shifting from sandy wastelands to a place where things could grow. There was the occasional litter of prior camps or lost belongings—it meant that fresh water was near.

Moluck told the others that by mid-morning of the next day they should enter As-Samawah. This announcement seemed to calm the group, and their demeanor toward me was one of relief, as if their plan was nearing its end—and their fears of discovery could safely relax.

"As I told you Bassam," Khan said. "We are approaching the river and there we'll take a boat and you'll be freed in Terdon."

"Don't sell me, let me stay, Khan," I pled, "I would rather be your ransom than traded to some distant caravan."

Khan nodded with a big toothy smile. "Maybe we will," he said. His eyes smiled a trust in me that had been slowly growing.

The bandits pushed their camels to a fast pace, well past sunset before stopping to camp. I sensed their growing excitement. They even treated me kinder as if the prize was already theirs.

For evening meal, they loosened my bonds and invited me to laugh around the cook-fire while tea was made. I made a point of asking them about their adventures, and trying to engage each of them in telling something that could challenge the others. With swelling pride, their comparisons grew with shocking tales of bravery and skill, until the night had slipped well beyond the middle of first watch.

Habib was cautious about all of the late-night bragging and called them to quit for the night. Things settled down, and each spread his mat to dream of the treasure awaiting them at the end of their long trek.

When the snoring began, I stretched out my fingers to the stars and counted. When the right stars appeared I knew it was the start of second watch, and reached over and pulled on Khan's rope.

"Uh? What is it?" Khan mumbled.

"I must go to toilet, will you come?" I whispered.

"Uh? No, you go, but don't be long."

My heart nearly leapt into my throat. *Four nights, four awakenings.*

He slipped the rope from his wrist. "I'll be just a moment," I hushed. Khan only grumbled and turned over.

I gathered up the rope's coils and stepped lightly away.

Beneath the stars, I tried to reconstruct the path I had already mapped before dark. Having spied a clump of leafy plants some 30 paces away, I quietly stepped beyond, feeling about for shadows and shapes, to pluck some stalks until I had a handful.

I circled around downwind of the camels, discerning by contrast that my camel stood with two others, with their reins secured to rocks. The others knelt, watching my quiet approach. My camel was tied farthest from the others as a precaution, but for tonight, that would aid in my escape.

I approached with my offering of foliage and put it right to her mouth before she could growl. She sniffed and then lipped the greens into her mouth while I loosened her reins and turned her carefully to lead her quietly toward the rising stars.

We walked gently, me humming the song of the watering trough. I paced her as she chewed, slowed when she began sniffing for more, hurrying again with the next mouthful. This kept her complaining voice otherwise occupied with eating.

When we ventured in this fashion more than 200 paces from camp then I pulled her into a slow run.

For two days I had been struggling with an escape route, wondering if I could survive through raw desert going north to catch Zafir. But, without supplies and a good idea about their location, I might put myself into another trap more dangerous than hurrying ahead to As-Samawah. Perhaps I could find safety in numbers, or at least become lost in a crowd, there. Balancing the risk and danger, I decided to head for civilization.

As I hurried into the darkness, I found it easier to run for a short while and then walk, alternating through rest and effort, for as long as I could keep it up.

I didn't dare mount up in the dark, at least, not without some bright moon to light the way. It was not a good time to risk stepping into a hole or rolling my bakra's hoof on a sharp stone.

The eastern horizon showed the signs of a waning moon about to rise, and soon, the path to As-Samawah would be lit. At half-gallop speed, I should be within the safety of As-Samawah by the time the camp of Habib and Moluck had awoken.

Habib was Al Murrah, he could track my every step. I carried no illusion of hiding my route, only to get ahead of them as best I could. My greatest concern was their determination to close the gap once they found me missing and determined my direction. Could they gallop that far that fast before I could reach help? I couldn't risk the least advantage to them and urged my camel along, pulling her forward. "Hut hut!"

37

THE PRAYER

The eastern horizon swallowed its stars in the soft brightening of dawn as we hurried over a rise. As-Samawah revealed herself for the first time. Even from a thousand paces I could see it was a poor herder's town, ancient with buildings to match, spread out as shadowy shapes hardly distinguishable against the silent and formless hills beyond.

Small plantations and grazing pastures greeted me first—vast stretches of life that surrounded the town like an expansive green moat. I found myself on one of dozens of worn animal paths that broke from the flats like so many spider webs, joining together at the main boulevard leading directly to town. From this vantage, I could see no river and supposed that it lay beyond the other side of the town.

I pulled back on the reins as I neared and slowed my bakra's run to avoid unwanted attention from the camping grounds. They were occupied like a patchwork quilt of several hundred slumbering men. Little movement stirred them, most beneath blankets, others in sagging tents that leaned against their poles like sleepy sentinels set to attention in the rush of night. Two bull camels lifted their heads with interest at our passing but made no noise.

Despite its image of poverty the city had every appearance of being a popular stopping place. The campgrounds were designated with short rock walls that stretched off toward the hills in straight lines, separating the visitors according to size or clan.

The adobe huts I passed crouched together under adjoining thatched roofs, their walls painted white or blue or faded brown. Some had woven canopies of stripes or solids, others not. Each of them looked empty—no doubt diners or places of merchandize that gave brisk business during the day-time hours.

There was no gate at the opening into the city. I guided my ride down the pavers of the main street, between taller, white-washed structures with lifeless windows that watched me pass. The buildings were thick, built together in long rows with alleys.

Just past a gap between two of the building, behind a narrow inn with brown shutters, I spotted a corral of split-beam rails to the back. *Perfect*, I thought. *I will leave my bakra there while I look for help. If I must leave her, she'll be payment for the inconvenience.*

I steered her into the pen, knelt her at the far side, then pulled another rail to close her in. "I'll be back," I whispered, and hurried to the deserted main street.

My first view of the river was thrilling. A smooth velvet sheet of grey stretching far to the opposite bank—its mirrored surface reflected the rolling hills beyond, and tufts of grasses lined the shores on both sides. The masts of small sail boats secured to the wooden posts of dilapidated docks stood unmoving along the still waters. A few early risers were out, laboring to load and unload amidst the pre-dawn mist that lay all across the river.

Even at this early hour it appeared that some of the boats now docked had arrived just that morning. Men worked about the boats talking softly, collapsing the sails, preparing. Other crews were just awakening, dressed warm, relaying supplies up ramps to other hands that waited on board. I hurried to the side of one lateen-sailed dhow and asked a man directing his helpers.

"Please sir, are you preparing to depart?"

"No passengers, boy," the man replied.

"Is there another here sailing up-river today?"

"NO passengers, boy!" and then he turned to scold a man for not hurrying the ramp enough.

I saw a smaller dhow, brown with age, single-masted, square-sailed, and large enough to carry six men and their supplies. A father and son worked to off-load several wooden crates.

"Sir, please!" I called, hurrying to the old man. "Are you leaving upriver today?"

The old man wore white robes and was barefoot. His white beard was lost in the veils of his headdress that hung below his shoulders. He stopped and looked at me with tired gray eyes. Handing off his box to his youthful helper, he frowned. "Why do you ask?" he said.

"I need to make An-Najaf—as soon as I can."

The old man rubbed his whiskers and looked to the east for the rising sun.

"I don't take passengers," he said.

"I'll pay you sir, I'll pay you to make that journey for me." There was desperation in my voice. And suddenly I panicked inside. *Pay? With what will I pay?*

The old man thought a minute and pulled his son aside. They engaged in conversation for a few moments, the boy pointing back to town, the old man pointing upriver. And finally, he turned to me with a smile.

"What is your name?"

"I am Bassam, a stranger to this city."

"All right, Bassam the stranger, this is my price. You pay two silvers and we'll take you to An-Najaf. But we carry trade there this day—you must wait for us to load it."

I breathed a sigh of relief. "I can wait, thank you sir."

"Then, God's blessings on you. I am Amin, and my son, Esam." We exchanged greetings.

"When should I return?"

"Mid-morning, and don't be late. The trip to An-Najaf will take at least all day, *if* the winds favor us for the upriver."

I nodded and turned toward town. My hope brightened that I had some time to find work and gain two silvers. How this could be done I had no idea. But trusting that my care was in the hands of another, I turned up the first street of shops in search of a job.

Village economies along the trade routes were both simple and complex. Simple because a man's oath was as good as his gold. Complex because gold could buy an oath.

I hurried to the stoops of the various shops that prepared to open. It wasn't an hour before the sun finally splashed over the eastern hills, and so did the rejections.

"Excuse me Sir, I'm in need of passage on a boat this morning, may I perform any labors for you?"

"Not here, beggar."

"Greetings to you sir, I'm an honest worker seeking passage on a boat, may I wash this floor and sweep the kitchen?"

"Be gone and don't waste my time."

"Hello sirs, I'm offering my excellent labors for a morning's chores, are there any ... "

"Away from here!"

I exhausted my good cheer in no time, discovering for myself that no matter who I approached, no one could spare a coin for labors. Indeed, the merchants of As-Samawah traded as tightly with their purses as they did their patience.

After another hour and the sun was well into the sky. I knew the time for departure had almost arrived. But I had failed at every turn—*it had to be a conspiracy.*

Worry began to weigh heavy. Coming off the desert sometime soon, those kidnappers would be boiling with anger and probably slay me rather than trade me. I wondered if I should retrieve my bakra and try venturing upriver myself? Was there a safe passage along the banks of the mighty Euphrates? And what of robbers? Could the old man and his boat carry me to safety for the sake of safety, or once out on the water might they rob me as well?

As hard as I fought otherwise, doubt and discouragement found me, my hopes began to cloud. I had to escape this village or I would certainly be overtaken and captured again. Could the men of this place guard me from that kind of danger? No, there was no one who would pay attention to a young boy in their midst, a suspicious thief who might even be accused by his masters to be an escaped slave. That's exactly how those kidnappers could regain my capture, by declaring me their escaped property—deserving of severe punishment, which Moluck would gladly administer himself, for all to see.

Disappearing into an alley that smelled of damp waste, I traced its foul-smelling interior until I found a shadowed corner and slumped against the cool stone of a wall, hiding from discovery and suspicious eyes. My mouth was dry and my heart was pounding—dark tentacles of doom began wrapping around my lungs. I couldn't breath, they reached dangerously close into the sanctity of my faint hope and courage. Tears were stinging at my eyes, and my skin started tingling cold. Hopelessness was falling on me fast.

I wanted to be alone, and quietly slipped behind an old wooden barrel and hid in a littered corner of abandonment, then crumpled to my knees in the blackness of despair and buried my head in my hands, begging—*I have tried, oh God, I have tried—I cannot steal it for my covenant. Please help me in this time, I know not where to turn if I am to be saved at all. I have so tried my best and these, my weak efforts, have failed me. Oh please, help me please, oh God help me?*

It was all I had left—I was at the end of my rope, and so I let go of any remaining hope of rescue or help. I surrendered to a certain demise. A beggar I was, reaching out from my most inner reality for what seemed to be the last honesty I had from my short years of life. In the weakness of my trembling plea, my mind became washed of any plan or notion or preconceived solution, and went quietly silent behind the blackness of my tightly shut eyes. For the first time in my life, I was truly fearful and truly alone. Sorrow and surrender washed over me like crashing waves of a storm slamming against cold rocks. I surrendered to my fate, and wept.

And then? *Just* then—something quite alien made a whispering visit—a gentle, fleeting, unfolding of something near—passing over me, or perhaps around me, I didn't know, though inwards it drew itself through me like gliding silk cutting the grey maze of my discouragement. The unidentified something became a sliver of a thought, a slight thought, softly dim and sparkling that sifted mildly to draw together the loose ends of my confusion, knitting them quietly and kindly into tiny embers that seemed to shine upon shapeless forms within the folds of my awareness. They scattered and joined again, fanning faintly into a thought that rose above the waves of my fear, whispering about as a feather in the wind until settling, finally, to carefully congeal into a vague idea. And the idea slowly swelled and solidified and matured until it formed into a memory. And the memory stood up within the center light in my mind as a true possibility. Then suddenly I opened my eyes in shocked surprise. *No, could it be*?

I wiped the tears and looked down at the goat-hair coat that Fawzi had given me for warmth back on that windy sandstorm night. It had protected me from the cold and provided security during the long days of riding with the bandits. They had not taken it, thanks to the threatening commands from Habib. It served as my only covering at each night's camp.

I anxiously pulled it off for the first time in five days and began fingering along the stitching, around the collar, up the sleeves. My anxious kneading found nothing of note—stitches, rolled lining, nothing more. The long seam enclosing the back was more of the same, overlapped after the fashion—loose, sagging, nothing more. Then I felt along the bottom edge where the weave was tucked under as was customary in such garments. Reaching the union of the back seam and the under fold, I suddenly stopped. At the intersection of the two seams a hard nodule of multiple layers did not yield to my probing. It stood firm and by my heavy press it revealed the outlined form of a circle.

My heart raced. *Gold in the clothing, gold in the saddle, gold in the tents*, I remembered him saying. And gold in the goat hair wrap?

Pulling at the stitching with my fingers and then my teeth, I frayed the threads and pushed the flat, round object until its edge poked through to reveal the yellowish gleam of a gold piece. I pushed it from the garment and closed my fist around it. Tears welled up and I bent over clutching the wrap to my face. "Thank you God, thank you God, thank you, thank you, *thank you*."

In an instant, there played out in my mind a rehearsal of the events that prepared and came together beforehand to bring me the coin—just a week earlier, pure charity from my friend who worried that I might be cold. And now, *this*.

I rose to my feet, sniffing and wiping my eyes. With the gold piece firmly in hand, I pulled the covering over my head and wore it with a reverent respect, as a garment of God-given salvation. I knew now that I had to fight for my survival, that I wasn't alone.

Walking briskly with a new-found purpose, I broke into the sunlight and began to cautiously explore one alley of shops and then over to another until I found it at last. I called out to the seller of knives, "Excuse me sir!"

"I said go away boy, no beggars!" the keeper scolded.

"No sir, I'm not here seeking employment as before, I wish to buy a knife."

The shaved man stopped and looked at me slyly, his round bulging cheeks pursed in distrust, with dark eyes that betrayed his greedy consideration. "And buy with what?"

I held out my hand. The gold piece glistened in the simple light of the shadowed alley. "This is for my ride on a boat. I'll give you part of it in exchange for a knife."

The old man's eyes widened then he tried to hide the thrill. He glanced hurriedly up and down the alley as if to capture the secret to himself. "I'll give you a good deal and the best knife that I sell. The finest bronze, fresh from the boat this week. It will sell fast, I guarantee you that, you must buy it today if you want it. For you, I make a good price for two of your coins."

I rolled my eyes with impatient disbelief. Oh no, not this again, not now.

I reflected back to Suoud and knew that bargaining was the only way this deal could be done. I shook my head and asked to examine his collection. I pointed out the knife I wanted—a long war knife with a poker-straight, sturdy bronze blade, lightly sheathed for quick use. Its beautiful ivory handle was slightly curved and smoothed for a comfortable grip.

"Two silvers for the ivory knife," I offered, and extended the gold piece.

The shopkeeper shook his head and pushed the coin away. "No good, it's not enough for this fine blade, I give you a special deal that can be yours for the one gold piece."

I shook my head and closed my fingers shut. "I will not, it's too much. Two silvers or nothing."

"The best I can do is 15 silvers, for that is what I paid for it."

"If that's what you paid for it, then where is your profit?"

I pointed out the knife I wanted—a long war knife with a poker-straight, sturdy bronze blade, lightly sheathed for quick use. Its beautiful ivory handle was slightly curved and smoothed for a comfortable grip.

The merchant was caught in his lie.

"Okay, 12 silvers, but you must allow me some profit. It will serve you well."

I laughed and slowly returned my hand into my robe, though there was no purse there. "No, it's too much. Two silvers or none—No, never mind, I will go to the other merchant of knives, he has what I want." I turned to leave.

The merchant put up his hands, "No! No! Come back, I make you a deal."

I smiled and then frowned before turning around. "What deal? You're trying to cheat me out of a fair trade."

"No, no, not cheating. I didn't understand. You meant this knife, no?" and the merchant pointed to another knife next to the one I had offered on.

"Not so, my good sir," I said. "The knife next to it," pointing to my original choice.

"AH, Yes," the man said, picking up my chosen knife and blowing off the dust. "Very good choice, yes, this is yours for three and one-half silvers, an excellent choice."

I rolled my eyes again, and turned away, saying, "Never mind, good day to you sir."

"Wait! Wait!" the merchant called me back. "I see that you are a man in a hurry. I'll make you a special deal. Two and one-half silvers, that is my cost, and for you that is the best I will do. But I'll lose much on the sale of this knife, you do not bargain with mercy as this."

I couldn't waste any more time and agreed. But first I wanted to see his change. The merchant called to the back, barking an order and a small lad appeared from the shadows, looking up at me with wonder in his young eyes. The merchant took from the boy the handful of a leather pouch and dug around inside, pulling out 17 large silvers and four eights of silver. I handed over the gold piece and the merchant bit it between his teeth. Finding it soft as true gold, he examined it in the light.

"Ah! This is an uncommon gold piece," he said. "This is the gold brought here by the Abdali-ud-din."

"You know the Abdali-ud-din?"

"Most certainly, they stop here often enough."

"When did you last see them?"

"Oh, not for a long time, now," the merchant said. "Maybe a year ago, maybe two. They used to stop here to cross the river, but not for a long time."

I took the silver coins into my hand, but with nothing to carry them, I asked for a purse.

"Yours for the four-eights of silver," the man said smiling, holding out a small purse of bright leather with a neck string coiled inside. I took the purse for the small silvers, and stored the rest of the coins into it. *Suoud wouldn't be proud that I paid full price, but I have no more time.* I resigned to closing the deal. *Besides, I have too many coins, the purse is heavy enough.*

Leaving the shop I hurried toward the eastern side of the village, to the river side. With the purse slung over my neck and beneath my robe, I fastened the knife to my side. Walking a fast pace, I pulled out my new purchase to examine its blade. The long sharpened edges reflected yellow, not as gold, nor silver. I tested the blade with my thumb. *The point is sharp but the edges need work. I better sharpen this soon. A proper edge, an edge like Suoud's.*

The center village by this time was filled with morning shoppers and merchants calling out their wares, and the traffic of people and animal carts was growing busy. The sun was near mid-morning and departure for the old man must be soon.

I needed a shortcut to the river and spied a narrow dark passage along the backsides of a long row of shops. It was covered over with stones the whole length of the alley, joining the two rows of buildings, making it a dark and narrow tunnel. Through that passage I could see its end where a stone arch framed the view beyond, a picturesque scene of the radiant sunshine glistening on the broad brown river. It was a timely shortcut that could let me bypass these crowded streets and race for the boat through that empty alley. I worried I was already too late.

Holding my skirts, I felt for the knife and took my first running steps. Into the shadowy cool of the dark, just a few dozen paces, when suddenly a massive hand hammered down on my shoulder, spinning me around in a whirl of surprise. "BASSAM!" roared a foaming Moluck staring down at me with eyes afire and his teeth seething in sticky rage. "You cursed vomitus wretch," he thundered with veins bulging and sweat flinging. "You die by my blade this day you leprous loathsome pest!" and pushed me deeper into the tunnel, pinning my head against the wall with his forearm. My heart raced and my eyes bulged. I could feel the hot rage pumping through the man's arm, crushing my throat against the wall, choking my breath, and suffocating me with the smell of evil rot spewing with his every word.

Moluck roared more cursings and then stepped back, releasing his prey, and drew from his sheath a long sword. Raising it with a white-knuckled grip of crazed determination, Moluck spit more cursing oaths. "You die *now*, kin of Zafir, you *die*."

He reached above his head with his other arm for a sure and fatal strike, his angry eyes widening, taking the stance of an executioner, but also unaware he made a target of opportunity that I instantly spied in the middle of the terror.

Reaching across my chest with my right hand I pulled the knife from her hiding place in a lightning motion of fluid instinct. Flashing its blade for a blink, I raised my elbow before Moluck could react, swiftly took aim, and thrust the blade with all my might directly into his breast bone. The long blade sank smoothly, all the way to the face of its ivory hilt.

The screeching Moluck suddenly gagged on his oaths and the scene slowed to a stop, each painful moment frozen in time.

The anger on Moluck's grimaced face faded and paled—his jaw dropped open in slack, shocked surprise, and his eyes bulged with fiendish hate. His shoulders caved forward as he took a staggering step toward me, fighting to keep his lost balance. Then his upright arms slumped to his sides, and he fell backwards against the opposite wall, letting go his sword that clanged onto the stone pavers. Moluck's angry eyes locked onto mine, yellowed with denied vengeance.

I pulled my knife out in a downward slicing motion, and the monster's eyes rolled up as he slipped down to his knees. Reaching feebly to clutch at the wound, he finally slumped forward, falling into a sprawled heap at my feet with a heavy thud. The killer breathed out his venom in a final exhale of putrid failure—and a single heartbeat later, all was still.

I stood back, my heart pounding in my ears, the knife streaked with human blood, the limp form of a full-grown man draining out at my feet.

The horror of the scene took away my breath and all I could feel was my stomach knotting up to vomit. My mind raced—should I run or stay or tell? I looked down at the knife again—it was a *human life* I had taken, should I call for help? Was the beast dead or pretending? Will he rise up? Suddenly? To finish his vow? Was his band close by to attack me? Did anyone see?

I stared wide-eyed at the carnage. In a flash to escape, flight overtook my senses. I crouched quickly to wipe the blade clean on Moluck's robe, and staggering for balance, I sheathed the knife and broke into a panicked escape, half running, half stumbling toward the alley's end that opened toward the river.

Looking back once more into the dark to see if I was followed, I almost stumbled when I leapt from the pavers into the full morning sunlight, landing on loose sand with a crunching thud, almost tumbling toward the river bank.

Scanning the shore for the old man and his boat, I spotted it a short distance away—he was just pulling in the ramp. I ran hard toward the small white sail, waving my arms desperately, and calling out.

TELL-TALE WINDS

It was a favorable day for sailing—the sky clear blue, a steady strong breeze, a place of serenity along the smooth waters. The sails billowed as the little dhow skimmed along the Euphrates in a steady smooth advance. My pounding heart had not given me rest for the better part of an hour when finally I could calm myself. Thinking I might be safe out on these waters, I positioned myself on the shaded side of the sail, watching as the little dhow's smooth speed could overtake the camel riders who, trudging by land, ignored the river traffic passing them by. I had barely caught my breath when the old man who was studying me finally made conversation.

"So, you make for An-Najaf?" the old man asked.

"Yes, I hope before night fall."

"And you have family there?"

"I hope so," I said honestly. "I'm meeting a caravan that should be passing through there just about now."

"On its way to Babilu?"

"Oh yes, how did you know?"

"The great caravans from the west cross the river near An-Najaf. They used to come here to our As-Samawah, but that stopped a year ago."

"Oh? Why is that?"

"The sheiks of our village," the old man said. "The trains keep to the safe roads, and when I was a boy, As-Samawah was safe at the river crossings. We protected the strangers and the trains. Why, one year, my father and I ferried more than 1,000 camels and their riders across the river. Just us, alone, with our rafts. It took us three days and two nights. You don't see such traffic any more."

"Is it because they became greedy and took the tax, but offered no protection?"

"Why yes, how could you know such a thing as that?"

Yes, how could a young man my age know such things? My pride in association with the Abdali-ud-din and Zafir with his elders, and their reputation of respect and integrity that preceded them into all villages, it all began to make a connection. Truly the honored ones will draw unto themselves the accumulation of wealth because where honor goes, enduring trust and lasting trade will follow.

"I have a good teacher," I told him. "He tells me about the ancient trading throughout this whole region. The greedy sheiks or the greedy elders, it's an old story, an old problem."

"Then you know somewhat of the caravan and its dangers?" asked the old man.

"Only a little. I haven't been out more than two months."

"And already you have had serious trouble?" the old man asked.

"Trouble?"

"Yes. The blood on your sleeve. You have had some trouble already?"

My heart froze. I looked down at the sleeve of my cloak and the front of my goat hair cover. The droop of the sleeve was drying to a rusty red as if it had been dipped in blood. It *had* been dipped in blood. And the goat hair covering carried spots on its front. I had to formulate an excuse lest the old man think I robbed for the boat fare. The body of Moluck would be found, people would ask—it would point to the crime of thievery and murder. The shopkeeper could produce the gold piece from a young man who just minutes earlier had come begging for work, and then a wealth too sudden for a boy's morning labors. The suspicions could point to me, and surely a witness would have seen me running to the boat of Amin. Such a shame wouldn't rest well on the village, and I could be hunted.

It was a puzzle I needed to solve lest such men came looking. At least for now, I should clean it, and reached over to the edge of the boat and dipped my sleeve in the cool water.

"There were robbers," I began honestly.

The old man put up his hand. "Do not tell it to me, I'm just concerned that you're all right."

"Yes, God has blessed me on this trip. You are a blessing for me Amin, and you don't know it. But you're a blessing from God to me this day."

The old man just smiled and trimmed the sail to catch a change in the wind, and looked upstream.

"Young Bassam," he said, "don't think that God only blesses the anxious. He blesses the hungry, too. Your two silvers for this trip will feed a widow I know, and her five children when we arrive at An-Najaf tonight. Do you not think she will find in *you* a blessing?"

I sat thinking, suddenly curious about an old man moving crated goods unguarded, with his son, these many stadia where mishap and pirates could out-sail them and steal their wares, leaving them murdered in the waters. Who was this sailor of the great desert river who took such courage alone in his small boat and could surrender his fare for those of less fortune than he?

I felt for the purse. It was money I didn't need as much as could a family I didn't know who was missing a father I never met.

I removed the purse from my neck, hefting it again, and handed it to the old man.

"If two silvers will feed a family of five, then let this feed twenty more," I said.

The old man was visibly touched. He accepted the purse and tucked it away. "The name of Bassam will be honored at many cook-fires in the coming days," he said. I just smiled. It didn't matter giving the money. It felt good to help. People needed help once in a while. In fact, giving that money gave me just about the best feeling ever.

We were both quiet while the old man's son went to curl up in the front to nod off. It wasn't much later that the accumulation of my sleepless night, the exhausting trek, and the difficulties of the day finally linked arms with the warmth of the sun, the slapping of the water against the hull, and the gentle rocking motion of the boat. I was soon lulled into a deep and needful sleep.

بـ هبصه 39 محبوب

REDEMPTION

It was just past sunset when the small dhow bumped against the dock of An-Najaf. I suddenly awoke at the jolt and sat up, the deep sleep still clinging to my muscles and my head.

"Are we here?" I asked.

"We are here," the old man answered.

A torch was already lit and attached to the front of the boat, and his son was on the dock pulling us in tight to tie off.

"We made good time, the winds blew in our favor," Amin said. He explained that An-Najaf was not exactly on the river but was a short donkey ride from there. He needed to take animals to reach the village.

"Bassam, may I trust you to watch here and safe guard my boat?" the old man asked. "I'll fetch help to unload and then get you to your caravan. I'll be but a short while. We'll take another torch, you won't be in the dark," he smiled.

Amin left with his son by foot and disappeared up the bank, the warm yellow light of their torch casting long shadows that danced across the river bank and then disappeared over the knoll.

I sat with the boat and looked out across the river as the thin orange band of fading light to the west was slowly swallowed into the horizon. A few other boats with torches labored toward shore as the diminishing light forced their rest. I observed that the opposite bank was much closer back in As-Samawah. Those sheiks, what fools for losing that business. It seemed that greed was the great common destroyer on this trip. Crossing here was much more difficult than downstream, and pushing the trade away created more danger between these wider banks. Here at An-Najaf the rafts had to be more involved over a longer span with dangers of loss and drowning much greater for the distance added.

The last cooling embers of the sunset faded into the west, and the night stars twinkled to life. I stretched my head back and found the polestar. *I wish I had Ammar's kamal right now,* I thought. *I'd like to prove his knots.* And then I remembered—the tattooed map down my arm.

"I wonder ...." and rolled my sleeve to begin an experiment. I stretched out my arm, just as I did the string, resting my cheek on my shoulder, closing one eye and lining up the horizon with my arm. Taking two fingers close together in estimation of the width of the kamal, I moved them up and down my arm until from that perspective the polestar touched the top edge of my top finger.

"All right, Ammar," I said aloud, "make me proud." I held my fingers to my arm, exactly where I had spotted them with the polestar, and moved to the light from the torch. Looking down, I carefully rolled my fingers over to reveal one of the black spots directly beneath.

"Ah-ha for you, Ammar! At least I find this river place on one of your marks." And then I counted down the number of marks, reciting the villages that Ammar ordered me to memorize many weeks earlier.

"First, it was Leuke Kome to here," I said, pointing to the first black dot, "and then Al Jawf that we passed to the north of, for the second. And the third ..." My jaw suddenly dropped and I took a breath. "No, it can't be can it?" I started again from the top: "The villages are Leuke Kome, Al Jawf, and ... and ... Noooooo. It's not An-Najaf! Can it be so?" I smiled out loud. "It *is* An-Najaf, exactly! Ammar *you genius*! It works!"

An hour passed and I found myself pacing up and down the wooden dock, my hand on the knife, wondering whether Habib and Khan might be hiding in the shadows, waiting for their chance, summoning robbers or elders for my capture. Looking out across the blackscape of the river I saw that many of the tiny lights carried on other boats had been snuffed out. I felt very alone and not very safe.

Should Habib and Khan find me, I wouldn't fare very well against the sword of Al Murrah. Those kidnappers were probably looking for vengeance, and no doubt discovered my escape. Need they but ask to learn about the boy who traveled upriver? A boy running as if from an unseen pursuer? Surely they had to be near, in the shadows, in the dark. Perhaps old Amin was in confederation with them and was just now fetching them. In my mind I mapped a strategy in the event they suddenly attacked. I mapped a leap into the river and where to swim from them into the darkness, or push them into the river and then run into the dark, or thrust the torch at them, keeping them cornered until ....

At that moment I saw the yellow glow of torches just over the knoll of the hill beyond the river bank. *At last*, I breathed.

"Bassam!" Amin called out, leading a group that followed behind him. "I have help!"

I squinted into the closing distance at a host of some two dozen men in robes, two donkey carts in tow, and others with torches, their walk was brisk and deliberate, hurrying toward me. *What is this? Such a crowd to off load a little dhow?*

Maybe it was a trick. I backed up a step with caution at the onrush.

And then another voice called out. "Bassam, my boy!"

REUNION

What? Could it be? *It was*!

"Zafir!" I called out and broke into a full run. "Zafir, it's me, Bassam!" And I ran as fast as I could into the old man's open embrace, almost knocking him down. The other men circled in close, laughing, smiling, calling out a welcome, patting me on the shoulders, tugging at my cloak—it was all my friends, Fawzi, Ammar, Humam, everyone.

"Bassam, Bassam! You're safe! We worried you were hurt or worse," Zafir said.

I stood back clutching my old friend's arms, my face broken open wide in a thrilled smile ear to ear.

"No, no, I was taken away, it was Habib and bandits—they took me. They wanted to sell me. I have so much to tell."

And then Fawzi stepped forward, "Welcome back old camel breath!" I turned and threw my arms around Fawzi, ignoring the hand put forward in welcoming friendship.

I stood back holding Fawzi by the shoulders. "You don't know, oh, you don't know," I said, fighting back tears. "I have so many things to tell you, Fawzi. I have so much to tell you."

Each of my friends came to me, taking me by the forearms in welcome, slapping my shoulders, grinning with relief at my safe return. And then suddenly the commotion fell quiet and the men parted a step to let Zafir gain access again.

Fawzi looked puzzled and looked over at Zafir who just smiled and shrugged. "We will all hear about it soon enough," Zafir said, "but for now, we must get you back to your Bakra, she's been complaining these five days for her master—and a good ear scratch." The men smiled and voiced their agreement, but still, no one moved.

I looked around at the friendly faces. *Home, a home away from home,* I smiled to myself.

"But first," Zafir said, "I want you to meet my steward and agent along this western bend of the Euphrates."

The men parted once more to make room, and in the yellow warmth of a dozen torches, now it was my turn to be amazed. I looked in the direction of Zafir's outstretched hand and there stood .... *no, could it be?* There stood old man Amin!

"What?" I said aloud, now confused. The old men broke into a laugh.

"I knew you the moment you came to my boat," Amin said.

"But why? I mean, why ...?"

"Bassam," Zafir said, "when you went missing we knew they had taken you for ransom, else we should have found your body instead. Al Murrah detected exactly the route your kidnappers took, and as the hawk flies, it was directly to As-Samawah."

"It was blowing sand, how could they ...?"

"It wasn't that difficult," Fawzi spoke up. "From the tracks we learned they had seven camels with riders and two pulled by rope that had been shadowing us since Al Jawf. One camel for you, one for Habib. They followed the slope of the hill in the dark, and made too much headway before light for us to pursue. The prints showed they traveled light—and fast. It was carefully planned a long time ago."

"I hurried three riders to An-Najaf," Zafir said. "They notified Amin and he sailed immediately to As-Samawah with his son, and these three," he said, pointing to three grinning coconspirators. "They were in the boat just behind you, didn't you see them following behind?"

I just shook my head in disbelief.

"You're fortunate, Bassam, you almost missed them."

"I saw no Al Murrah," I said.

Amin smiled. "I had them in the village already, looking hard for you when you found me. Had the winds not been favoring me, I might have missed you this morning."

I couldn't believe what I was hearing. I was in shock, my jaw almost hanging open.

"I would have given you transport even without silver, young Bassam, but Zafir asked of me a favor."

I turned my blank, unbelieving stare from Amin to Zafir.

"My boy," Zafir said, "I had expected you to make an escape if possible. If Amin had found you a prisoner, his men could have freed you right there. But there are other forces at work in that city, Amin had to be cautious. None of us knew what confederations the traitors might have formed in An-Najaf."

"His men?"

"Oh, yes. Amin has many friends and business associates in that city. He tried to spread the word to be on the lookout for you. Fortunately, you found him first."

"So, why didn't you just take me then and there, Amin? And tell me who you were?"

The old man grinned and shook his head, looking for an understanding spirit from young Bassam. "I wasn't sure you were you, and not a trap for me," he said. "An-Najaf is not the city I knew as a boy. Today there are many wicked secrets. For a price I keep my place at the river harbor, and though I have many friends, the darkness there grows. If they knew I was arranging you passage, it could have been a deadly trap for me *and* for you."

"A trap? Me?"

"As Zafir said, there are other forces at work in this city. I had to make time to test that you were not some impostor working a plan against me and my son. There is too much deceit. Had I known you personally, I wouldn't have taken such steps. I gathered, by the way you were behaving, that time was important—but you seemed safe enough. I needed time to gather my men to check on you and any others that might be cohorts, or just following you. There is no more trust among the wicked of our little river home."

I shook my head in confused disbelief. "And Al Murrah?"

"They waited behind looking to see that we were safely on the water. They followed in another dhow, perhaps you saw them coming to shore in the dark."

"But, but, why didn't you just tell me, I mean, do you know what happened back there?"

And then my smile at the clever ruses dissolved. The thought of killing suddenly boiled back into my conscience and my conscience clouded. The feel of the knife pressing into human flesh and bone was revolting. I had killed a man, me, myself, it was an ugly burden, a heavy burden. Could I tell them? Should I tell? I so desperately wanted other arms to lift it from me, I didn't like being the carrier of such crimes.

"Zafir," I began, suddenly sullen and looking at the ground, "there is something about this morning ...."

"My boy," Zafir interrupted, putting a hand on my shoulder. "There is yet something else you must be told for your continued safety." He walked me a few paces from the men who then surrounded Amin for more of the story.

"Bassam, these many weeks, I knew I had a traitor. But such men hide well in the community of the caravan."

"A traitor?" I was shocked, but had wondered for a long time.

"Yes, and there is little to be done when a traitor is at work on the road," Zafir said. "So, I tripled the watch at each of our stops. I had those at the fire who watched as usual, and other eyes watching in the dark for me. But it was you who led us to a clue that night with Ammar."

"When Fukara attacked me with the knife?"

"Yes, that was the night."

"But that man, wasn't he a new hire from Leuke Kome?"

"Yes, he was new, but he wasn't the traitor I was seeking."

"Then who was?"

"Many of my men were visiting in Leuke Kome the night Suoud was murdered," Zafir said. "Many eyes and many knives. I was almost sure of who was involved in the murder, and had narrowed it down to two. The night of the Fukara, it was then that I knew who I was after."

I held my head in disbelief and looked directly at Zafir. "No, it couldn't be. Habib couldn't kill one of his own, could he? Not with his oath."

"Habib did not kill Suoud," Zafir said, "In fact, he did *not*. He was on watch that night—it was his turn, he didn't leave his post."

"I don't understand," I said, and felt a pain began to grow in my gut, a sense that there was news I didn't want to discover.

"The man I seek met with Habib in Leuke Kome, and shadowed us to the place of the Fukara. The two must have communicated in the night, beyond the eyes of the watch. But you and Ammar, you exposed their rendezvous. That night, that company of bandits was there to take you, Bassam, probably to Al Jawf, and then east."

"Me? Am I such trouble to you?"

"No, you're not trouble," Zafir said. "They believed that a ransom for your life would be a king's ransom—even the scrolls themselves. They hoped the long planning could have paid well."

I took a step back to catch my breath. How could I be of such terrible consequence to my honored friend, Zafir? Had I only known, had I only understood that the *kin of Zafir* was a prize, not for my own self, but for the ransom, for the value of a promise and a love like a father's.

I swallowed and suddenly realized how dry my throat had become. My stomach groaned from lack of food.

"Then who is it you seek if not Habib?"

"I still seek Habib," Zafir said. "And the man from Leuke Kome who escaped the night of the Fukara. He is named Khan, I also seek him."

"Khan?" I gasped. "*Khan* killed Suoud?"

"Oh no," Zafir continued. "Khan is a little man, he was the messenger from Habib to the bandits. But the other, the man who murdered Suoud, he is a powerful man, cunning and wicked, there is already much blood on his hands," Zafir said. "He will be difficult to find. His name is Bazma, but among his bandits he is known as Moluck."

Moluck? *Moluck?*

The shock hit me like a rock in the head. My world of faces and freedom and stars and torches suddenly swirled around in a blur of black, and the wretchedness of the long arduous days knotted my stomach and I bent over, pushing away from everyone to find the water's edge and fell to my knees vomiting.

RESOLUTION

Amin took the blame, holding my head up as fresh water was brought to my lips.

"The boy hasn't eaten since I first saw him this morning," Amin said.

"He slept all the way here."

"And who knows the trial that brought him to As-Samawah," Fawzi said, leaning over in concern.

"What is this?" Fawzi asked with his torch, lifting my limp arm to examine the faded bloodstain on the sleeve. Amin looked across at him and just shrugged, shaking his head.

The water made me sputter and cough.

"No more excitement for tonight," Zafir said. "We must feed you, boy, and get you rest."

I raised his hand wearily. "No, not yet, please," I said, reaching for the clay mug of water. "I have to tell you, I have to say it, I can't hold it inside of me any longer."

I sat up on the ground, hanging my head. The swirling dizziness had stopped with a roaring headache that throbbed between my ears.

Humam handed me some dates. "Eat these," he said. "You need some nourishment." I took one but couldn't eat it, I couldn't eat anything, not now, and pushed them away.

In stuttering sentences, I tried my best to piece together the splintered events of my kidnapping—Habib's debauchery of trust the night of the storm and my fight in the sand. The days on the trail and the wickedness of Moluck, and how Habib had stood up for my protection, but only for the reward that awaited him at some distant place.

I told of my strategy, my ruse each night at the second watch, and how it had worked among the bandits. And my all-night run through the desert until the rising of the moon, and the near gallop over many stadia. And the lone boatman and his son, willing to give me an escape for a price.

"I prayed to God to help me, to help me find passage on the boat. And when the thought came to me to look for gold in the goat hair coat, *I know* that was Him answering me, guiding me."

The group had gone whisper quiet, leaning in to hear.

"I bought a knife, and it carries a stain upon it that ... that I must explain."

I told them of my terrifying encounter with Moluck in the alley, and how the man had sworn my death and raised his sword in rage.

"You would have been foolish," Zafir said, "to let Moluck decide for the both of you whether he was scaring you or wanting to kill you."

"He has killed in his rage many times before," Fawzi said.

"But I didn't *know* he was the assassin," I said. "All I knew is that he told me he was going to kill me, and he raised his sword to do it."

"Do you remember, my boy," Zafir said, "when I told you that if you take up the sword of another man, you take up his honor over the decisions of life and death?"

Oh yes, I remembered, and nodded.

"Suoud must be grateful and proud," Zafir said. "You decided with wisdom, my son."

I looked away to the ground. The distasteful act still clung to my hand, the knife and its handle, and the diluted stain on my sleeve. "I knew I had but one chance," I said. "When Moluck came at me, I saw the place for striking, it was not guarded."

Fawzi elbowed the man next to him. "I taught him that," he bragged.

"I drew my knife with my right hand, I took the stance and raised my elbow. The knife did her work."

"I also taught him that—the elbow thing," Fawzi bragged again.

There was a long silence as the magnitude of the confrontation spread to the listening ears. I felt to a degree that I had exorcised my guilt, now that it was fully shared with those I loved. I felt the beginning of some sense of resolution and escape from that moral dilemma, a conflicting struggle between choice and consequences.

Zafir saw the struggle in my face and broke the silence to address the group. "Enough story telling for one night," he said, it is time they returned to their donkeys, return to town, and go to bed. The men began to disperse toward the knoll, caught in pleasant banter among themselves. "Young Bassam, he has tested his knife," said one. "Baptized in the fire of a murderer," answered another. "That axe man would have beheaded Bassam," spoke a third. "But not the student of Al Murrah!" said the first. The group spread out as they walked up the bank toward the knoll, some lingering behind to help Amin secure the goods from his boat.

Helping me to stand, Zafir wrapped an arm around my shoulders. "That coin, the coin that God helped you find ..."

"Yes?"

"You know that gold did not belong to you," Zafir said.

I was too tired to fight a philosophy and just sighed, "Yes, I know."

"And it wasn't yours to give away to Amin for the hungry families, either."

"Yes, I know that too. I'll work hard and pay it back as quickly as I can."

Zafir smiled. "So that I am fair with you as I am with the others, I must make you aware of my reward. For whoever finds and brings to justice the man who killed Suoud, a gold coin."

"And that murderer would be Moluck," I said with half a grin, "and he is dead."

"At your hand?"

"Yes, at my hand."

"Then you have fulfilled the contract. The coin is yours, you may do with it as you please."

I smiled at the old man's tricks, it was so good to be back home. "Thank you," I said. "Then I make a gift of the silvers—no, not a gift, I leave the silvers in the wise care of Amin, to use them honorably for the hungry he might find tonight, and for those in the days to come."

"That is well," Zafir said. He helped me into the donkey cart, snapped the little stick across the donkey's hind side, and the two of us rode toward the knoll, his torch burning steady, and a light to our path.

Lingering behind were nine Al Murrah following us with hands on swords, watching keenly for dangers in the dark.

"Day 91—Dear Rasha, I am back with my bakra, and it is good to be home. I was taken by the hand of treachery and kept for almost a week, but I am safe now. I was compelled to save my life in a fight, and the life I took was the killer of Suoud. Suoud's life has been avenged and men think highly of me for it.

I don't feel honored for taking a life, even a life so evil as Moluck. Fawzi says I've stopped a killer from killing again. I can still feel the warmth of his blood on my hand, I do not like it. Zafir sees this torment in my eyes and keeps me close. He said the cost for safety in this world is sometimes higher than those protected could ever understand. I think I understand now what he means. He says no more adventures for me. I agree. We are close to Babilu, and will camp there tomorrow.

I am back with my bakra and my writings. She missed me, but won't show it. She still complains.—Bassam"

"Dear Bassam, Our garden shows some growth. Small, green leaves split their seed pods and poke from the soil. I water them daily. We may have something to harvest. Faris is showing me how to tend the furrows and recognize the tares. He knows a lot about growing things. He says he hopes to raise a large farm in the eastern plains outside of Rekeem. He comes almost every day now. He wonders what my hopes are, my life goals. What shall I tell him?—Rasha"

LESSONS OF THE RUINS

I awoke to the pleasant activities of our company setting camp for a long stay in Babilu. For me, I wasted no time catching up on new flavors, new food and new sights.

"What's this? You want to be a cook or something?" Fawzi asked. I ignored him. I was capturing with my journal the latest recipes we had eaten and I was trying to remember them all.

I had my writing supplies spread out on the ground, a few notes here, a menu there—too many adventures in eating around Babilu to let the new flavors and spices escape my journal. It was only mid-day and already the smells of delicious meals wafted from the city center all the way to the rolling, grey grassy foothills of our camping place.

"No, I'm making a list," I said. "We should bring samples of these foods and seeds back home. We could open a diner."

"Women's work, Bassam, just look at yourself," Fawzi mocked. "Like I said, you must be practicing to be a cook. …"

I was too absorbed to acknowledge his tease. "This is great, Fawzi! Pomegranates, quinces, all these different grapes, and apricots, they're bigger than any I've seen."

"It's no secret, camel head—it's not hot here, more rainfall, too."

"But these melons! And spicy rice dishes with chicken and beef and lamb—there's a treasure of food in this place."

"Wait till you get some mee pok …"

That was new, I'd never heard of it. "Mee pok? What is that?"

Fawzi refused to answer, that treat was coming soon enough.

The caravan would stay five days, resting from the exhaustion of my rescue. Their hurried desert journey and river crossings had forced the men to consume supplies and patience. And so, the peaceful recreation in the pleasant, warm climes of Babilu was especially welcomed. While Zafir and some elders were working some trade, the rest of us enjoyed the city's bountiful pleasures.

As for me, I was the unwilling center of attention. Each evening my friends obligated me to regale to curious listeners around a cook-fire the tales and intrigue of my brush with death—and I found that my story grew to greater extremes with each telling.

Zafir and Ammar smiled as they passed by, remembering how their own harrowing adventures had added richness to the spice of their own campfire stories.

On the day before departure, I was awakened early from a perfectly restful sleep.

"Get up Bassam!" It was Ziyad—*all* of us knew his voice from anywhere. "This is our last day, will you sleep it away?" he said, standing over me in the morning light. The large man spread out his shadow as wide as he was tall. "You're going to see some ancient ruins before we leave, you won't want to miss them."

"I've seen plenty already, Ziyad. What's another city in ruins?"

He could not be put off. "Dress, prepare, and bring water, I'll be back to fetch you."

Ziyad was right. I might never pass this way again. I prepared, and strapped on Suoud's sword and found that he was not alone—a dozen Al Murrah waited with him. The new rule Zafir had imposed was that in these lands where conspirators could join forces to execute patient plans, no one was to go anywhere alone. "Twelve men with swords, at least," Zafir said, "or find your own way back to Rekeem."

With Ammar, Fawzi, and the dozen swords in tow, Ziyad led us beyond the city walls, north and upriver along the banks—toward the toppled stone and brick remnants of a great empire past. A slight breeze from the river cooled us, flattening the tops of grasses with irregular, fluttering strokes, stirring dust into the cracks of corners of ancient and collapsing stone ruins.

The hills rose slightly and then flattened into a great plain where the ancient foundations of Babilu once stood. A lone dirt road had been cleared ages ago, and we followed it under the hot sun, winding through more rubble where our group followed on foot. I saw two long rock lizards scurry to shelter when we passed.

Traveling more than half an hour, we found ourselves completely surrounded by the wrecked walls of hundreds, no, tens of hundreds of foundations. The skeletons of structures that were laid flat by some fantastic force in ages past.

"There was greatness here," Ziyad said as we passed toppled clay-brick walls and foundation stones of assorted buildings—all of them within easy distance of the river's refreshing shores. "Long ago, this land of gardens was well watered. There was a day when this was a fortress city. Massive terraced walls surrounded it. Atop these walls grew gardens of all kinds: trees, fruits, vines and orchards. So great was the prosperity of this place it could not contain its wealth. Legend says that the low-hanging fruit could be had freely by any man on foot or beast within reach on the outsides of the walls. Hanging freshness for the taking."

"The hanging gardens, I have heard of them!" I said.

"Indeed, and so had the world. But that was centuries ago, maybe longer."

The place was huge, larger than any city we had visited. "What great power destroys a mighty empire like this?" I wondered.

"The same that destroys all empires," Ziyad said. "Come, let us walk some and I will tell you the story."

We continued climbing the slight rise until it leveled out to an expansive plain, the very foundation place of history, a magnificent stretch of rubble, the toppled remains of a civilization that had been erased, its handiwork strewn as far as eye could see.

Ziyad headed directly to one building that was a good 30 paces square, also facing the river. Its short foundation stones remained, a course of three blocks high, double-wide, outlining the structure from girth to width.

The floor was amazing—some tens of thousands of decorative cut tiles, wall to wall, front to back. The intricate cemented mosaic was the most amazing work of art I had ever seen. It was as flat as still waters with dozens of images partly covered over by wind-blown sand—others faded with time. We walked about the tiles in silence, observing the dimmed images of happier times—colorful portrayals of fruit platters, animals fighting each other, ships set for sail, Grecian columns, household scenes, servants offering baskets of breads and melons.

"What is this place?" I asked.

"Watch," Ziyad said, reaching for the water skin slung over his shoulder. He brought it in front of him and splashed water onto the floor, washing away the dust.

Instantly the faded tiles burst into colorful life—vibrant reds, blues, whites, browns, and shades in between. The platters became grey and silver with fruits of yellow and red, purple and blue. The animals took form, their fur a rich brown and black, their teeth white and sharp, their yellow eyes angry. The ships billowed with majesty in the wind, the waves beneath them whitecaped in an ocean blue. Lacy ribbons of decorative streamers in shades of gray framed the center pieces with prideful esteem.

"Ahhhhh!" we exclaimed in unison as the hidden visages suddenly awoke. Ziyad splashed more water.

"Wash a little desert dust and see the grandeur of ancient Babilu!" he smiled.

I bent down to examine the massive masterpiece. Each little tile was no larger than my thumbnail, with smaller chips carefully cut and inserted in between. Multiple shades of various colors gave the images a reality.

A few paces away was the image of a man putting a wreath on the head of a woman, but the tiles of her face were all missing.

"Look at this, what does this mean?" I asked, pointing to the woman's obliterated face.

Ziyad stepped closer and splashed water on the tiles. Suddenly the creamy colors of the man's face and his hands and arms took life—his eyes brown, the wreath forest green, their clothing elegant in browns with yellow trim. The woman's shoulders and arms came to life in beautiful ivory flesh so real I almost expected it to move with life. But her face? It was gone.

"I've wondered the same," Ziyad said. "I can only imagine, but do not know. I think this grand house, whatever it was, belonged to a wealthy man depicted here. It was he who put the image of his travels and luxuries into the floor as you see. And perhaps at the end of a journey, he found disfavor with his wife—there could be many reasons. But why he didn't replace her face with that of another? It is a mystery, but I think part of the answer is in her face. Look closely!"

I bent down and ran my fingers over the rippled straight edges of the dozens of small tiles that filled in the woman's face, a shadowy mixture of creamy colors, dark and light, neatly set into a blur of nothing.

"Oh! I see it now!" I said. "All the colors of a face, of hair, eyes and lips—are these the tiles of a face, just all mixed up?"

"That's what I think," Ziyad said. "If he wanted to replace her, if he found another woman, why not put on the face of the other?"

That would make more sense, I thought.

"That is why I think she betrayed him, and rather than replace her image, he left it disfigured, to scorn her—an insult to her family as well."

"And those who visited this place could see her face ruined," I said, "and no doubt would tell others, and keep her shame alive."

"Certainly. And perhaps the man dined with others for that very purpose, to send a message."

"Strange ..." I said, running my hand over the woman's face tiles. "Putting it together, I wonder what she looked like?"

"There is a great lesson, young Bassam," Ziyad said. "Life is no different today than a thousand years ago or ten—every man and woman walks this earth just the same, in any period of time and history. These images tease us with a story that seems very human, but we will never know except that same truth—it is not whether they were born or they died, it is how they lived that matters."

What did I just hear?—did Ziyad just quote the scrolls? He did not make eye contact with me, and spoke it turned to the others. Does he know the scrolls?

"Gather around, over at this wall," Ziyad announced. "I will make this telling very short because the sun is hot and we should start back soon."

We followed him to the marble facing of a tall stand of bricks, high enough to cast a shadow large enough to let us sit in shade on the tiled floor. I rested my back against the marble—its smooth, streaked whiteness showed the tooling of care and engineered perfection—soft, sculpted moulding along the bottom, carved long ago by artisans who knew the patient secrets to cut ornate reliefs of vines horizontally—that were now worn with the passage of time.

Ziyad stood before us and swept his hand across the scene as if by his magic he could recreate a majestic city of many thousands of dwellers—some of them riding about in fine clothing on gold-trimmed chariots drawn by well-bred horses harnessed with silver and leather. And the people, a clean people in their rich draped clothing, filling the swept paths as they carried themselves about to destinations within the safety of those magnificent walls beyond. Ziyad unfolded the story—

THE STORY OF BABILU

Ammu ("Ah-moo") was loved by his people. They called him their great healer, a senior kinsman to all. Because of his wisdom and military might he was the sixth king of Babilu and became the first king of his great empire. He won several wars and gained control over the entire watershed of the great Euphrates and Tigris rivers—all the way to the sea.

Babilu was his headquarters. He built up its walls wide and high, into a huge, impenetrable fortress. With treasures he built out his city to either side of the river and stretched the fortress walls across, allowing a tunnel beneath through which the great river flowed. He built underwater pylons of such complexity and strength that only the passage of the waters was permitted while armies were prevented from finding a way in.

With the city secured, Ammu built roads, expanded the temples, enlarged the stocks and herds, and created a glorious place of industry and peace.

There seemed nothing he did not do. Sudden floods common to the area that washed through the land presented no problem. Ammu had his people cut canals and cisterns to control the flow. From such care the city flourished and foods in abundance grew here—even the high walls could not contain the gardens that hung from them with rich perfumed flowers, ripening fruits, and shade from the sun.

Visitors traveled for months to trade here—to behold the wonders of Ammu's kingdom. In time, Babilu became an important stopping place for traders from the sea or those crossing toward the great deserts. Its fame and envy spread to lands far and wide.

Ammu found his place in history because of his great wisdom. Unlike those before him, he governed his kingdom with a written law. It was one of the first times such a law had been put to parchment, even before the writings of Father Moses.

Ammu taught there should be one law, one law for all—that no man should be above it, not king or pauper, it is the same. He knew the wiles of his subjects and insisted that if one man accused another, he is innocent unless there is proof. If no proof materialized, the accuser was punished for his unwarranted attack. And if a man injured another, he had to pay twice or four times that which he stole or ruined. All men had to obey this law. It was the Law of Ammu.

He had these laws cut into stone tablets and sent all over his kingdom. They were placed at the center of all cities and towns to guide the justice of every household and neighbor. This order brought peace and civility to Babilu. Hence, he became the great healer of strife in the land.

I sat spell bound through the telling. *The wisdoms of good government had roots long into the past. The tools were theirs to grow and prosper if they would use them, although many did not.*

"So tell me, Ziyad," I asked. "Why then did Babilu and the empire collapse?"

"As we leave, I will show you one of the tablets of stone erected in this very place, a stone with his law cut into it. It stood as a monument to the great progress of Ammu, but it also tells the sad truth that virtue is not inherited, it may not be passed from father to son. Such virtue must always be learned and earned."

Ziyad looked at the sun, it was late. "But know that when Ammu died, his son did not rule by the Laws, and lost the empire. Enemies came and knocked down the walls and it was no more."

"These walls?" I asked. "How was it possible?"

"A great general knew Babilu's weakness. Do you?"

I thought a moment but could not fathom a city of ruins this size to have ever been weak. "I couldn't guess," I said.

"A thousand years after Ammu, a general came who saw what others before him had missed. He went upriver of Babilu to a turning place in the river and ordered his men to roll great stones into the river and tear down its bank. They succeeded in turning the river's course out into the desert just long enough for them to make their move. At the water gates of Babilu, the river became low for a few days. The men waded into the river at night. Instead of the water rising over their heads, it came only to their knees. They found the pylons of stone and broke through—and took the city."

"And no one was watching?"

"Why keep up your guard when you have such walls as these?"

"Day 121—Dear Rasha, I saw the place of the hanging gardens today. It is all a ruin. Zafir is right—only that which is built on a strong foundation will endure, even a place so glorious as once stood at Babilu. I replaced my sandals here. I had worn the leather to strands and they finally broke. The Euphrates is beautiful—narrow where we camped but fast flowing. My bakra says hello. She is showing wear for the journey. Her eyes are gray. I am bringing home seeds and recipes. The fruits grow well in Babilu. I cannot forget the image of a man and his wife I saw, like a painting but made in tiles. The story is that he erased her face for reasons we can only guess. Love once found should never be lost.—Bassam"

"Dear Bassam, Our garden grows better. The squashes are sending small vines, but no blossoms. Faris says two more weeks and we should see blossoms. I think that is too soon. I carry water to it each day, and it is a lot of work in this heat. I enjoy school. Dalal taught it here this past week. A man came through with 11 camels and more honeybees. He raises them. He is trying to sell them to Kateb. Your father is thinking how to make a business of it, and has been talking to farmers outside of Rekeem. He said bees are the bearers of new life. Dalal doesn't want them, nor do I. For all of their sweet work, they guard it with their sting. It made me remember our time together looking for honey treats. It made me smile.—Rasha"

44

WALLS THAT TEMPT

It was early and a dozen stubborn stars refused to yield as the sky grayed toward morning. Zafir sent messengers to rouse the camp for departure. There were no fires—he wanted his men out of the valley by sun-up.

The route ahead was long between supplies, and each man had loaded up as much as he could manage—dried dates and fruits, nuts, breadstuffs, cheeses, jerked meats. And water—double the skins, and then some.

I could hear complaints from hundreds of camels climbing to their feet when the signal was given. They growled at the riding stick but complied—snorting and wheezing, rising in chaotic massing, jangling, rustling, pushing, to form themselves into several plodding lines, one behind the other.

The shrouded shapes moved slowly at first, as if trying to summon the courage to carry another day's load. But they found new footing as they pulled their heavy burdens away from the damp river mists. The beasts crowded each other up the narrow funneling pathways to the main road, making it thick with man and beast as we set out toward the dark rolling hills eastward.

The caravan never took long to find its stride on the trail. As if built for the rhythm of the road, the camels came up to speed in brief time. It was another hour before the day was upon us—enough to climb the weary slope to the broad pass that led away. And there began our daily race with the sun.

At the very moment the rising sun peaked over the eastern hills, glaring directly into our faces, the caravan had reached the apex—the last climb leading from Babilu's slumbering valley.

I turned in my saddle for one last look. From my place high above that grey ribbon of river that snaked south, I could discern the ruins of the ancient city on the far side. Its silent stone ruins of ancient wealth and forgotten glory stood as motionless and eternal as the surrounding hills. From my vantage I could see the old city fading into the brown of the horizon, its appearance was like stumps of gnawed-down teeth, row behind row of faded and forgotten glory. The ancient city stood vacant, like it was rubbed from the earth, obliterated like the face of the scorned woman in the tiles. Its ghosts were audible, calling to me across the great expanse in whispering warnings—*All things give way to the dreamers and those who will build them. A city a thousand years strong cannot stand—for, the hand of man without virtue does not endure.*

I rode on with the voices echoing their haunt in my head—Nothing endures without virtues, *nothing.*

How many ancient travelers departed this way, this very road, turning at this very place toward other villages—how many had removed this way during Babilu's glory days, but with a more magnificent vision shrinking behind them?

Spotting Ammar ahead of me, I hurried to catch up for the companionship. My wandering imaginations were getting out of hand and I needed something to bring me back to reality.

"What's the best calculation for our next stop?" I asked.

"Plan on four weeks," he said. Ammar had his maps spread out on his lap, trying to measure a distance.

"Four?" I asked in dismay. "Such a long stretch ...."

"It's not many stadia distant," he said, sweeping his arm at the next range of mountains over the horizon. "With those passes to conquer, it will take longer—the Sagartians ("Cigar-she-uns") and the Saka ("Saw-kaw")—and we'll have our share of muddy streams to forge. Extra days? Yes, we'll need ten or more."

I leaned over to see the map. "And more valleys?"

"Oh yes, the Mountains of Medea ("Ma-Dee-uh") here, with Mouru ("More-ew") there, at the end. Have you heard of it?"

"A little. It's a main trading center, isn't it?" I asked.

"Very large, yes. Visitors from everywhere—the sea north, the southern caravans, trains headed west. It's an exciting passage from western culture to eastern. You'll enjoy it. New smells and tastes—different goods, great spices, and colors and flavors—a sort of culture gate from here to there."

A culture gate. I took a deep breath of the perfumed desert air, and realized things were already different—the angle of the sun, the fluid indifference of the heat, the slight crisp to the air. I smiled to myself, "I love this place. I wonder what's next?"

On the third day out of Babilu, Fawzi caught me dreaming atop my bakra.

"Camel breath! What are you doing?" he barked.

It made me jump. "What?"

"You're riding like you have another scheme cooking. Will you force me to save you again?"

"I'm just thinking about Saka. I've seen their carpets," I said. "I didn't know they traveled so far through this waste to reach our Rekeem."

"Not by camel they don't," Fawzi said. "What you saw in Rekeem was brought by caravan up from the sea—after they had already traveled halfway round the world by boat."

"Boat? Zafir told me boats don't do well."

"The boats do fine on the short hauls. There's too little profit shipping the Saka rugs on caravans like ours. But the captains on their boats? They're the bandits who make the most profit! They carry many hundreds, *thousands*, at a time, and their journey is faster. These four-footed whiners of ours are good for a few dozen small carpets each, too heavy for more, but *why*? The things we carry are worth a thousand, no, ten-thousand times the weight in carpets. Carpets are not profitable for Abdali-ud-din."

"Seems to me the captains have it best," I said. "A life at sea, it makes me wonder ...."

"You should try it one day, Bassam," he said. "A boat trip on the sea is nothing like your little sailboat play to An-Najaf."

"I slept through that trip."

"On the sea, the waves are not forgiving. You could sooner die from a storm or the rocks on the shore than pirates boarding with long, curved blades."

Images filled my imagination of floating bodies and debris, war-ravaged survivors of a pirate raid. "Fawzi, you have this habit of throwing camel dung on the best dreams."

"You're welcome," he said. "But the captains have no wind through these deserts. This is where the people live. Such boats could sail for a distance up rivers, but at the end, only our caravans can reach the people. And only our caravans can endure the trips overland."

Fawzi pointed his riding stick at a wide sweep of the plateau that flattened out far beyond. "We carry east to west through places like these, while a boat must fight storms and distance in the southern seas. It's still an expensive loss in those storms, when a boat is lost—such storms come quickly."

"So the boats don't carry much trade? I thought that you said…"

"The boats *do* carry the trade, Bassam. A great deal. Some day when they're large enough to carry more, when they can travel from the eastern coasts to our fair climes, you can expect men like Zafir to buy into a line and control the seas as do such men the desert roads."

We rode along in silence for a few minutes more, passing between lifeless dirt mounds and stretches of salt flats—more dead terrain leached of life—and gravely underfoot, the waste for which the region was famous. I watched a strange bird floating on hot updrafts above us.

"I think I'll buy a carpet for Rasha," I accidently said aloud.

"R-a-s-h-a?" Fawzi asked with a grin.

"Well, uh, and my mother, too." I felt a blush come to my face. "My mother, she asked if I could bring her something, and I thought …."

"I see," Fawzi smiled. "And she probably wants two if you brought her one."

"Certainly," I said.

"Or three if you brought her two."

"Naturally."

On the sixth day out of Babilu, the route led us through Rhagae ("Raw-gay"), an ill-fated, nasty path of struggling settlements and wandering herdsmen. The village and its surrounding region were enveloped by dark-rock mountains and rusty-brown hills, canyons and gray stretches of dry salt flats. An oozing black mud that never dried in these flats made the off-road tangents dangerous for its sticky quicksand. Such sands had doomed countless travelers of earlier times.

Rhagae was watered by the runoff from the higher snows that fed a thousand streams—but this time of year they ran light or were already dried up. Those that flowed washed brackish the whole distance to the sea.

Local badawi hoping for a trade happily steered the caravans toward freshwater stops along the way. They stood at the roadside, large and toothless smiles on whiskered faces, gesturing with enthusiasm toward this way or that, begging in exchange a small payment of only a few fractions of silvers, or some trade.

A route from the west had to pass through the mountains, or detour around them through hill country. There was no better direct road to Rhagae. It was the cost of expediency—Zafir knew losing many days by traveling the length of inhabited valleys could delay him, but it was safer and that was paramount here.

The mountains and valleys meant a welcomed relief with lush, green pastures, patches of green farms, clear, running water—in stark contrast to the washed-gray wastelands we had traveled.

On the tenth night out of Babilu, Zafir bought several long-haired sheep from a local herder, partly to pay for crossing his clan's valley, but also for a feast to urge the men through the coming harsh days. Fresh meat was a welcomed pause, and the night of roasting was a needed reminder of the familiar ways—a reminder that hardships could be endured when balanced with refreshing pause.

With the sun almost set, the men staked out their camping place on the easy slope of a grass-covered hill.

After Zafir's tent was erected, he called his elders to consider their route toward Mouru. He dispatched Al Murrah to scout the paths ahead, and others to secure any threats from behind. It was time to make necessary adjustments now that we had arrived at the higher mountain passes. Zafir wanted to ensure our readiness. By the time dinner was removed and tea was served, it was past dark, and the elders remained discussing with Zafir in his tent.

Near the center of camp a cluster of men had gathered at a large fire telling stories.

"We were just boys," Talib began, unfolding an adventure from his youth. "Our father lived in a coastal village and we sneaked away one day and hid aboard a merchant ship from the Indus Valley."

"Those pirates never take passengers, especially boys," a man said. "How did you get on board?"

"We pretended employment—cargo tenders, and nobody asked. It was a two-day trip down the coast. Our parents knew we were hunting work, they didn't seem to notice our absence. And then a storm blew in. It hit hard and fast, waves pouring over the side, we were sick at the rail. And then the winds blew us into the rocks, smashing the boat."

"You swam from that wreckage?"

"We floated on debris. Others floated with us, but many drowned."

I stood listening, awestruck at the near catastrophe of life, wondering if I could be ready to float in the sea as had Talib. Could I have fought the tides to swim toward a landing that was safer than the sharp rocks and pounding surf?

From there the conversation drifted to other acts of stupidity that boys tended to employ while testing the adventuresome barriers between growing and dying. The taunts triggered a memory—a time in my father's youth, a story he had repeated many times to me, a means to teach me a lesson.

But rather than a happy ending, father's tale was usually shared with shame—a shame that his boyhood sense of caution had not steered him otherwise. And a fear of what had nearly happened, a fear that Father had carried with him all his life, like a stain—permanent, that he couldn't wash off. And he shared it frequently all through my growing-up years—

When father was a youth of 12 and traveling with his uncles, they passed through the high country where sheer cliffs dropped off a thousand cubits straight down. Ages of storm and weathering had smoothed the cliff's sandstone edges clean, and any living creature that ventured too close perished on the sharp rock piles deep into the sinking shadows beneath.

Father had seen these very cliffs from the trail that ran through the valleys far below. Leaning back on his camel he allowed his eyes to scale the sheer cliffs, ascending the straight walls, all the way to their tops that disappeared into the clouds.

On one trip through that same area, the men found themselves on the topside of those very same cliffs, passing over the high land, crossing the plateau with the great drop-off to their west. When father realized it, he hatched a plan he kept private—he planned to view those same cliffs but this time, from the top down, and know the cliffs from both sides—top and bottom.

After camp was set and the uncles sat about the cook-fire with tea and talk, the sun had not yet set. Young father escaped the attention of his uncles and went to the cliff's edge to see the upside of this fantastic spectacle of height.

Nearing the ledge he found the view opened up in a spectacular expanse that he had never before seen. He could see far to the distant south, even the clouds bowed below his vantage at that great hazy distance beyond, following the curvature of the land.

Drawing his view nearer to the range they stood upon, he could see the closer valleys, the routes normally taken by the caravans in the green blur of canyons below. Thin, winding threads of brown showed the wide boulevards they traveled in the valleys beyond.

But what of the immediate depths that fell below these cliffs?

He paused to examine the edge of the cliff in front of him. The rounded ledge sloped away, its rough bare rock not anywhere near the edge that young Father had imagined. Instead of the sharp edge like from the top of a cut stone wall, he found the sloping edge rounded like the curve of a large boulder. He stepped near it and tried to lean over and peer to the bottom but he wasn't close enough to cleanly look down the wall of the cliff. He had to lie on his stomach.

The rough sandstone was warm through his shirt and he felt the grit tug at the threads as he scooted closer to the edge. Straining his neck as far as he could, his eyes still couldn't see down the rock's edge.

He slid closer, the slope now angling his body in a downward position, head down. He peered again, jutting out his neck, straining to see.

Not yet.

A slight move once more, and then yes! His eyes saw the streaks in the rock immediately below him, he could almost reach down and touch them where the erosion of rain had smoothed the sheer sides. His eyes followed the descent deeper, trying to land his focus part way down, but the view kept dropping away. He focused farther down, but still the view kept dropping until the magnitude of the tremendous distance that gaped open below him, shouting deeply an emptiness just a breath away, was too far down to discern and the immensity of the cavernous descent that was right then just at his fingertips suddenly sent a shiver of fear coldly into his very soul. Fear grew to panic as the reality of the dropping vision had no end. Casting his frightful gaze far below, his eyes suddenly discerned countless numbers of sharp rocks heaped up at the bottom and masked in the swirling mists of mystery and dark, beckoning to him, calling his name in evil whispering taunts, *come closer*.

He felt an unholy urge from the air around him, from the very rock itself, to slip off the sloping drop and fling himself into the open air, tumbling over and over to a long and silent fall to the rocky rubble in the deepening shadows below. That's when he realized that his body's center of weight had shifted forward. His own body was pressing down on his neck and head, and all across his shoulders. He was leaning too far forward to get up, to move, even to breathe. His heart started to pound in his head and he knew that foolishness had brought him to this brink of a certain death.

Fighting the urge to panic, he forced himself to lie breathless and still. His palms began to sweat as slowly—ever so slowly— he pushed back to test the resistance against the smooth, washed rock. Beneath his hands he could feel a few singular granules of sand indenting into his flesh as he pushed back steady, carefully. The crystals rolled from flat side to flat side, almost audibly clicking, tightly pressed between his flesh and the stone, offering little resistance. He pressed his chest into the rock and tried to slide back, upwards and back—slowly, so slowly, nothing hurried, patient. His muscles began to tighten, his breath held still, he felt his shirt drag into tiny folds of resistance with each push backwards, bunching up beneath his stomach and legs. Another slow, careful push one more time, the sand crystals rolling under his palms, some sliding, his pressure against the ledge delicately paced according to the degree of resistance he could exert.

He dared not inflate his lungs to call out, he could hardly move, but move he would, too slow to disturb his precarious balance, a little at a time, slowly at a time, focused on but one thing, his palms and the rock, his only brake and leverage away from that edge. Immediately from his face, the rounded edge into eternity was gone and the streaked details of the sandy surface took the drops of sweat dripping from his face. Fraction by fraction the rounded drop moved away. He carefully lifted one leg to allow his clothing to unbind, and then the other, and pushed back slowly a little more. Father felt his center of weight shift from his shoulders to his chest, and then to his torso. He pressed more, testing the resistance of his palms with each new placement. And then his weight shifted to his hips, and finally he could back up slowly on his knees to the flatness of the rock that was but a short length past his feet. Backing up with another two deliberate and slow pushes, he cautiously turned his eyes to anchor on something safe behind. He turned about and crept low on his hands and knees to the level rock, and crawled five paces beyond before standing to a shaky sure footing. Without looking back, he returned to the camp.

An uncle spotted his approach and his smiling face turned sober. "Kateb," he said in concern, "What happened to you?"

"To me?"

"Yes, you're soaked and dirty, did you fall into a swamp?"

Father looked down to see the whole of his front, his shirt and his trousers were soaked in sweat, his palms rubbed red raw, and a sprinkling of sand dusting his shirt. His hair was matted down, cooling droplets of sweat congealed off his ear, his chin, his hands.

"I'm okay," he said in a shaky voice. "I am okay." And he headed for his camel, his blanket, and his sleeping mat. In the darkness of the privacy of night, he pounded an angry fist to the ground. *That was stupid. That was stupid. That was stupid. Never again will I look death in the eye, never. For the foolish reason of curiosity. Foolish. Stupid.*

At the end of the telling, father always gave me a sermon about the risks of walking on the dangerous side, that there is no safety, and not all have escaped the inevitable that awaits them. "The balance between life and death," father always said, "is literally in your own hands, there on the edge of that cliff, or any cliff in life. The destroyer is always lying in wait to deceive the foolish into his sure and certain trap. Too many have fallen for lack of caution, for lack of wisdom, for lack of self governance. You be better than that, my young Bassam, you be better than me."

45

THE THIRD SCROLL

Zafir stood impatiently at his tent door, holding it open so the yellow light poured from behind him, casting a long shadow across the trampled grasses.

"Bassam!" he called out. "Do you sleep, boy?"

Some ten paces away, I sat crouched around a dying cook-fire, lost in thought—my gaze fixed on the glowing ashes that I stirred with a stick.

"What?" I said, standing up. "I didn't hear you!"

"You didn't hear me three times? Any one else might think you were ignoring me!"

I shook my head apologetically. "Sorry. I was lost in a memory, what is it?"

Zafir gestured to his tent. "Weren't we going to talk tonight?"

"Oh yes!" I dropped the stick and went immediately. He let the drape close behind us, making a dampened place where whispers could not be heard.

The spacious enclosure was lit by half a dozen oil lamps hanging by cords from the top of the high canopied fabric. The flames bathed the brown walls in the warmth of flickering light. On the ground, several faded red carpets decorated with blue and gold were spread wall to wall—half a dozen brown pillows lay scattered. A small table with maps stood in one corner, chests and luggage were stacked in another. The ancient but cozy aura drowned the shadows and illuminated the colors in the woven rugs.

Zafir tossed me a large pillow, inviting me to recline. "My bones are as old as me," he said groaning as he laid down. "I've kept that secret from them for a long time now. Someone must have betrayed me and told them the ugly truth. Now they protest daily."

He had the scroll sack in front of him, and in the usual fashion, began with the little ritual I had grown accustomed to—

"This bag," Zafir began as he unlaced the top, "was my father's when he was a boy. It was new then but it shows wear today. I may have to replace it."

I closed my eyes at the familiar lines, reciting them to myself. They had more meaning now—speaking of a love and trust that endeared the old man to me as a friend and as a father. That leather bag was a token, an emblem of rites of passage—reaching across the centuries through the families of generations, the generations of faithfulness to the teachings of the scrolls. It was a ritual, and I liked the friendliness of it.

Reaching inside, Zafir lifted out a long bundled pair of spindles, the larger of which was of the same girth as the handle of Suoud's sword. It was tied in three places and had three leather tassels dangling from the top.

He laid it on the rug in front of us.

"Most men," Zafir said, "hope to find in these scrolls some ancient and lost guide to riches, …"

As the familiar declaration unfolded, I could almost repeat it myself.

"… I think your heart is ready, Bassam. Do you understand?"

"Yes, I do."

"Then let us begin."

He carefully unrolled the parchment to the first passage. The beautifully penned characters appeared the same as before, laid out in neat and straight lines, the lettering clear.

"You will do the reading, Bassam, and I will listen. If you have a question, you may ask me. But some things I will not tell you. It is part of the test."

I began:

> "The Song of the Stranger. To the prosperous, prosperity is not in the possession of things, but in the power of control. Control is not the type the tyrant wields, like a chain restraining a dog. It is gentle as the guiding oar of a ship or sincere persuasion with trusted words. The earth has treasure enough for all, too grand for any one man to exhaust, and yet such treasure has no value unless sent on its way, exchanged with others. To keep it hoarded chains a man to his wealth. It puts him in a cage of distrust, a fear of loss, and blind to the true power such wealth can bring when put to good use…."

The words unfolded gently, weaving a dozen carefully rendered ideas together that drew the first two scrolls into a complete whole.

The scroll spoke of those who finally learned to see beyond their own selfishness—to see that all men bring value to this life; that no one is a wasted birth who strives to carry his own weight.

Even so, dependence on others comes to every man—once, twice, a hundred times. It must come to all, it *does* come to all.

> "The man who learns the teaching power of failure is no longer afraid," I read. "He has come to understand fear. Fear is faith in failure. And so he rejects fear and replaces it with confidence that he will succeed. Confidence cannot materialize without experience, trials, resolutions. He therefore doesn't fear the problems that come to him in his life—he sees in them new opportunities. Looking for opportunity from his failures is how he removes his blindfold. With new powers of discernment, creativity, hope and perseverance, he uses failure as the most powerful tool available to improve himself.
>
> "The wise man counts profit not in treasure but in the worthiness of the effort. He understands that losses in a worthy effort nevertheless bear great returns. Lessons from losses are invaluable, therefore, they are not losses at all.

"Such a man has learned to live simply. He knows that any treasure built up by the labors of others, he has no claim to—he isn't owed any part of it simply because they possess it and he doesn't. The self-governed and humble man understands he has no claim on the labors of others.

"Treasure does not bring lasting joy. Joy can only be had in the work of his own hands, and the lessons he gains from that. All else is temporary and expendable. For when he dies, what is there left of him except love and respect, or shame and disdain? No man's worth is measured by the wealth he accumulates, except by greedy and lazy people who lust."

The scroll helped me see something I had already believed but never put into words—that true and enduring happiness is never founded in material things, it is only in people. Thereby are the prince and the pauper equals. Those depending on material things for happiness will live their entire lives disappointed.

And then I came the riddle. "We are at the end," I said.

Zafir smiled. "So I gather." There was a curious tease sparkling in his eyes. His brow was furrowed as if he was expecting a surprise of some sort. Perhaps there was one, a surprise yet to come.

"Read it aloud, please," he said.

I cleared my throat.

"The sayings of The Third Scroll, the Song of the Stranger.

"A virtue of wealth is this for thee, One branch one limb on the self same tree; The coin and palace all men may gain, But woe is life when spent in vain. For joy that lasts and doth not cease, Embrace the virtues thou Prince of Peace. One branch one limb on the self same tree, A virtue of wealth can be for thee."

"I see now that each of the scrolls teaches a virtue. Just as the tree is stronger with many branches, so is the man stronger with many virtues, is that it?"

"That's correct," Zafir smiled. "And each cannot stand alone without the power of the other six. So, do you have any thoughts about the importance of the 'Prince of Peace'?"

"I thought of it ... but not yet. Not just yet ...."

"Then," he said pointing, "proceed with the riddle."

"Oh wisdom, behold now the Song of the Stranger:

"A night that was damp, it blew and it thundered, A stranger had come, both thirsty and hungered. The drifter put forth his plea for relief, No door there was opened, they held the belief: The beggar's own acts, these were his undoing, His sins, his faults, his foolishness accruing. But then there came one, his purse he did open, to give the free gift, no words need be spoken. The beggar took gladly, and gave to him back, treasure found only in the wealth of their lack.

"What meaneth this the Song of the Stranger?"

Of course, I thought, *I know this already*. "This riddle is no riddle, Zafir," I said.

"Oh?"

"I know this one myself, the beggar is not a man or a woman or an orphan. It is man's prejudice that came knocking."

Zafir's eyes widened in surprise. I could see from his expression that he was wondering, *How did Bassam come up with that?*

"This riddle talks about me, exactly me," I said. "When a beggar comes calling, I think he's the victim of his own folly. And begging, he doesn't want to change himself. He wants the easy way out. Begging brings a coin for a day but nothing for a lifetime. And because that is exactly what people think when they see a beggar, the riddle says it precisely—it is their prejudice that has come knocking."

Zafir just watched as I waved my hands around, admitting my own remorse in the privacy of his tent.

"That's me, that's me from start to the end. I see a man in rags, I say 'Get up you fool, go work somewhere.' I see a woman with her child, begging. I say 'What did you do to offend your husband?' Or worse, 'Do you deceive with your begging, do you squeeze my heart to buy for your drunken husband who awaits your labors back in his tent?' I see the drunken fool fallen in the street. I say, 'Lie there in your vomit, that's the reward for your indulgences,' and I walk on. Those closing the doors in this riddle, they are me."

Zafir nodded. "Bassam," he said, "don't be so selfish with God's gifts. Those feelings are in every man—they must be removed so you may grow. Now that you know that, how will you do it?"

"I want to," I said truthfully. "But I don't know how. To those I find disagreeable I turn my back. A drowning man could wrap his arms around his rescuer and sink him as well."

"Exactly," Zafir said. "That's exactly how people treat people. And the fact that we all haven't killed each other to the very last man because of this disdain is one of God's many miracles."

It was true. Each of us looks out for himself first.

"Why don't you look to the riddle again, tell me if there isn't a clue how we answer the door when prejudice comes calling."

I pulled the scroll toward me like it was a confessional—a papyrus revelator of my own weakness.

> "But then there came one, his purse he did open, to give the free gift, no words need be spoken. The beggar took gladly, and gave to him back, treasure found only in the wealth of their lack."

"Can you explain it?" Zafir asked.

"This exchange," I said, "they do it without even speaking."

"Do you suppose they are acquainted?"

"They must be, why else would he make the exchange?" I stopped to think. "You know, Zafir, it's strange but I get the feeling the riddle is trying to say the man wanted to open his purse as if he *needed* to give, not from his generosity but more out of some sense of selfishness...."

Zafir's eyes brightened. "Selfishness?"

"Well, yes ...." *Selfish*, I thought. *Why would it be selfish to give? How is giving to a beggar being selfish?* "Perhaps it wasn't selfishness that shut those other doors. Perhaps they only feared him."

"You almost have this," Zafir said. "What is it about fear and prejudice and selfishness that opened this one door?"

"They all come from the same root, don't they? A lack of knowledge, a lack of history, a lack of understanding?"

"Think about fear for a moment," Zafir said. "Does fear always threaten from outside? Do they shut the beggar out, or do they shut the beggar ...."

"Shut it *in*!" I interrupted. "They didn't want to rid themselves of the beggar, he wasn't trying to break in—it was their prejudice looking to get out and they refused to let it go away from them."

"Away from what?" Zafir asked.

“Get out of their hearts, out of their lives, their attitudes, their fears of the unknown,” I said. “These doors are like prison doors, and so long as the prejudice is held inside, they feel safe in their own fear. It’s familiar to them, it is predictable to them, it spares them from dealing with the beggar. Shutting him within is so much easier than loosing prejudice and trying to help.”

Zafir was smiling now.

“And when their feelings to judge and reject come knocking at their doors to be let out,” I said, “the man refuses and keeps those feelings pent up inside, thinking that’s easier. But it cankers and eats at him, and ... Oh, that’s it!” Suddenly I saw it—“It destroys his ability to trust.”

“Yes!” Zafir said. “Prejudice robs a man of a *virtue*, his virtue of trust. Hear it again: prejudice robs a man of his ability to trust.”

I had never considered it before. When we can no longer trust, and worse, when we are no longer trustworthy, then there needs come new masters to compel us to correct action.

“Read these last lines one more time,” Zafir said. “They tie these beautiful thoughts together into one.”

> “But then there came one, his purse he did open, to give the free gift, no words need be spoken. The beggar took gladly, and gave to him back, treasure found only in the wealth of their lack.”

“In this riddle,” Zafir said, “the man didn’t ask for any specific information. He didn’t challenge the beggar. He didn’t examine the use of his charity. How do you explain that?”

I thought a moment. *Selfishness.* Could selfishness ever be a good thing and not bad? “I was thinking that a wise man always enquires after he makes an investment, to see that it is well worked. But the man who does not check on it, like here, must be buying something instead, something he really wants. In the riddle the beggar has that *something*, and yet ... the beggar has nothing.”

“Yes, yes,” Zafir said. “Keep talking, son.”

“So, there must be an important purpose in the exchange that made both of them feel prospered. Both of them must have needed or wanted. The beggar took but it’s not clear what he gave.”

Zafir started to smile. “Read that last line again,” he said.

".... and gave to him back, treasure found only in the wealth of their lack."

I rolled the last thought around in my mind. "Oh!" I said. "*Their lack,* that means no treasure at all. It says both of them had 'lack.' It's a negative."

Zafir nodded. "And?"

"The man who gave from his purse was lacking something. He gave because he needed something, something that wasn't money."

"And what was he lacking if it wasn't money?" Zafir asked.

"Oh! It's making sense now," I said. "The beggar wasn't actually looking to take alms, he was looking to actually *give* alms—a gift. Yes! He was looking to give a gift that could open this prison door to the outside world. A key, so to say. A key that could free the man's prejudice, so he could heal. The key was ... well, that key was ...."

"Their lack?"

"Yes!" I said, sitting up tall. "The steward who gave the coins knew he had a lack of love and trust in his heart—he carried prejudice in him. And the key to repairing that flaw was to give away his treasure. The act of giving is what brought him the only true treasure. He needed nothing back except the sincere opportunity to *simply give.* That was the gift from the beggar."

"My boy, you've got it!" Zafir said.

"And that's how selfishness was good, right? It was his own heart that needed repair, and he knew it! And there was no tool except to help someone else. And that someone was the beggar."

Zafir nodded and smiled. "Tell me then, my boy," he said, "what is the secret of the third scroll?"

"The key to escape our own prejudice is to give—to help the poor among us, those we reject for reasons of our own fear and ignorance. We give to them not because it helps them, but we give because it helps us—yes, that's it, we give because it helps us ...."

"And that's how a man can both stand strong in self-governance and show humility at the same time, by giving of himself," Zafir said. "That is the secret to wealth, to bring balance to your greed. To give away a few of your coins to help them retain their value and power in your heart—and not let them consume you with false promises. We give to help ourselves stay humble. I say it again. *We give to help ourselves stay humble.* And staying humble serves us how?"

"It opens us to learning true knowledge," I said.

"I want you to remember that your hope might fail and make you discouraged. And your faith might fail, your faith in others. But remember this, that charity will never fail you, my son. Because, in truth, you are the beggar, Bassam. You desperately need the true opportunity to receive the gift that comes when you freely give to another. And so dies your prejudice, and so is born your true inner strength, the most real power you will ever possess."

Zafir ended the reading by climbing to his feet.

"Remember that a man who gives of himself, who gives because he sees a need and wants to help, such a man is never sad or angry. Giving makes him happy. Giving makes *you* happy. And what of happiness? Happy people work harder, they work better, they serve others happily. Such is the man of prosperity, the man of humility, the man of happiness, the man with no prejudice—the man who gives."

"Day 130—Dear Rasha, I learned many things tonight. The third scroll teaches that the virtue of charity serves three important needs. First, all men are beggars and receive charitable help every single day from God. Second, the wise man knows that only by giving can he remove the scales of selfish greed that blind his judgment. Giving keeps him humble. Then, he is open to learning.

Third, giving brings joy, joy brings industry, and that brings success. Others seeing this will view the giving man as a leader, he serves others first, and becomes leader as a result.

We saw a large black viper today. The camels would not go near. We had to kill it before the camels allowed us to continue. If my bakra was in front, all could have been fine, we saw vipers all the time in Rekeem. No camel is as smart as mine.—Bassam"

46

TRUE WEALTH

The landscape separating the western deserts from the regions of Mouru was flowing with fresh-watered valleys and canyons that offered plenty of nourishment for both animal and man. The watering stops were delightful, offering as much as we wanted from cool and sweet mountain streams. Local farmers and merchants welcomed us with kindness. It was wonderful to see green growing things, again, even if just for this short transit.

Dinner around the cook-fire was energizing. Cooking fresh foods after eating our supplies for so many days gave all of us a good boost of renewal. Even the camels had more of a skip to their normal plod.

One crisp morning I found Zafir traveling to the side of the caravan and I pulled up next to him.

"Bright morning to you, my young son, what brings this day for you?"

"I wondered if this was a good time to ask you some questions about the scrolls."

"Certainly. Follow me to the side so we may speak openly."

We steered our camels toward the outer edge of the caravan, letting the others pass, and followed from a dozen paces back.

"You call these scrolls the seven scrolls of wealth," I began. "I wanted to ask you how they helped you gain wealth. Are they truly scrolls of wealth or are they scrolls of good advice?"

Zafir smiled. "Advice? Yes. Wealth? Not in the way that you might think."

"I suspect there is much more that I don't see," I said.

"Yes, you don't see it yet, but you understand better than you realize."

A gust of wind suddenly whistled past, surprising both of us to put scarves to our mouths. We watched a wind devil swirl by, lifting its horde of dusty followers into a slender yellow column of swirling sand and debris that danced down the trail in front of the caravan.

"The ideas are basic, Bassam," Zafir began. "Too many people define their lives by what they have, by their possessions—a large tent, many servants, many camels and horses, riches from far distant places, many wives, large estates, even homes in a city or shops by a river. These things do not define a life at all, they only reveal the choices that a man makes."

"But are those not the tokens of the wealthy?" I asked. "Don't others look upon such things as evidence of prosperity and treasure?"

"They do, but for what purpose do these possessions serve?" he asked. "If a man buys such things to further his prosperity, or if he buys them just to lift himself above others, which of those is the right way?"

"Pride doesn't serve anyone well."

"That's correct," Zafir said. "A man who seeks to lift himself above another by accumulating things, such a man is squandering his blessings, and no man is rich enough for that. He doesn't know of the first scroll of self governance because he wastes his resources, and therefore is not teachable according to the second scroll, and fails the third scroll because he gives to himself and not to others."

"But isn't it okay to get things just because you want them?"

"Yes, that's the privilege of him who has mastered wealth in his life," Zafir said. "But for purely prideful reasons, to show up the man in the other caravan, that is not the virtue of wealth speaking, that's a great lie."

"A lie?"

"Prosperity that is not put to use to benefit others soon falls in on itself."

"Well, okay, I think I understand ...."

"Let me say it this way. Imagine you live in a far distant place where water must be brought by caravan," Zafir said. "The camel drivers carry heavy water skins for many days and upon arriving, they empty them into your cistern. They do this for many months—the camels come to deliver, and you have water to draw."

I nodded.

"Now suppose you cut their wages in half. You tell the camel drivers you will start using half of their wages to build a beautiful desert palace. The palace will have many rooms and gardens and pools. And for this, they had to go without half of their wages. But you will share your beautiful palace with them whenever the camel drivers come with their loads of water. And they could stay and rest from their journey to eat from the gardens and cool in the pools of abundance."

"All right, I understand," I said. "I'd hate that if I was one of the camel drivers."

"Exactly. So—what does the camel driver do? When he returns to his home on half wages, he doesn't have enough to buy for his camels or prepare for the next trip to carry water. So, he doesn't travel out to you on the next turn—he can't afford it. And you, why you are sitting in the desert needing water but it doesn't come at the appointed time. Your cistern goes dry, your gardens wilt in the sun, and all becomes nothing but dry bones. The lesson, Bassam, is that to keep your paradise alive, you must share your prosperity. You can't consume what creates your strength. You can't consume what supports your strength. You can't consume what perpetuates your power, or you yourself will die."

"The first scroll does teach wealth," I said, "because a man who can't control his appetites will consume his coins as soon as he finds them. If he could get the whole world, he'd try to eat that too, and still not have enough."

"And my first wife," Zafir said, "Rasheeda, did you know about her illness, that rash on her skin?"

"I heard of it, yes."

"Rasheeda uses the mineral mud from the salty sea north of Rekeem. No other cure can help her condition. These mineral muds are rich with healing power and stop the spread of the illness on her skin. We depend on another camel train to bring us the mineral mud two times a year. Do you think I want to pay those camel drivers to bring the help for my Rasheeda?"

"Without question."

"And do you think I want to see Fukara working in that land to rob and plunder such trains?"

"Certainly not."

"Then you see how I work hard to support the elders of the whole land, to trade with them, to do what business I can to support them," Zafir said. "This helps keep them strong so they can afford to keep peace in their lands so the camel drivers with the mineral muds may pass through freely to deliver help to my Rasheeda."

"So, it's not just what you want, but helping others get what they want. That's how you really get what you want—by helping others?"

"That's the way," Zafir said. "The first scroll teaches that the wealthy have learned to control their wealth by controlling themselves, their selfish greed that excludes others. Treasure is like water. So long as it flows, all the farms and fields it waters grow and benefit. But dam it some place and all else suffers. The farms die, the workers move away, there are none left to harvest or protect the land. Self governance means to control what you consume voluntarily, sell or trade to give others what they need, give and take for there is abundance, enough for all."

Amazing, I thought. I could never have attached self-governance to the idea of becoming wealthy.

Ahead of us we watched the dusty men riding in their long lines, talking, laughing, exchanging. The giving of friendship and trust opening the gate for everyone. What I might have given that morning for a boat ride out of As-Samawah before Amin came along to test me.

"So I ask you, young Bassam," Zafir said. "If I handed you two talents of gold right now, what would you do with them?"

Oh my heavy bakra hooves! That's the last thing I needed. I looked away a moment and then frowned.

"Why—nothing, really," I said. "I suppose I could put that money into some enterprise—a caravan like this, or a farm or a shop in a busy city. I can't imagine much until I reached home again."

"What about your clothing?" Zafir said. "Those rags are beginning to look more and more like the hair of your camel! Or your food, how much longer will you insist on living in that little blanket of yours each night, eating your dried fruits and bitter water from the cistern? Don't you want to buy nicer clothing, a better knife, a large tent with carpets and pillows, a more comfortable saddle for your camel, a few other camels to follow behind you carrying fresh water, breads, fruits?"

"That sounds wonderful, especially a softer saddle, but if I had two talents of gold, I couldn't be happy spending it as you said. All of those things make me feel heavy, like a slave chained to my belongings, sentencing me to drag them about, so much luggage and care and extra work. I couldn't feel free to do as I pleased. It might require me to turn my energies from our great adventure to care for too many belongings, to see that thieves didn't steal or soil them, and watch to see them packed properly each day and night, that they did not show wear. Oh my heavens, I don't like that idea. That's too much work for my vanity. I can be content with what I have."

"Then you know the wealth of the first scroll," Zafir said. "You keep your two gold talents and use them to make more. That's wise. Managing your treasure is what the wise learn to do, to have sufficient for your needs. Consuming your treasure is what the fool does. That's why self governance is a virtue of wealth—the first of the seven. And the most important."

"Dear Bassam, we ate our first squash tonight. I sat by Faris. He showed me how to make the squash tasty with salt and a spice. He won't tell me about the spice, it is a secret he says. He is such a tease. He always teases. A large caravan of 370 camels came to Rekeem two days ago. It was more kin of Zafir, so that makes them kin to me. I met cousins of uncles and nieces of aunts, but no one I had ever met before. They said I look just like my mother. They are traveling south, they will go to Saba' and see her. I sent with them a long letter to mother. I hope she is well, I have not heard anything since you left. —Rasha"

BASSAM

The final two weeks of travel into the oasis of Mouru passed with hot, enduring days through the worst desolated barrenness I've ever seen. In comparison to the drudgery of the west, the regions of the black-sand desert stood apart as land where no man was ever meant to be.

The place was marked on Ammar's map as the great Garagum Desert. It stretched both north and south as far as a caravan could travel, and was a place of windy passes among rolling mountains and mounds of weather-washed sands and rock.

White crusty crystals atop washed soils created salt pads oozing to the surface. The dried patches crumbled to dust wherever we stepped. On either side of the great valleys there rose blackish foothills at the base of the mountain ranges that heaped upon one another like giant cattle crowding shoulder to shoulder. Each slope was etched with the deep eroded furrows from ancient floods.

Upon this barren waste the sun beat down hard—relentless with his anger, like an oven.

No growing thing dared root itself in the parched soil. Baked death encrusted all the land. Lifeless soils like burned crust on bread was delicate to the eye but crumbled at the lightest touch. It was no place for man or beast. Had we not carried the right supplies, I saw no way that cisterns and wells could be dug into this earthly waste. The drawn-out days through this region were made more difficult for their harsh emptiness.

Each day I spent time counting the long hours. Step after step, plodding along at 200 stadia a day, crossing broad, gravel-strewn washes and crumbly crystalline soils, leached salty rivulets—the scenery never changing.

It was with great relief, then, that one morning, we noticed the air beginning to freshen with subtle and faint perfumes of life. The morning breeze brought earthy smells of growing things—living things, and *green*, just beyond view, just over the next rise.

We quickened our pace to crest a small rounded hill. Reaching the top we discovered we had came within the outskirts and settlements of that delightful garden land of Mouru.

I loved the scene. Here must be the world as God intended it—green valleys, animals pasturing, curious villagers standing at the roadside watching, kind gestures to trade beckoned by herders and men of the fields, children, women with their shawls.

The life that water brings began to emerge from the bleak of desert waste. *At last*, I sighed, *there was life in this part of the world.*

Our caravan passed near a narrow rushing river that followed us to town. Occasional huts lined its banks, and melted snow flowed from a hundred peaks to the green valleys beyond.

I could smell the sweet of newly cut grasses, wild flowers, and the raw life of herding cattle, sheep, goats and penned animals.

We continued to the lowlands where homes and their small, tidy farms had been standing for centuries, at least.

Curious children and barking dogs hurried to the dirt road to greet us and beg, or just gawk. The familiar scenes of the young and the curious reminded me of Rekeem and its friendly warmth that was always in the full bloom with life and living.

We settled on Mouru's southern side near the banks of the river. There was plenty of grazing green spread out like wild grassy blankets draped lightly over the hillsides and plains near by. It would be a three-day stay, and this time I chose a camping place near Zafir's great tent. I didn't mind any longer the intense security of the watch—for once I welcomed their attention.

MODU

The boundary construction of Mouru was a short walk from our camp. Its walls of white baked bricks and dwellings stretched across the palm-shaded settlements for half a day's ride—a barrier to invasion and a monument to prosperity.

Fawzi was already setting camp when I arrived.

"This is where you begin to feel a new part of the world," he said. "Just don't get yourself kidnapped again, fish bait."

I smiled and unbundled my supplies. "I see real opportunity here, maybe I'll sell you to the Huns."

"Watch your threats, camel cud, or I'll have a hard time explaining to Zafir my newly acquired bag of gold."

We busied ourselves with the camels and took inventory.

"What is this place?" I asked. "It's beautiful, but in the middle of nowhere."

"Mouru sits perfectly centered in the middle of many roads," Fawzi said.

"What roads?" I asked.

"The sea trade comes here from the west delivering their copper and brass to the caravans headed farther east. And from the south, the trade from the Indus people deliver their cottons and ivory the other way. And those coming from Chang'an travel through here to send their silk threads and porcelains and jade to buyers west."

"And we bring the frankincense and gold ... So, does Zafir do much trading here?"

"No, this is where he links with one of his eastern friends for escort," Fawzi said.

"Escort?"

"Oh yes, we're out of our element around here," Fawzi said. "Too many warring tribes, robbers, thieves. Zafir has many friends who join us for the trip to Fergana. And—speaking of friends, look—here they come now."

I looked up to see Zafir with a group of a half-dozen men headed toward me and Fawzi. The men wore a strange dress of beautiful silk robes of blue and black, with swords girt about the stomachs with wide leather belts at least a palm wide.

"Fawzi," I hushed. "Look."

"Be nice, dung face."

"Bassam!" Zafir called, waving his arm in greeting as he approached with his guests.

Fawzi whispered under his breath, "He likes you better than me."

"I know."

"Bassam, I want you to meet my dear friend, Modu ("Mow-dew")," Zafir said.

Modu wore a brilliant white turban tightly wound against his head. The smooth skin of his paled face bore no beard or stubble, and his eyes smiled with the slender of the orient. His long robe of royal blue silk was embroidered with purple flowers on long green stems, and slender stalks of green and blue that showed different hues in the changing light. It was trimmed in beautifully intricate patterns of red and black that hinted of tribal tradition and legacy. His pointed-toed boots of soft leather looked comfortable and durable. And the billowy cotton of a finely woven shirt blossomed with brilliant white from the open front of his robe.

Modu took a step forward and bowed, a look of new friendship was pleasantly set on his whole countenance. I returned the gesture and smiled, "Hello!"

"Modu," Zafir continued. "This is Bassam, my young apprentice of whom I have spoken."

"Bassam, I am Modu," he said in an accent of broken words. "I'm honored to meet the young prince of the house of Zafir. These are my personal guard," he said, sweeping his hand. "You may count them your trusted friends."

I looked each man in the eye, and that same distrusting and guarded alertness common to Al Murrah was returned.

The sword hanging at each man's front was different, very different, in fact, than those of Al Murrah. The blades were wide and curved, and somewhat shorter. No doubt perfect for close battle, but not as effective as the extended long sword like Suoud's. The sword of Al Murrah was suited for the western desert battles when a man had to reach across a camel to strike a fleshy target before the enemy could come close.

"Modu is an old friend," Zafir continued. "He is Xiongnu ("zhung-new"), travelers of the far eastern deserts and mountains. He and his men will accompany us to Fergana Valley and then beyond to Chang'an. He comes from a family of great warriors, Bassam. You may learn much from him."

"I'd love to learn," I said. "Thank you, Modu."

The chieftain put a hand to the hilt of his sword with a friendly smile. Zafir invited the friends into his tent, leaving me standing alone to watch them file in. Four of Modu's guards remained outside, taking up positions around the tent for a full view of protection.

After the draping closed, I turned to Fawzi. "I've never seen clothing like that," I said. "Do all such Xiongnu dress like that?"

"It's their formal attire, my young and naive friend," Fawzi said. "For the trail they will put on their cottons and heavy tweed, not much different from ours. And I do like those boots."

"Me too," I said. "I wonder if I could buy a pair ...."

NAJEEB'S

At evening time of the first day, Malik, Fawzi and I headed toward a crowded diner called *Najeeb's*, a busy eatery they told me was their favorite place to eat.

It was a long brick building with timbers and thatch for the roof. The entrance was an arched-stone doorway that led into a large ornate dining hall with hanging lamps that were lit. Many of the tables were already filled with an odd-looking collection of some 80 or so foreigners. Each of them was dressed after the manner of his own country, and were quietly talking in strange tongues. The customers were crowded all the way across the width of the room to the yellowed plaster walls that carried murals of faded images of seascapes and horses. The back of the room opened to a patio with stone pavers and more tables and lamps. Beneath the yellow light the diner was noisy, busy, and glowed with a friendly feel of spacious expanse within cozy walls.

The hubbub was sprinkled with laughter, discussion, calculating or dealing. The servers carried trays of meats and rice, fruits and salads, breads and fishes. The smells of new and exotic foods, the foreign dress like none I had ever seen, and each man carrying a sword of a different make, a different nation—all mingling in soft prattle, was just delicious to watch. Pipe and strings made quiet music that settled my nerves. My escort of eight armed Al Murrah sat at two tables adjacent to me. Just watching them made me nervous. The whole time they sat there scanning for danger, even as they ate.

"Malik, tell me something," I said, leaning over to lower my voice. "Doesn't Al Murrah ever relax? Look at them, they can't sit still—even when they eat they're looking around like the lion that has spotted his prey."

"That's no extra work for them," Malik said. "That's their job, to watch. And yes, even when they eat. You would watch too if the lives in your care were yours only to protect."

"It's *nervous*, it makes me nervous," I said.

Malik smiled. "And that's a good nervous," he said.

The conversation drifted back to Fawzi and Malik who picked up from the interruption.

It didn't take long for my attention to drift into daydreaming and then boredom. I could stand it no longer and had to excuse myself.

"I need to walk. I'll stay close, don't worry."

And just like that, just as I stood, Al Murrah locked eyes on me and stopped chewing. I couldn't help but notice and became very self conscious. I stretched my legs and brushed a few bread crumbs from my shirt. Stealing a glance, I saw that three of them still watched, not twitching a muscle, the food locked in their mouths—staring alert with caution.

I turned toward the patio and felt their eyes glued to my back as I sauntered outdoors. *This is just a little bit strange*, I thought. *I could go crazy with a job like that.*

Through the portico and down the steps, other patrons sat at tables, quietly drinking coffees and dipping their rice bowls. That's where I spotted the serving girl who was delivering a tray of breads to a table.

The girl was about my same age, and she had the most beautiful oval eyes, so young and bright. She was nearly the stature of a grown woman. She smiled when she saw that I was watching from behind the columns, and my heart climbed into my throat. I quickly turned to escape the awkward exposure with a dozen steps towards some privacy beyond the yellow glow of the lamps. I found some empty tables and stools and a view of the sleeping city beyond. Searching for my usual bearings, I looked up and noticed the night sky was cloudless—with shimmering stars above.

Just then a sweet, young voice asked, "May I get you a tea?"

Turning around, there she stood at the top step, an empty tray tucked beneath an arm, her beautiful long black hair framing a pleasant but quizzical look on her face.

"May I get you a tea?" she repeated.

"A tea would be nice," I said. "May I, um, may I take it here, uh, right here at this bench?" I stammered.

"Yes, I'll be right back." And she turned toward the kitchen near the entrance on the far side of the diner.

I couldn't believe it. I was actually nervous. I checked the bench to make sure it wouldn't collapse beneath me when she returned, and saw that it was far enough away from shadows yet close enough to be within eyesight of Al Murrah, and that my hair wasn't poking out funny, and no food was on my face.

When she returned, a small porcelain cup of gentle manufacture clinked against a saucer.

"This glass work is beautiful," I said as she placed it on my table.

"These are from Chang'an," she said. "We received them some time ago, as a gift from some traders passing through." She poured the hot tea and set a small cake at the side.

"Chang'an?" I asked. "That's the same place we're traveling to. This must be costly."

"No, not around here," she said. "We exchange with the caravans—food for plates, drink for cups. It comes cheaply enough. Most of what you see here was bartered for, or a gift. Many nice things. So, tell me, from where do you come?"

I felt a blush growing inside. I hadn't had much experience actually engaging in conversation with girls for a very long time. In fact, none at all in recent times unless these hundred days with my bakra would count for something.

"I'm traveling with Abdali-ud-din," I said. "I live in Rekeem, near the eastern sea."

"I know of Rekeem," she said. "You bring the incense, right?"

"Yes, frankincense. We'll fetch a good price for it," I said. "If I had some I would give it to you, uh, um, well, I would give it to you right now." *Oh my heavens.* I started to blush again, tripping over my words. *What is this confusion*?

The girl laughed. "I would like some," she said. "So, I'm Kalila," she said, introducing herself. "My father and my uncle run this diner."

"I'm Bassam, and I'm pleased to meet you."

"So ... do you not like our tea?" Kalila asked, smiling.

"Oh! The tea! Yes," I said, taking a sip, finally. "The tea, it's a very good tea, you make an excellent tea, the finest tea, a very good tea."

Kalila smiled again, giggling at my discomfort. "I'll bring you more if you would like."

"Oh yes, thank you," I said.

The girl turned away and I sat back on the bench with an audible sigh, a rush of relief washing through me. *Girls*, I grumbled, *what am I supposed to do next? What if she wants to talk to me? I'll ask Fawzi, he knows everything.*

An hour later, the dining and visiting was done. Malik, Fawzi and I walked the dirt path back to camp. Al Murrah was at the lead and followed behind, torches lighting the way, their hands on swords, their suspicions alert.

Malik turned to me, "So, you enjoyed your tea back there, eh?" Fawzi looked away, smiling.

"Yes," I said. "It was good tea."

"And did you like the cup?" Malik said.

"Yes, fine workmanship for a cup."

"You know they get all sorts of goods here in Mouru, they barter for them."

"So I gathered."

"And did anything else seem interesting?" Malik asked.

"Well, the diner, it was nice too."

Malik and Fawzi could stand the game no longer and they broke into a laugh and slapped me hard on the back. “It’s all right, Bassam! Her name is Kalila,” Malik chuckled. “We’ve known her these many years since she was a child, she’s like our little sister, and she’s grown into a beautiful young woman, don’t you think?”

“I guess so,” I stammered, “I didn’t notice.”

The men laughed again.

“Don’t worry about her flirting with you, camel face,” Fawzi said. “She’s waiting on her fiance’. He’s on a caravan trek, just as you are, and when he returns, her father has arranged a marriage.”

A rush of relief suddenly washed over me.

“Of course, that is, unless,” Fawzi drawled, “unless she could be won by another, a distant traveler, for example, a dashing swordsman or such—if he was determined for it.”

Malik learned forward, his arm on my shoulder, and spoke around me to Fawzi walking on the other side. “It has been awhile since we left home, no?”

“Oh yes,” Fawzi said. “More than three months, maybe four, and that’s not a long time.”

“No, not long at all,” Malik said.

“Especially for old men,” Fawzi said.

“Yes, especially,” Malik echoed.

“Or young ladies,” Fawzi mused.

“Or young ladies,” Malik grinned, “—young ladies hard of hearing, wasn’t that your trouble back home, young Bassam?”

My face felt beet-red and burning hot. *Girls*, I thought. *They are so much work*.

THE DINER GIRL

On day two at Mouru, Zafir began integrating his camel caravan with Modu’s armed guard of Xiongnu warriors.

The 200 warriors arrived early that morning, dressed in full regalia, riding their lightly armored horses in all of their dress and formality.

They sat tall in their saddles, a fierce look of stern determination chiseled into each Oriental face, a leathered hand tightly gripping the reins, their other hands holding the hilt of their sheathed swords.

The ceremonious parade was impressive and stirred feelings of respect among all of Zafir's men. Malik told me this association was very old, going back dozens of decades—and the annual meeting I was witnessing wasn't between strangers, but between dear friends, the sons and grandsons of dear friends, faithfully meeting at this very place at this very time, every year.

The groups flowed through each other, many men smiling in acknowledgement of others, clasping hands, stepping off horses to embrace, greet and laugh.

"Tell me something, Fawzi," I asked as we watched the glad welcome. "Why does Zafir buy this escort? Are not the 400 swords and Al Murrah *swords* enough?"

"It's more than swords," Fawzi said. "Zafir needs to make a showing. He needs to make an impression, to be a large band, a train of great influence, a force to be dealt with. When we meet up to trade, everyone will know that Abdali-ud-din has arrived with wealth—wealth so precious it demands such a guard."

"So, it's mostly for show?" I asked.

"Mostly for show. Protection, yes, certainly. But it's to impress the buyers. A band of robbers sells their dirty goods in the corners and alleys of the villages, looking for the quick profit from stolen lucre," Fawzi said. "Zafir is honest but he also knows when he must make an appearance of prosperity and strength. He knows how to make an appearance in a village, to win them by fear or by respect. He works the hearts of the sheiks and their scribes in these parts like the pieces on a game board."

I was amazed that two wandering groups could intersect at this distant place with such precision and timing. "So they knew we should be here this very day?"

"This escort was with us a year ago, and every year for decades before that," Fawzi said. "We meet here during this week, give a day or two either way, each and every year."

"And if they don't show?"

"The bargain is to send a message by fast horseman, or to wait ten days. Modu has never failed us, and we have never waited."

I watched Modu's men with delight and respect. They looked splendid, everyone of them—prancing about their parts as warriors, parading their prowess among the men of Zafir's caravan.

Their dress was well suited for the mountainous terrain and this cooler climate. The Xiongnu packed light, bringing only saddle bags and a little food and water. They wore heavy-weave pants and animal hair coats with leather guards across the shoulders—protection against a glancing blow from a sword. Their heavy cotton-weave shirts were dyed red or black, and they carried a leather helmet hanging off their saddle bags. And each had that same soft leather boot as Modu's.

Where do I buy a pair of those? I wondered.

The Xiongnu sword was ornate. It was worn across the front of a man. The sheath was embellished with pieces of broken colored glass, brandings and other markings that honored their many battles. Bits of metal were pounded at the corners to secure the seams.

Such sheaths were much fancier than Al Murrah's, perhaps too much so. I wondered if such bravado in their workmanship could match their courage in the heat of battle—a bravery that Al Murrah had already proven in regions much more hostile than these.

On the evening of day two, Fawzi and Malik invited me to join them for another visit to Najeeb's for dinner.

"They're serving white fish tonight," Fawzi said, "an excellent dish not to be missed, will you join us?" I could read in their eyes some form of conspiracy, but couldn't discern what it was. I didn't resist and joined them.

This time we were met right at the entrance by a bright middle-aged man with a trimmed black beard who sported a broad robe with half sleeves. He welcomed us warmly.

"Greetings to you again, my friends," he said. "I'm thinking you're here for the white fish tonight!"

Malik returned the greeting and pointed at Bassam. "Najeeb, I want you to meet our young friend, Bassam."

"Ah ha, young prince Bassam, I have heard of you," Najeeb said. "You're the avenger of Suoud, are you not?"

I felt the blood start to rise in my cheeks. "Thank you sir, I am he," I said softly.

He grabbed my hand and clasped it firmly in formal greeting. "I knew Suoud. He was a great friend of mine. He came here for many years. I was saddened when Zafir told me of him, but I'm pleased to hear of your escape from his killer, and avenging the death of our friend."

"Well, it wasn't quite like ...."

He turned me about and took my arm. "Then you must dine with me and my friends tonight," Najeeb interrupted. "And you must meet my daughter."

Oh, great.

"She must be about your age," Najeeb said, and then called her to the front. "Kalila! Come, I want you to meet the avenger of Suoud, a new friend of mine."

Kalila emerged from the kitchen, pulling back the drape that hung in the doorway, brushed at her hair and wiped her hands with a towel.

"Coming, father," she said without looking up, and almost bumped right into me.

"Oh!" was all she could say, stopping abruptly and looking up at me.

"Kalila," Najeeb said, "meet the brave warrior who found and slew the monster who took from us our Suoud. This is the valiant fighter who was kidnapped by traitors, tortured, punished, and dragged for a week through the worst deserts ever, and with clever scheming won his escape to hide and avenge the blood of Suoud, the hero about whom Zafir was speaking yesterday."

Kalila looked at the group, wondering who this great warrior was, and searched the face of Malik, and then Fawzi, and then each of Al Murrah who stood smiling at her.

"Well?" she asked.

"Him!" Najeeb said, pointing. "Him, Bassam! He's our honored guest this evening. He will sit with me, and you go tell mother to prepare something special so we may honor him this night!"

Kalila looked up at me, her jaw dropped, dumbfounded at this nervous young man who stood a good four palms taller than she. The puzzle on her face shouted loud and clear that she couldn't believe it was *me*, the same one who was so clumsy and bashful the night before.

"You?" she said in astonishment.

I just nodded, the throbbing of embarrassment pulsing near boiling point in my throat.

Kalila looked about suddenly, patted her cheek a moment and then took her breath.

"Well," she said. "I'll tell mother," and turning, went back into the kitchen, stealing another glance at me as I watched her leave. I tried to shrug a smile, but she just glared—and then smiled.

I looked over at Malik and Fawzi. They were chewing their smiles into submission—they could hardly wait to begin the teasing. With my reaction around this pretty, young girl, I was quite positive I had earned from them weeks if not months of torment that I'd *never hear the end of.*

"So, Najeeb, lead the way," Malik said. "Your wife is easily the finest cook this side of Alexandria! Let's see if this white fish can taste better than her last dish, a feat that I can't imagine possible, but still, let's try!"

Before the delicious courses had finished, Zafir and Modu arrived with another delegation of guards—Xiongnu warriors who joined Al Murrah, and more room was made to seat everyone at tables pushed together. In short order a regular party of reminiscing was well underway.

"Now Modu, listen to me, I must tell you about our friend Najeeb," Zafir said. "When we first came here to this diner ... when was that, Najeeb? Some 21 or 22 years has it been?"

"Twenty-seven years, old friend!" Modu said.

"That many? Why the years, they just race by," Zafir said. "When we first came here, Najeeb was sure you had taken me captive, you and your broad swords."

"You looked much too stern in those days, Modu," Najeeb said. "I might have fled for the hills when I saw that sword of yours! I wasn't fast enough to escape my wife, I would have fared worse running from the tip of your sword!"

The men talked and laughed for another long while, leaving me to just listen and enjoy. And then Modu interrupted and leaned over to me and lowered his voice.

"Bassam, I think you're being impolite."

"What?"

"Yes, Kalila left two cups of tea on that back table. I think she wants to talk. You're being rude ignoring her."

"I didn't ask to talk to her," I whispered. "I don't want to talk to her. I think she's ... well, I think she likes me."

"That's not the point. She wants to talk to someone her own age. Go ahead, brighten her day, go spend a few minutes. You'll be okay, we'll keep an eye on her, if anything happens, I have my guard to protect you," he said stone-faced.

I audibly sighed and stood up. This trick had been played on me before.

As I made my way to the patio, I felt 40 sets of eyes following me, and knew exactly what each man was thinking. My worry was, what was *she* thinking?

"Do you mind if I ask you something?" she said.

"Um, sure, no problem," I told her.

For the next many minutes, we began talking about my kidnapping, the death of Suoud, my meeting Moluck, and the very private experience I had in the alley of As-Samawah.

"And you didn't know the coin was in your own coat?" she asked.

"No, not at all. It was a prayer and it was an answer. It saved my life," I said.

"It bought you passage and it bought you a knife, both to save a life," she said.

"That was their plan, or at least Amin's plan. What none of us knew was that Moluck had been hunting for me in the village, looking and hiding in places for probably an hour at least. Moluck didn't think I would be among the shops. It caught him off guard when he found me."

"And so you killed him, you killed the murderer of Suoud …."

"I didn't know who he was," I said. "I knew he had sworn an oath to kill me, but not until he raised his sword to commit the deed did I truly believe it was my life or his."

"Such a man should not be allowed to live," Kalila said.

"There are more such men. Another man I knew is part of that conspiracy, his name is Habib. He is Al Murrah but he betrayed his oath to Zafir. And now he puts his specialized skills in the service of darkness and dishonor. I don't understand him."

"And he is still out there somewhere?"

"Somewhere."

Loud laughter erupted in the dining hall as Malik reminded Modu of a robber who acted so bravely in the middle of three Xiongnu warriors, and pretended he was Modu's close cousin.

"You may have such an ugly in your family," Modu laughed, pointing at Malik, "but all my children, they're handsome, they're intelligent, they're swift and clever, indeed, one would say each of them bears a suspiciously striking resemblance to *Zafir*!" he said, pointing a scornful finger. And huge gales of laughter radiated out into the night like a warm fire.

Catching her attention again, I asked, "So, will you always be here, serving the guests at Najeeb's?"

"I hope not," she said. "My mother tries hard to teach me her cooking skills, but that's for later—after I marry. My dream is traveling the great caravans."

"*You*? You like to travel?"

"Of course, oh *yes*!" she said. "I don't like being stuck here, staying put in one place. They say a house is just a grave for the living."

"So I've heard," I said. "Where have you traveled?"

"I've seen enough in these parts. I want to go west, to *your* homelands, over the great sand deserts to the sea," she said. "I want to sail the Nilus and stand between the paws of the great sphinx. I want to climb the marble slopes of the pyramids."

"The west? Why not the east? There is so much there …."

"I've been to the east," she said. "Chang'an, the ocean, south to the great mountains, the Indus and their blue water, I've seen enough."

"You? Really?" I was actually surprised at this.

"Yes, certainly I have! And you're surprised? A girl can't ride the caravan?"

I smiled and apologized. "What I meant was—the families of the Abdali-ud-din, the wives and the daughters, they travel between places that are close to the main roads, in mahmils, under heavy guard. Always. When it's safe, and …."

"But that's when it's known that they're family," Kalila laughed.

"You mean you *stowed away* on a caravan?" I asked.

"I wanted to learn," she said. "Every year, all year, long columns of camels and horses pass through our village with sacks and pouches of mysterious works of art and foods and gems. I wanted to see for myself those lands where those treasures were discovered."

"So you stowed away on a caravan? Well—how did you—I mean didn't they ..."

Kalila laughed and blushed. "I was young, then. They thought I was a boy, a son of a steward. It didn't bother me."

"I don't see how ... well, I mean you're so very ... uh..." I was caught.

"Yes?" she asked.

"What I meant is how could you take such a trip? Did you think the caravan might not return? In fact, most caravans don't follow the same path back home, it's not profitable. We won't pass through here again. We'll be far south, past those great mountains among the Indus people."

"It was my uncle's caravan," she said. "I knew we would return."

"Did you tell your uncle you had joined him?"

"After a few weeks, two or three, yes, I told him. But it wasn't until after a terrible sandstorm. I think we were about a week outside of Fergana Valley. I was nearly lost with a dozen others who stopped for shelter. Two days later we caught up with my uncle at a wadi—we found them resting and eating. I was so relieved to find him that I ran to my uncle and cried."

"Was he angry with you?"

"Oh yes, very angry," she said. "He told me that if we had not been so far from home, he would have sent me back with escorts—at two-day speed!"

"How far did you travel?"

"All the way to the Gobi Desert, the villages there. But we didn't make it to Chang'an on that trip. And when I returned home, it had been two months."

"Your parents must have been sick with worry."

"No, not really, and that was the trick on me. Uncle knew from the start that I was with him and he talked it over with my parents that very morning as we departed."

"Ha! Then they wanted to teach you a lesson or something?"

"Yes, a lesson," she said. "I was a difficult child and created too much mischief. Mother and father worried over me and wondered what to do with their wandering young girl. When they learned about the trip, they decided the hardships would be good for me—and it was. They made it easy for me to pack and run away. My uncle knew it all along. It was a wonderful trip."

I couldn't help but smile at her escape. I knew those crowded feelings, but running away on a *caravan*? "Perhaps you'll join us on one of our trips some time," I said.

"Perhaps."

The traffic of clients into the diner had quieted, and the warmly lit café was almost deserted except for the central tables where the guards listened as Zafir, Najeeb and Modu continued reminiscing about years gone past and tales of travels too risky to leave unsaid.

The pause in our conversation grew long and I stirred uncomfortably. I stole another glance at Kalila. She was pleasant to look upon.

"So, do you still travel? I mean, with your uncle?"

The girl laughed. "Travel? I go out once a year with him," she said. "We'll be leaving here in a week or two for Kashgar and on to Lhara. I heard Uncle planning something with Zafir, I guess it was the same, I will have to ask."

"Lhara? Towards the mountains?"

"They are magnificent, Bassam! It's a long trip, I've made it twice before. There's snow in the higher lands—everywhere snow, and it's *cold.* We trade our camels for donkeys or yaks—they're the best, and other animals—sometimes by wagon. But Lhara is warm enough this time of year."

"And what will you trade?"

"Uncle has a large order for cotton or textiles, I'm not sure what, but it will be a larger than the usual—maybe a hundred camels."

"Then you'll go ... I suppose follow the routes south while Zafir takes us north."

"Yes."

"And return back here?"

"This is my home. At least for now—but like I said ....."

"For now?"

"I love to travel, Bassam!" she said, sweeping her delicate hand through the air as if to paint a picture of the world. "Those great mountains, they can't be crossed you know."

"So I've heard."

"They're a wall—a mighty fortress of snow that climbs right to the sky. They call it the top of the world. We can't go through them so we must go around."

"That's something I want to do one day, and trade with the people, perhaps …."

"Then you must join us," Kalila said, smiling with invitation.

"That would be a wonderful trip."

"One day you will return to Mouru and I will point the way," Kalila smiled. "And you will be our guest."

"I want to see the mysteries there, and snow." I glanced up to catch her looking directly at me. Her beautiful oval eyes smiled with a youthful brightness that sparked for adventure. I suddenly noticed the slender smoothness of her cheeks and nose, her soft gentle lips relaxed part way through a breath, a tangle of shining black hair framing a face that was young and innocent, beckoning but casually guarded, a mystery of feminine allure that suddenly showed in the flickering warmth of the oil lamps.

For a few short seconds she allowed me to look but hid her thoughts, wondering if the brief exchange would betray other things not spoken. I caught myself, my jaw hanging slack and closed my mouth as a blush erupted again. The unspoken uncoiled fast enough until the tension became too much. Kalila suddenly stood.

"Well, thank you Bassam, now I must tend to the tables," she said, picking up her tray and stealing another glance at me. I sat straight, almost puzzled, almost wishing, and said nothing as she turned to walk away.

"My friends are jealous of my freedoms," I finally said.

"A short rein, is it?" she asked, stopping to turn.

"Yes, they keep a short rein, it's all silly, really."

"Silly?" she said. "The avenger of Suoud is silly? Ha!" and she turned abruptly, letting her long black hair swish from one shoulder to the other, and carried her tray to the center dining room where she began plucking empty platters from the tables. I tried not to watch.

That night, the last night in Mouru, I collected my thoughts and got my priorities straight by writing them.

"Day 168—Dear Rasha, I befriended the daughter of Najeeb here in Mouru. She is Kalila. We talked for a while about her life and adventures. She wants to visit Egypt. She is promised to someone who is traveling as we are. I must make this time pass quickly. I keep your veil with me always. I sometimes wish you could be here with me and see these magical places.—Bassam"

"Dear Bassam, I busy myself helping your mother. I am learning so much, you will be surprised. I love your mother and father, they are as parents to me. I care for them and they care for me as their own daughter. I visited Faris at his parent's home. They are a very nice family, five children with twins. They have a dog and a large home with many rooms. His father invited me to dinner some time soon. His family has invited

me to join them on a short trek south. They have relatives and a farm. Dalal isn't sure I should go. Kateb tells me to have a good time. What do you say?—Rasha"

ب هبعه 51 محبوب

THE ANCIENT ROUTE

It was still dark when I climbed into the saddle and ordered my bakra to the path eastward. I fell in place among the hundreds of other camels and horses. By the time the last star faded, Mouru was already a distant shadow. The grasses on either side of the road slumped beneath a heavy sheen of morning dew. I felt a cool current in the air. The seasons were on us again.

In a strange way, the steady rhythm of my bakra's gait and the predictable grunts and growls made for a comfortable and familiar start to each day. Every camel had its own voice and personality, even a smell that the rider grows accustomed to. For me, my bakra had become my dearest friend in these strange places, a reminder of home, who faithfully came alive each morning I took saddle and ordered her forward. It reminded me that even in this faraway place where the passing panorama of new sights and smells changed so quickly, for just some cud and an ear scratch my bakra remained a faithful part of home who I could count on, a friend to share in the newness of the adventure.

With that I leaned forward and scratched behind her ears. "Some of the men have traded out their bakras for the horse," I told her. "Don't you worry, there will be no strange camel pen for you."

The trip east to Fergana was well underway—it was our next planned stop. But still, I had Kalila on my mind—and last evening, at Najeeb's.

"Once a year, maybe two years," I said to myself. "It's difficult to keep friendships for the men of a caravan."

"What are you mumbling to yourself?" Fawzi asked, pulling his animal next to mine.

"Only that I made friends here," I said, "... and coming back again one or two years from now—it seems safer to not make friends at all," I said.

"When I settle down, I want to bring my Rasha—that is, I mean, bring my family to these places, safely, to see all that we have seen, the foods we've tasted, and the beautiful land and sights we've traveled through, and enjoy these wonderful adventures."

"It's not as bad as it seems right now," Fawzi said. "The time slips by faster when you work on growing instead of waiting. I know, I've been there."

"Really?"

"Yes, but in the opposite way. I left my bride of six years and two young boys waiting for me," Fawzi said. "This trip—this two year trip is a long time to be gone and my boys will be growing without their father—and my wife is raising them by herself."

"Why make the trip, then?"

"Because it pays enough to carry us for another seven or eight years, maybe longer. It's that way for many of us. Our wives find each other, they share the burden of loneliness and difficulty, and help one another, and it seems to work for everyone."

"Two boys?" I asked with a big smile.

"Oh yes!" Fawzi smiled back. "And they're *just* like me."

* * *

The briny soil that swept by at a camel's pace was no longer loose as before. It was compacted—heavy with the footfalls of caravans from untold centuries past. Only a rare rainfall could have washed the soil in such fashion, leaving in patches nothing but gravely sand, pebbles and a few stones to bother my bakra's steady plod.

The ancient roads were all this way, and it was simple to separate them from other roads that scattered toward the east and west. Each was a witness to magnificent fortunes of silk, spice and commodities that were forever on the move—like the wind, carrying things from here to there. And when the seasons changed, the travelers returned, stronger because of the trek and the labors it required.

Sitting tall, I looked all about me—and smiled.

The rolling hills pointed us toward our intended destination as clearly as the lines on Ammar's maps. The riders ahead of me hardly worked their animals to negotiate the direction. The terrain naturally funneled the traffic into the paths of least resistance, winding through crest and crevice into patches of pleasant, flowing meadows and over long stretches of salty marshes.

It was the fourth day after Mouru when the rolling hills flanking our left finally evaporated into plains of a broad and flat desert. It scampered far from us, out so very far—horizon to horizon, and without hills or mountains to disrupt—so flat it revealed the curve of the earth.

I could see in the far distance the peaks of tired mountains, though none high enough to snag any clouds with their rounded summits. The lush valleys of the Fergana lay beyond, and from Ammar's reckoning, we had more than four weeks yet to ride. The path to Fergana lay through the passes of that distant range.

Unlike the deserts near home, the roads through these realms were better marked with the abandoned litter of old camps—half-buried skeletal remains of collapsed horses or camels, tufts of shredded clothing clinging to the brittle stubs of chewed-down greenery, patches of broken pottery scattered, and the blackened stains of cook-fires.

Such tell-tale signs of human passage conjured in my imagination the stream of adventures that must have accompanied the thousands of camel trains passing along those routes. And what wealth had crossed the way for so many reasons.

"Bassam!" Fawzi called out, steering his horse over by me.

I looked up, surprised—"Hey ... where's your bakra?"

"This is horse country, *camel cud*—you're always behind the latest fashions, Bassam. But never mind. You must meet my old friend Tou."

Trotting up on a handsome black Arabian horse was a Xiongnu warrior. I had seen him with Modu the other day.

His face was smooth and square, a tense smile to match his eyes. He was about the age of Fawzi, and was dressed in a thickly woven shirt with a tight blanket of white yak hair yarn looped diagonally across his chest. His leather cap had a white wool trim and his broad-blade sword hung at his middle. There was a bow and quiver of arrows tied to the saddle, with a skin of water.

"Greetings to you, friend," Tou said, tipping his head toward me. "Fawzi has told me many things about you."

"I hope it was all true!" I said.

Tou smiled. "He tells me you're his young student, no?"

"Student, yes," I said, frowning at the idea I was still *young*.

"This is your chance, Bassam," Fawzi said. "Zafir said learn the way of Al Murrah. Xiongnu is no different, they will teach you the bow and arrow." And pointing to Tou, "Here's your teacher."

"I'd like that," I said. "But why doesn't Al Murrah carry the bow and arrow?"

"Because we have Tou!" Fawzi said.

Tou nodded and they both grinned at me.

"But not before we had reached Mouru! Why not?"

"In your great deserts," Tou volunteered, "the bow and arrow are never so strong as the sword of Al Murrah and a swift war camel."

"Exactly," Fawzi said. "We've got bows but they're better used when an enemy is confined to close quarters. And then Al Murrah is effective."

"So, where are they, where do you keep them?"

"Among the baggage, donkey dung—never far from us," Fawzi said. "We string them for the mountain passes. Suoud had one, I'll show you later and let you try its draw. Did Zafir say you could use that, too?"

"I didn't ask."

"It's probably too strong for you," Fawzi said. "It's a man's bow, and you, Bassam, will need the help of a girl to pull its string. Perhaps you will shoot a lizard for your dinner."

"At 100 paces, and dare you to do the same!" I said.

"Two with one shot," Fawzi bragged, "a lizard for you, and one for your girl!"

I abandoned another insult, Tou was getting impatient.

Fawzi gestured to Tou. "Tell Bassam about this new bow that your chiefs have been working on."—

For centuries, the nomadic Xiongnu lived in the northern highlands of the Far East, scattered in clans claiming the high valleys where they could raise horses, oxen and sheep. Their smaller ranches raised camels and mules that they traded for labors among friendly families. The Xiongnu had no fixed homeland, and moved with their animals to greener pastures and fresher water as their circumstances changed.

As a youth, Tou and his boyhood friends mimicked at play their warrior fathers by riding sheep, and in pretend they used their homemade bow and arrows to shoot birds and squirrels. Although a sheep wouldn't obey as does a horse. Still, they played the part of the fighter and hunter. What little flesh could be picked from the tiny bones of their small game was cherished as the prize of conquest.

When Tou grew to manhood, his prowess with the bow brought down foxes and hares from a distance of 30 paces. As an adult he could finally employ his strength to bend the large bows and bring down full-sized game. The men of his clan wore the large skins and furs as tokens of their prowess and cunning.

The bow of the Xiongnu had improved over the centuries. War and trade with those of the far east had introduced new ideas into their weaponry, and Tou's clan was innovative.

In ancient times, their fathers used a single stick of wood, flexible, and gripped at its center. Such bows began as weak and inaccurate tools, good only for close-range fighting or hunting. In some lands, a flexible metal was developed that kept a strong spring longer than wood, but the cost was high for any one group, and was rarely found among the nomadic Xiongnu.

The bows of Tou's childhood showed the evolution of a technology of greater sophistication. The upper and lower limb were separate bands of wood, each curved of its own accord and joined at the grip. The bow nock where the string attached was strengthened with bone or antler to allow maximum tension without breaking through. Instead of one mighty spring to launch the arrow, the new design acted as two springs working together.

Tou's bow had antler pieces or rib bones for stability and strength in the draw. Strings made of animal sinew and tendons worked the best, but Tou's ancestors replaced these whenever possible with plant fibers of several varieties, carefully woven and treated. These proved superior to animal products because they could bear more weight and power on the pull without breaking, and they did not stretch in damp weather.

The arrows had not changed as much. As a boy, Tou helped gather shoots and suckers from certain trees, or reeds growing near the water, or animal bones. He watched as his father turned the shafts, shaving them with a knife until they measured straight. And then split one end to accept a pointed stone or shaped bone that was pinched in place with animal sinew. The back of the arrow was notched for the string. Tou remembered his father applying many kinds of tips—blunt for use when hunting small birds, or hooked for fishing. His father carried an assortment of arrows with different tips—small triangular stone or bone tips for use in war, larger points for larger game.

“Our people are horseback archers,” Tou said. “Our skill is in speed and accuracy, and many battles have fallen to our favor because of the bow.”

“How is it you can carry such a bow on horseback?” I asked. “Doesn’t it get all tangled in the reins, or...?”

“That’s the challenge I’ve come to show you both,” Tou said. And with that, he reached behind and produced a bow that we had never seen before. Its lower half was shorter than the upper half, and the limbs were deeply curved.

“Just as you said, Bassam,” Tou explained, “seated on our horses, we have little room to move side to side without the horse or saddle getting in the way. Before now, the Xiongnu had to hold their bows sideways to keep clear of the horse. But this shorter hang gives us the power of a large bow without the awkwardness of its size.”

Tou held his bow in front of him and pivoted side to side, demonstrating how he could hold his bow in drawn position and not be hampered by his horse’s neck or the saddle.

And then I spotted the strange addition of split bamboo layered into the bow’s limbs.

“You see the layering?” Tou asked.

“The bamboo—and, is that more bone?”

“We are still working on it,” Tou said. “Six, maybe seven other woods—layered, glued with animal glue, bones at the tips, wrapped in sinew—it makes for a powerful draw.”

I studied the design and saw advantages to the stiffness the new layers brought.

“But there’s more,” Tou said. “Forged tips for our arrows. Bronze is sharper. We make it in many shapes and sizes.”

Tou produced half a dozen arrows, each with a different head. “The larger the tip, the more heavy its flight. The arrow shaft must be stronger to support that weight, so these are for close combat or close hunting,” he said.

He handed a large-tipped arrow across to me to heft and test the point.

“How do these feathers attach?” I asked.

“We use glue made from animal hide. And we wrap thin strips of sinew.”

“So much work, and so many arrows lost,” I said.

“Yes, but these hooks on the points,” Tou pointed out, “hold the points inside so that we may pull the shaft out for use at another time, and the point stays inside to finish our work."

"If I'm hit with one," I asked, "it's made to stay and not pull out?"

"Better yet," Fawzi said, "we get it out of you by pushing it the rest of the way through."

I grimaced at the thought.

"And I'll be happy to push it for you, Bassam," Fawzi said. "Call for me any time."

I remembered the knife in my shoulder. In and out, damage done, leaving me with no strength. Carrying an arrow tip inside would do its work in a terribly painful, prolonged manner.

"When we stop, will you let me try?" I asked.

"If your teacher approves," Tou said.

"I approve," Fawzi replied. "If camel breath here will promise me not to shoot an arrow into his bakra ... or more likely, his foot."

After evening meals the practice began.

My first dozen arrows failed to hit anything worth mentioning, or missed the target altogether.

"You fetch my arrows," Tou laughed, "I'll show you what you are doing wrong, and we'll try it again."

As I grew more comfortable with the bow's powerful pull, I learned the value of an arm guard. My exposed forearm holding the bow's grip was rubbed raw from the repeated action of the string.

"Why do you think we wear these long sleeves?" Tou laughed, "To keep the insects from biting?"

I put on a covering with sleeves and resumed our practice.

"You learn the action of the arrow according to what tip it carries," Tou said. "The heavier tips are harder to push and the arrow will bend or wobble in flight," he said. "If you don't plan for that, your arrow will veer to the right every time."

How am I supposed to guess this? I drew a small-tipped arrow and adjusted my aim to account for the width of a man at the distance of 10 paces, and let the arrow fly. It struck with a swish-thud. I had hit the target dead center.

"What?" said Fawzi, turning in shocked surprise. "Bassam, your luck follows you everywhere, let me see you do that again."

I was all grins and mounted another arrow on the string. I drew back, aimed a width of a man to the left, and my second arrow dropped four finger-width's below the first. By this time, even Tou was impressed.

"Not bad for a beginner," he said. "We'll make you an expert marksman on the ground, and then teach you to hit your man from a moving horse."

I was excited and didn't want to lose my knack. While others sat about with their teas, I kept perfecting this new-found skill, hammering the target with increasing accuracy—a swish-thud that continued until there was light no more.

محبوب 52 بجبعه

SOUTHERN PASS

Approaching the Southern Pass we could see the Fergana Valley eternally barricaded by continuous ranges of brown granite mountains. The fortifications rose majestically from deep canyons that appeared impassable to any but the birds that nested in the sheer cliffs or floated on hot updrafts. The mighty stone slabs yielded to no one and nothing except the relentless determination of the Yakhsha Arta ("Yawk-shaw Art-a") River. For ages its rushing deluge had been wearing a path through these mountains, leaving a snaking, twisting gorge that roared heavy with grey foaming torrents. Ammar told me that between seasonal runoffs there are passable river banks along this mighty flow, passageways where the caravans wend their way through nature's gargantuan maze.

The trail through the Southern Pass offered us two routes. One led deep into the canyons themselves, through the twists and turns of thick, green overgrowth, bogs and snares, sharp piles of broken granite slabs fallen from above, overgrowth, and the dangerous competition with wildlife looking for new prey in these shadowed difficulties. At its terminal, the river basin awaited.

Ammar said that given the obstacles of the lower trail, few men traversed it safely. Scattered bones proved the futility of those inexperienced in such regions.

The other trail led upwards, along narrow paths cut into the sides of the foothills. Those stretched across the face of the mountains themselves, switchback paths, wide enough for a camel and her load, narrow enough for one-way passage.

Such trails avoided the mistakes and mysteries in the perpetual darkness below, but presented another danger. Along the steep sides, a fall off the trail could never be recovered. Those in times past who had lost their footing became quick victims to the slippery slopes and tumbled helpless into the disappearing darkness below. The remainder who keep to the safe side eventually climb their way farther upriver to a much safer and easily-approachable meeting with the Yakhsha Arta. The duration on the trail taking this upper route was farther in stadia, but shorter in time.

There was no question in Zafir's mind about taking the upper path. It was the usual way unless heavy snowfall prevented it. This time of year, when the summer melt was well underway, he cautioned us to be wary of the runoff—it would make the path that much more treacherous.

I followed the rider in front of me, staying in single file, admiring the beautiful rocky terrain of this amazing place. With every step forward, it seemed to me that we were climbing higher. But for all of our progress, I wasn't winded or faint from the altitude.

"It's a trick," Tou explained as he followed along behind me.

"Trick?"

"We're not really climbing. We're not going up the sides of these mountains," he said, pointing off toward the clouds that hung behind the highest peaks. "Watch those clouds," he said. "They neither rise nor fall, but stay the same, as do we."

"I don't understand," I said, peering off toward the distant horizon.

"It's simply that the canyons below us do not mark level ground, they slope downwards. We're not climbing higher, they are sinking below us."

And then it made sense. Except for the occasional switchbacks, the path was alarmingly easy. "And all this time I thought I was getting stronger on this climb!"

Tou laughed and nodded.

The snow-capped peaks loomed high overhead like old gray-haired guards, looking down in amusement at the teeny winding line of camels and horses as we wrapped around the hillsides. The long stretch of men required nearly an hour's ride for the last to pass the place of the first. We crept with caution, working our patience to the other side.

"Tell me Tou," I asked as we slowed to pass a particularly slippery stretch of mud. "This is such dangerous ground, why don't we circle around north? Is it like this all around Fergana?" I asked.

"This is the best way," Tou said. "There are places where we approach from the desert plains, but there's been fighting."

"Xiongnu?" I wondered aloud.

"Splinter groups," Tou said, "warriors defending their claims. If we came down from the north we'd drive right into the middle of that fighting, and there are not enough swords in all of the world to defend from the forces that hide there."

They live by the sword, a terrible way to live, I decided. "Then tell me, do these mountains *ever* end?" I asked.

"We are coming upon the Khudjand ("Kewd-john") Pass. You'll see it—it's the western portal that connects the old silk routes to the roads back to your homelands. The pass is popular, but also the entrance for raiders—that's where they launch their attacks."

"I don't see any surprise attack *ever* possible from these mountains and canyons," I said. "Especially where it takes an entire day to travel 50 stadia, and *that* with an accidental fall always waiting for one misstep."

Having said it, I peered down the slope, following with my eye its steepness. The foothills were raked with crevices cut by the eroding streams rushing in foaming fury into the shadows that were hiding the river below.

"Very true," Tou said. "But you'll see differently when we arrive. We are ready for action—we're always prepared to extract a great cost from anyone so foolish as to try Zafir's patience."

The pathways narrowly hugged the mountainsides, and wound around into shadows and out again—climbing, descending, negotiating. Far below in the gorge, moving splashes of yellow sunshine illuminated the tiny meadows and painted the overgrowth and tiny groves of trees in beautiful frames of green living colors. Winds pushed the passing mounds of mist into piles of gray and gloom—but only for a moment before parting again to let bright sunshine warm the view.

"Mountain sheep made the first path," Tou said. "No one knows when, the land changes so rapidly around here—maybe centuries ago, maybe last year. We've been following it since Zafir and his fathers, and their fathers before them. There is never enough time for the path to grow over with neglect. Men come—and will always come through these passes, like they've done for ages."

"The goats know these best," I mused.

"Yes, the best. We should pay them for this work—they save us many days with their shortcuts."

"But shortcuts meant for sharp hooves!"

"Indeed!" Tou said.

By mid-day the caravan had worked its way to its highest loft and then downhill from there, for at least six, maybe seven more days.

At the peak Zafir slowed the train to enjoy the outlook. Twisting, folding, crowding humps of layered mountains and hills tumbled down into the shadows of the river rushing below. The Yakhsha Arta was cradled in the gorge somewhere, out of view—but its roaring voice was heard all the way up the mountainside.

I peered into the distance to the front of us, following with my eye the thin line of our trail running to the east—I saw it disappear around a bend, reappear farther down the distant hills, and lost again around a large mountain. More patches of yellow sun streamed between the sailing mass of puffy clouds, lighting the path before us. I estimated that we should find ourselves somewhere there below, before nightfall, in the warmly-lit gardens that seemed so inviting from above.

It was windy. A stiff, unrelenting breeze scolded us all through these lofty heights, growing especially brave around the end of an exposed hilltop or canyon edge. I thought how much cooler the breeze might make the shadows below. I was glad I carried extra blankets.

The camels couldn't negotiate the rutted paths and slippery washes as well as did the horses, and most men not already on foot were obligated to dismount to lead their beasts by rope on the downward trek. We found no rest along these haphazard routes—no flats or widened turns in the trail. We had to keep marching our way to flatter ground.

By day's end we found a wide, gently-sloped field suitable for camping. It served adequately well, but none of us slept. The hard, lumpy ground was strewn with the elbows of large buried rocks, and no tuft of grassy cushion could blur the uncomfortable lumps beneath our sleeping mats.

53

EDEN

On the sixth day the caravan approached the entrance trail into the bottom of the great gorge. For half a day more we staggered along the black soil path that was mostly covered over with grasses and ferns. As we descended into the shadows of the gorge, I felt the air become cooler and damp. The light dimmed to dusk between the walls of this canyon even though the sun shined on their peaks above us. It was like night during the day.

The splintered summits of the cliff tops jutted into the sky like grey fortress walls, jealously leering over the pearl-colored river. They gave us just enough of a sandy bank for a natural road that we followed close to the Yakhsha Arta's edge.

The river's voice was deafening—like a continuous waterfall that pushed through its milky-foamed panic an unending collection of shredded trees and floating debris. It rushed opposite us, as if escaping the danger into which we were determined to go.

Tou told me the summer melt created flash flooding upriver and the debris washed into Fergana Valley with an annual renewal of nutrition for the soils there. We rode along in utter amazement, having never seen so much water flow so rapidly for so long. Any valley should be grateful for the gift, I thought. But for how long can a river strip the land of its soils before there is none left to take?

But this much was sure—my bakra seemed happy to be back on safer ground. She stopped her snorting and quickened her pace to keep up with those in front of us. The mists of the water rose high over us, drifting to earth in a gentle wash that was refreshing to man and beast. I let my eyes close to a sleepy slit and inhaled the smells that rivers bring—the organic splash of cold-washed rocks, the sweet of wild grasses and blossomed greens, and the occasional rot of decay that accumulated in creamy flotsam atop ponds of standing water that escaped the torrential current.

And then I saw something above us. "Tou!" I called out, pointing up. "Look at the beautiful patch of blue, and the bird!"

Tou looked straight up and smiled. "We should do better if these beasts of ours sprouted wings," he called back.

"My thought exactly," I said. "How do they stay afloat up there, not a wing moving...."

"It's the drafts," Tou said, pulling alongside so I could hear him above the rush of the river's torrent. "The winds pile up along the bottom of these great peaks and with nowhere else to go, they push up the sides to freedom. The birds take the ride, rising high with hardly any effort at all. They loiter to spy on us. Drop a crust of bread and see them drop from the sky like an arrow, and then there will come others, from nowhere—and fight for it."

Each night we camped, Zafir had us climb a short way up the nearby hills to escape the damp. At first light each morning, we returned to the basin and continued our long trek along the river.

"Day 168—Dear Rasha, I befriended the daughter of Najeeb here in Mouru. She is Kalila. We talked for a while about her life and adventures. She wants to visit Egypt. She is promised to someone who is traveling as we are. I must make this time pass quickly. I keep your veil with me always. I sometimes wish you could be here with me and see these magical places.—Bassam"

"Dear Bassam, We ate the last of the squash and maize. It was a good garden for us. I must tell you we had a small earthquake a week ago. It shook our canyon and gave everyone an alarm, but we are safe. Do you remember the old pillared crypt at the north end? It cracked. Part of the front sloughed off. They had a meeting about the safety of the caves. No other cracks, we feel safe. There has never been an earthquake in Rekeem that anyone can ever remember.—Rasha"

BASSAM

ب هبعه 54 محبوب

NIGHT VISITOR

It was darker than dark. Only a ribbon of stars showed between the tops of the cliffs above us.

An alert listener could have heard the twigs break in the black of night, or felt the hot panting of something large on the prowl through the dark of such a night. But those on watch, those paid to be alert at such times, were not so keen as those creatures that hunted while others slept. And because of the river's loud call, and because of human frailties, the eyes and ears of our guards missed the tell-tale signs—the signs that sent other creatures racing away for their lives.

There is only one force strong enough to send an animal into a camp of humans. Only the arrogance of hunger could coerce a creature's investigation far into a camp as large as Zafir's.

And hunger can play many tricks. For the flesh eaters in the narrow gorge, this place was a cornucopia of fresh meat. And because of it, the ease of the kill easily overpowered the good sense to stay clear—risks that animal instincts cautioned against, warned against, and usually fought against. But tonight, there was a scent in the darkness, a heat of fresh flesh, and the power of the hunt drove this particular hunter dangerously close to our camp.

It was the fourth night in the mountains and our train had made excellent progress. For lack of an adequate view of the sky, Ammar had trouble knowing with accuracy our place on the map.

"It's never taken us more than seven days," Ammar mumbled with the kamal string tight between his teeth. "I think we're on schedule, maybe a half a day late."

"The runoff?" I asked.

"Yes, the mud and the caution delay us ... but it is nothing new," he said, making a note on his map and coiling the string around his fingers to stow away. "Three days, we should arrive, probably by dusk."

"Have you taken the lower path?" I asked.

"Three times, maybe four," Ammar said. "It's beautiful, sometimes, other times the air is thick with insects, biting and bothering. One year we had to wrap ourselves in blankets like a makeshift mahmil, and kept our fly swatters thrashing about like a camel tail, all day, all night, to stop the biting—it was bad."

"Is it a manageable path?"

"Not at all. You heard Tou talk about the broken rocks? They are huge slabs of granite, the length of ten camels and the thickness of five men standing atop one another. And these fall from the mountain peaks and pile up so high in the bottom of the gorge, you cannot see if they are fallen from the mountain or if they are the mountains themselves."

"Can you climb over them, or must you go around?"

"Too slippery to climb over, too rugged and steep. We have to cut a trail along the hillsides to get around them. And beneath those slabs are thousands of dark crevices and corners, shadowy dens for the animals who live here. No man wants to explore the darkness beneath the massive fall. It's not a safe place to be, and Zafir chooses the lower trail only if weather prevents us from taking the upper path."

"Big animals?" I asked with concern.

"Only for those without their knife unsheathed!" he smiled.

That night I laid awake peering into the blackness. The sword of Suoud was unsheathed and rested across my chest, and my bronze knife laid at my side. There was no light from the stars or moon above, and only the small fire of the watch gave proof that men camped here—its yellow flames cast faint flickers on the cliffs jutting upwards on the other side of the river. The watch was camped on the other side of a small knoll that separated the camp into two sections by some 100 paces.

I tried to close my eyes but crawly things kept finding me, going for the moisture in the corner of my eye or my mouth, or they buzzed close to my ear, lingering there until I swooshed them away.

After swatting at the invisible invasion for half an hour, I woke myself in exasperation to pull a thin blanket over my head so I could breath in silent slumber—and then I drifted into sleep.

Suddenly, a loud screaming from above bolted me from a dead sleep and I sat upright holding my sword in front of me, calling out, "What?" Other men likewise sat up, and a great hubbub of concern spread all the way up the hillside. The scream came again, and then again, weaker this time. The men started shouting.

In the blackness I could discern nothing but the sounds of men around me stirring to action. And then the scream again—but it was no animal, this was the scream of a man, followed by the scratchy growl of a deep-throated cat yowling in defiance—and then the man screamed again.

All the camels suddenly rose up in excitement, snorting and stomping. The horses began to whinny and pulled at their reins tied to logs. Everywhere the camp was awakened by the screams and the men fumbled through the darkness calling out, shouting, slipping over stones to stand, trying to run to offer aid but tripping on snagging branches in the dark.

And then a watchman came running from afar, a torch lit, lighting a great circle of clarity as he leapt over shrubs and camps toward the screaming of a man and something large, in a terrible fight. And then another torch followed the first, hurrying to the sound. "We're coming! Where are you? We're coming!"

In seconds, every man was scrambling for his sword and chased after the lighted way, calling, shouting, frantically hunting shadows against shadows, shooting questions to one another for news of the noise.

When the torches arrived up the hillside, the runners stopped having lost the direction. Others joined them, a cluster of shapes, dozens, gathered in a great mob, obscuring the light with more men shouting, many hurrying back for more fire, passing torches to any who arrived, and spread out across the hill in lines—looking for what, I wondered?

But then something more frightening could be heard, something more ominous than screaming. It was the panicked urgency that came with long and deadly silence.

By then the hillside was covered with torch-bearers, casting dancing shadows that jerked about the slope as men raced through the shrubs of undergrowth. The flickering lights littered the camping place with sharp shafts of confusion.

I held my sword in front of me and watched from my camp, not knowing if I should help or stand my guard as a defense at this lower part of the hill. Thinking it better to watch the downward side, I remained poised, hoping that I was ready for anything. My breathing raced almost as fast as my heart, and I kept calling out to others for answers. Those around me had climbed already and I was left standing there alone.

When one of the torches came within distance, I saw the familiar large bulk of Ziyad—his fondness for food was extracting a price for the night's sudden exertions. Beads of sweat glistened across his cheeks and forehead, and a look of rushed anguish was branded over his face.

"What is it?" I called out. "Ziyad! What is it?"

"A lion," he said breathlessly. "A lion of some kind. He has dragged away our friend. There is blood."

"My friend?" I anxiously asked.

"Yes, it's Fawzi—he is gone."

THE BELT

"A torch! A torch! Give me a torch," I screamed at the men up the hill. I had to hurry but I needed light. Feeling about for sticks near my smoldering fire, I found the warm end of a branch and blew it to life. The little light could never do, so I ripped a shred of cloth from my shirt and wrapped it about the stick. Finding my oil lamp, I poured its contents on the cloth and caught up with Ziyad.

"What do you mean, *gone*?" I asked with panic.

"Dragged away," Ziyad said, waving his torch for more light as he hurried through the tall grasses, hunting. "He can't have gone far."

And just then a man shouted from the far side of the hill. "He's here. Come! Come! I found him here!"

I exploded into the dark toward the shout, hurdling the saddles and shrubs and camps of others, running uphill through the heavy grasses as fast as I could, slipping then falling, climbing to my feet again, running.

I was huffing and panting when I arrived at a group of men standing in waist-high grasses, circled around something—some of them were crouching down, others standing, holding their torches to illuminate whatever it was that called to their attention.

As I came to the scene I wasn't sure I wanted to see what lay there in the grass. The men saw me arrive and parted as I neared to let me close.

Lying in the matted grass was the stretched form of Fawzi, prostrate on his side, his head bent back, his eyes closed, and his mouth hanging open. The grass around him was splattered with blood, but nothing pooling beneath him. That was hopeful.

One arm stretched away from Fawzi, clawed and bleeding, his other arm clasped about his chest. Men bent over him attending to his wounds. His clothing was shredded, spotted and soaked with blood, ripped from his bare shoulder to show five or six puncture wounds that dripped red down his chest. A deep slash above his right eye oozed heavily. There was blood everywhere. I held my breath, fearing the worst.

Just then Humam arrived, breathing heavily from the climb. "Give me some room," he ordered. "And light, I need light. Bandages, I need bandages." Instantly, men ripped the hem of their shirts or robes and handed them off to Humam.

The old physician worked quickly, compresses on the most severe wounds, dressing the others, cleaning the blood from Fawzi's face and shoulder, wiping the gash on his forehead to examine.

And then, as if coming back to life, Fawzi groaned and opened one eye. He saw the men about him, their torches held high, and concern showing across all of their faces.

And then he saw me, and he smiled weakly.

"Camel brain," he gasped, "look what I caught," and turned his eyes toward his outstretched arm.

A man with a torch pushed up the hill through the grass to the side of Fawzi to light what lay there beyond his reach. As soon as the yellow flames brightened the place, all the men suddenly gasped in unison. There, behind the low branches of a shrub and almost hidden in the tall grasses, lay the still form of a large cat. Fawzi's knife remained stuck in its throat and his sword was pushed clean through the animal's breast—its blood freshly pooled beneath it.

"I got him," Fawzi smiled again, and closed his eyes.

"Is it a lion?" I gasped.

"A lion of the mountains," another said.

"Fawzi has killed a mountain cat!" a man boasted.

"Enough, enough," Humam ordered. I need six men to carry this man to Zafir's tent, and torches to light the way. The rest of you, back to camp. And make fires, we don't want more visitors like this one tonight."

I followed the men down the hill holding my torch high in one hand, and my sword in front of me with the other, to guard lest another surprise leap from the shadows.

The group found its way safely to Zafir's tent and carried Fawzi inside. I stood by the mat where they laid Fawzi and before Humam shushed them all away, Fawzi gestured me to lean in close. "What is it, Fawzi?" I asked.

"Go get that cat," he said. "I want his skin."

"Of course," I said. "The whole thing?"

"I need a new saddle cover."

"I'll scrape it tonight," I promised.

"And clean that fur," he said. "I don't want the smell of *cat* spooking the animals ... one more thing—bring me his tail."

"What?"

"Yes, and clean it up."

"Of course, but ...."

"It's my prize, donkey breath. Can't you see?" Fawzi said, pointing to his waist. "He slashed my clothing, my robe, my shirt, everything. His tail will be my prize—I need a new belt."

STRINGS

Not a man slept that night. When the sun finally lit the sky above, Fawzi remained restless with pain. Humam spent the night treating the wounds and emerged at first light having completed his task. Standing at the river, he was refreshing himself when I asked for a report.

"We sewed him up last night," Humam said.

"*Sewed* him?"

"That's an idea from Chang'an," he said. "I might have done it to you, but we needed to keep your deep wound clean."

"And Fawzi?"

"Except for his shoulder, his wounds were not serious, at least not life threatening. We stitched him—a lot."

"That must be difficult work ...."

"Yes, it can save a man's life. In the past, the best we could do was bind up the wounds and hope for the best. But sewing like a garment—great idea."

"My mother has such needles."

"No, we don't use needles like hers," Humam said. "Mine are smaller. I like the thin bone needles unless the flesh is thick."

"And thread?" I asked.

"Hair—yak hair, horse hair, human hair, plant fibers. Some people use animal tendons. If we were a rich caravan, I'd use silver wire, but only for large wounds."

"Do they stay? The threads?" I wondered.

"Oh no. After the wound closes and starts to heal, we take them out. They usually fall out on their own."

"So, what sort of lion was that, Humam?" I asked. "I've never seen that kind before."

"There are many," he said, throwing water on his face and burying it in a dry cloth. "I'm no student of the animals, perhaps Ammar knows. But I've never seen a striped cat this far north ... these barren places make for poor hunting grounds."

"Maybe he was chased here, by hunger?"

"Maybe ...."

Humam gathered his things into his arms and started back toward camp.

I was worried for my friend and had to ask. "So, is Fawzi ...?"

"Oh yes, should be fine," Humam said. "He's pretty sore, I'm watching that shoulder ...."

"Can he travel?"

"Yes, but he'll hate it—for a few days. Those bites are not too deep. He's rugged. He's *Al Murrah*. He'll be in the saddle today—but those cuts are dirty. Do you remember how I kept your wound clean?"

"I'll never forget it," I said, reaching for my shoulder.

I found Fawzi awake in Zafir's tent, sitting alone, a bowl with hot rice and sliced fruit at his feet. "I brought you something," I said.

"Ah-ha, a stranger bearing gifts to ask forgiveness for sleeping while his friend was eaten," Fawzi said.

"Rescuing you? What were you doing camped up that hill, so far from the rest?"

"Fewer insects," Fawzi said. "You were attacked by every flying torment God ever invented, no?"

"Well, yes, but …."

"See? You should listen to Fawzi. Fawzi knows best."

"Sure, the next time I want to be eaten by a lion, I'll come ask your opinion," I said.

"Look at yourself, *yak mouth*—your face is pocked with insect bites. And look at me! Hardly a bite on me …."

I laughed. Fawzi grimaced through his pain, smiling weakly.

"So, Humam said he sewed you up."

"You slept through that, too—it's a pretty good trick those threads of his. Except here," he said pointing to his shoulder. "Lion teeth are dirty, he said."

"So … the brine wash?"

"I'll have two good scars above my eye," Fawzi said. "Opened me right up. Humam closed them with his tricks. These are the damages that make men look ferocious."

"You look like my bakra," I said. "Not as pretty, but close."

"You watch it, *donkey rot*, I can still give you a piece of *this*," Fawzi said, holding up his red-bandaged arm.

"Speaking of girl arms, I have something for you." I handed over the lion's pelt and tail—the tail was stiffly coiled in a circle.

"Ahhhh, my new seat covering *and* my new belt. I need you to bone it for me, do you know how?"

"Well …."

"All right, get your knife, cut all the way down the underside, and do a neat job. It's your payment for not rescuing me. Pull the hide—be careful to protect the fur, the leather isn't strong."

"That I can do," I said, and turned to leave.

"Hey, *yak jowls,* not so fast."

I stopped at the door. "Yes?"

"Is that lion still in camp?"

"It lays where you killed him—I skinned him for you. And he's quite without his tail, of course."

"Then get me his right paw as well."

"His paw? What on earth for?"

"To save the claws. Perhaps I'll string them to put around my neck, or something. They'll prove the scars above my eye—and bring me luck."

"Luck?"

"Of course. So when people ask me about the scars, I can show them my belt and his claws, and tell the entire story of my fight in the dark, and how I killed him with my knife and finished him with my sword. And then they'll know, after I tell what happened—when my story gets to the end—to the tail end, that I'm not lion."

I looked at him a moment—blankly—looked down, paused, and then shaking my head, I walked out of the tent.

FERGANA VALLEY

On the sixth day through the river gorge, our escape finally revealed itself—a massive natural gate of sheer cliffs that marked the entrance to Fergana. We could feel it even before we saw it—the wind from behind was stronger, rushing past as vigorously as the river we followed.

The sun had just set when we rounded a final bend and the great cliff walls ended, framing a spectacular panoramic view of the immense Fergana Valley. A great sandy incline spilled out of the river gorge that gradually dropped to the valley floor beyond. The air was warmer here, dry and sweet.

The settling dusk was already masking the valley's treasures—long shadows stretched over the valley's patchwork of distant farms and settlements. The people of Fergana had returned home from their labors with thousands of tiny lights blinking to life. Even in that darkening sky I could see the valley was hemmed in by blurred-grey peaks that marked the farthest boundary, a distance, Ammar said, of at least seven days' ride to the other side.

When the last of train joined us, Zafir sent Al Murrah to find a convenient place to camp. The enormous sandy plateau descended for half a day's ride, a trip that had to wait for tomorrow.

I couldn't contain my excitement—Fergana Valley! Why stop? Why not continue toward the old villages, why dally?

Then I caught the wonderful smells drifting on the evening breeze—the smells of life and growing things, animals and diners, excitement and trade, just beyond our reach. A new energy lifted our spirits and camp was set quickly. With the camels circled around, our fires lit, the excitement was vented through new conversations and story telling that lasted as long as the sticks they burned.

I laid out my sleeping mat with a perfect view of the valley. The feeling there was delicious, surrounding me like warm arms. Our presence seemed to stir ancient feelings as if I were in the presence of something historical and exotic and hidden. It felt heavy with time, reverberating with the echoes of untold passages of human experiences long past—soaked and seethed in a culture overflowing with magic and surprise. I wanted to explore—would anyone notice if I stole away in the night? There was a time, and not too long ago, when that's exactly what I would have done. Indeed, I had.

I pulled my blanket around me thinking how nice it was to be back on soft desert sands—the sand was home. I propped my head on a folded blanket and watched the tiny flickering points of lights of a distant village. Their torches and cook-fires and lamps shined like stars across the darkness. And then, after a while, they slowly blinked off, dissolving into a veil of invisibility.

The night breeze turned cool while the stars shone steady like watchful eyes, protecting the safety of this place, the safety of this beautiful and wonderful garden—a garden of Eden.

TA-YUAN

We rose early that morning to make our first long-term camping place by midday. Our landing place was the outskirts of the very village I had watched go to sleep last night.

Ta-Yuan was the oldest settlement in Fergana. Dozens of brown-brick buildings surrounded its market place—one and two floors high—and gave visitors a warm and inviting welcoming place.

"Notice around you, Bassam, that everything is an art," Tou said. "Even those buildings ahead. When we arrive, you will look closer and see those bricks sag with more than five centuries beneath the baking sun. You will see their artistry when we get closer."

I whistled in astonishment.

"The newer structures are still more than two hundred years old," Tou said, "erected for the increased trade brought by the larger caravans."

It was the strangest feeling for me, almost like every step forward was a leap deeper into another world, like passing through a gate into a garden. On all sides were green pastures and orchards, streams and meadows—lively growing things that welcomed us to their paradise.

What a pleasant change, I thought. Sweet smells filled the air, the fresh smells of grasses and ripening fields of grains. Birds of many varieties were singing their songs in the branches of wild blossomed shrubs, and flying things, insects and such, hovering from near and far, flying close, too close at times, to investigate.

The C'ina people welcomed us with kindness. Friendly families with round, kind faces, and dressed in modest but simple wraps—tunics, or light-weight baggy pants wrapped up about them. They came excitedly to the roadside to wave us in—farmers and craftsmen smiling for an exchange, women with their children holding up foods and flasks, blankets and sandals, homespun clothing, scarves, cloaks and fruit—for trade or purchase—I had no idea the price they asked, I couldn't understand a word from their sing-song language. I needed Tou to help, but he was busy with others.

I watched in complete amusement as our men gestured with the people who thronged about us. Modu's men came to the rescue but showed no patience for bartering amid trinkets and wilted leftovers. Behind their gruff rejections and snapping words, our men smiled at the welcoming party, anyway. We tried to communicate our peaceful intentions as best we could—waving, smiling, shrugging shoulders, hand to heart, whatever we could do to politely decline their offerings. They didn't discourage easily and ran alongside in spite of Modu's men.

"They're persistent, Tou. Are they that desperate for business?"

"In this place? They're rich beyond belief. Maybe not with gold, but the average family has enough to outfit a palace twice over. The traders who pass through often surrender their commodities at far too good a price just for some fresh food."

"I can see why. I'm ready to move here and settle down!"

"It's a magical place my friend. But don't forget that a serpent loves a garden just as much."

The nomads' homes were made of cloth—tents not meant to move. Each was built around many tall poles planted in a circle with white or brown fabric wrapped about. The roof was fabric, pitched high in the center, with small windows high up the wall to vent the heat. Children ran in and out making me wonder if more than one family lived in each.

Yak were to be found everywhere, and served as the main engine of power—pulling loads, walking the presses, ploughing the fields, giving rides to children who guided them forward with sticks, and stood in pens, patiently being combed. I saw two dozen white ones on the mountainside, foraging near a large patch of old, crusted snow. They almost disappeared into the scenery.

"A rare breed, very prized," Tou said. "The white can be dyed any color, so it sells for the highest price. But its not so good for the animal."

"How is that?"

"It's the sun, Bassam. Very hard on their skin. No protection for the white hairs. Skin problems make them ill and they don't live as long. The dark haired live the longest."

"I saw a woman combing a black hair, what is that for? Are they pets or something?"

"In a way," he said, taking hold of his blanket wrapped over his shoulder. "This blanket? It comes from combing. They care for their animals a great deal—many gifts come from the yaks. Blankets, milk, cheese, power to pull. My shirt, these boots, and we make many uses of the hair. I'll show you how we comb out the short hairs."

"Oh, I see. She was gathering and not grooming, like wool from sheep?"

"Yes, like sheep. When they molt, a woman combs out the short hairs and twists them with patient hands into soft threads. I watched my mother do it all my life, and today, so does my wife. I have done it myself—it is patient work. See this shirt? You feel how soft?"

I reached over. It was soft—comfortable.

"And the long hair?" I asked.

"For strength—ropes, saddle straps, reins. That's it over there," he said pointing to a yak whose long hair was dragging on the ground. "That long hair is the strongest."

The people of Fergana were distinctively different. I detected no western features in any of them. They were of slighter build, narrow eyes, fair skin, and every part the descendants of the Qin Dynasty that ruled the whole of C'ina.

Their manners, their clothing, especially the food they ate had a distinctive difference. The cuisine was deliciously attractive with new aromas and colors of assorted tastes and smells.

Closer to town I saw a multitude of little donkeys everywhere.

I called to Fawzi, "Look, some animals just your size."

He glared and swatted the rear of my bakra, making her jump, and me with it.

"They use them for everything, donkey brain," he scolded. "Don't make fun. They're smarter than you and I'm sure work a lot harder. You're so much trouble, I'm sure Zafir is considering a trade."

"We use these little beasts for just about everything," Tou said. "They're more maneuverable and thrifty inside the cities, sure-footed on the mountain paths and can pull tremendous weights of grain and commodity through places our yaks have faltered. But when it comes to strength, these little friends must yield to their big brothers."

The buildings of Ta-Yuan were constructed in rows and carefully designed. They were linked wall to wall and ornately covered with blue and turquoise tiles, each hand painted with emblems or letters that tell a story about the painter or the city at the time they were made. Reading the tiles was like reading their history. They were fastened everywhere—archways, domes, walls, any place they could make them stick.

Zafir signaled his captains of 100 to choose a camping location just outside the walls of Ta-Yuan, and they promptly divided the group into five sections. The camp was a large grassy flat that overlooked the city. My spot was among Al Murrah.

It didn't take long to fall in love with this ancient place. A multitude of flowery perfumes wafted past me with the scents of cultivated plants, wild flowers and grasses. The sun was hanging lower in the south, a sign we had traveled into the north lands.

Fergana was surrounded by tall snow-covered mountains. High clouds stretched out in long streamers and a haze hung over parts of the valley where evening activities were already underway.

After dinner I joined Ammar at his cook-fire to look at the maps. "Beyond the Fergana," he said, "Zafir must choose."

"This?" I asked, pointing. "Another desert?"

"It's the Taklamakan, he must decide if we travel north or south of it."

"Why not just pass through? It looks passable enough."

"It's a different sort of desert. Ours are stony places, we can dig cisterns, chart paths, create rendezvous places," Ammar said. "But here in these lands, the Taklamakan is pure drifts, giant dunes—a massive sea of sand that is forever moving. Men must carry everything for at least seven weeks. It's impossible."

"Then how do we cross it?" I asked.

"Have you been listening to me at all? We *don't* cross it. We go around, north or south, that is what Zafir must decide."

"But it's just another desert ...."

I had made him impatient. "You may ask Tou about this, but the name Taklamakan means 'he who enters does not return.' So don't enter, go north or south of it!"

The name struck me as odd, a curious combination of ideas. I wanted to see it closer. "Alright." I said. "Then what makes Zafir's choice, the weather?"

"No, it depends on the trade here in Ta-Yuan. If Zafir is as profitable as his last trip, we'll travel south, around the lower part of Taklamakan, and then east to Chang'an. And if not, we'll travel north into Tou's country. We have business in four markets to the north, very profitable the last time we traded there."

Ammar's map gave few details about this region. The Taklamakan was drawn as a large, empty oval stretched east and west, with an arrow and the words, "Seven weeks west to east."

"Day 202—Dear Rasha, We have come to the valley at last. It is fertile, many farms, villages. Mountains all around that captures the snow to fill their rivers. We bought fresh grapes and peaches. They have a strange bread here that I love. Fawzi was hurt by a large cat. He killed the animal and will be all right. We had no wood for fires on the last part of our trip, the nights are cold in the mountain canyons, even this time of year. I will bring you here one day.—Bassam"

"Dear Bassam, The earthquake broke more than we thought. Do you remember the white cliffs at the north end? These have split and are waiting to fall. Men have climbed on top with ropes to drive wedges. The broken slabs are being used for building in the market place. This opens a new passage into Rekeem. Perhaps this will change life for us around here. Kateb believes more traffic will come, more caravans because of the new outlet. Faris said the quarry workers were all sent to clear a passage in the walls, to open it. I bring him lunch each day to help him work. I wonder, do we want to lose that northern fortress? Perhaps we will need to rebuild that fortress with bricks one day. —Rasha"

MEE POK

Ta-Yuan was divided into two parts—the old town with its ancient sagging-brick buildings, used for poor shops or diners. And the newer part of larger shops and brighter buildings. It was an amazing congestion of traffic and merchants. I was caught by surprise at how many Westerners I saw.

"Where did they come from?" I asked Tou. "Look at these fair-skinned people—some with red hair others with green eyes, all speaking the same tongue." *How could this be*?

"This is an amazing city with an amazing history," he said, and unfolded a story about a great general from a western empire who built Ta-Yuan.

"He needed a place to rest his wounded warriors—and chose this part of the valley. After the people had rested, they decided to stay rather than return to their homelands."

"I've thought that very thing!"

"It is a captivating place, and has trapped many for the same reasons," he said. "From this garrison grew an important trading place. The Westerners who were transplanted settled down, had families, and their children grew up not knowing any different. They became a part of Fergana Valley's storied past—and part of that throng you saw greeting us as we came in today."

As we pushed through the hustle and bustle of the market square I could hardly cast my shadow on the door of a shop without local merchants initiating their busy rituals of welcome, almost forcing their goods on me. I learned quickly to avoid eye contact.

The smells were strong—raw fish and slaughtered animals, roasted birds, deep fried roots, and spicy rice dishes that drew me like a hooked fish into some of the small diners. I couldn't resist the experience, and pulled on Tou's sleeve to follow me into a few places. As the afternoon wore, I made him stop as frequently as my stomach allowed.

At one such table Tou suggested the order, and our waiter delivered a large porcelain work of art steaming over with dark-skinned rice. He left another with shreds of chicken, and others of various dried spices for sprinkling.

"Here," Tou said, pushing the bowl toward me. "Taste it without the meat."

I scooped a corner of it with a piece of bread. "This looks more purple than black ... is this *the* black rice?"

"It is the same. It starts black and turns purple after cooking. You like it?"

I chewed and smiled. "It has a rich flavor, very nutty—heavier .... more substance—*I like it.*"

"I knew you would! Now, with meat and spices ..."

Finishing my portion, I wasn't full. "I could do with another," I said. "I really think I could!"

"Then you must try another of our favorites!"

Tou caught the attention of a passing server and exchanged a few words. The young man nodded, and left for the kitchen.

"Now," Tou said with a broad smile. "Now I introduce you to something new. Here is something you can make back in your Rekeem—you will like it."

A few moments later, the waiter delivered two small bowls of steamy chicken broth. At the bottom were flat, narrow ribbons of *something* that were curled about with a few shreds of greens.

"What is this?" I asked. "Worms?"

Tou laughed. "No, not for you, but maybe later—Taste!"

I dipped with my bread and scooped a few, eating them with suspicion. "Ummmm, this is fantastic! What is it, I like it!"

"We call it mee pok ["may poke"], the most popular dish in all the land."

I was too busy enjoying to ask more.

"They grind grain, sometimes rice, mix it with water, and make it into long strings and boil it."

"Boil?"

"Oh yes—mee pok."

I slurped more of the long, tasty treats. "Very soft, excellent. I could eat this with just about anything."

"Then we officially welcome you to Fergana Valley, home of *mee pok*."

I grinned at him. "I'm sold! Tell me the secret, how do you make them?"

"Ah ha, not so easy my young friend!" Tou said with a toothy smile. "Some things are not for foreigners! But—if you *happen* to get four parts flour from your wheat, and one part water, and knead it up and rest it a while, and stretch it to the spread of your arms, fold it and dust it with flour and stretch it again, and repeat until your back aches and your arms burn, maybe forty times, and you have made a hundred strands, it is mee pok."

I was laughing by the time Tou finished. "Slow down, let me write it!"

"Sorry, too late. I have told you nothing, it is our exclusive, godly and mystical secret, not for foreigners!"

"But these here, they're flat like ribbons, how do you do that?"

"It is another secret, foreigner! You must not know that we add a couple of eggs, take away a little water to be one part to four, and you spread it thin and cut it with your knife."

"My oh my, Tou. Such secrets. I could never figure that out!"

"And you won't. It is a *secret*."

"And do such secrets need to be cooked?"

"With the eggs, yes, the other, no. You let the mee pok dry and save it for a day, a week, a month—keep away the insects and it will stay a long time, unless there is egg in it. And then drop it into boiling water for a short while to cook. Serve with meat. And there you have it—Fergana Secrets!"

"You are suspiciously smart about *mee pok*, Tou. Are you hiding a talent for the kitchen that you have kept from Fawzi and me?"

Tou smiled. "At my home, my wife sits and sews for our babies while I prepare such masterpieces. Were it not for my duties with Zafir, I would be at home making mee pok, and growing out my belly as your big man Ziyad!"

I laughed and dipped my bread in the broth and was left with mee pok and slivers of chicken at the bottom of the bowl. I was just reaching with my fingers when Tou slapped the top of my hand with the pair of short slender sticks.

"Hey, what?"

"No fingers—it is rude, an insult!" Tou scolded. "You use the sticks."

"For these little bits of meat? This ... this mee pok?"

"Let me teach you. The slivers of meat are not to starve you," he said, "but to save the precious firewood. Smaller pieces cook faster, and a smaller fire can cook many such meals in a short time. Firewood is costly, it is economics not nutrition that declares our small portions."

I rubbed the top of my hand. "What are these for?" I asked, pointing to the sticks. "Everyone is using them to eat. Why?"

"You must learn the sticks—not your knife or your bread," Tou said. He positioned the sticks in my hand and worked them to show. Like all beginners, it was a hopeless endeavor.

"An ancient teacher long ago decided against meat," Tou said. "He declared that knives at the table were gruesome reminders of the workings of a slaughterhouse, and ruined appetites. He told everyone they should use sticks as a replacement. Sticks worked well—cheap, easy to make from wood, they can be burned, and the idea caught on. So, we make our food small, so the sticks can serve."

I was already focused on manipulating the sticks without much luck—I did manage to flick some food across the table.

"Harumph," I said in disgust. "Too much work," and I picked up the bowl to my mouth and slurped its contents away.

By the end of our walk, both of us were so full we felt like we were waddling back to camp. I brought a variety of uncooked black rice and spices to take back to Rekeem—and a pleasant memory of a dessert too delicious to forget, something to be eaten as often as I could find it: yak milk poured over boiled rice with honey. It was my favorite treat during our week in Fergana.

"Day 216—Dear Rasha, I have never eaten so well in all my days. My friend Tou wanted me to taste the foods of his country, and he gave me them all in one day here in Ta-Yuan. This evening by the fire, he taught me about their teas. Tea leaves grow wild, they are easy to find and prepare. Their teas include anise or ginger. I am bringing some to taste. The secret is the combination of leaves. Some recipes go back a thousand years and are carefully guarded. I have learned some of their secrets. You and mother will love their teas. And mee pok.—Bassam"

"Dear Bassam, Today Faris asked me to be his friend, to send his father to speak to mine. I told him that is not possible, Zafir is gone for another year at least. And besides, I have made a promise. He wants to make a life with me. I will say no when he asks.—Rasha"

60

BIG SANDALS

It was the morning of the fourth day when Zafir slowed long enough to spend time with his men. He was busy meeting with strangers for barter and trade.

I learned his problem was a delayed caravan from the south. They were supposed to meet in Ta-Yuan, but after four days there was still no sign and no word. Zafir told his captains that we could wait two more days before releasing the bulk of his valuables to merchants already bidding high prices. And that is what brought Zafir to camp in the middle of the morning.

"Bassam!" Zafir called out as he approached. "Let us walk some."

I was surprised to see him with the bag of scrolls slung over his shoulder and the two mats under his arm. In fact, he looked somewhat anxious.

This is a change, I thought. *It's not dark—it's not night—can we find privacy in this busy place?*

I strapped on Suoud's sword, and with two pairs of Al Murrah behind, I followed Zafir up a dirt path to a grassy knoll beyond the walls of Ta-Yuan overlooking our camp.

"These scrolls make too many sleepless nights," he said smiling as we worked our way above a pasture to the wild growth in the foothills.

"I wanted to thank you for that," I said. "The short nights have been well worth the exchange."

"We can find our solitude in the empty desert," he huffed as we climbed, "but here? Here we find a busy, crowded place with many eyes and more ears."

"And *mee pok*."

"Ah yes! I see you have discovered Fergana's special recipe. These eastern people, are very inventive don't you think?"

"Inventive and filling," I laughed. "Thanks to Tou's generosity, I've been introduced to just about everything different and new, and eaten it all in one day!"

"You'll find more new things as we continue east. You're keeping a good record of this in your journal?"

"Yes sir, down to the exact recipes themselves."

We stopped at a clearing that offered a beautiful view of the valley's delights, and within warning shout of their distant camping place. From this vantage I could see Ta-Yuan stretch out before us, heavy with traffic and trading. The sun shined warmly and the steady march of lumpy clouds above painted the valley with patches of shadow and light that glided over the terrain.

Zafir dropped the two mats and invited me to place them. "Tell me, what do you think of this business?"

"This is the most amazing business I've ever imagined. And the fragile balance between success and failure."

Zafir raised his eyebrows. "Failure?"

"Without you to guide this company, how could we make it through those deserts and mountain? Ammar's maps are not exact enough, we need you."

"It's not that difficult, Bassam," he said. "Traveling over the desert is not so complicated. But you just wait until we arrive at Chang'an and you can meet the boat captains. Then you'll see how going anywhere is difficult without old travelers like me who do it the old way. I shouldn't worry, my son. There is Ammar, Falid, any of my captains of 100, and others, who know these routes as well as I do. However, those maps are not as abbreviated as you might think. The way forward is always best made with a map. Know well your goal, your destiny, and your path there is always straight. There is safety in that."

"How then do people make it around on the open oceans?"

"Sea trade is as old as the pyramids. But getting it from the dock to market has always been our job. The boats can only go so far, of course. There is a very large profit, but the costs and risks are so great. They carry expenses that we do not. For us, the greatest cost is time, and while time is treasure, our time in the desert is a treasure easily found."

He dragged the scroll bag to him. "So tell me, my son, what now do you understand of these scrolls?"

"Wonderful new things—that true wealth is not what I had always imagined it," I said.

"And how is that?"

"I thought the treasure brought to Rekeem, those black leather sacks, was the wealth that made Abdali-ud-din powerful. And now I see that's not exactly true."

"Then what is the source of wealth, Bassam?"

"It's a way of living, an attitude, a way of looking at things. It's not the accumulation of coins, it's the control of what coins there are—be they few or many. I've come to understand the number of coins matters less to one who lives by the virtue of the first scroll."

"That's right," Zafir said. "True wealth is mastery of self and all that comes your way, for the betterment of others with whom you trade."

I looked at our camp. Mingling at small tents and cook-fires, more than 600 men and their great herd of horses and camels rested ready to take the trade farther east as soon as Zafir gave the word. "I've watched how the words of the first scroll lay at the root of all things."

"Such as?"

"The men and their pleasures," I said. "At our stops, I've noticed that some of them try to be first to eat and drink, sleep and laugh, wander and explore. And they are the same who are also the first to be offended—easily offended. Some are like children, afraid there will not be enough, jealous of anyone who accumulates more, or is in line first."

"So is it all around the world and through the ages," he said.

"And then there are the others who wait behind patiently, spying out the lay of the land, the merchants, the dangers, the opportunities, their chance at the cistern. These others are in no hurry. They wait and watch, and they seem so calm and peaceful, not carrying around worry and consumption."

"And you?"

"I try to wait and watch, like the others, but that mee pok and black rice with their spices, well—it's especially hard!"

Zafir laughed and nodded. "Yes, the foods here are something wonderful. It grows on you after a while," he said patting his stomach, "and calls you back at the most unusual times."

"So, what is this quiet strength I see in those men who linger behind, letting others crowd forward?" I asked. "It's as if they have this power over their appetite, their urges—and I see it shining in their eyes, it stands beside them—like a watchful guard ready at their command. It's in their countenance."

"You're looking at integrity," Zafir said. "Those are the traits of honesty, devotion, control and strength. It's the permeation of reliable honesty showing in their lives, in their attitudes, in their daily stance."

"Then I want to be like them."

"You will be. In many ways you already *are*," Zafir said. "These experiences have taught you good judgment. And your experiences came because of your poor judgment. You need some time to fill those big sandals you brought along on this trek."

"Big sandals?"

"Yes, your expectations of yourself—and of others. Did you think I wasn't aware of your disappointment in Al Murrah? I was watching you. I know of your disappointment in some of them."

"I always thought Al Murrah to be iron men, at their posts always, never letting down their guard, always watching."

"Most of them are, but others are simply hired thugs. I have them both in this company, Bassam. All I ask of them is loyalty to our purposes, and for that they're well paid."

I grew thoughtful and looked at my hands. "Zafir, I always thought my life was defined by my possessions, things I could buy and show, I suppose to show off the tokens of my wisdom and intellect, or so I thought."

"And that has changed?"

"Oh, yes sir. Now I see that I can be content with few possessions, and with modesty in my way of living because it's not in the *having* that makes me happy. It's in the control. Mastery over *me* brings this new confidence. It needs no audience or acknowledgment. Self governance is its own reward. I don't need many things to be contented. I didn't understand that before."

"I'm glad to hear you say that, Bassam. You're letting the teachings of the scrolls distill into your heart, to teach you how this short life that God has given us must be used for reasons more lasting than the mere acquisition of things."

"And so much work, I didn't realize it," I said waving my hand through the air. "So much work to keep it all safe. The houses we pass once meant security. But now, they are more like anchors in this vast wonderful land, and the dwellers like prisoners or guards or defenders of those things that make them feel secure. It's so much work. It seems that *less* is *more*."

Zafir grinned. "You're a wise old philosopher, my young Bassam. You see the world through new eyes, now."

"Well, at least I want to," I said with honesty. "Or see with eyes that did not see before the scrolls."

"You'll see that many of these wisdoms are learned after a lifetime of trial and error, and most men who live to an old age and taste the fruits of right living after many wrong choices, eventually become content with less. The material things really don't matter as much once you get that true perspective. We all want enough to live, but we don't need to live like a king!"

"Which king?" I grinned.

"The scrolls give you that perspective. They teach that these principles have the power to make bad men good and good men better. And you, Bassam, you are made better."

Far below us the tiny figures at our camp were hurrying about their business like so many insects scurrying for reasons that meant nothing from this distance.

After a few moments, Zafir pulled the scroll bag in front of him, set it upright, and unlaced its top.

ب هبعه 61 محبوب

THE FOURTH SCROLL

"This bag," Zafir began, "was my father's when he was a boy. It was new then but it shows wear today. I may have to replace it."

Was the bag truly his father's, or was this another lesson from the scrolls?

Zafir lifted out another bundled scroll, this one with four leather tassels dangling from the top. Placing it on the mat he untied the cords and let the scroll rest untouched. Its yellowed papyrus clung curled to itself with visible edges worn from use.

"Most men hope to find in these scrolls ..." he began, repeating the very same words. I could repeat them if he asked.

".... I think your heart is ready, Bassam. Do you understand?"

"Yes, I do."

"Then let us begin."

He unrolled it to the first passage.

"You will do the reading, and I will listen. If you have a question, you may ask. But some things I won't not tell you, it's part of the test."

I took the scroll as before. "The Song of the Judge," it began.

> "To the prosperous, prosperity is not in the possession of things, but in the acquisition of good judgment. Judgment must discern between the extremes of the impractical. The place of prosperity is not at one extreme like an excess, nor is it at the other extreme where there is deficit. Prosperity is balanced between them. It is patient, it does not vacillate, it is steady and finds the central current for the greatest velocity toward any particular goal. The wise understand when the path is well-trod for reasons of experience. Or, for reasons of lost initiative and desire, the two traits of the soul that has died ...."

The words flowed in kind phrases and ideas, a gentle balm of calming resolution—oil on troubled waters. It was the instrument for addressing conflicting choices throughout life, to steer from life's many extremes toward reason and sensibility. The scroll offered the tools of right reason to choose between want and need, having and having not, patience and impatience, darkness and light, life and death, joy and woe—the constant argument between *this* or *that*.

The scroll taught that principles are unchanging, they are eternal and never contradict each other. If they do, then one or the other is not a true principle. "That's a test, isn't it?" I asked.

"Most men trip over this one," Zafir said. "There's a great Natural Law always at work. It's difficult to come into harmony with the Law until we learn and understand it. And when that happens, all else falls into place—government, justice, economies, the market, family life, child rearing, personal governance, all of it managed by Natural Law, we just need to find that harmony."

Natural Law—it was an idea I hadn't considered. "If all things are meant to obey this law, then joy is simply living within its boundaries?"

"That's it. But I wouldn't say *simply*," Zafir said. "It seems that very few ever discover the deeper tenets of Natural Law because some dictator always comes on the scene and disrupts it."

"I'm thinking that many people try to skirt around this Law and try to use another wrong to make a wrong a right."

"Have you ever seen this work?" Zafir asked.

"Not for very long," I confessed.

"I see! You have some experience here?"

I smiled and waved away his chastisement. "The fourth scroll talks about extremes," I said, "that a defect on one side is not repaired with an excess at the other side."

"That seems to be the universal problem," he said blankly.

"I've never been happy in the extreme of anything."

"The reason, my son, is that it isn't possible to stay in the extreme. Have you ever witnessed anyone *in excess* enduring it very long?—it always exhausts itself early. And living with *defect* cannot long endure because the creature or the endeavor quickly dies."

He was right. My kidnappers kept me starved to keep me weak and being weak I was easier to control. It was both extremes at once.

"I think the scroll will do a better job of explaining it," Zafir said. "I see you're at the riddle. Let's hear what it says."

"A virtue of wealth is this for thee, One branch one limb on the self same tree; The coin and palace all men may gain, But woe is life when spent in vain. For joy that lasts and doth not cease, Embrace the virtues thou Prince of Peace. One branch one limb on the self same tree, A virtue of wealth is this for thee."

"Oh wisdom, behold now the Song of The Judge.
"Betwixt two paths the choice hangs sure, of this or that, corrupt or pure. The choice is one or one it's not; dawn or the dusk, cold or the hot. With a dearth of life, the fool is he, who solves with glut in hope to flee His scorn, his woe, his hungry vice; take all, take all no matter the price. Then seated there above the rift, he thinks he's given himself a gift. From stem to stern he says 'I've Fled!' But lost is he amid his dread. A vice for vice will not redeem, so look for the middle, the golden mean.
"What meaneth this Song of The Judge?"

There it was again, the middle, the mean, the balanced center. "'... Look for the middle,' that works well for me," I said. "But I usually can't find it."

"Let the scroll guide you, Bassam. Try the second passage again, read it carefully."

"'With a dearth of life, the fool is he, who solves with glut in hope to flee ...'"

"Stop there," he said. "Do you understand what it means by *a dearth of life*?"

"I suppose it's little or nothing of life ...."

"And with what do most people seek to escape their problems, their many and assorted *dearths* in life?"

I wasn't sure. "It says the fool seeks to solve it with glut."

"Yes!" Zafir said, raising both hands. "A gluttony. An over-abundance, an extreme. Is gluttony good?"

"No, it is not self governance."

"That's right, but what else is gluttony?"

"What do you mean?" I asked.

"If you have a dearth on one side, is gluttony any better?"

"Both are bad, I suppose," I said. And then it hit me. "This part, '*take all, take all, no matter the price,*' he's deciding to go to an opposite extreme, from dearth to gluttony, another mistake."

"That's right, and that's the problem," Zafir said smiling. "Where there's a defect, the fool tries to fix it with excess, it's that basic."

"I see it—*'A vice for a vice will not redeem'* means that two wrongs do not make a right."

"You've got it," Zafir said. "I want you to understand that too much of something can be just as bad as none at all. A defect is not corrected with an excess. Shall we find examples?"

He thought a moment, tapping a stick on his mat. "I'll give you some examples of defects and you find for me the extreme, and then tell me the balanced choice, the golden mean."

I nodded.

"Since you insist on growing so fast, tell me about starvation."

I laughed. "Starvation is what I feel most of the time! I'll say the opposite of starvation is gluttony, but what do I say for the middle?"

"Think of it as a virtue," Zafir said. "What does the man of virtue choose?"

"Just enough?"

"Excellent!" he said. "That's it in a nutshell—just enough, or sufficient for your needs. The virtue is sufficiency. Let's do some more. How about slavery?"

Slavery. *What is the opposite of total control*? "Not enough control? Anarchy?"

"Right again, Bassam. What would the golden mean be?"

I couldn't find the right words.

"I'll give you this one," he said. "*Freedom*. That's the middle ground between total law and no law. However, a better word is liberty because that puts boundaries around your freedom. You have freedom to swing your riding stick at me, but you're not at liberty to strike me, even if I deserved it. You may safely say that liberty is the key virtue of a free people."

I laughed. "Okay, I get it."

"Another ...." he said. "How about being a coward?"

"Its excess is probably just rushing forward, leaping before looking, not looking ahead ... being rash?" I said.

"Good! I'll take that. Between the two, cowardice and rashness, what would you call the virtue?"

"Courage? Because courage is measured, not blind or foolish?"

"Very good Bassam, you're getting it. How about chaos?"

"Chaos is everything out of control, that's the defect. I'm guessing the excess would be too much control, suffocating, regimentation, strict regulation."

"That works. And the virtue?"

"....I'm not too sure," I said.

"How about *order*?" Zafir said. "Chaos is not order—being overly regimented is suffocating—but simple order seems to cover it. A man of the scrolls makes his house a house of order."

I liked it. The golden mean was a balanced way to consider the many extremes in life.

"Here," Zafir said, "I'll give you one that I use to govern my caravans. What would you say to the excess of too much government, of ***total*** government?"

"Well ... it's like freedom and liberty, I would say the defect is too little government."

"And the virtue?"

"A little government, not too much?

"Or limited government, that is how I govern my caravans. I have representatives, captains, at all levels. They deal with their own problems. I get involved only when the grievance is too difficult, otherwise they handle things. That is how Abdali-ud-din has run its thousands of caravans for more than a dozen centuries, with limited local government. And it works."

It was an amazing concept. "Why would *all* people not want to govern in this fashion? It is so much better."

"So ... let us try another, something that strikes closer to home," Zafir said. "Consider our homes in Rekeem. If your father accidently poked out my eye, and as punishment the sheiks brought a hot poker and took the eye of your father, how is Rekeem helped?"

"I'm not sure," I told him. "The crime was paid for with a suitable punishment."

"Is Rekeem better with two men who are half blind? Or is it better with only one man that is half blind?"

"Well, yes, just one, but ..."

"The words in this lesson are poorly understood," Zafir said. He held out his hands like the cups of a balance scale and dropped one hand down, the other high. "Two wrongs do not make a right, Bassam. The ancient words about an eye for an eye have been misunderstood. Two half-blind men hurt Rekeem no matter what injustice has transpired."

"But all my life I've heard that the punishment must fit the crime." I looked at him with some honest astonishment. "Is that wrong?"

"The correct understanding is this: for the loss of an eye we must ask for the *value* of an eye. And for a tooth, the *value* of a tooth. Do you see the difference? Then the victim receives some gold to compensate for his loss, the criminal is punished, and Rekeem suffers just one, not two half-blind men."

"I see it. That is balanced, that is good justice." I said. "But how do you decide the value of an eye? Can an eye have a value?"

"No, it's priceless, so I judge it as this—I ask the victim, 'Do you require both eyes to do your labors and sustain your family?' The victim says yes, and I ask, 'How will this injury slow you in your labors?' And the victim tells me it will hurt a great deal. He is angry, of course, and I keep that in mind. I learn how much his work is hurt and from that I estimate a price for lost services and labor. I compel the perpetrator to pay that sum."

"And if that sum is too high, what then?"

"I arrange payments over time. After all, the perpetrator must care for his own family and obligations, and if all the fruits of his labors went to compensate his victim, the burden to care for his own family would fall to the others in the caravan. I still need all my men, and all their labors."

"And putting him in chains," I asked, "that's not punishment enough?"

"Putting a criminal in chains or prison does little good unless he is a danger to others, his crime makes that clear," Zafir said. "For non-violent offenders, sitting in prison does nothing to heal his victim of the loss. The criminal can't work off his debt, and another cost comes to his crime when others must care for him in his cell. The loss is added upon. If he is sincere—we watch for that very carefully—then it is better that he be compelled to work off his debt and the payment go to his victim. If he falls behind on his payments, we keep the poker red hot—that is his motivation."

"What about a man who kills?" I asked.

"For them the Law of Restitution, which is mercy, cannot help because no restitution is possible," Zafir said. "The killer must face the Law of

Justice that knows nothing more than the most severe of punishments. There is no escape for taking God's most precious creation, especially for wasting it twice: the killed and the killer."

That night I tried to sort out the Fourth Scroll. The words made me look at life, at choices, at errors and corrections in a new way. I see now that justice and mercy are virtues on the same tree, and together, they bring great order to life. They *are* the virtues.

"Day 225—Dear Rasha, the fourth scroll has opened my eyes to judging. It teaches the foolishness of extremes. There is moderation in all things except knowledge. There is always a deficit in learning, but never an excess. Knowledge brings forth all the best virtues in men. On some days, like today, I wish you were here with me to see this beautiful place and learn these wonderful things.—Bassam"

"Dear Bassam, I must share this in writing and with no one else. Faris tried to kiss me tonight. I did not let him. He became angry. I told him not to be angry, that my kiss is promised to you, it is my promise. He said that maybe you are gone and not ever coming back. Are you there, Bassam? Does the same moon shine on you that shines on me? I won't let you go.—Rasha"

BAMBOO BIRDS

The morning hangover from a short night finally released its grip. I slept longer than usual, and woke slowly to the smooth breeze of the fresh valley scent that carefully caressed our camp.

Without opening my eyes, I could tell that the days were growing shorter. Earthy perfumes in the air signaled the approaching end of harvest time in Ta-Yuan.

The sweet smells of cut grasses and grains mixed with cook-fires and breakfast foods and the sound of an awakening town combined in a pleasant warmth of delightful temptation. I opened one eye toward the ragged mountains. They were black with the sun rising directly behind them, and long shafts of shadow splashed across the valley floor. A few minutes more and the warm rays would shine on our camp, stirring us to life and melting the light frost that covered the ground and tents.

Then something caught my eye. There, directly overhead, *what is that?* I'd never seen anything like it.

I called across to Fawzi who lay slumbering a few paces away.

"Fawzi, wake up, get up! Look!"

His night was shorter than mine, and from the sound of his deep snoring it should have been clear he'd be in no mood for my exuberance this early in the morning.

"Bassam—leave me be, and I'm not kidding. Come back when the sun is up."

"The sun *is* up! But look!"

Fawzi pulled down a corner of his head scarf and squinted over at me with one eye. "What is it?" he mumbled.

I was excited and pointed. "Look! Look in the sky! There are birds hovering over our camp!"

Fawzi leaned back with great suffering and pain, and looked up. "Oh my heavens, Bassam, don't you know anything?" he said, pulling his blanket over his head.

"Anything? I don't know about those birds. What sort of creature hangs in the sky, and such colors!"

Fawzi groaned and rolled over, burying his head. "Fetch me a coffee and some sweetbreads," he mumbled, "and I'll tell you about the *muyuan*."

When I returned, Fawzi had woken himself and sat at the cook-fire stirring the coals. A small yellow flame ignited the end of his stick just as I set the clay mug and bread at his table.

"That's more like it," he said, and sipped at the hot brew. "Ah yes, perfect. I had forgotten the good coffees that are to be found in these parts." And he sipped again. After a few moments his voice was warmed enough that he could tell of the muyuan.

"It's another wonderful part about this place, young Bassam," he said. "Before our trip is finished you will learn many more new things."

"So, tell me of the muyuan!"

Standing still in the sky above were twelve beautifully painted-silk birds floating high, tethered to earth by a tight line of twine. I could see the other birds, more distant, fluttering in the sky all around Ta-Yuan.

"It must be a festival or celebration," Fawzi said.

"A festival? These birds? Why this early in the day?"

"Early is when I got to sleep, Bassam. And I should have been left to finish."

"Then tell me of the muyuan, and then go back to sleep," I said excitedly.

"All right. But don't interrupt."

Fawzi stirred the coals and held his hands around the warm mug.

"No one really knows how the muyuan first came. One story tells of an old farmer who was working his ground and kept losing his hat. One day he tied a cord around his hat to keep it secured upon his head. But that did not prevent the wind from catching it again, but this time the hat didn't fly away as it had done before. No, this time that hat was held with the cord and that's when the farmer noticed the hat could ride upon the wind. No one really knows, but this could be the beginning of the muyuan."

"I don't see the connection."

"What I'm saying bird brain is that the idea of things being held aloft on the wind has been known for a long time. Whether it was a hat and a string or a tarp tied at one corner and flapping in a wind storm, or papyrus shreds between your ears, no one knows. But what you see above you is not a real bird."

I stretched my neck to study the vibrantly-colored creatures standing above us with their shimmering wings colored in rich reds, gold and blues.

"How does it work?"

"Have you never been on a *dhow* and watched how its sails fill with the wind and it moves forward?"

"Yes," I said.

"When the wind passes by, it pushes all things before it. You see this, don't you Bassam, or does the wind whistle through your ears, too?"

"Of course, but not like this, in the sky."

"A muyuan is no different except a man keeps a leash on such a bird so that it doesn't fly away," Fawzi said. "Such a line is what gives the bird its strength, and it will climb higher into the windy sky. Cut it loose and it drifts to the ground again. If you will let me be, give me a chance to wake up, we'll visit Ta-Yuan. I'm sure we'll find a shopkeeper who sells the birds that fly on the twine."

An hour later, we met with Ammar and Tou who were also looking for an excuse to visit the market. We gathered an escort and strolled into the village looking for breakfast.

We found some tables in an open-air diner and sat. I enjoyed the chattering din that surrounded us—so many patrons from so many lands, seated for a meal and talking casually in an assortment of strange tongues.

"I like it here," I smiled to no one in particular.

"You want to move here?" Tou asked. "Many have."

"We'd be happy to drop you off," Fawzi said. "Big help you are keeping your friends *safe*."

"You shouldn't have camped so far from the rest of us, Fawzi," Ammar said. "There is safety in numbers."

"I *was* in numbers, only they were camped farther down among the insects, with Bassam."

"That's an ugly scar above your eye, Fawzi," I said. "Must have been a pretty large insect."

He glared and then winced at the tenderness the expression imposed on his recent wound.

I picked up a piece of bread from the basket and turned it in my hand.

"Tell me something, Tou," I asked, "tell me about the breads here. This is so dense and chewy—no offense to the cooks, but I'm wearing out my jaw on these."

"You should ask Zafir about that," Tou said. "His forefathers first brought wheat to our lands."

I hadn't heard *that* before. "You didn't have wheat?"

"Many centuries ago travelers brought kernels of wheat, and found it grew well here. You saw the green fields coming into Fergana? That's wheat, barley, and in the paddies among the ponds is our rice."

"Yes, it was a beautiful—green!" I said.

"The problem is wood—we have too little of it, not enough to run an oven."

"I saw that in the mountains," I said. "The river rushing through, but nothing growing. It was amazing—no trees anywhere. Grasses, maybe shrubs, but where were the trees? Saplings close to the river, but nothing else. Very strange to me."

"This region has always been that way. Without the forests, fuel to cook is expensive. So they make flat bread. Unleavened."

"And the C'ina like it?"

"Here in the north they love it. But farther south they have plenty of fuel but they don't make the bread you like."

That seemed crazy to me. Everybody loves bread. "Why?" I asked.

"Too soft, too empty. They call it hollow food. The poor people live on what they can boil. They boil the wheat and the grains, and that is their main food."

"So this flat bread, it seems a waste of work to cook it, why not leaven it and make nice bread?" I asked.

"It takes more fuel to keep their ovens hotter for a longer time. Instead, we use small baked-clay ovens. Every home has a *timuru* ("team-ew-rew"). Just a few sticks can keep such ovens hot for a long time, and we press our kneaded dough against the walls and they cook fast enough. That's what we ate today. It is our custom in Fergana."

I suddenly noticed no one seemed anxious to get going. I was impatient and noticed the sun. "We're at midday, let's start looking," I said. "We can eat more bread later, can't we? I want to see how these flying birds are made."

"It's not that difficult, my very rude and impatient insect," Fawzi said. "Give us a moment, let us finish. We'll have to search a little, we haven't been here before."

"So, what exactly will we be looking for?" I asked.

"A shop, Bassam, a fabric shop," Fawzi said.

"That sells muyuan? We can buy one?"

"No, but they're easy enough to make," Ammar said. He was enthusiastic about the whole idea. "It just takes some patience—and knowledge about the wind."

We went strolling off the main road a short time later and found a silk shop with colorful sheets of red and blue draped from an awning in front. Inside we were greeted warmly by three smiling women who clasped hands and gave a slight bow, extending their hands toward their selections. It was a colorful feast with shelves and tables overflowing with bolts of reds and blues, gold, green, sky blue, forest green, blood red, more colors than I thought possible.

"Did you know this is *our* weave, Bassam?" Fawzi said.

"Our weave? I don't understand."

"Yes, they don't make this quality fabric in these parts, but we do."

I was astonished. *Our* weave?

"It's the thread," Ammar added. "They send us their silk threads and we make the fabric."

"Then why are we here so far from our homes," I asked. "Isn't it cheaper to purchase this on our way back?"

"If you want to wait, my impatient friend, then that is exactly what we'll do," Fawzi said. "But for today, calm down. You remind me of my dog back home. Can't wait for a thing, not even the sun. Let's buy some silk and *make* a muyaun."

With fabrics of various colors, a ball of twine and some long, thin rods of split bamboo, we headed back to camp and sat down in a circle by Ammar's cook-fire.

"You think you can really make something of this that will hang in the sky?" I asked.

"Oh, it will fly all right—it's the size that matters," Ammar said.

"Size? Such as those birds?" I asked.

"No, nothing that large. But if you like we can make one large enough to carry you aloft," Ammar said smiling. He was laying out the cloth on the ground, measuring with a piece of charcoal.

"Ha! That's not possible. No man can fly like those birds," I said.

Ammar had a different story to tell. "According to wise old men in these parts, in ancient times the military had a lot of use for the muyuan."

"A weapon? How?"

"During a great battle that was at a standoff," Ammar said, "a creative general floated a muyuan from his position and sent it floating over the walls of an enemy's fortification. When the muyuan was past the walls, the general knew by how much twine he let out, and how far from his place the fort walls stood. Unknown to the enemy, his men had finished tunneling toward the fort. Knowing how much farther to dig allowed his men to accurately measure where to surface inside for a surprise attack."

"And did they?"

"Oh most certainly," Ammar continued. "There is also talk of a muyuan so large that it could carry aloft two men to spy and watch an enemy while floating beyond the distance of their arrows."

"That I'd like to see," I said.

For the better part of the morning, we crafted a muyuan with red silk. Fawzi crossed the bamboo sticks to make a large X that stood almost the full height of a man.

"The tall stick," he said, "is the spine, it's the backbone of our bird. As for the wings, this shorter stick will lie cross ways, equal on both sides of the spine, and we tie the two at the center, tightly."

I watched Fawzi and Ammar work as if they had done this many times before. Fawzi took a long piece of twine and tied it to the top of the tall stick and pulled it taut to the tip of the cross member and back to the bottom of the spine and up the other side to the top again. And then he laid the stick and twine skeleton onto the silk and with his knife he cut out a shape of cloth.

"You help sew, Bassam," Fawzi said. "I'm not going to do this all by myself."

"What do I do?"

"Fold the silk over the twine like this, and stitch it in place," Fawzi said.

Fawzi gently folded the silk around the twine and smoothed it out. With a needle and silk thread the edge of the fabric was sewn around the twine, securing it to the bamboo frame. Additional knife work finished our creation, and the shimmering crude thing actually resembled a bird.

We tied another twine tightly on a bamboo to put a slight bend on the center piece, and with an anchor twine tied to the front, we headed to a breezy hillside. There we let our creation catch the wind. As the afternoon breeze lifted it out of reach, I had to smile as our red bird joined the others in the sky. It danced up high, rolling to one side, sending the men racing one way and then another, darting high, falling, and hanging.

"We're no experts at this, Bassam," Fawzi huffed after half-an-hour of chasing, "but these people are great craftsmen with such things. And such things take skill and time."

It was more than skill, I decided—it was magic.

BARTERING

"Bassam!" Zafir ordered. "Come, it is time you learned the business of bartering."

I stood and fell into line with his little band, leaving my knife-sharpening for another day. Zafir led an escort of bodyguards, and four men pulling 18 camels by rope who followed behind.

"You're selling?" I asked. "This means your rendezvous with the traders didn't work out? The traders from the south?"

"They never showed," Zafir said. "I've met them right here for the past three years. Something must have happened. They probably found another use for their gold, or there was trouble. I will discover it soon enough, but for now we must sell our goods here and take the rest north."

North. So that's his plan, I thought. That meant taking the upper road around the desert—into Xiongnu land. Suddenly I was very glad to have Modu and Tou as escorts—and friends.

We turned a corner onto the main path toward Ta-Yuan and its market place. Zafir made it a time for learning.

"Do you know the difference between barter and sell?" Zafir asked.

"Not really."

"You can *sell* your goods to just about anybody," Zafir said. "It's not difficult, just a matter of the price. There are places where it's wise to accept gold for your goods. But to *barter*, to trade item for item, is a secret that can magnify your gold many times over if you know when and how to do it."

"And how can I know that?" I asked.

"That, my young son, is the secret, and such secrets don't manifest themselves if you stay at home all your life. My southern friends always barter with me, and my load changes accordingly. When I sell those goods farther east, I always make more profit."

"So, you're really just saving them a trip farther east, and for that you gain the added profit?" I asked.

"That's my business," Zafir said. "It doesn't get any more complicated than that. But a man must know the market to make it work."

"How do I learn this?" I asked.

"By watching, and that is what you'll be doing today."

I heard about Zafir's expertise at the bargaining table, but never watched him do it. *This should be interesting.*

"Some ground rules, Bassam. I want you to know how I balance my decisions."

"All right," I said.

"Let me tell it this way. Suppose I had the greatest pearl in the world. There is no one in the northern villages we'll be visiting who has enough gold to buy it from me. They don't want a large pearl, they don't need it, so they wouldn't offer much. They don't value it. Do you see how *they* fix its value, and not the thing itself? Do you understand?"

"Not yet," I said.

"People value things according to their own wants and needs. What's a pearl to a village starving to death or suffering from an outbreak of some kind? But if I brought food, or a balm that cured them of an itch or rash, such a thing is highly valued here and the people willingly barter all they could to find relief."

"And with that you leave a much richer train," I said.

"Yes, richer in commodity, not gold. But I must find a market for that new load, or I'm stuck with inventory nobody wants. My water skin filled to the top will fetch a higher price to the thirsty man lost in the desert than my grand pearl."

"And in the desert, I would rather have water than a pearl," I said.

"So is it if you were dying of thirst. Here I barter. I sell for gold later, but more importantly, bartering for goods lets me deliver commodities that are bought and sold many times over to strengthen the economy of small markets."

Strengthen small markets, I thought. That was a new idea. "You're such a philanthropist? Why care about small markets?"

"This is not philanthropy, Bassam. By keeping economies active, prosperity follows and the next time I pass through, they will be strong enough to buy my goods with gold. That's how Abdali-ud-din builds a market that pays back for decades to come. It's our investment in ourselves. And from that, many others also benefit. They benefit with new goods, better goods, quality goods."

"Isn't that more selfish than clever?" I asked.

"Don't be fooled, Bassam. Selfishness is the power that drives all good things forward. Balanced with honesty, selfishness is what drives all things to become better. All people want more money for themselves. Is it selfish to create better goods and lure the gold away from others?"

"Well, I didn't see it that way ...." I said.

"The answer, Bassam, is yes! It *is* selfish, but look at what good comes from it. The selfish man wants more gold, but being an honest man, he knows he can't steal it, he must lure and tempt and draw it out of others.

So he creates things that others are willing to buy. He receives their gold, they receive his product, and everyone benefits."

"And what if someone came along," I asked, "who competes with a better product or a better price?"

"That's how it works! And the men who buy the goods find these prices dropping and the quality rising, so they are thrilled. What a great market that is. Unless, of course, some sheik steps in the way to take away the profits in the form of a tax. But letting this competition run freely is how all men may become wealthy."

The two of us grew quiet as we neared the market place. My young appetite awoke at the beautiful display of foods we encountered. It had been different each day of our stay. *Where do they get all of this prosperity*? The day's catch from the river was spread out, fresh vegetables and fruits picked before sunrise were piled in baskets in all their assorted colors and sizes. Small fires heated aromatic coffees and boiled water for teas. And the hubbub of daily living filled the streets with cattle calls, chatter, the raucous grumbling of many voices speaking at once.

The hot morning sun beat down on the square as animal and human traffic intermingled, seeking a place, a sample, a bargain.

But in that cornucopia of delight, an undercurrent of flies and stink exposed the imperfections of such markets and the rush of competition in all its forms. Zafir didn't tarry in the general marketplace where the haggling for a day's meal unfolded with such drama each morning. Instead we headed to a different kind of market, a place much quieter without the mess and noise.

It was in a broad dirt field where stood many large tents—staked for a prolonged stay. Each occupied space with room enough to keep pack camels securely penned while negotiations commenced. Servants delivering tea to keep the discussions civil were seen coming and going from each of them.

As we neared one of the larger tents, Zafir sighed. "Our journeys to places such as these will not last."

"Not last? Why do you say that?" I asked.

"Moving our goods by sea must become our new venture. It's ancient, it's new, it's expensive. It promises the greatest profit, but still, it's difficult."

"I thought that was the way things should go. Fawzi speaks of pirates …."

"Yes," Zafir said, "and other concerns such as the storms at certain times of the year. When one of our boats takes to the rocks, a great treasure is lost to the deep."

"What stands in the way?" I asked. "Better pilots, experienced men who know those rocky shores?"

"Even with the best, such accidents still happen. Oh, it's successful enough. I expect the majority of trade over the seas to expand as more ports of call are created and our ships are stronger. Such losses are quickly recovered with the high demand. They call for us from all corners of the world," Zafir said.

"Then why continue traveling overland?"

"When our ships grow large enough to improve the profit from port to port, and when more camel trains can carry goods from the ports to places inland, then the long trips such as these will be replaced with many short treks—fewer camels, fewer men, less risk. Even our sea trade—many smaller boats are less costly if we lose one. It will take time to build a fleet."

"What becomes of Abdali-ud-din? Do they become masters of the seas and leave the overland trips to the badawi?"

"One day, Bassam, perhaps soon, you should take a voyage from the southern coasts to our western homes and then you will see the problems. The sea is a cruel teacher and the sea takes a prince's ransom for the least carelessness while in its care."

"How are such accidents prevented? Do we play odds at sea?"

"It will take time and investment. It has been going on for a thousand years, the sea is the way of the future for us as well."

For the balance of the day, my mind was preoccupied with visions of shipwrecks or being lost at sea as I watched expert salesman do battle with expert buyers.

All those who came to negotiate with Zafir in the great tent knew the price that such quality goods could bring, and all men knew that Zafir would settle for no less than top price. Even so, that is where Zafir's expertise came to play—

"You ask too much, Master Zafir," said one buyer. "I can buy your offering for half the price from the traders south, and they bring me twice the load."

"Yes, you are wise and you are discerning," Zafir replied. "I see that you cannot be convinced for old time's sake to deal with a friend long and humble on the trail to present his cherished wares for your consideration. I will think again of my price lest my suppliers lose faith in me."

"Lose faith in Abdali-ud-din? Never! You shadow our lands far too often as old friends. No one could lose faith in Abdali-ud-din!"

"Then I must be fair to them as I must be with you. I can reduce my price by a fourth of the profit. But let us be open about this. If I reduce it more than that, then I will need to thank you for letting me make a new friend and talk business with you today, and bid you good day."

"You are too kind to your buyers, Master Zafir. You travel far too long to give way so easily. But I know that honest men do not cheat, and we have always profited handsomely from our dealings with you. I will take your offer and hope to be more generous with you on your next visit to our village."

Hours later, the exchanges were not much different—

"Men of the desert! How can you think that we are so gullible to swallow any trick you bring to the market?"

"We bring no tricks," Zafir would say, "only treasures and goods from the west that we carry here to sell for profit so we can afford to venture farther into your land."

"Profit? What thievery is this? We've never paid such high prices. And look at this, these are merely common goods we buy all the time from other traders. And you ask for such prices?"

"Only what I have paid plus a little to make it worth our while."

"You say that, but in your heart I know you are trying to rob me of my gold."

"Then good day to you sir."

"What?—Hey, wait a minute. What do you mean?"

"My prices are too high for your liking? I am so very sorry. Then good day to you sir."

"Oh no, you're up to something. It's a trick."

"No tricks. Thank you for stopping by. Perhaps next time my prices will be less disagreeable."

"Oh, oh, oh, you're trying to trick me, yes you are. I know it."

"I said, no tricks, my friend. You may leave and perhaps I will have better luck with others not so discerning as you, others who will not see the truth as you see it. I must make some profit, else why come this far? But you, you are too wise for me. Let us salute with a bond of understanding and perhaps I will buy you a dinner. But free me from my oath so that I may try to sell to others."

The buyer stood to leave, and then thought a moment, and sat right back down. "No, I think if you will reduce your profit to half, then I will still buy, even though I think you're trying to cheat me."

"If you believe I am trying to cheat you, then no, I will not reduce my profit by half. I will by a fourth, but not by a half. A half is cheating me. So, my friend, release me from my oath and you may keep your gold for another train. And thank you for coming to this tent today."

"See? Do you see it? Do you hear you? You are trying to get rid of me. Oh no, oh no, you have put a price on the table and you may not take it back. I will accept your offer."

"But I was only trying to free you to trade elsewhere, not to ...."

"Don't you tell me what you were trying to do. I know exactly what you were trying. I will accept your offer and if you try to back out, I will make it known all across the land, Abdali-ud-din are cheaters and thieves, their goods are polluted and impure. There is blood in their trade, do not let them in your villages."

"We are none of those. And if you will retract your words—words that I know you did not mean because you spoke with passion and anger—which of course is my fault, and for that I offer my sincere apology—then I will feel better about losing so much on this trade."

And with that, Zafir drew to himself gold coins by the hundreds, and commodity by the camel-load, and made enormous profit with every trade. I watched the sly old fox work his magic time and time again, analyzing his every move, memorizing his every response. It was like a game—playing dead to the buyers, rolling over and letting them take all. But all the while hiding the real profit he was making, a real profit that was rich indeed. I smiled after their departure from each trade concluded. Zafir truly was a master of the hidden upper hand. By the end of the day, his load was exhausted and the bartered items became his new load for trading at the next stop—the distant village of Kashgar.

The last evening in Fergana Valley found me sitting with Tou in a diner, finishing a large bowl of mee pok and chicken—this time eating with the sticks.

"I think you've got those figured out," Tou said.

"Yes, I'm getting better with them," I said. "I like the food in this place, Tou. It fills but sits lightly. I'm satisfied but not uncomfortable, and I'm sure I've eaten more than my bakra's share!"

Tou smiled. "We're not finished with the foods in this place, my young friend."

"I couldn't take another bite! This is a wonderful valley. Peas I've not had, cucumbers and cabbage—never as these. The oranges and lemons, peaches and apricots! Is there no end to it?"

"Before we retire, you must try one more," Tou said.

He called a waiter over to ask the cook for a sample. It was delivered on a small platter.

"Here, try this," and he picked up with his sticks a green, tender shoot and let me take it with my fingers. A drop of dark, brown liquid was on the end.

"These are shoots of the bamboo, you will like it especially with the shoyu ("shoy-ew")." and Tou handed over a small glass container.

I looked at the brown liquid and took a hesitating bite. It was fantastic. "Very delicious, Tou! What is this sauce?"

"It's made of a bean that grows in these parts. We cook the bean for nourishment or grind it for flour. We squeeze it for oil, and that's what we serve you here, that's what you see in the bottle."

"It's salty but rich—a roasted flavor."

"In some villages, shoyu is as sacred as the black rice—received with thankfulness from the gods. You may store it until a famine, and in times of hunger, whole villages have survived on it between growing seasons."

"Amazing. I must take some home. Where can it be bought?"

"Follow me," Tou said, standing to leave. "You may have better luck with these beans than with our black rice. Let us go find some shoyu."

SCARS

The week-long stay in Fergana Valley ended far too soon—the caravan had to move on. As morning broke, Zafir was already far beyond the city with more than an hour's length of men following behind. By sunrise we were well down the main road that stretched the entire length of the valley, a road that took us past other towns and stops before turning east.

I pulled my camel next to Fawzi. "You bring an incredible souvenir from this last stop," I said.

"You like my belt?"

"Very much. I'd like to get one myself."

"And I know just how to make that happen, donkey head," Fawzi said.

I laughed and we rode along in silence for a while.

"You never did tell me how you killed that lion," I said.

"You never asked."

"I'm asking now. How did you manage it, and in the pitch of black?"

"He was sniffing around my face, that's what woke me," Fawzi said. "I felt his breath on my neck, in my ear. It woke me."

"And that made him attack?"

"I was startled and suddenly rolled to my side. I sleep with my knife in my hand. All of us do, don't you?"

"Well ...." I stammered.

"Never mind," he said. "The lion grabbed me by the shoulder to pull me, and at the same time I was swinging around with my knife. I thrust it into his neck and he bit down harder. It was paralyzing, I could hardly yell."

"Sounded more like screaming to me," I said.

"No. It was yelling," he said flatly.

"Like a girl."

"You want to hear this story or not?"

I stopped.

"He was so strong, even with the knife in his throat. I was helpless. He dragged me with my shoulder locked in his jaws like I wasn't even there, just a play thing."

"Why did he drag you?"

"I don't know, it's a cat thing I guess. But I fumbled around with my good hand trying to find something, anything to defend myself and found my sword caught up in my blankets."

"Still wrapped around you?"

"Yes, tangled up, a corner caught in his teeth against my shoulder. I found the handle and started punching it against his jaw, his nose, his eyes, anything to make him to let go. Then he released me."

"And fled?"

"Oh no, he wasn't finished. He put a paw on my chest but I kept hitting him with the hilt, and that's when he began clawing me, trying to find another place to bite down, I guess to pin me down or something. I was worried for my throat, he kept going for my throat."

"How did you manage to drive your sword into him?"

"In all the hitting the sheath came off and when he bit into my shoulder again I was able to turn the point to him and just pushed. I couldn't see where, only that he was to my side and there was enough of something big there to stab at. I knew I just had to get my point into him far enough to make him drop me."

"And he fell dead on the spot?"

"Not at all. It just made him mad. He slashed at me again. It was so fast, all at once, heavy blows, like a bath in hot oil, pain everywhere, at the same time."

"And you let go?"

"I felt his hits weakening. The blankets took a lot of the thrashing or I might have been frayed like jerked goat meat. It was him or me, so I held tight and just pushed my sword deeper into him. It wasn't until the torches came that I saw I had found his heart."

"And pinned him to the ground."

"And pinned him."

"So, I don't understand it, what is this lion doing in this place? I've never seen that kind of cat before."

"There are many lions, I told you. Some fast, many furs—striped, black, spotted. Some very large, others sleek. I don't know why a striped lion lived here. He was a young lion, maybe wandered from his pride, but big enough to kill a man."

I looked over at my friend. He looked tired. He was thin. The travail had extracted a price that showed in his countenance but not in his courage. And with the bandages off, I could see the cuts were red and deep, still healing. Without the sewing by Humam, he probably would be dead.

"Then it is a belt and a paw—his right hand of power—that is a worthy prize in a fight to the death," I said.

"A pair of claws for each of my boys," he said. "My wife won't have anything to do with me when I get home. Probably won't let me bring dead animal parts into the house. But I will. The boys will know about the night their father killed a lion."

I was thinking his boys might never really know how close to death he came that night. Looking at Fawzi I saw the scars of survival and victory permanently etched into his face.

He saw me looking and an expression of "what's with you?" spread across his brow.

"Camel vomit," he said.

"Donkey bowels," I replied.

THE WORDS

With the death of Suoud, the near death of Fawzi, and all the other dangers we had experienced on the trail, I wondered about messages to home. It made no sense that so many fathers and sons traveled so very far, and for so very long without some way to be contacted. I decided to ask Ammar about that and see what he knew about messengers.

I found him near the front of the train, making a note on one of his small maps. I steered my camel to his side.

"What if Fawzi had died," I asked.

Ammar was concentrating and kept writing. "What are you talking about, Bassam," he said.

"What if Fawzi had died from the cat, do we really wait to send word?" I asked. "What if there is an emergency. Or worse, an emergency at home. Is there no way to send messages?"

Ammar put down his map and looked at me like he had something to share.

"Has Zafir told you about *The Words*?" he asked.

"What words?"

"*The Words,*" he said. "Al Kalimat, *The Words*. The relay for messages."

"No, what is that supposed to mean?"

Ammar seemed to be weighing a decision, like the other times he divulged things he wasn't sure I was supposed to learn. But he also knew I wasn't going away until I had an answer, and seemed to become less restrained about sharing.

"Al Kalimat," he said, "is code for a message system that spans this entire land."

"A message system? You mean—why wasn't I told?" I asked, throwing my hands in the air. "All these things, no one ever tells me."

"It's not that big of a concern," Ammar said, "but it is wisdom. It's not really a secret but it's something we don't talk about openly."

"So tell me," I said. "What is *Al Kalimat*?"

"It's complex, expensive and rarely used," he said. "Yes, there are times as you say, times when we need to receive word from home or deliver to home, or to other caravans."

"So, for example, to avoid dangerous lands," I asked, "like the Xiongnu wars?"

"Exactly, and that is why Zafir put into play *Al Kalimat*. There are only three ways for us to send and receive messages while we're out here on the trail," he said. "The first is too outdated and isn't used very much. They called it the *sirr-g'bal,* or Secret Mountain. In ancient times when military campaigns were long and difficult, messengers had time to relay word all across a country that if you see the light on a mountain, a man-made light, those who knew the code could then know that we are victorious, or under attack, or a new prince is born, or the old has died, or our army is on the move—whatever the signal might mean. And when the action took place, word was sent to a guard on the nearest mountain and a large stack of wood was lit on fire. Far away, maybe hundreds of stadia, guards atop other mountains saw the flame and lit their own, and so on, all the way across great distances."

"But just one signal," I said, "either lit or not lit—a yes or a no?"

"Right. So other ideas were tried. The most obvious idea, of course, is an actual messenger, a living human who has memorized a message and must deliver it in person at the other end—he ran on foot or rode a camel or horse, racing from one point to the next. The problem here is that such messengers became perfect targets for robbers or enemies to intercept and be tortured for their message. A man can run 40-50 stadia a day. To protect these runners they used to set up guard towers every 40-50 stadia, but this didn't always work. If the runner never showed, how were they to know one was ever sent in the first place?"

"A man could be killed part way," I said, "and no one would know it farther down the line?"

"That was the difficulty, Bassam," he said. "They tried to solve it with birds—pigeons, usually—then falcons. If a message was expected and never came, the receiving end released trained pigeons that flew to the starting place, signifying they didn't receive the message in the allotted time, please send again."

"Why not just put the message with the bird?" I asked.

"Because birds could be caught and messages stolen or changed," he said. "They encoded the messages but they had another problem—bigger birds. One solution was invented by the people of Chang'an. They attached whistles and bells to their birds to scare away predators."

"Brilliant!" I said.

"Yes, for the short run," Ammar said. "But for longer distances, a new idea was needed. And that's when the Greeks came to the rescue. In those days they had 24 letters in their alphabet and divided them into five groups. If they wanted to send one letter, they held up a torch for the group number and a torch for the letter number, and even at a great distance, so long as the fires could be seen, the message could be read. Do you follow?"

"I think so," I said.

"For example, *omega* is in the last group—the fifth. The guard held up five torches on the left to show which group the letter was in, and if the letter was fourth in that *group*, he'd hold up four torches on the right side. Five and four, number 24, omega. Get it?"

"So they could spell out words!" I said. "In Greek!"

"Yes, except—anyone else watching could read the torches and figure out by trial and error how the Greek letters were grouped. So, the Greeks and others started to mix things up, adding codes and confusion. It is quite an art today, and very difficult to decipher if you don't know the key. We call this system by its old Greek name, *fryktos*—their word for fire."

"So tell me about Al Kalimat."

"Like I said, very complex," Ammar said. "Cooperation and capability vary in all the lands we visit. Zafir buys loyalty with gold, but still, there is a question that people don't just take the gold and cheat him."

"Can't he check?" I asked.

"Yes, but it is costly. He usually sends a message once a year and on his next trip to that area he checks with his stewards to learn if they were delivered."

"And if not?" I asked.

"If not, he challenges the steward and those in the chain of delivery—he withholds gold and tries them again the following year," Ammar said.

"Do they all use the same system?"

"I don't know if you noticed but at each of our stops where Zafir has a steward, he is always checking for messages. While our train travels overland, he pays his friends to deliver messages by boat. The messages are copied 20 or 30 times and dropped off all along the part of our route where a river or ocean is close enough for a boat to meet one of Zafir's stewards. That way, as we travel, if something urgent needs to go out or come in, it can move faster than our slow line of beasts."

I whistled in dismay. "You're right, Ammar," I said. "It sounds complex and expensive. What does sending a message to Rekeem involve?"

"It depends where we are when we send it," Ammar said. "For example, in Chang'an, it goes out on a boat to the ocean and travels all the way south and then west. That can take six months to a year. That's about the same time it takes our train to travel from Chang'an to the Hindus and then west to home. But there are stopping places by rivers that empty into the south ocean where we could dispatch a message. These usually reach home before we do."

He reached for his larger map and circled with his finger the lands of the Greeks and Romans.

"These are controlled by emperors and armies," Ammar said. "They use messengers inside the land they control. Down here through our deserts, it's a waste to send messengers across the long deserts so it's worth the time to trek down to the coast and use boats."

He pointed to the places along the southern coast where the rivers intercepted Zafir's usual route. Anywhere along those places, messages could come or go.

"So, all these people, all along these routes are being paid to sit and wait," I said, "to run messages if they get one."

"Yes, very costly, but they don't just sit—they are merchants or farmers or fishermen," Ammar said. "Nobody knows where we are at any given time. They know generally because there are schedules to keep. But still, one message must be delivered to many places hoping to find us. Things change, and Zafir plans accordingly."

I shook my head in disbelief—cost, complexity, distance, difficulty. A letter to Rasha would have to wait.

66

EASTERN KASHGAR

The long ride to the oasis of Kashgar demanded dangerous travel through steep mountain passes.

“There is no other way,” Ammar said again, trying to stop my questions and complaints. We are at the top of a grand plateau and these mountains will stand in our way for the next two or three months.”

“Months?” I couldn’t believe it. “A boat on the sea is sounding more to my liking all the time,” I said.

“And that’s why you will always be poor,” Ammar scolded. “The places we visit now? Most of these villages have never seen men from the west—we foreigners in our strange costumes and silly manners and curious appetites.”

“Will they trust us? Enough to trade?”

“Certainly. Everyone knows the incense, there is no hiding the value of what we bring. And they will be happy to exchange it for their gold.”

Zafir always chose the river valleys through the ranges, finding a steady path eastward where runoff from the snowfall gave plenty of drink and greens between villages. Some rivers ran shallow, others were dried.

“This route is on every map,” Ammar said. “No kamal strings needed here,” he said.

“I keep hearing about Kashgar. What’s so exciting about Kashgar?” I asked.

“It’s the dividing place. For as long as the caravans have traveled east to west, this is the place where they choose north or south. North toward Turpan, or south toward Hotan.”

“I’m still not convinced we couldn’t cut right through the Taklamakan, you’ve said it before, I think we should go east.”

"Oh my holy goat milk, Bassam, must I argue this point with you again? The Taklamakan is a tomb of endless sands into which a man may enter but he will never come out of again. You will see it—there are dunes as tall as mountains, sand that blows across weeks and weeks of travel. No water, no growing thing, just dunes, dusty nothing, as far as the eye can see. No, we don't just pass through. We go around it, Bassam. Nobody ever comes out of that place. We go around."

Ammar told me the old villages of Kashgar were more than a convergence place for two paths to the east. The mountains also protected the place from the rise and fall of empires that had been boiling south for many centuries. The caravans were safer along these routes.

Kashgar sat high among the plateaus. The over thrust was smooth, well watered and scenic. Massive mountains clawed at the sky on all sides. The higher altitude and the lateness of the season meant cold temperatures. For the last three days of travel, I unpacked my goat-hair coat and a spare blanket—I needed them.

As the company neared the Kashgar, Zafir announced we would rest for two nights and a day before resuming along the upper road to Turpan.

"This is home to you, isn't it?" I asked Tou as we rode along with Fawzi between us.

"It's near home, but not home," Tou said. "Kashgar is historic, an old place. Many visitors for a long time. In fact, there are ruins, Bassam. Old ruins. With paintings. I will show you when we arrive."

"Ahhhh, ruins," Fawzi said. "Your favorite tourist stop."

More ruins. I pondered. *These lands are filled with the graves of the ancients—eons, ages, eternities. How many have come and gone through these places? And more important, why? Why didn't they stand the tests of time?*

Kashgar finally presented herself to the slow approach of the caravan, coming into view at the gentle foothills of the blue mountains, just as the cloudy sky darkened for dusk. From our vantage on a mountain pass that led directly to the city, I could see from a distance the whitewashed, mud-brick shacks that leaned against each other in long lines. The dusty road led us directly to the center of the merchant square, past open-door shops with scant supplies stocked for the visitors. A few cook-fires in small diners gave the only allure. It was a poor town. I looked at the scene passing by as we followed single file to the pastures on the far side. I decided this would be a very long and trying two-day stay.

"They don't look happy," I almost whispered as we passed villagers in dirty robes and wraps, lining the road with their hands extended.

"The people don't have much trade," Tou said. "They see us often enough, and it is always like this."

Their thinned, sun-baked faces looked up behind shawls, scarves and headdresses, holding out for a morsel, a coin, or piece of bread, with trembling, wrinkled hands.

"Don't be fooled," Tou said. "They are expert beggars. Zafir would agree with me. They are neither warm nor cordial, not friendly or conspiring. Just lazy and poor."

"Poor because they are lazy," Fawzi added.

"For a coin they will feed our animals," Tou said, "and perhaps provide some hot meals and a place to sleep. When Xiongnu conquers the whole land, it is the villages like this one that we want to free, to show them prosperity instead of handouts."

The caravan exited to the far side of the town and circled around to the west of the main center. There we found suitable pasture to set camp. Zafir did not put up his larger tent because of the short stay.

As night fell and the watch was set I sat close by my cook-fire, looking for some warmth and enjoyed a bowl of mee pok. And try as I might, plucking the slippery nourishment with a pair of sticks was an art that still refused me with any degree of coordination. But there was *bread* in this place—and with a few slices of that, I was able to catch enough to satisfy a hungry boy's lament. I huddled close to Bakra, scratched behind her ears for a few moments until she relaxed, and then I tried to sleep.

THE KISSING STONES

Our first morning in Kashgar found Ammar up early. I opened one eye to see him blowing coals to life to prepare a quick breakfast. Then I felt all my muscles protest at once—too little warmth in the dark, I decided, and pulled my blanket tight to watch Ammar's morning routine. He hurried about as if he could hardly contain his excitement over something.

I was curious and leaned on an elbow. "Just what are you getting ready for, Ammar?"

"Ah, my young student spies on his teacher, that's not wise, Bassam!"

"I'm not spying, you goat herder. How can I sleep through all the noise? What are you doing? Packing to leave?"

"Yes, to the market—just to visit the market place."

"What's so exciting about the market at this time of day?"

Ammar stopped for a moment and looked right at me for a long time, as if weighing something in his mind. Then tipping his head to the side in consideration, he snapped back as if he had decided something important. He continued his preparations.

"There are tools of my trade I haven't told you about, Bassam."

"What tools?"

"It's not like I've been keeping some secret from you, or been silent ... silent by request of Zafir or something like that."

I shook my head. "Secret? What secret?"

"It's simply a secret that belongs to the navigator who wants to keep his job."

"What on earth are you talking about, Ammar?"

"I'm saying that there is more to my kamal strings and knots than I have told you," he said.

With that, I sat right up and looked at him dumbfounded.

"More? *More?* I figured so! So you *have* been holding out on me!"

Ammar smiled. "No, not like that, but I do hope to find something in these parts. We don't normally travel north, this is a rare treat, I've wanted to go this way for many years."

"What secrets do you have up your sleeve, Ammar?"

"So … Zafir has not told you about my kamal and my strings?" he asked.

"Told me what?"

"Well, this is interesting!" Ammar said, grinning like the cat that caught the bird. "I know something you should know, and Zafir has chosen not to tell you. And now you want to know, and this puts me in a good bargaining position. This will cost you, Bassam."

"Cost me? Why, you old goat herder, I'll go ask Zafir myself!"

"No, he wouldn't tell you, either. But for the cost of a dinner I'll tell you the secret of the *south pointer.*"

"What? A *south pointer*? What under heaven is a south pointer?"

"Come by the fire and I will tell you," he said. "When this water boils for tea, then I am leaving. You may come if you want. But let me first say that the south pointer has changed everything. It came from a man many hundreds of years ago who lived east of here, another 30 days' ride. This man was nothing of note except that he came to the most extraordinary discovery quite by accident—"

According to the ancient legend that was passed among traders and merchants along the routes beyond the great deserts east, there lived in the region of Cheng an old man who knew the art of metal works. He had melted and cast, he had formed and polished, he had crafted and sold. And from such works he kept enough coins to put rice on the modest table for himself and his aging wife.

One day his neighbors tending to crops in their fields observed the old man carrying toward his shop a basket of common black sand. Such sand had always washed down from the mountains upstream. Being black, the sands had once been an oddity that the locals had gossiped about long ago—but not any longer, they had lost their mystery. For what value is there in the sands of the sea, let alone the sands of the rivers, be they black or white or any other color for that matter? It was all *simply sand.*

Not until that day when they saw the old man laboring under another heavy basket did the black sands spark any discussion at all.

It turned out the old man was working an idea. For all the years he lived in his home, it was his grandfather's great flat rock that had intrigued him—intrigued him since he was a boy.

From the iron mountains his grandfather had hauled a large black rock to his little shop to study it. The value that grandfather placed in the rock was that it was of the same kind from which he had taken the "kissing stones."

The kissing stones were so named because they were attracted to each other, and given the chance, they did just that—kissed. Large or small, it mattered not. Put two near each other and they slid, tumbled and snapped together—a kiss. Certainly they could be pulled apart. And stranger still was the fact that other objects with iron in them drew themselves to the kissing stones until they clicked together and held.

When the grandson inherited the old workshop of his grandfather, along with that large strange rock, he used the cozy little place to craft his own artwork.

Every so often, the grandson's attention turned from his labors at creativity to grandfather's large slate-gray, black-mottled rock. But it wasn't an ordinary ornament—he put it in a prominent place in the corner of the shop to use for his art work.

Periodically, as if to play with its magic, the grandson took sand from the floor and sprinkled it down the side of the black rock. As if by some unknown power, silky black webs and threads took form, created from a black powder hiding in the sand. It grew into tiny lacy strands thanks to the rock's magic.

Such slender webs stood as stiff as boar hairs, but a dash of water washed them off again. Indeed, grandfather's rock held a power that was puzzling—the power of the kissing stones.

After many years of tooling and working across its top, the old stone surface became smooth and polished. It served as an anvil, a work table, a sanding surface and so much more.

It was on this solid, unmoving surface that the grandson made detailed engravings and filigree for his metal castings. The rock served as a second pair of hands—holding in place, just like magic, any iron objects while he worked them. Over the years he learned a great deal about the properties of the rock and its relationship to other iron objects.

And then came that day from the beginning of our story when neighbors observed the grandson, now a grey-haired, old artisan, hauling black sand toward his shop. It was especially odd because everyone knew the black sands never showed the same mystical qualities as the chunks of rocks that "kissed." It wasn't the same.

The old artisan emptied his muddy burden into a large clay pot where he washed out the mud and impurities.

Draining away the waste, there remained a sparkling mixture of black crystals and glimmering diamond-like particles. He reached into the black silky treasure and let the granules flow between his fingers and cling lightly to the creases in his hand. If there was magic in these sands, he hoped to unlock it by melting them down and creating something wonderful.

The old man had melted ores for other projects, many times before, but never the black sands—he was curious. If the sands that had once been kissing stones could unite once again in his furnace, would they yet kiss again? He hoped to find out soon enough.

But first, he puzzled over what object of art he could create for the experiment.

The solution came to him unexpectedly, at a feast to honor the marriage of the daughter of their good friends from a nearby village. The old man and his wife joined the celebration and found themselves seated at a table watching the new bride and the festivities. Suddenly, he realized a cumbersome irritation began to repeat itself over and over again. It had to do with soup.

There was simply no way to serve soup without making a little mess. His hosts made the pot of soup the center piece of the meal, bravely honored on a small ornately-carved, dark-red wooden stand with individual bowls stacked to the side. The father stood behind the pot and graciously dipped with a ladle to serve—one scoop into each bowl, and passed it to the guests.

When the last bowl was served, what was to become of the ladle? And why should this annoyance create such attention?

Left to itself the ladle slipped into the broth on its own, or had to be laid on the wooden stand. Either way, there was a mess. Fishing out the ladle was embarrassing. But laying the ladle on the table dripping its delights onto the cloth was a likewise unsightly litter. The solution they reached was simply to lay the ladle on a saucer.

The old artisan watched the best efforts at serving go awry, and stroked his chin as a new idea began to form in his mind. Could he address that little annoyance in a way that might win him some sales?

It was weeks later that he fired up his furnace and pumped it with the bellows until it smoked white hot. He poured the black sand into his largest crucible and placed it between the bricks and pumped more air until the glowing coals of the little furnace did their work. The sands began to smoke, then glisten, then wilt, and finally melted into a thickening pool of shiny black.

When the melted ore was ready, he skimmed it of the dross and called to his son. Together they removed the crucible from its fiery containment and carefully carried it to a sand-and-plaster mold that was already carefully anchored atop his grandfather's large black rock. Tipping the pot slowly, they poured the molten mass into a small opening at the top of his mold until it filled to the top. He packed sand and straw around the mold, and covered it with a thick layer of cloth. He wanted it to cool slowly lest it crack.

For the whole of a day he waited, busying himself with other chores.

That next morning, he let it be, checking it often to see if his creation was cooling, but not too fast.

On the third day, he found it had cooled enough to touch.

Curious, he took his tools and carefully pulled apart his mold to reveal his creation.

It had cooled so he could handle it and clean it up with his brush. Seeing the finished product made him proud. He set it on the rock and stepped back—rubbing his chin, wondering.

It was the oddest looking soup ladle ever invented. Its bulbous, fist-sized cup was oversized on its bottom, and elegantly rose to a fluted top where a squat handle protruded opposite its pouring lip. The ladle's rounded bottom gave it an unsteady look, yet it was exactly the opposite. It stood upright, perfectly balanced.

As the ladle cooled its shiny blackness dulled to that same tone and hue as grandfather's rock. *Shale grey*—no object had yet been created with such odd coloration.

And so began the finishing work. He smoothed the seams left from the mold, flattening them, scraping and polishing to hide. He smoothed off the ridges on the handle, and put a wet mixture of hard powders inside the bowl swirling around with his cloth, polishing, smoothing, polishing—until the glass-smooth surface darkly mirrored his own image.

"It looks mystifying," he said aloud. "People will not know what to make of my black sand ladle!"

He crafted a story to lend mysticism and lure, and decided to tell others that it held a mysterious energy—power to defy the gods of nature, to commune with the stars.

Giving it one last polish with his rag, he held it up again to examine. The final test, of course, was his wife.

When evening arrived, the old man joined her at the table for food. After a nice talk about how the day went in the shop, he brought his creation from his hiding place. He presented it in a way that mysteriously eclipsed the yellow light of their oil lamp.

At first she said nothing and just looked.

She took if from his hand and held it carefully to examine the mysterious shape and study its beautiful finish, turning it about slowly.

She placed the bowl in her cupped hand and found it cold to the touch. She closed her fingers about its fullness and lightly touched the harmony of the hemisphere that elegantly curved upwards to the top. And then held it by the handle and hefted it as if serving.

After several long moments of silence, she held it at arm's length. "The bowl on this ladle is too large for the handle, my husband. You should have asked me for the design of a proper ladle. For what dish will this serve?"

The artisan smiled, his eyes twinkling. He took the ladle from her and pointed out its unique features, emphasizing that the genius in the design was its natural balance.

Then he set it on her table and after wobbling a bit, it came to rest perfectly upright, it's handle jutting out—no tipping over to spill its contents. It was perfectly balanced and unmoving, a perfect solution to the soup-serving mess for all occasions.

"Do you see?" he asked. "Do you see it needs no saucer to catch its spilled contents, nor a hook to keep it to the edge of the soup pot?"

The woman's skepticism was growing.

"This will stand on its own, always balanced upright so that nothing will spill out. Its balance is its appeal," he said, "and this will bring something new and different to the messy boredom of ladling soup. If the handle was longer, it would lose its careful balance and tip over toward the back. And any shorter, it would slough to the side, or forward."

She picked it up again and turned it around in her hand and set it back on the table. As before, the ladle rocked side to side, slowly, coming to rest upright with the handle level with the ground, the lip of the bowl perfectly upwards. It was magnificently balanced.

"Do you see?" he asked. "Do you see that after the ladle is dipped for as many times as there are guests, when it has finished its purpose, the host simply sets it on a flat place and the contents inside do not spill out."

"Forgivable?" the wife asked. "Is this joke forgivable?"

The old man looked at her, shocked at the rejection.

The wife took the ladle from the table again. She hefted it once again by the handle, finding no balance as a serving tool, and complained that it was awkward.

She mocked her husband for creating a large flower bulb with a little stem, making it hard to control when full of soup, and called it a joke that friends would laugh at once they caught wind of this crazy idea. For the time he spent, she scornfully asked, "and this is all you could create?"

She put it on the table and watched it rock slowly into a perfectly upright attitude as a tired look of disbelief spread across her face.

It was precisely at that moment that the discovery manifested itself.

As the old man stood there, absorbing the wrath of his wife, and she stood there venting her poverty, their mutual attention was suddenly arrested by an eerie and unnatural movement.

As the ladle slowly rocked into its upright and balanced position, it pivoted ever so mysteriously in a gradual but deliberate circular motion.

As the rocking motion dampened the dip and rise of the handle, the utensil finished turning until the handle pointed opposite to where the old woman had placed it on the table.

"That's odd," the old man said. "It must be unbalanced. And yet I worked on that so carefully . . . ."

He looked at its bottom, rubbed it with his sleeve, and placed it on the table. Rocking back and forth, finding its balance once again, the ladle pitched up and down, slowly pivoting around as if some unseen finger had lightly pushed it until the handle pointed the same direction. The motion was so exact, so precise, it caused both to take a breath.

"It points south," the wife gasped.

"Indeed," said her husband. "Indeed it does. Perhaps it's the slope of your table."

Taking the ladle to the hearth stone, the husband blew away the soot and carefully placed his work on a flat spot. Gently touching the handle he set it in rocking motion. Just as before, it softly turned until it pointed south.

His wife broke into a superstitious panic. "It's the spirits," she whispered. "That blackness, it's a thing of evil, you have summoned an evil! It's black as the soot! The soot calls to you to destroy it, return it to the place of its birth, it is possessed!"

"It is not black, it is grey," the old man said, hardly hearing her complaint, and sinking into a deep quiet. *The black sand*, he thought. S*omething about that black sand.*

"It's made of the kissing stone sand," he said aloud. "It's moving because of the kissing stone sand." And with that he carried his curiosity back to the shop to his grandfather's stone. *Could it be?* he wondered.

He placed the ladle and started it rocking. But this time, instead of pivoting, it simply rocked back and forth—and stopped. No circular motion whatsoever.

That's when the old man suddenly understood. "The stone!" he said aloud. "The stone, it imparts its traits into my ladle! Atop the mother rock the ladle is at home, it doesn't point anywhere."

And with that, he took it to the far corner of his shop and placed it on a shiny flat plate of bronze. Pushing it into motion, the ladle pivoted around with greater strength than before, and stopped—it was pointing south, *not toward his grandfather's stone.*

Next, he carried it to the hut where he kept the cow. He found a smooth plank of wood and placed it there. The ladle behaved just the same, slowly turning to point south. "Grandfather's stone," the old man mumbled, "it is indeed a kissing stone, but to what does it kiss?"

He spent the next day performing experiments. Unless it rested near to the rock, the ladle always pointed south. Could it be the iron mountains? No, for they stood in the east. It must be the drawing power of the sacred stars that rose in the south.

He also observed that the power that turned the ladle was weak. A smooth surface assisted its fluid-like rotation. A rough surface prevented the same accuracy.

Once the oddity was shown to friends and neighbors, and finally at the palace, it took but two weeks for word of the old man's discovery to spread throughout all the nearby villages of Cheng.

Visitors worked their way through fields and paths to discover his home. They wanted to see for themselves this wonder that could point them toward the high place of worship. The old man's ladle pointed there, designating a power beyond all mankind. Some found worship in the ladle and they brought offerings to encourage its work.

Next came the wealthy requesting such a ladle for themselves. Would the old man oblige? The poor followed after, also desiring prosperity from the magic pointer. Would the old man make for them one that was small, and could he make it cheaply?

The man and his wife grew busier and wealthier than they had ever dreamed possible. His little shop became filled with molds of different sizes and types. And the work of his bellows ran all the day long.

When 30 days had passed, the old man and his woman had to hire more help to meet the demand.

And then others came. They wanted to examine the workings of the magic ladle. They took from the black sands to make such objects for themselves. Strangely enough, they could not make theirs work.

The old man decided it was the stone in his shop that made the difference—that while the molten sands cooled atop the mother rock, her powers infused themselves into her child-product before the metal could congeal.

Failing to achieve the same effect with the black sands, the visiting craftsmen ventured to the iron mountains and took large pieces of the kissing stone, and using the craft of the jade cutters, they worked the rough stone into similar shapes as the old man's ladle.

Within six months of the discovery, a regular train of distant laborers was seen traveling into the iron mountains to extract the black rocks and haul their treasures away, determined to duplicate the old man's magic.

A year passed and ladles of all sizes and shapes began appearing in shops just about everywhere.

Eventually the oddity took on a name, and they called it the *zhe'nan*, meaning the rock that points south—the south pointer.

"So what was it?" I asked. "Spirits? A trick?"

"No, not spirits. It's something in the earth," Ammar said. "Since that ancient time, many varieties of the south pointer have been made. Indeed, I carry one with me as does Zafir."

"*What?* What is this?" I couldn't believe he had kept such a secret from me, *me* his good and close friend. "I've never seen you use anything like that, or Zafir. Where is this instrument of yours? Let me see it!"

"Perhaps another time, Bassam. Perhaps I've said too much. So, Zafir hasn't told you of the south pointer?"

"Not a single word. I once asked him how he could travel from cistern to cistern with only your kamal and strings. He said he could get us there simply because he knew the way, that was all!"

"There is more to a destination than what you have been taught, young Bassam."

"So I gather."

"Zafir knows the desert paths as well as Al Murrah."

"Better than you?"

"No, but he is often too occupied with other business to master the science of navigation."

"Could he make his way without you and your strings? Without a south pointer?" I asked.

"He would do better than most. He knows the wind patterns and how they shape the dunes. He knows the change in the color of the sand, its texture, he knows the constellations at night. He can track stadia and his place anywhere along the trade routes, he is knowledgeable."

"And the south pointer?"

"I've probably said too much if I've betrayed a secret," he said. "If Zafir chooses not to tell you, it's because it's a protected secret of the Abdali-ud-din. Few other men know of this instrument. No, that's not correct. Many men in these parts know of it, but few use it to find their way around a map."

"Secret? Why must I always stumble upon these secrets! First, the gold—scattered everywhere in this train but seen nowhere. And now this south pointer? So, this is the secret, this is the tool that directs Abdali-ud-din east and back, or south to the Indus Valleys and north to Fergana?"

"Sometimes, yes," Ammar said. "Most of the routes are well known throughways, there is no reason to leave those tracks except to avoid robbers and tax collectors. So, in truth, Bassam, there rarely is reason to use the south pointer."

"But there are places where I see no path at all!" I said. "It looks to me that sometimes, like in the deep desert, we're the very first."

"That may seem so, but the roads are direct and true. They may be a day's ride wide in some places, but still, a straight road."

"Then tell me, have you used your south pointer on this trip?" I asked.

"Oh yes, several times," he said bluntly, throwing a hand in the air as if I was boring him with my questions.

"When?"

"This morning," he said smiling sheepishly.

"*This morning*? I never saw you with anything resembling a ladle on a flat board, Ammar! What are you telling me?"

"Oh Bassam, so much impatience, so much to learn. We use a small needle that we float. I'll show you one day, if Zafir wishes it."

"A needle? Then why all this bother to get the ladle if they work the same?"

"My heavens, boy! Let it rest or we'll never get out of here! It's because the ladles can only be bought north of here. To most it's just a piece of odd history. But you will see, they are curious devices, quite ornate. It's always been part of a spiritual movement among these people. They use them to predict the future, to tell them where to put a building or how to arrange their furniture."

"That's silly," I said.

"Perhaps to you, not to them. Such ladles and the bronze plates are intricate beautiful works of art, I'll show you. I'm told they come in all sizes, all shapes, and matched with beautifully etched plates of brass. It's a religious artifact."

"And no navigation? That seems so backwards."

"Perhaps at sea," Ammar said. "I've not seen that myself, I'm not even sure they've considered it, but who knows? For them it's spiritualism, to know true south, the place at night from where their sacred constellations rise."

"Then we'll find a shop that sells the south pointing ladles and I'll let you use it to serve me yak milk over rice with honey."

"Beware young boy," Ammar said with a gruff. "I also know the recipe for poison bark oil, I'll gladly serve you all you want!"

"Then teach me the way of the south pointer before I die!"

"Then get your sandals on, let's go," he said. "I think Zafir should be made aware that we have had this discussion. He must have his reasons for not telling you."

"I'm sold," I said. "If this is all that you say it is, then I want one as well. Let's go look."

KASHGAR SHADOWS

Another village, another market, another stop. And more fending off the barking smooth-talkers who blocked the narrow pathways through the market places with their calls to buy this, see that, special deal, this day only, for you twice for half. Some beckoned with no shame—others exchanged for the bargain in almost a whisper, clasping hands to seal the deal, passing coins unseen by anyone but themselves.

I felt as if I had seen these sellers, heard them, and fought them for these twelve months only to discover there was no magic over the next hill, no hidden treasure in their shops, no unappreciated relic of old or of curious workmanship that was anything worth stopping to examine. It was, simply enough, all the same.

In fact, I no longer felt compelled to engage the shopkeepers in a duel of wits, but simply ignored them without guilt. Ammar and I strolled through the narrow alleys crowded with sagging tables, bending beneath the weight of foods and wares, rudely ignoring the merchants who called to us.

We stepped aside for a herd of sheep, then donkeys carrying stick cages and squawking hens. These clusters of noise stopped for nobody. It was a busy day.

Following directly behind was our contingent of eleven Al Murrah and Xiongnu warriors. They didn't seem to mind the trip into town, and actually looked relieved to get out of camp.

The morning air was already filled with the aroma of roasting mutton and the curious seduction of sweet eastern incense.

"What kind of shop sells south pointers?" I asked.

"I expect any place that sells brass and copper goods," Ammar said. "Or religious artifacts. We'll see."

"So, this spiritualism—what's so important about south?"

"They believe there are forces in this world that balance good and evil, right and wrong, hot and cold, light and dark, all things. They try to be in harmony with those forces by aligning their lives, their houses, their decisions, their actions, even their inactions."

"What?"

"Oh yes, certainly," Ammar said. "You can find a man leading his family, choosing a corner of his land, building their home, all according to the south pointer—and where *not to live*, and how *not to construct* such a home, and just about everything I can think of."

"All I care about is which way the water flows after the rain."

"Precisely."

We pushed through the crowded bazaar past tables of raw flesh—birds stripped of their feathers clinging from a twine, hog's heads, snouts, tongues, ox tail, the pink gleam from skinned rabbits, and black bothersome flies buzzing everywhere.

Turning down a shadowed alley empty of shoppers, we escaped the noise into pleasant quiet. It was lined to either side with sparse tables of fabrics and sandals, brass and carved objects, a variety of manufactured goods set neatly outside the hustle of noise. The calm made me more alert to the shops we passed.

And then, Ammar spotted it suddenly. "There!" he said, taking a hard right into an open shop. "There!" he said pointing with his eyes, almost in a whisper.

I followed with half a smile, bewildered at Ammar's mesmerizing infatuation. This unusual passion was in such contrast to his normal intellectual and mildly condescending ways.

Ammar stepped into the shop and went directly to several deep shelves on a wall. There displayed for all to see was a neat collection of eight small but statuesque south pointers in assorted sizes and shades of black and grey. Each had that rounded, bulbous form with a short stem, and rested still and unmoving, untouched, all of them balanced in their own unique way—and all of them pointed in the same direction.

"Look at that!" I said in astonishment. "They all point south!"

"Naturally!" Ammar said, "That's why they call them south pointers, didn't you hear a word I said?"

"Yes, but still—look!"

The elderly shopkeeper rose from his stool holding a pleasant look of neutral disregard. It masked his long experience of smelling a deal already done. He could see in our eyes the *buyer's hunger*, and already knew that we had made the purchase, it was now just a matter of the price.

One of the Xiongnu warriors stepped forward to translate.

"I see that you are seeking after the *zhe'nan*, do you want to try it?" the old shopkeeper offered by way of the translator.

The old man gently took one of the bronze plates from the shelf and carefully set it on the table and placed one of the larger south pointers in the middle. He smiled and gestured to us. Ammar reached out and carefully touched the ladle to start it rocking. And just as Ammar has told me, it turned about slowly and came to an easy stop—pointing south.

That was the most curious thing ever. "It's just like you said!" I blurted out in surprise. "And it serves soup!"

Ammar said nothing and carefully picked up the ladle and turned it around in his hands, studying its shape and balance. He set it down on the bronze plaque and set it rocking again. Sure enough, it pivoted about slowly until the squat handle pointed directly south as before.

"It really works!" I said, smiling. "That's the most amazing thing I've ever seen."

"Then you haven't seen much," Ammar mumbled as he looked closer at the bronze plate.

I watched over his shoulder and was caught by the intricate engravings on the plate. A number of lines radiated out from where the ladle was supposed to be placed, and each line carried labels in a script neither of us could decipher.

"What are these etchings?" I asked the translator.

The old man smiled and began to describe. "This is called the Ladle of Majesty, and it is made of the five elements of the earth, and copper. It will guide you to your wealth and prosperity—in all things! It will guide you if you will follow."

"And this," I asked, pointing at the square bronze plate. "What is it?"

"The heaven-plate," the old man said. "This is marked with the pole star, and you see the shape of the large dipper from the sky?" he said pointing to the north. "The Ladle of Majesty is also shaped as the dipper in the stars, and as you can see, the earthly ladle, it will align itself with those very stars and tell you where fortune lies in your way."

He set the ladle down and after it rocked side to side, pivoting slowly about, it came to rest pointing south.

Ammar elbowed me for attention. "The south pointer that we carry is small and thin," he said. "Ours is shaped like a skinny fish or a tadpole, almost a needle—a miniature ladle such as these but smaller, thinner. In fact, we sometimes float them on a piece of wood. A fish out of water always points south, Bassam."

I stood silent, staring at the heaven-plate, sorting with my eyes the engravings, lines, the mysterious filigree that mapped a secret with detailed precision and care. It was a code of such complexity—I couldn't take my eyes away. The old man saw my fascination and was happy to point out the additional details.

"The lines that radiate from the center, each points to one of the 15 celestial stars," he said, looking to the translator to make sure the message was delivered correctly.

"Ammar!" I smiled. "You told me of those 15 stars, these are the same, right?"

"Yes, they're the same everywhere," he said. "But you must listen to what he is saying, Bassam. They don't use this device to find their way around a map, they use it for energy, for their worship."

The old man watched us speak in a tongue he did not understand and when our attention turned back to him, he smiled and continued.

"These markings speak of the northern dipper and the key star groups in the sacred constellations. And these twenty-four lines," he said, pointing to the radiating engravings, "These are the seasonal periods of the earth, two for each of the twelve Earthly branches."

I grinned at Ammar. What mystical philosophy was this? But the old man was pleased to continue—he knew he had us caught in a web of our wants, and continued to embellish the tale with detail and mystical connections.

"The earth is a square within the circular heaven, and the gods direct its movement among the stars. From this you are guided through the days of your sorrows to the World Pillar, the Broad Palace, the Revolving House, the Hanging Garden, the Cool Wind, and the Hedge Forest. Climb the World Pillar and find the carved-out garden with the yellow water. Drink of such waters and you will not die."

The old man's eyes sparkled as if he was revealing a great secret. I stood there fascinated with the hypnotic telling of the mysteries in the south pointer through the deep melodious tones of the translator.

"Climb a mountain that is double in height of the World Pillar, the mountain called Cool Wind. Climb to its top, and you will not die. Ascend double again a mountain to the Hanging Garden and you will have power over the wind and rain. Climb a mountain yet double again and you will be above Torch Dragon and Thunder Marsh. There you will meet Yin and Yang and become one with heaven. It is the *qi* ("chee") the turbulent, or qi the subtle. It is the qi in all things, all ten thousand forms of life from the father heaven to the mother earth. The Yin and the Yang become your fishing net with which you gather all things. And to this, my young foreign friend, the south pointer will lead you."

My smile had dissolved into a lost look of confusion while Ammar grinned at my bewilderment. "What is qi?" I asked.

Ammar answered before the translator could query the old shopkeeper.

"*Qi* is the name they give to the power that gives motion to all things. It can be a good power, or a bad. To get more of the good, the C'ina believe you can draw it to you with colors, spacing, movement, positioning, all according to what the south pointer directs them."

"He speaks about a complex philosophy I've never heard of," I said.

"Well, well, Bassam, congratulations. You have just received a complete and start-to-finish religious philosophy about the creation of the universe and your place in it. Do you feel like searching out such a mountain to climb? And such waters to drink?"

I shook my head. "I'll climb mountains later. I want to buy one of these south pointers. But this one, this is too large," I said, directing my comments to the translator. "Do you have something that will fit in my pocket?" I gestured with my hands to convey the desire.

The old man smiled and bent down to a stash of small crates stacked in a corner, covered over by a dusty shawl. Feeling beneath the stack, he grunted and then smiled, pulling from the dark corner a long palm-sized rectangle about as thick as a thumb and hinged on one side. He turned it over revealing a latch that he unlocked and the object unfolded into a perfect square about a palm wide on each side. He laid it on his table and from the shelf he plucked the smallest of ladles, not much longer than a finger, and only a thumbnail wide. Placing the ladle on the brass plate, he gave it a touch and after a few wiggling motions, it came to rest pointing south.

"I'll take it," I said.

"You're a foolish trader in these parts," Ammar said. "You hand him an easy deal like that and they will be looking for Bassam by name at all the remainder of our stops. The buyer must always force the seller to make first claim on a price. Now you must pay full price."

"And what is full price?"

The Xiongnu guard relayed the question and a deal was struck. For the price of four silvers, I took my new south pointer and examined it closely.

As for Ammar, he purchased a large and more finished south-pointer with an ornate brass heaven-plate with movable parts and small embedded gems. He didn't argue the price down too far because, after all, it was going to be the centerpiece of his wife's entertainment room, and the price he paid will be part of her brag to her friends.

With the deal completed and the purchases in hand, we left the shop to make haste toward camp. As the group filed out, down the dark stone walkway, a Xiongnu warrior checked the safety in the opposite direction and spotted unusual movement. He snapped a gesture to a brother warrior and the two watched. Far up the dark alley way, beyond the shops with their colorful awnings, and over the bobbing heads of a few buyers mingling, he caught sight in the shadows of two distinct and shrouded figures that stood watching from afar. When they realized it, they slipped smoothly from view and disappeared into the shadows of a side passage.

The heart of Kashgar was a maze of such narrow streets, centuries old, where only a local could navigate with any hope of finding a way out. It was immediately clear that pursuit would be fruitless and certainly would diminish the number of swords presently at hand.

Our escorts exchanged messages and placed hand to sword, drawing them out part way as we walked, on the ready should danger befall us. In this manner we worked our way back through the market streets, past the village center, beyond the gate and walls, and into the open fields that led back to camp.

I was unsure about the presence of a south pointer in Zafir's camp, and didn't know how it would be received if word of it got out. Or did no one else care because no one else understood its power and significance?

That night I set up my little tent and within its privacy I began experimenting with Ammar's maps and strings. For several hours I sat writing about the actions of the south pointer and how it helped me understand the other markings on Ammar's maps—markings I had earlier ignored for lack of knowing their true purpose.

> *"Day 310—Dear Rasha, I learned today about the most amazing tool for my maps. We measure our direction with precision using the south pointer and the heaven-plate. Knowing how many stadia we travel, and the direction, Ammar can track our place with accuracy. Now I understand why my estimations of travel and distance differed from his. Ammar let me practice with his maps tonight. I've estimated the trek north and then east around the desert. Our next stop at Tumushuk is 16 days away. Qiuci lies eight days farther—Yanqi is 14 days more, and Turpan 10 more. We'll complete our detour around the great desert in seven weeks. And we'll follow the main silk road directly into Chang'an.—Bassam"*

It was late when I extinguished the lamp and quietly pulled down my blanket and buried myself in it. The night was cold and I wore the goat-hair coat. As I closed my eyes I heard the careful padding of feet over the sandy ground as the watch shuffled in exchange. I drifted off to sleep unaware that three Xiongnu warriors stood guard only ten paces away, peering into the darkness, hands on swords for the least unusual movement. Zafir was apprised of the earlier sighting and responded by making other plans in these remote parts that held us so far from friends.

ب هبعه 69 محبوب

TIJM URNAK

I decided Kashgar was my favorite among the many villages near the Taklamakan, the most mysterious and unexplored. It was famous as a fitting out place for caravans going west, but this wasn't always the case for those headed east.

Tou told me it was probably the strange dress and manner of the Westerners who headed toward Chang'an that struck the inhabitants in so dark a way, like so many invaders coming for gold and leaving behind their trinkets. But Zafir was hardly an invader, and always prospered those he met.

For whatever bother Zafir's men had been, we apparently had exhausted our stay in Kashgar. As we packed up to leave, I could see envy and greed eyeing our goods that we could sell for much gold in the northern places. Fawzi said the men of Kashgar always entertained the dark plot of overpowering our train and taking what they could. That was another reason so many swords with warriors wielding them were present, to make the prospect a bloody one, and none showed enough exercise to attempt it.

On our last morning in Kashgar we filed out unmolested, consuming the better part of midmorning to clear our camp and find the road headed east.

I rode my bakra in line with the others near the front, but my mind was far removed. The cold was climbing closer and this goat hair coat was just not heavy enough. I wore my blanket for the morning ride and pulled it tight for warmth.

Spotting me shrouded like a religious man, Fawzi steered his camel to my side.

"You need a yak-hair coat, you donkey head!" Fawzi said. "Goat hair, ha! Yak is suited for this climate—I buy one in these parts every year. They don't last the trip, but you won't need it long."

"I'll get one at the next stop," I said. "And why won't I need it long?"

"When we get to Chang'an you'll see that the sun finds us again, and such smelly baggage isn't worth the trouble."

"Then I'll borrow yours and you can buy another."

"Ha!" Fawzi laughed, and steered his camel back into the pack.

As the day waned, Zafir moved our long snaking line from the lower foothills to the flatlands. It was a broad, wind-swept plateau that stretched between the rim and the lifeless expanse of hardened soils bordering the dunes. Our caravan assumed this forward place for the rest of the day, plodding eastward at a quickened pace until the sun dipped into the hazy mask of the lower western sky, signaling a camping place was needed soon. The wind changed direction shortly after, and the air grew decidedly colder.

One last long upwards climb labored the end of that day's energies. A gentle descent took us down the other side to a small green oasis that grew in the shallow valley of low, white-bleached hills. Some two hundred paces beyond stood the skeletal remains of standing walls. Like so many other such sites, these ancient ruins hunched over like tired old men, leaning on their courses of sun-baked bricks, longing for something to prop them lest they fall into a heap.

"Gather round," Zafir said, signaling our attention for a quick update. "Especially you, Bassam," he added.

"Those walls yonder," he said pointing to ruins 300 paces to the west, "once housed the merchants of Tijm Urnak. It was a fair enough stopping place, always friendly, always welcoming. When I first began trading in these eastern places my men and I stopped here for two or three days in preparation for the long stretch to Tumushuk. We had many great friends here. It was here they introduced the stirrup to our men, an idea that serves our horse riders well. For several years I came here to renew old friendships, do some trading, freshen ourselves, fatten our camels. But look at it now, men. What is left of it now?"

All eyes followed his outstretched arm that swept across the ruins as if to breath life into them again.

"Nothing but ruins. These are the ways of the desert, my friends. Those of you who have ventured with me before have heard these tales from my lips many times in this exact place. Those of you new to our enterprise, I count this stopping place the grave of a good idea, and those walls the marker of its demise. While all men may plan and work, toil and conspire, no matter the cause, there are forces in this life that yield to no one. These mighty sands have crept through the years until they washed over the green fields where I once camped. They spoiled the spring I drank from. They drew the moisture from the orchards, leaving stumps where shade once beckoned us, and fruit once fell. They smothered the life here and destroyed its history and its memories until all that remains is what you see. And those walls, they're not long for this life in the presence of the advancing desert dunes. We'll bed here for the night and resume our travel at sunrise. But listen to the wind that whistles past the forgotten genealogies of this place. Dream of what was and what is. And let this place and these dry bones rattle deep into your souls as they did mine—that there is but one thing that can outlast the moving sands of time. It's the permanence of the good idea, the good idea that is passed from generation to generation. That's what shapes men on this earth. And with such good ideas, all men shape their lives if they so choose. Let this place become a monument to your own hopes and ask yourselves, are your best dreams built on the rock of a sure foundation as these mountains north of us? Or are they built on the sand, the moving sands that smother, bury, and destroy?"

With that, Zafir turned his camel and directed his captains to disperse the groups to various camping spots.

"Fawzi," I said in hushed tones. "That's the kind of talk I get when he has me reading the scrolls. What's bothering him?"

Fawzi shook his head. "Zafir is a good reader, and I don't mean the written script," he said. "He reads more than scrolls and terrain and the night stars. Zafir also reads the spirit in the land, the hearts of men he does not know, the dark conspiracies of his enemies, the good works of his allies. I don't know about him tonight, I just don't know."

We caught up with Ammar and Malik. They had secured a flat piece of ground and relieved their animals of their loads.

"May I join you?" Fawzi asked. "And this young donkey cud who keeps shadowing me?"

"Sure, pull up a piece of ground and relax," Malik said. "That was an, uh, an interesting speech tonight."

"This place means something more to him, doesn't it?" I asked.

"It sounded so," Ammar volunteered. "I myself don't know, but I have heard."

Fawzi jumped off his camel and ordered her to kneel. "Heard what?" Fawzi asked.

"This place, this Tijm Urnak, is more than his former watering place."

"What did you hear? Did you hear it from Zafir?" I asked.

"No, but from the other elders," Ammar said. "The name, they said, it's a local tongue, their version of the bedawi tongue, and it's not some name from some place back in time. It's a name he gave it and had it drawn on all of the maps. This all happened many years ago. But the others told me it means 'my heart bleeds here,' or 'my love bleeds here,' something like that."

"Then some tragedy happened in this place?" I asked.

"That's what they say, but I've never asked, and Zafir has never offered to tell," Ammar said.

The evening was subdued and the cook-fires glowed warmly. The beasts fed on the sparse greens, and we took turns drinking from the little spring.

When darkness finally spread her ink, no stars shown above—the haze that was stirred in the wind obscured the night sky. To the west, the weak sliver of the moon quietly gathered up her long shadows leaving a muted splash across the distant mountain peaks and the tops of the higher dunes beyond the ruins.

The fading grey lingered just long enough to usher in the sleeping time. Before the last of the light faded, I put away my journal writings, snuffed out the lamp, and prepared my sleeping mat and blankets.

Then, on a whispered hunch, I decided to take a last look of our surroundings before going to sleep, and stood up to scan the whole territory. I stopped to peer at the old ruins, grey monoliths almost invisible against the shadowed sand.

And then—just then I saw someone out there, the unmistakable form of a woman—small and distant, shrunken in size between the lone stone sentinels, walking slowly in flowing white robes, a silky silhouette against the obscurity of the dunes. It looked as if she was reaching up to touch one of the old walls when the night breeze suddenly sprayed the camp with a light dusting of sand. I looked away for the hem of my headdress, and when I looked back, the figure was gone.

70

HIGH WATERMARK

On the tenth night out of Kashgar, Zafir ordered his large tent set, and invited me for evening meal.

"The wind finds a way into my place," Zafir said, chewing a strip of boiled yak meat, then reached for a bread. "By morning, half the desert will have flowed through the threads of these walls, and my men will lose valuable time sweeping it clean."

I sipped some water and took more rice with my bread. "I can help," I offered.

"Oh no, I'm only joking. I've done battle with this desert sand for many years, and while it seeks to beat me through patience, I'll beat it because I am *more* patient."

The oil lamps swayed to and fro as another gust pressed against the walls making the beams squeak and groan as they moved.

"My hope, Bassam, is to teach you two more scrolls before Turpan. Do you think you can handle that much more?"

"I'm ready when you are, Zafir."

"Good, then let's finish our meal and talk more about what you have learned."

I was grateful for the long trek. It gave me a chance to ponder, question and challenge the words we were reading and see the principles in action. And each time Zafir asked me, "What new have you learned?" I could answer that life itself was the teacher, bringing to light the deeper meanings of the scrolls. Zafir told me that complete understanding of the scrolls was a lifetime pursuit—but one worth risking because the rewards could bless my life in ways I could never comprehend.

"There is something at work in this great caravan that makes me wonder," I began.

"And what is that?"

"You don't drive, you don't force, you don't coerce," I said, "and yet this great enterprise moves forward despite its failings and problems. How is it that so much peace can attend a mass of so many different men with different dreams and goals and pursuits?"

Zafir looked at me and smiled as if caught in a thought. "You're witnessing the power that comes when men are free to choose."

"Are not all men free?"

"In one sense, yes," he said. "Agency is their natural gift, I neither give it nor can I take it from them. But to survive in this great journey such agency must be used for only one thing."

"To do their job?"

"No, to serve others," he said bluntly.

"Serve? I don't see that …."

"That's the only way to make this caravan prosper across this vast continent, Bassam. Anything less is just too much work. Giving others what they want so you can get what you want is the principle at work. We have discussed this before. But now you're seeing it in a whole new light, aren't you?"

"I suppose, I'm not sure," I said.

"The great circle of prosperity in this life is not a solo endeavor, Bassam. I had to use my inventive ideas to create value as a young boy. I earned my first silver at a sheik's stable cleaning his horses, raking out the straw, keeping it clean."

"You? You worked as a stable boy? I thought your legacy was the son of a mighty Abdali-ud-din sheik."

"Yes, but why should that matter?" Zafir asked.

"Well, your father was wealthy, and he could have ..."

"Could have taught me in other ways, with the scrolls, with teachers, with travel, to set up a large enterprise myself?"

"Yes, something like that," I said.

"Father knew I had other lessons to learn. His gold could spare me the troubles of daily life, so he put me to work in the stable to teach me for life," Zafir said. "He was wiser than most men."

"What did you learn about life?"

"That *all* labor is necessary in this world," he said. "All labor is always worth something to someone. The challenge is to match up desire with ability with opportunity. Some men ignore many opportunities, looking to match *only* their desires with opportunity. Ability takes time to develop and to prove. My father knew I was capable of much, but it needed a beginning place—as it is with all things. And so, I learned the importance of cleaning stables for the truest and most faithful beasts of burden."

"I haven't had to work like that," I said.

"I know," he said. "And it shows. It's an odd cycle between the generations. Parents work hard to make life better for their children and forget that leisure is not a teacher, leisure is an earned reward. A youth who begins life in leisure misses the important lesson of earning his rewards, and will never rise above that level of mediocrity. The same can be said for a youth who is raised in a household built on handouts and charity. Without struggle and enterprise, a youth is off to a terrible start."

"How can poverty and destitution not be a worthy struggle?" I asked. "That describes most of the world, doesn't it? Do the poor not strive hard to improve themselves?"

"Laziness is in both rich and poor," Zafir said. "And when a man spends all his days living off the handouts of others and never produces a single thing on his own, that is not building a life. That is passing time, that is wasting life. Each man must face his own challenges, no matter what they be, and learn that only by climbing out of his pit by his own sweat and toil will he truly find the joy of achievement of his own making. Even if those heights are no higher than just cleaning out the stable."

"Are there stables for everyone?" I wondered. "We've passed some poor places where they have no stables to clean, nothing to perform, nowhere to strive for except to beg. What of them?"

"There is a great lie in this illusion, my son," Zafir said. "It is natural to believe the boundaries of survival are set within the realm of the here and now. Destitution is a great teacher. It pushes all of us to creatively consider beyond those boundaries. Too many surrender to the prison of their circumstances, blaming their place on other things, other forces. We must reject those boundaries, use our minds to invent the un-invented, to analyze and consider, to look everywhere for new beginning places. Even so, too many accept their circumstances. A hundred reasons why—no courage, discouragement, lack of will to get creative, all hard work of course, but the best work ever engaged."

"But don't those ideas take time to build?" I asked. "And don't people need food today, right now?"

"That is the trap," Zafir said. "A handout must be a diminishing crutch, not a way of life. A wise steward isn't casual about his generosity, tossing a coin here or there, thinking he's assuaged his conscience in the eyes of God. A wise steward feeds the hungry and clothes the naked as part of a plan to stand them on their own feet. But to continue the handout without a path for escaping the poverty is to keep them slaves."

"Then I'm guessing that your stable work wasn't satisfying for very long," I said.

"Not necessarily so, Bassam," he said. "I call it the high water mark in a man's life. It was for me at that young age. You have seen how men will cut or paint on a tree or on a post the highest flood level of a river? This high water mark becomes the standard, a measure of how high the water once rose. For years afterward, men will measure each spring runoff to this high water mark and know what to expect because they have seen what the most severe run off had done in years past. And if a new flood exceeds the old, a new mark is made and all seasons have a new standard to be measured by. And now look at a man's life in the same way. You carry in your shoulder the scar of a near-death knife attack. Are you stronger or weaker because of it?"

"I hadn't thought about it," I said. "I don't want to take the knife again. But instead of fearing it, now I respect it—and I can fight what I respect."

"Then you are stronger. That's a high watermark in your life. That event taught you about real battle. Could you now charge into danger for something you believed, with courage and integrity?"

"Yes, I think so, it's different now."

"Before the Fukara you might have bragged how brave you could be, promising all sorts of prowess, power and loyalties. But on the battle field, when the first swords came at you, I know you would have run away. Your high watermark before this trip was nothing more than childhood pranks or an easy caravan trip that lasted a few weeks."

"Well, I don't think I would run," I said.

"You don't know what it's like," Zafir countered. "It will surprise you how desperate you feel with fending for your own life and safety, and the choice to help others comes at you harshly, to help at the expense of your own life. These battles test the mettle of every man. But my point is, hardships are what make you a man, to face such things. And that is why stable work is good work."

We both fell quiet a moment as the wind gathered herself and whistled past the tent, scattering sand that hushed against the woven walls. The suddenness ignited a few grunts from nearby camels that were bedded for the night.

"Let these lessons work their magic inside of you, my son," he said. "They build high watermarks that prove we can overcome challenges—we know we've been there before, it is worth moving forward and not giving up. You will have yours, indeed you have had some in recent time, and there will be more. If you take them for what they are, they will teach you that your many trials are not setbacks at all. They are events that refine you, strengthen you, congeal you, like a stone with many edges rolling down the river of life. Every obstacle it hits knocks off a flaw until you become round and polished, refined and beautiful—a life well lived, a man of full stature, a son, a father, a husband of integrity, virtue, and durability. That is the work of the high watermarks."

THE FIVE TEACHERS

Zafir's tent was a work of art. The gracious feel within its walls created more than pure comfort. Such tapestries displayed the artwork of many hundreds of years of desert culture—travel, exchange, greeting. His was a portable monument to the legacy of a family and its dealings with countless generations of traders spanning dozens of centuries.

The poles that held the enclosure were inscribed with patterns of palms, almonds and ferns, inlaid with thin leaves of gold and rows of dark obsidian beads. The walls and hangings were no less refined—woven with rich threads of red, golden blue, and orange.

As we sat on the carpets I inhaled the lingering aroma of incense meant to cover the mustiness of faded luster. It was an old tent, carried on too many trips, a witness to so many negotiations among strangers. It was a reflection of Zafir himself, enriched with the signs of honor, history and a life well lived.

Zafir brought over the scroll bag and picked through it for another lesson. I watched without speaking as the curious little ritual unfolded.

"This bag," Zafir began, unlacing its top, "was my father's when he was a boy. It was new then but it shows wear today. I may have to replace it."

Reaching inside he lifted out a long bundled scroll. "Most men hope to find in these scrolls some ancient and lost guide to riches," he began, just as before. And then one of the memorized phrases caught my attention: "... But such a key is only for those who know what true riches are."

True riches. I let the idea roll around in my mind. What are the *true* riches? Do I really know? I would give it more thought.

"... I think your heart is ready, Bassam. Do you understand?"

"Yes, I do," I said.

"Then let us begin."

He turned the scroll to me. "You will do the reading, and I will listen. If you have a question, you may ask. But some things I will not tell, it is part of the test."

I took the scroll as before, and began reading aloud:

> "The Song of the Wise. The virtue of wisdom is a light given birth in the dark shadows of sorrow. It is the collection of life's lessons unfolded through choices that have led to prosperity and poverty, to joy and terror, to peace and contention. It leads the wise down pathways of deliberate calculation, and the foolish into traps that snare them until they learn the lessons. It can hardly be a pathway to wealth—for what is carried in one man as wise is foolishness to another. But the wise do not see themselves in a mirror as wise, but instead as deliberate thinkers with deliberate associates. They know true prosperity is not in the possession of things but in the wise dispatch of what possessions one has—invested for the most good. Putting them to such good is not easily done by the ignorant and the impatient, but by those who have been made patient from the scarring through poor choices, accidents, or any of the five teachers of life. While others cower in fear, the wise have gained the fruits of the deliberate life that graces their every day with true prosperity, lessons that gold and treasure can never buy. ..."

The five teachers. I had not heard of them before. Farther into the scroll I read that they served as shared experiences through which all humans must suffer. I wanted Zafir's explanation.

"Then ask me," Zafir said.

"The first—the *Teacher of Failure*, speaks as if failure is a good thing. How can that be?"

"It shows you that your pursuit was wrong. It teaches you that you did something you shouldn't have. Or you failed to do something you should have. Or someone else's failure has done you injury. For circumstances that you control, failure teaches you that you lacked wisdom—from that mistake you learn you should have chosen differently. Because you made the wrong choice, that is the painful proof you have something yet to learn."

"Must I fail so that I can learn? Can't someone simply tell me?" I asked.

"You have been told all your life, Bassam. Had you listened the first time, or any time, your list of problems and failures would not be so long. Some do learn to be wise early on, but most people do not, and they are kicked around until they learn."

"Ah-ha, the second scroll—be thou humble and learn," I said.

"Precisely. A lesson learned is foolishness avoided."

"All right, what are your thoughts about the *Teacher of Self Denial*?"

"It is self-governance," Zafir said. "When you deny things that are not good for you, you are building your life. When you indulge, you are dismantling your life. But the real test is when others deny you what you want. Some greedy men view this as selfishness and feel justified to use force to take what they want. This puts them back under the whip of the *Teacher of Failure*. No good will come of taking things not earned."

These teachers, I decided, had to be the scrolls themselves. The first, the second, the third ....

"The other teachers," he said, "will introduce themselves soon enough. We've discussed some already—the *Teacher of Extravagance* and the golden mean, the *Teacher of Renewal*, and the *Teacher of Death*. These will become friends."

"This *Teacher of Renewal* sounds vaguely familiar," I said.

"You've heard this already. It is your new chance each and every day to start over," he said. "Too many of us drag the baggage of yesterday's failures behind us like a train of stubborn goats, as if they were trophies of our stupidity. We should leave them behind, and go forward, erring no more."

"And that's it?" I asked.

"Not quite, you must repair the damages of yesterday, apologize, restore what you uprooted. It speaks to the first scroll, Bassam. Every day is the beginning of the same struggle. If you have been wise, you are stronger each day. If you have stumbled and failed, a new day is your chance for renewal, to try it again—a clean tablet, no markings or records kept—just keep trying. The *Teacher of Renewal* will give you another chance until you don't require another chance."

"Require?"

"Yes. It means you have *learned*," Zafir said. "You stop making *this* or *that* mistake. It has become a strength—no longer a weakness. We call it having wisdom."

"What about *Death*?" I asked.

"Most men ignore the *Teacher of Death*," he said. "They look at their fathers and think, 'When I am an old man, like my father, that is the time to think about the *Teacher of Death*.' But when they come to their end, perhaps early on the battlefield, on a sick bed, or on the tail of a snake that bites—the *Teacher of Death* comes with short notice to deliver his last great lesson."

"What do you say that lesson is?"

"It is this—that at the end of life, all opportunity to advance yourself in this life will stop—completely. This life is the time to prepare to meet your God because when death comes, there may be no more work performed. All work for you ceases. When that time comes, you *are* what you *were*—and no more may be consumed, changed, altered, corrected, or perfected by you."

"But Zafir, I don't want to go around all day thinking about dying ..."

"That's the point, Bassam, the very point! Prepare yourself, fill your life with so much growth, so much positive action to help others, that death is the least of your concerns. Its certainty drives you to be *as* good, *as* productive, *as* growing as you are able. Build, help, encourage, conquer, strengthen, support, enjoy, weep when you must weep, laugh when you can laugh, but *build*. Build the positive not the negative. And the rest? The rest will take care of itself—even the *Teacher of Death*."

I let the words settle in my mind like windblown chaff drifting back to the threshing floor. *Was Suoud ready for his ending when it came?* How could that be? How could any man be ready for his ending? And then a thought drifted into my mind.

"Zafir?" I asked. "A man should not look to his ending as just that—as his end. It's a beginning? Do you think?"

"Very good, my son. That is precisely what it is. Nothing less. And to be ready for that, you must make this life all that you can, so work hard, work with joy, work to give of yourself. Your preparations are within these scrolls—please, continue."

72

THE FIFTH SCROLL

We had arrived at the riddle. "It's the end again," I said looking up.

Zafir was lost in thought, his eyes looking afar off at nothing, his mind traveling on a memory, or was it a calculation?

"Yes? Oh. Yes," he said without excuse. "We are at the riddle, are we? Then continue, please."

"May I ask?"

"Yes?"

"Of these five scrolls we've looked at, why is the scroll of wisdom shorter than the others?"

"That's a fair question," he said. "Let the scroll answer that—it comes next."

"All right. The riddle ..."

"The sayings of The Fifth Scroll, the Song of the Wise.

"A virtue of wealth is this for thee, One branch one limb on the self same tree; The coin and palace all men may gain, But woe is life when spent in vain. For joy that lasts and doth not cease, Embrace the virtues thou Prince of Peace. One branch one limb on the self same tree, A virtue of wealth can be for thee."

"What do you think of this passage now?" he asked.

"These past weeks I've been thinking about peace—and all of its counterfeits."

"Counterfeits?"

"I see the men leaving at night to go into the villages to buy their way into some diversions."

"Some more than others," Zafir said.

"Yes, but still, the end is the same. They come back late, they sleep off their party, and in the morning nothing has changed."

"How is this counterfeiting?" he asked.

"They try to get the one thing they want but can't," I said. "It's as if they're looking for the joy that peace brings, and look everywhere except where it can be found. They drink too much thinking *peace* is there. They party too much thinking *peace* is there. They risk their coins on people and foods and chance, thinking *peace* is there. And still, in the morning, *they have no peace*."

"Very good, Bassam. Nothing can mimic true and lasting peace," Zafir said. "Only through becoming the man or woman about whom the scrolls teach can true peace be found."

"It looks to me like everything that takes our coins also takes our time, pretending to offer peace, but in the end, it doesn't. All of it always disappoints."

Zafir looked at me for a long moment. "Bassam," he said, "sometimes I think you're much older than your years. Now, I hope my student hasn't turned into a dusty prune who doesn't know the virtue of good recreation, has he?"

I shook my head, *that wasn't it*. "I haven't decided," I said. "I don't know if that Prince of Peace is an idea or a man, but I can see the power of it coming together."

"Then you will come to know this Prince of Peace before our journey is through," he said, "but that can wait. For now, maybe the scroll will help."

I continued.

> "Oh wisdom, behold now the Song of The Wise:
>
> "Father Wisdom came late, so late in my life, To succor the years I wasted in strife. With words that were calming and gentle to hear, Soothing my losses, my anger, my fear. Said 'Be glad, be glad of the gift you gained; Remorse cost you dearly, your life was left stained. But such is the price for this hard won treasure: Experience to judge, a right way to measure. For wisdom is born from being amiss And suffering in loss, that terrible abyss.' I choose not to fail though fail I must, For that is the teacher that teaches this trust. Else how could I know lest error I wrought, that Father Wisdom was me, it was me that I taught?
>
> "What meaneth this, the song of the Wise?"

It was me that I taught. "That's exactly what happens, Zafir. But what am I learning? I work so hard to be prepared for what might befall us—the goat fat to save my parched lips, my goat hair coat, sleeping with my knife unsheathed. I was thinking I'm always hiding away from the little trials that come because I don't want to suffer. Is that weakness?"

"Bassam, don't confuse the *teacher* of wisdom with the *teaching* of wisdom. The scroll doesn't say go the edge of the river and leap in just to have the experience of drowning. It doesn't say that at all. Think about this—why do you administer the goat fat?"

"To prevent the bleeding," I said.

"Did you venture among the dunes in the heat so your nose and lips would crack and bleed?"

"Well, no ..."

"It just suddenly happened, right? And you learned a great secret from Humam about the help from the goat fat."

"Well, yes, I did," I said.

"And when you slept at night in these cold parts, and your goat hair coat didn't protect you, what of that?"

"Fawzi told me that a yak-hair coat is perfect for this cold clime and I should buy one at the next stop," I said.

"And your knife, it's uncovered and ready for you at night?"

"Oh yes."

"These choices are the lessons of wisdom changing you for the better, do you see it?" he asked.

"Well ... I think so," I stammered.

"Not think, you *must* see it, Bassam. The teacher was the hot wind, the teacher was the cold night, the teacher was the enemy with short swords. These are the teachers of wisdom. You learned lessons—one of them nearly killed you. But you learned. You learned wisdom. You learned the heat and the cold and the danger are real and lethal. And because of that very personal experience, you altered your life patterns to be prepared for them. You *learned*! These are the lessons of wisdom."

"You're right," I said. "They did show me the wrong path—"

"Look deeper, my son. They helped you understand the right path. That is the teaching, to show you the *correct path* through the heat is with the goat fat, the *correct path* through the cold is the yak-hair coat, the *correct path* to prepare against ambush is a knife at your side. When you pick up the solutions to your challenges and employ them to spare you discomfort, you are then being wise. When you ignore them, you're being the fool."

That was the definition of my life, I thought, always ignoring the danger signs, thinking somehow I was smarter, or, it would be different this time.

Zafir could see me chastising myself. He smiled at the self rebuke and counseled, "The teacher of wisdom finds the holes in your life, the weaknesses that don't get enough of your attention," he said. "Most men neglect a few holes in the guard walls. Wisdom sends her armies to enter through those neglected gaps to destroy you. When you secure yourself afterwards you declare, 'I will never let down my guard on that weakness ever again.' And that, Bassam, that's the teacher of wisdom giving you a lesson in wisdom. If you don't employ it, those kinds of failures continue as proof that you don't yet have wisdom. The wise *do* have the fat, a coat and a knife. The fools say, I'll handle it later."

My brain was spinning. The scroll was true power, I had learned so much, new pieces were falling into place. Oh that I had learned these truths when I was younger, how might my life have been different. But would I be here today? Probably not. It is good then, the path I've followed. And my respect for Zafir ... I could see his integrity, his honesty and trustworthiness. This great man had become the personification, the very embodiment of the scrolls.

When I left Zafir's tent, two Xiongnu warriors had been waiting and escorted me to my camping place. I thanked them and they went to their usual posts to keep watch in the dark.

Wrapping warm, I rested my head thinking I should write in my journal while the words of the scroll were fresh—but it was cold, so I etched the teachings into my memory—the idea that lessons of life come daily, and the wise avoid injury by applying their experiences as life-changing lessons, without delay. Just then, I realized the irony, and with a determined sigh, I reached over to light my lamp, do my duty, and write in my journal.

OWL

Fawzi caught me deep in thought as he steered his camel over to talk. The terrain before us was endlessly barren and flat, no wind, just the cold—and boredom. No villages, no stops, nothing for three more days. The bright sun did little to warm our skin.

"These scrolls are ruining your health, Bassam!" Fawzi said, poking me with his riding stick. "Why don't you let me sit in for you for a while? Zafir might appreciate somebody awake and listening."

I looked up surprised, reacting to the poke, and gave half a smile. "It's not that," I said. "Something just doesn't fit."

"Oh no, not another of your famous theories!"

I smiled. "No, just wondering."

"Okay, let me give it a try. What are you wondering?"

"None of this fits," I said.

"None of what?"

"This harm, these dangers—the killers of Suoud, my capture, Zafir's distant caution whenever I discuss it with him...."

Fawzi said nothing. He looked forward without reacting, watching the group ahead, rocking atop his loping ride as if that was his preferred place in life.

"Maybe it's my imagination," I said. "No. It *must be* my imagination. That's it, that's got to be it."

Fawzi furrowed his eyebrows. "Not fair, Bassam. You can't just start something like this and then end it."

"I don't know what I was thinking, I'll leave it alone."

Fawzi sighed and cleared his throat. Lowering his voice he finally confessed. "Bassam, I know what is bothering you."

"You do?"

"You should be aware of things that are organized, men and their wicked designs, plotting—always plotting against Zafir, against Abdali-ud-din."

"Men?"

"Follow me," Fawzi said, steering his camel to the side, out of the traffic.

He led me beyond the eavesdropping of others, far enough so that other riders could not hear. He motioned me to pull up close.

"You remember the Tauri of the Pontusl, the Fukara—raiders, bandits, organized thieves?"

"Of course."

"What you found in the murder of Suoud, your capture, the concern in Zafir—all of it is a dark world, a different world, different than what you think."

"What are you talking about?"

"Abdali-ud-din has been master of the trade routes for centuries," Fawzi said.

"Yes?"

"And all that time, there have been many different groups rise up to challenge them."

"Is that the real reason for the Xiongnu warriors?" I asked.

"Exactly. No longer can the trade move freely across these great lands. New forces seek to take them—and not for what we carry in our bags only, but their place in the trade, their place among the villages and the coasts and ports, to replace us with them."

"And the scrolls?" I asked.

"Especially the scrolls."

We both stopped talking to watch strange dark birds circling slowly overhead—too thin to be hawks, too slow to be any other.

"Then what is this shadow that clouds Zafir and even *you* every time I ask about it? It's as if we're being followed, attacked—with purpose, with design—a plan, but no one will talk to me about it."

Fawzi tightened his jaw and chewed on the inside of his lip as if to weigh a decision.

"I'll tell you Bassam," he said. "I'll tell you this much but the rest must come from Zafir, do you understand?"

"Okay," I nodded.

"They call themselves the *Order of the Crescent*."

"Who does?"

"Don't interrupt me, camel brain. Just listen."

I held my words.

"They wear a small ink drawing of a crescent in their skin. Most people think of the moon in phase. It's not—the crescent is a sword, a curved sword from the east."

"Where do they wear this sign? Why not check the men, check them for their betrayal?"

"I said *just listen* for a moment, donkey dung."

"Sorry."

"There are two marks, usually. The one is the crescent, the other is the eye of the owl. "

"An owl? Wisdom?"

"Wisdom, but also a bird of the night. Night meaning hidden, masked, buried, unseen .... It's an odd gathering. More of a religion for most of them. A large band of zealots who take directions for which they are willing to die."

"Who gives these directions?"

"No one knows. They hide among the villages and the caravans, committing their heinous acts, unseen, unknown. Probably tied into the old Egyptian worship of *Ka*."

"I don't know *Ka*," I said.

"It's their idea of the life force in every living thing, their worship of the dead. When something dies, the *Ka* is freed. They believe it becomes theirs, infuses into them to make them stronger. It is their haunting in the night, these children of the moon."

"How does that connect to the Order of the Crescent?"

"It's all the same idea, really. The plan is to execute in the dark of night and dispatch *Ka* from whomever stands in their way for wealth or power. The owl is their guide through the dark, the *Ka* is the great universal force, the crescent can signify both the moon at night or the tool of their debauchery—the sword. And they harvest the *Ka* by taking lives."

"So, Suoud was . . . ?"

"Yes, probably. His killers were most likely sons of *Ka*. Had you known it, you might have looked for their crescent on the body of Moluck. He must have been one, though the members guard their allegiance carefully."

"And so, Zafir was suspicious of the men of Leuke Kome, suspicious they were sons of *Ka*?"

"We often call them the *blue ring*. That dates back a while, but they once inked the crescent in the folds of the skin at the base of a finger in the palm. Over time such inkings faded to blue, hence the name. But people started looking at hands for proof of trustworthiness, and that's when the markings went elsewhere—on the scalp, behind an ear, inside a thigh. Receiving the mark was ceremonial with many witnesses. That's because one's oath is not enough among such bandits. The inscribed token became the currency, the proof. This ensured secrecy and trustworthiness in identifying one to another."

"And the eye of the owl?"

"Much more difficult. Those inkings can appear as simple moles or freckles on the skin. Those are hard to find and can be easily denied."

"And finding them, discovering them, a difficult task ...."

"Yes, that's why Zafir never discusses it openly. He doesn't want you going around examining all the men you meet for small dots and crescents—it could raise suspicions, although suspicions already exist."

I fell quiet again, considering the problem.

"Moluck," I said finally. "He and the others, they were a band?"

"We all suspected it. Sons of *Ka*, following after the Order of the Crescent. It's really the only way such evil can survive in these places—they must hide in plain sight so that men will miss looking for them."

"Until they kill?"

"Until they kill."

SMALL INVADERS

The way-station of Tumushuk was clustered in the flatlands of grasses and sparse, scattered trees beyond the foothills of the mountains. Signs of a great but losing battle against the blowing sands stood weakly in the form of more stacked rock walls to the south. It was a boundary the Taklamakan did not respect, its sands burying the foundations of ancient ruins as they spread away from the winds. These marked the entry way into the deserted way-station of Tumushuk.

Zafir was anxious when we arrived, dismounting quickly and directing the traffic left and right to circle about into suitable camping places.

It was a good enough place—near several clumps of huyang trees that stretched westward following the small river. I joined Fawzi and Ammar who settled at a small grove where a silky stream escaped the boundaries of its mother source and meandered nearby on its own.

The trees helped windbreak against the cold. Already their iridescent green leaves showed weak and flat in this weather. I was sure the changing season was upon us again. I had always wanted to see leaves change colors, a passage I had heard about but never witnessed during my life in Rekeem.

With Fawzi and Ammar dropping off their gear on a flat spot, I spotted a lush carpet of wild grasses just begging for my sleeping mat. I was happy to oblige and knelt my camel nearby, and spread out my belongings for the night.

As night fell the frivolity that normally accompanied our group at a day's end was unusually subdued.

"This fire isn't doing its job," I said as I sat cross-legged and scooted closer to the flames, pulling my blanket tight around me again. "The wind blows the heat away."

"You're being a girl again," Fawzi growled as he pulled his yak-hair coat up around his ears. "All you do is complain, Bassam!"

"Well, you're the one with the good coat, you should let your younger friend have it to prove your manliness."

"I prove my manliness by enduring the suffering guilt I feel by watching you shiver so," Fawzi said. Ammar just laughed, shaking his head, and stirred the fire with his stick.

"More wood will help this fire," Ammar said. "Why don't you go fetch some?"

"It's always me, isn't it?" I said half scolding, half joking as I stood and wandered to the outskirts of camp for more fuel. Finding a dead shrub, I kicked at its trunk until it snapped off cleanly and dragged it through the dark.

Night had fully enveloped the valley flatland and I could see many dozens of fires scattered for 200 paces all around, most of them obscured by the huddled men who sat about them closely. And in the middle, Zafir's tent stood against the wind, a lone tower in the midst of the mounds of camels and men.

Fawzi cut up parts of the shrub and stoked the fire. "This will smolder until the end of second watch. By then, Bassam, you had better be wrapped up and warm!"

I peered from the edge of my blanket and said nothing as I watched my two friends spread out their sleeping mats and wrap themselves in warm blankets. The shadows cast by the flames danced and darted and the cracking took hold, flared to life, then burned out like black fingers slowly curling in the smoking heat. Finally, the sleeping time was upon the camp.

I couldn't doze off, and opened an eye every little while to check the fire that grew sleepier with each exhausted moment. It kept me awake—and watching. The wind was a bellows, blowing the fuel into a hot and burning blaze with its furious whistle—and then exhaling afterwards, leaving no flame but a tight bed of coals. With each passing swell those coals would glow and cool, the hot breath giving them life, then dying again.

Just as my eyes began to close for the last time, I felt a light hesitant tickle on my temple, just below the band of my headdress. I sleepily brushed at it.

A few moments later it came again. This time it moved across my cheek. I was irritated and brushed again. *My bakra*, I thought, *she carries fleas and I'll be tormented if I don't get her brushed with the liniment.*

I began to drift again.

Suddenly I felt across my ear the distinct feathering of little legs scattering down my jaw.

"What?!" I said brushing at my face again. And opening my eyes, I sat up to chase down the annoyance, brushing at my chest and then my head and then my chest again. And at that moment another feathery creeping hurried partway down my left cheek, and then—gone.

"Ah!" I said and began patting down my neck and head and chest and shoulders. "What is this? Flies at night?"

"Bassam!" Ammar mumbled. "You're too noisy."

"What is this?" I exclaimed and quickly jumped to my feet. From the glow of the dying fire I could see the ground all around me undulating in shadowy black motion—vibrating, dancing, black movement in dark puddles as if pelted by brown hail—but it wasn't hail, it wasn't falling, and it certainly was no puddle.

"What is this?" I asked again backing from the fire. And then I felt another feathery tickle climb up my chin and around to the back of my neck.

"Ah!" I almost screamed and grabbed at my neck, throwing my blanket down, brushing my hands all over myself. "They're all over me!"

Fawzi was awake by this time and Ammar was sitting up. "Spiders!" Ammar said, standing suddenly and brushing at his clothing.

Fawzi jumped up in a daze and backed off, nearly falling over backwards against his saddle. "Spiders?"

The three of us retreated from the fire trying to avoid tripping over each other and began brushing at our clothing, swatting, stomping, swatting again at anything moving, even the shadows and creases in our clothing.

"What are these?" I asked, brushing hard.

"I can't tell," Ammar said, "but the ground is covered in them. Look at that, like a living carpet."

We backed away some more, looking to our footfalls, kicking at anything that moved. Gaining some distance we felt removed enough to examine our camping place by the retreating light of the fire.

"They're very large—long legs, look at the size of them!" Ammar said, pointing with a poker he held in front of him like a sword.

"They're huge," I said. "What are they?"

"Sun spiders," Ammar said astutely. "They're at home in these parts, close to the desert. Looks like we found a nest."

"Sun spiders? Do they bite?" I asked. "Are they dangerous?"

"They carry no poison but they hurt when they bite—oh they hurt," Fawzi said. "They'll take a chunk of skin when they do—I know, I've been bitten."

Just then Ammar whacked at the ground and knelt to examine it in the dim fire light.

"Yes, that's what they are, the sun spider. We call them camel spiders, Bassam. But these are little ones," Ammar said, picking at the remains with the tip of his knife. "That's our mystery guest all right—the ancient haunt has come to see what monsters invade their home. They won't bother you if you don't bother them."

"Bother? Do you know what you're saying? They crawled all over me, across my face, my neck, my hands, I was covered!"

"Oh stop crying," Fawzi said. "You weren't covered, probably just a couple of them."

"Fawzi's right," Ammar said. "The camel spider can grow as big as your hand, but it has no venom, and it's too timid to attack prey larger than itself. But watch out for the daytime."

"What happens in the daytime?" I asked.

"They're night creatures, hunting for food and warmth. They probably found you conveniently heating up their nesting grounds in those tall grasses, or perhaps you brought them with you when you dragged that shrub to the fire. In either case, during the day time, they don't like the heat and they'll chase you just to get into your shadow."

I shuddered. "Chase me?"

"Oh yes," Fawzi pitched in. "And they're fast! You can't walk away, they'll keep up, even if you run slow. Run fast and they can't keep up for long."

"And if they catch me?"

"They're not trying to catch you," Ammar said. "They just want to be in your shadow. They can see it, you know. They just want shelter from the sun. And when you move, they'll move too."

"I saw my first as a young boy. I thought it was trying to attack me," Fawzi said, hooking the remainder of the shrub with his knife and dragged it over the bed of coals. "Scared me to death!" As the dry branches crackled into flaming life, Fawzi retreated and stood with the rest of us some dozen paces away.

"And that's why the name," Ammar said. "Camel spiders sometimes take a ride in the hot day on the underbelly of your camel."

"My camel?" I asked, stealing a glance at Bakra, suddenly worried about what foreign secrets might cling to her undersides.

"Sometimes," Ammar said. "They find protection from the sun, a shadow they can keep instead of running alongside."

"Do they hurt the camel?"

"Oh no, they just go for the ride. But if you roll over on one in the night or try to corner one, they will bite."

We grew quiet as the fire's heat grew and its flickering light illuminated a large circle of short shadows about our camp.

"So, what now?" I asked.

"I suppose you won't want to lie back down there," Ammar said, "but you could get your sleeping mat and blanket and shake them hard, and find a place over there away from the warmth of the fire and that grass. That's probably where they made their homes."

Fawzi found a few more sticks and tinder lying about and tossed them to the pit, scattering the flames in a billow of sparks.

The activity and brighter fire sent dozens of the remaining long-legged creatures scampering about, away from the heat, and disappearing into the grasses and the darkness of safety. I stepped carefully toward my sleeping mat and gingerly retrieved my belongings. I worked them against a large, flat rock for several minutes until I was confident that no living creature could cling or hide, and wrapped my blanket about me as if to reclaim the territory as mine.

A large mound of solid rock protruded from the ground, and there I spread my mat across it—off the ground where the reflection of the stoked fire give light for signs of the returning desert patrol. Until I fell asleep, I saw no such eight-legged guard, and for a few hours of deep sleep, if they had indeed launched a patrol over my body, I did not awaken to witness it.

When the sun peeked over the horizon to warm the cold air, the camp was already stirring for departure. Zafir had nothing to bargain in this village, and no reason to try except to freshen our supplies, fill the skins, and prepare for another eight days travel to Qiuci.

When the long line of camels and horses finally roused and gathered into tired lines for the slow plod through the outskirts of Tumushuk, Tou caught up with his trio of friends. It didn't take long for the previous night's spider tale to be told in great detail and drama.

"They covered him like black on rice," Fawzi grinned, "crawling everywhere, and all he could do was stand there dancing like a girl to get them off!"

"I did not dance, and you acted as skittish as me," I countered.

"But they scampered everywhere," Ammar added. "I've never seen them that thick before. Chances are we've got several who found a ride underneath," and he stared at me. I suddenly wondered and decided that at the next stop, I've got to get off and check my bakra.

When the laughing and bragging died to silence, Tou furrowed his brow. "I was just talking to Zafir this morning. We must keep an eye out in this region."

"What is the danger?" I asked.

"This is Xiongnu land, but not all Xiongnu follow the same master," Tou said. "Our men who united with you are part of a much larger alliance that is forming to the south of the deserts. And north of here, we are all still Xiongnu, but a fight for power has broken out. It shouldn't be of any concern along our route, but if those bands have moved south toward these lands, it will not be safe. Then it will be a concern."

"What options does that leave, Tou?" Ammar asked.

"I have been speaking with Zafir about that," Tou said. "The last word I received was that the route we're following is protected by my people. And then a runner caught up with me yesterday to tell us of fighting in some borderlands many days east of here."

I asked, "How far east must we travel before we can turn south and drop into safer land?"

"Such fights rarely last more than a day or two, then they move on. We can turn to the mountains or continue our trek to the end of the desert. The mountains offer a place where we can disappear into a valley or canyon for a few days. By then, most fighters have exhausted their supplies and have retreated to villages. The fighting is easily diffused for lack of a supply chain, and the weather is on our side, too. The Xiongnu are a seasonal people and will return to their homes if there is no threat to their sovereignty."

"Do we pose such a threat?" asked Ammar.

"Not one that we couldn't buy our way out of should they wish to tax us for the trespass. We'll know in another few weeks. But now is the time to keep your eyes open, and don't stray from the pack."

Suddenly I felt useless. I wanted to do more than carry my own weight for the security of the caravan, and vowed to start up again practicing the sword and the bow. If Zafir's train faced trouble, I wanted to be that additional sword and bow.

As we plowed our way through the icy wind, I saw that Zafir's agitation grew more visible as the day wore on. This didn't escape the attention of Modu and Tou. They caught up with Zafir and suggested it was time to have another large roast at evening camp, to lift our spirits, and that Tou could teach the men some of the great traditions of the Xiongnu. Zafir accepted the diversion and made plans accordingly.

COLORS OF MUSIC

With the camp set for the night, a large fire was built and the men circled around. Roasted meat was served, greens and fresh drink. It was an excellent meal, a satisfying diversion from the cold—our first significant meal in more than three weeks.

Tou stood before them and called for their attention. With broken words he welcomed their attendance.

"Tonight I teach you the bells of the Huainanzi ("Who-ah-ee Nan-chew")," Tou said as he walked back and forth around the fire. The blaze had been so stoked that it was too hot for those closest yet warmed those seated on mats farthest back. Tou kept moving from the heat as he spoke.

"Tonight I must have you help me and we will find wisdoms in the bells and the strings!"

With that, his associates brought forward small silver bells of different sizes. Another brought forward a pair of squat stringed instruments of many strings on low hollow handles.

"The Huainanzi is an ancient teaching that comes to us from Liu An, the King of Huainan," Tou said. "His words are well respected in these parts. The Eight Immortals respectfully completed his writings that tell of the universal Five Phases. Tonight we will all share in drawing from these instruments the powers of joy and good so that we may have peace in our journeys."

He passed out the bells to create what he called Zafir's Happy Band of Musicians. It made the men laugh and smile.

Handing the first bell to Humam, Tou explained so all could hear, "Each bell rings a tone of the five-note scale, and each note means goodness and light. For you Humam, you have the tune of the Wood. Its song speaks from the east where the great forests grow, and it is the color green."

Humam held his bell and gently hit it with a metal striker that was attached.

He handed the second bell to me, what he called the tune of the Fire.

"Its song speaks in Red, and is from the south." I looked over at Ammar and raised my eyebrows as if to say, "South pointer, again?"

To Rakin a captain of fifty, Tou handed a larger bell he called Earth, "for its song is from the center, and its color is yellow."

Rakin tapped the bell loudly, its earthy tone rang clear and unwavering. A soft chuckle spread among the group.

To Sofian a captain of 100, Tou handed the fourth bell. "This song comes from the west and its color is white, the song of metal, shall we hear it?" Sofian struck the bell and its lower note resonated cleanly in harmony to the others.

The last bell was handed to Zafir. "This is the song of water, and its color is blue for it always points north." Zafir gave it a solid hit and a higher note rang out in beautiful solo.

"We have the Five Phases in these notes," Tou began. "Wood feeds Fire, those two notes blend one to the other. Fire creates ash and Earth as it burns, and its harmony is clear. From the ash the Earth bears us its Metal and the Metal carries Water. The Water nourishes Wood and we begin again. These are the five phases, the five notes of our players this evening."

The men smiled at the harmony of ideas and began to relax as Tou brought them the music that his little Happy Band of Seven Musicians started to create.

"It is said that when all things are in harmony, they can draw out of one another the good energy and light. For example, my strings, if they're tight in the right way, one note will draw out the same from my other instrument, like this." And with that, one Xiongnu warrior plucked firmly a single string and then placed his hand over it to stop the vibrations. The other Xiongnu warrior held up his instrument that was not plucked, yet all could hear the same note repeated on his own string—it was vibrating from the strength of the first in perfect receiving harmony.

Amazement passed from man to man as they saw the remote power of one string passing a note to the other, untouched, invisible, mystical.

"My Xiongnu warriors are as these strings. We know each other like the tunes of these bells. And your great caravan of wealth can be tuned as these strings if there is but one who sets the notes and the others wish to follow. Let us see if we can make music together."

For the balance of the fire Tou had those with the bells follow his lead to strike their bells while the stringed instruments plucked notes that harmonized up and down until a beautiful richness of eastern tones and notes blended in a gentle melody woven in softness upon the evening breeze. The musical notes flowed across the band of travelers like the curling smoke of the fire, carried aloft into the night air. The sound was ornate, simple, and rich, with many layers and multiple tones—as if a large army was sharing in the making of the notes. It was amazingly beautiful, the likes of it I had never imagined possible.

With some practice and laughter at the newness of it all, the little group managed to plink out a nice little tune that stuck in my mind and erupted with an errant whistle a couple of times that evening.

Tou explained further some deeper meanings into their philosophy. He spoke of the many layers in the five phases, not just the wood, fire, earth, metal, and water.

He spoke of an alignment with the five main planets, the four seasons, with Earth being the fifth for her role as the action of change, and the five livestock, the five fruits, and the five grains. Even the cycle of life came in five—from birth to youth, adulthood, old age, and death, represented in the bell he gave to Zafir.

"Oh, death!" Zafir laughed out loud. "So, Tou my friend of these many years, you give me the bell of water—of death—for I am the oldest man here? Such gratitude!" And the whole group roared in laughter.

"You might wish it so," Tou laughed. "Truly, I was thinking that yours is the last of the five beasts—the dog, the goat, the cattle, the chicken, and yes, the last is the pig." More laughter filled the cold night air.

As the entertainment wore the evening away with warmth and merriment, the night closed in damp and cold. Darkness was thick, and again no stars this night—high clouds veiled them from view. The nearby mountains wore no discernible edge chiseled between them and the sky.

And the band of men laughed and clapped their approval of Tou's amazing mastery of music and philosophy.

And for those many moments at least, more than 600 weary travelers enjoyed an escape from the hardness of the journey, the coldness of the region, and the dryness of the land. The universal language of music took them to a place where their souls could rest at ease, even if for but these few laughs.

But out there in the darkness beyond, behind the ridge of a black hill, peering from behind a large ruin some distance away, there was slight movement hidden in the shadows. Eyes of strangers looked on—watching, counting, and calculating. The weight of the caravan told the greedy eyes all they needed to know. In silence they crouched, watching—and in silence they disappeared.

A YAK COAT

As the cold of the coming winter washed over the flatlands leading east, the nights became distinctly more difficult. Every man shivered or slept, wrapped in whatever desert ware or local clothing he could purchase as protection during this long trek around the never-ending desert obstacle that kept us north. Eventually, the long expanse of sands to our right was supposed to end so we could move to the warmer south.

A week of endurance finally brought us to the walls of Qiuci, arriving there at dark. No fires burned for reasons of safety, and we hurried to set camp. It was going to be a two-night stay. I put up my little blanket as a tent to stop the wind so I could light the lamp and do some writing before wrapping up against the dropping temperatures.

And then came Fawzi, shaking my tent.

"Hey! Camel breath!" Fawzi said, speaking above the whining wind.

"What do you want?"

"I see your lamp burning, we don't need your beacon summoning more kidnappers. Qiuci is a prosperous but dangerous village, Bassam!"

"And so?"

"And so put out that lamp! Didn't you hear Zafir? This is the great crossroads. Keep your eyes open for merchants for the Hindi kings, they're always looking for slave boys to serve their great palaces."

"Write me a dispatch when you get there, Fawzi, I'll deliver it to your kin."

"No, I'm serious about this, this is slave territory. If their swords outnumber ours, you had better start learning Hindi."

"I know enough Hindi right now—*There's your man, Fawzi's his name*."

Fawzi frowned and declared his burden to keep a strong eye on me whether I liked it or not. A dozen Al Murrah, he said, might not be enough should we wander too far from their safety of numbers.

After Fawzi's departing footsteps faded in the wind I put aside my writings and extinguished the lamp. I felt around for my knife and held it close. For once the darkness brought a security of safety that before I had found only in the brightness of day. With knife in hand I dozed off warm despite the cold, curled up close to Bakra who was warm enough.

Before sunrise the animals began to stir. I peeked over my blanket wondering what daylight could reveal about this new place. And there crouched Ammar, already at a cook-fire, shaving sticks to start a fire.

"You're up early, Ammar!"

"No, I have not yet slept."

"What?"

"I've been in Zafir's tent going over our maps."

"What now?" I asked.

"Word will come soon enough, but for you, you should know that reports are coming from caravans arriving from the east. The Xiongnu battles are spilling over into the eastern lands. Villages burned, innocents driven, flocks stolen, much killing and slaves taken, the worst fighting. We must not be caught up in this."

A shiver of cold shuddered through me, only it wasn't the temperature. "What is Zafir's plan?"

"We have no strong options except to make haste to Yanqi."

"That's another 18 days, isn't it?" I asked.

"We can't take that long."

"Then Zafir wishes to depart now?"

"He takes one more day, maybe part of a day, to trade in this city. Much of his wares will be sold for gold, there is plenty of that here. We must lighten the load for the push through to Yanqi. If he must delay, we have no choice but to take our leave early in the morning."

At Ammar's caution, I decided to stay in camp for the balance of the day, not sure if Fawzi's warnings about Hindi kings was a tease or not. But I wouldn't take the chance because too many chances before didn't end well for me. I decided to stay close.

As the morning wore on, my boredom led me to visit other members of the train who also wearied of the wait. They spoke of the delay, some showing discontent that was more directed at the cold than at Zafir's time-tested trading techniques. It was a rule of Zafir's that the negotiations must never become rushed. The old trader was master at the waiting game, even when most other traders might take off running away in frustration.

Finding Tou, I passed the time by practicing more targets with the new bow. And then some jousting practice with several of the men whose own boredom welcomed the chance to demonstrate their own fighting stance and blows. I settled for the balance of the afternoon by a fire with several crusty journeymen who taught me casting lots for the game of twelve lines. Not knowing the strategy involved, I was just getting the knack of the knuckle bones when evening meal was called.

As the men gathered, Zafir invited all to circle close while they ate.

"The northern band of Xiongnu and an eastern alliance are fighting for land just ahead of us," Zafir announced. "I've been asked why I don't travel north and go around this fighting, but this is the wrong time of year through those snowy peaks and plains. Instead we'll press on toward Yanqi and work to make that trek in 12 days." At this a rumble of exchanged concern passed among the veterans, but for me it meant little except more hours before stops.

"For the protection of the train," Zafir continued, "we'll restock our supplies each night. That means your must fill your skins, pack breads and dried fruits. Buy them from the villages, from the herders, from whoever raises a petition to exchange. We must be prepared at any moment to survive in the mountains should trouble beset us and divert us from our intended goal. Feed your animals well, water them often, we'll move at a double pace and reach Yanqi in 12 days."

On the morning before dawn, Zafir rallied the train to the trail and steered toward the foothills. He dispatched Al Murrah and Xiongnu warriors to front and back, and with a protective line between the main body and the northern mountains and foothills. That remained our formation for the next several days.

At camp on the night of the fourth day, I was feeling the fatigue of the fast hurry. My bakra had hurried along faithfully at double-pace to keep up with the pack, but the jarring and jolting was more fatiguing on me than the long day itself.

With the sun set, the mountains to the north glowed cold in the silvery moonlight with snowfields ignited in pure white radiance.

Sleeping was as important as traveling, yet Zafir pressed on. He never let the night rest long as there remained several weeks of travel before safety could be found in the southern cities beyond the desert bandits and the rumored fighting.

Before sunrise each morning, he awoke his men to be on the trail before the warming rays began glistening off the frosted trail before us.

These passes, these great canyons along the folds of ancient mountains, were home to the occasional herdsman whom we passed, struggling to feed his herd of yak on what sparse green would grow there.

For Al Murrah, such passes were eyed with heightened suspicion as ideal for marauding bands of bandits, and their alert had remained keenly elevated. All through the days and nights since Qiuci, Al Murrah had dispatched fast riders ahead, into the hills left and right, lingering behind to guard the rear. Too great a treasure now passed through these lands to let a guard down at this late part of the trek. Some six hundred swords made for a formidable force, but these parts had many evil alliances.

I took inventory earlier in the day of the men as they rode in silence through the cold wind. For a desert people, these climes became most uncomfortable. Nearly every rider wore layered clothing or blankets about his shoulders or legs, with head scarves wrapped about them and pulled low to protect their eyes. To the north, the mighty blue peaks were dressed in deep snow while to the south, the constant brown horizon of mighty dunes stood static in steep, elegant repose. That barrier's end was soon enough. Kurla was a few days beyond that, and then on to Yanqi, another three days' travel.

It was Al Murrah's job to see that evening camp was always set close to a wooded area where plenty of fuel lay close by. Along these regions such a request was becoming difficult to fulfill, and several times the guides had to lead Zafir north of his intended route because of severe shortages in the wastelands through which he directed their passage.

I was grateful for detours so long as they brought the caravan within easy access to the forest and the wood. Seated about the fire I held out my hands for warmth and listened as Modu and the others discussed the route ahead. After an hour of such talk, fatigue and lack of experience in such things caught up with me. Tou saw my bewilderment and decided it was time to give his young prentice a history lesson.

"Yanqi is a large city," Tou said, kneeling beside me, testing the heat of the fire. "Many peoples have influenced it here. It falls within the 36 kingdoms. Zafir will probably have more trading to do here…."

"Many peoples?" I asked.

"Like those in Qiuci. They are wealthy traders from the Hindus and the far east who have been passing through Yanqi for so long nobody remembers any more. It's near the great lake. So many of them come here. From the north and in the foothills of the western mountains, all of them," Tou said. "All of them have come here for centuries to exchange and negotiate peace. It's not too different than your Rekeem. In times of peace, many roads cross here. In times of war, they move far north of the mountains, or south of the great desert. It's their punishment for the evil spirits that come to Qiuci and Yanqi and all the watering stops between."

Just then Fawzi called out and everyone turned to see him hurrying over to the fire, a look of a veiled prank pinched in his face. "Look at this, young student, explain this," he said, holding out a large, ragged chunk of black rock for me to take.

"More rock?" I asked, taking it in hand. It was as black as obsidian but didn't shine the same. I turned it over with suspicion, suspecting Fawzi was up to some trick. "What is it?"

Fawzi grinned, his eyes twinkled. "You will like this," he said. "Watch!"

And with that, he took the rock and reached to the cook-fire, letting it gently drop into the flames. He nudged it closer to the coals with a stick.

I watched a few moments wondering if it was magic or should I back away lest some surprise erupt.

It didn't take long for the rock's sharp, thin edges to glow red as little wisps of yellowed flame started dancing tightly atop them with furnace determination. Moments later, a rich, mineral smoke began to funnel above the fire, whisked away for the wind.

"It smells like burning pitch," I said. Fawzi just smiled, his eyes dancing with another secret.

"This black rock burns, and burns hot!" Fawzi said. "What other land has rocks that burn?"

For several silent minutes, me, Fawzi, Ammar and a few curious men who stopped by, watched a glowing incendiary creep across the black rock, etching its surface with glowing red threads and exuding a white crust as more black smoke swirled above. Fawzi had a leather sack filled with chunks of the rock and reported that local merchants sold it in great quantities for just fractions of a silver.

"They dig it from the broken sides of those hills yonder," Fawzi said. "They think it has magical powers and don't part with it easily to strangers such as us."

"May I keep a small piece, to take home?" I asked.

Fawzi handed me a chunk the size of my fist. "I've been watching your souvenir hunting, donkey head. Much more and you will need your own caravan to haul all of these home, if that's your goal."

"Just one piece is all I need," I said. I envisioned the possibilities of such rock in regions where both cooking and warmth was needed. I planned to show the rock to others and find if any could be discovered back home.

Fawzi dropped more of the black rock into their fire until warmth radiated with such intensity that we moved back to enjoy the surprising heat. I stashed my piece into my saddle bag before wrapping up to sleep, and went to bed feeling comfortably warm.

The stopover in Kurla proved profitable for Zafir and the elders. He sold, traded and bartered his way into a nice profit so he could bring plenty to bargain and negotiate with when we arrived in Yanqi. Most of the remaining goods we carried found buyers for considerable profits.

It was amazing. As I watched, load after load of clay flasks and the leather pouches with their precious cargo were carried away by others, and I was astounded at the growing numbers of chests filled with gold coins that the buyers left behind.

I smiled at Zafir's repeated performance, and the wrestling of persuasive deal-making. He was in his element, bargaining for the best price and playing the loser at the end. From his tent the strangers of that city came and left, some smiling for their fortune, others angry that their offer wasn't acceptable to the old man.

At midday, with Zafir still busy, Ziyad sent a group into the market place to find foods to carry us for several more days until the next village of farmers could supply us. For me this was my chance to buy a yak-hair coat. I asked Tou to help me do the shopping, with Xiongnu warriors in tow.

"You should trade for a yak and leave your camel," Tou said as we walked toward the market place. "Yak is made for this place. He can live where it's cold, and still he gives meat and coats for winter. And the *dri*, she gives plenty of sweet milk and the chhurpi."

I looked at the locals around me. All of them were dressed in long woven clothing or leather coats, products of the yak and his long hair and thick leathers.

"Chhurpi?" I asked.

"Yes, a hard cheese. And butter. You must try the butter tea with the yak milk, I guarantee you, you will want to make your home here, I warn you!"

"It's that good?"

"That good. The yak lives in these highlands because he is strong. His lungs are large, his heart is large, his hair, have you seen how it grows to the ground?"

"I've seen that," I said. "And yet they don't come down into the valleys."

"They can't," Tou said. "They die in the low valleys. They must live where the air is thin, the weather harsh, and the temperatures cold. It is good for them."

At that, Tou led our band past the heckle and noise of animals, fowl, traders and complainers, and into the more specialized shops down an alleyway. He spotted an open-front shop right on the corner that was warm with spacious windows and colors. The coziness of its wide doors and windows was inviting and curious, well-lit and well stocked with colors and leather.

"Here, young Bassam," he said. "This is a good place. We'll find a good coat for you here."

Colorful skins and long-hair robes dyed in reds and oranges, even a rich blue, hung with craftsman's pride on the walls and the entryway.

Several long tables stood in the middle with short stacks of three dozen or so leather coats carefully displayed. The long hair on each of them was neatly trimmed, some longer, some shorter.

I ran my finger over the tight stitching of the seams boasting the even-stitched perfection of an experienced seamster. A nice variety was available to choose from—assorted shades of brown, some black, a few in bleached white. I reached for a white coat.

"No," Tou said, "White is for the rich man to be seen by others. White is not for this cold place. Choose brown or black, those come from the wild yak, the survivors in the highest places."

Beneath the coats laid one dark brown with beautifully brushed mottled hair with strands of grey in a fluff of red-brown mixed with black. I pulled it from the stack and unfolded it for size. The coat was long enough, falling a little below my hips as I held it up.

It was heavy, even without the gold that Zafir might hide there. But this, this was the weight of strength and versatility. A wide leather belt of woven tail hair hung through tight loops around its middle, and was decorated with small wooden beads and matching strands of color. I slipped it on with comforting ease, and found the inside warmly lined with down.

"This is soft inside," I said.

"They line it with short fibers," Tou said. "These fibers are harvested every spring. I've done this myself, when I was a boy—brushing out the fiber and I let mother twist it to threads. It's very soft, no? Expensive too, but the best yarn in all the world."

"This is warm," I said, pulling it closely about me and securing the belt. "And pockets, it has pockets for my hands."

"Or your knife," Tou added.

"I like it, I'll take this one."

Tou translated the transaction and after some slight discrepancies on an agreed price, Tou handed my silvers to the merchant and the deal was done.

"You will like this coat," Tou said. "Yak leather breathes. It's supple enough but will become protection to you as it ages. It will keep you warm, but on a warm day, you don't sweat as easily as with other leathers. It breathes."

We left the shop with me wearing my new purchase. From a distance, I'm sure we blended with the mingling crowds. I felt almost like I was in disguise, just another shape, another local man moving among strangers, testing the wear of my new coat. We returned to camp where others in lesser wraps looked at me with envy. I smiled and gestured toward the market place. Some took up my offer and stood to venture out themselves.

By midday of our final stay, Zafir concluded his sales and returned with the other elders to camp. They found each man ready at his camel for quick departure. We loaded the foodstuffs, filled the water skins, and deployed the bows and arrows. Al Murrah and the Xiongnu warriors girded about leather armor, mantles, and layered epaulets as if ready to do battle that very day. And I was not to be discounted, and strapped Suoud's sword against my saddle. Zafir surveyed the readiness of his train and turned over the gold of that day's trading for distribution into safe keeping by his captains.

With half a day of light remaining, Zafir signaled for the company's departure for Yanqi.

WINTER

"Turpan means 'fiery hot," Tou said as we rode through a barren stretch. "It's a beautiful oasis in the middle of a large desert. Some men say it's the lowest place on earth."

"Does it have a winter?" I asked.

"Not like your desert winters. You can expect cold at mid-day, the water freezes in the shade. You should keep your water skins close to your beast—keep them from freezing."

"Don't you even get rain?"

"No rainy season but there has been snow."

"Snow? In this place?"

"Maybe once in a lifetime. I have seen it twice."

Snow. I had heard of it and wondered, could snow appear in a dry desolation such as this?

The climb north toward Yanqi grew difficult with steep terrain, twisting paths, dried creek beds and broad stony washes that hurt Bakra's feet. The wind was relentless, whipping us to silence as our beasts fought and snorted and grunted their burdens to the rim of the great Tarim basin. The usual route was a large river base, washed out eons ago, and dry as bones today. Modu didn't like the reports of warring tribes to the north and suggested another route. He said the low mountain valleys were safer than the river base, but would add several days to the crossing.

It was the evening of the second day out of Kurla when we drove into the broad vale of a twisting dried river. A cemetery of dead trees marked our camping place. Their gnarly roots clung to the stony soil, and protruded just enough to give us fuel for cook-fires. There was no water to be seen. "Drink with measure," Zafir told us. The animals sniffed out enough greens to make cud and seemed content to rest from the long climb.

As darkness fell I found Ammar and Fawzi at their fire. Fawzi was trying to tell me how I got cheated on my new coat.

"I know where you can get them a third the price, yak brain!"

"And a third the warmth," I said. "Tou says this coat is from yaks above the tree line. The dark color protects from the sun and keeps them exceptionally warm."

"Well, you just watch, another three or four weeks and you'll be paying a beggar a gold piece to take it away. It'll be too heavy, you'll toss it."

"You just want it for yourself," I said. "Forget it! Yours is embarrassing! That old rag insults the old sow that gave it."

Fawzi sat straight, pointing a finger, ready to launch a counter-insult when Zafir suddenly stepped from the darkness and into the inviting glow of our firelight. He smiled and noticed my new coat.

"Ah, you got it!" he said, warming his hands at the fire.

"Yes, Tou helped me, in Yanqi."

"Very nice," he said, and reached over to test the seams on the sleeve. Then turning to Fawzi, "You should replace that old rag of yours, Fawzi, it insults the old sow that gave it."

Fawzi shot me an angry eye and I could hardly contain my laughter.

"Come Bassam," Zafir said with a tired sigh. "We have a short night to cover a long subject." He handed me the two mats. "Bring your lamp," and turned to reveal the sack of scrolls slung over his shoulder.

The wind was noticeably calmer but the temperatures remained uncomfortably cold.

I strapped on Suoud's sword for the first time around the outside of my new coat, finding it poorly fitted over such bulk, and followed Zafir. Two pairs of guards fell in behind, surveying the distances of flat nothingness that bordered that night's camp.

After a hundred paces he gestured to drop the mats and prepare our usual arrangement.

With the lamp lit, we seated ourselves, adjusting to the hardness of the packed soil.

"I told you I was short on time," Zafir began. "Do you mind?"

"This is fine for me," I said. "I've been looking forward to it."

"Then—what can you tell me about the scrolls since we last talked?"

"Each new scroll helps me understand better the previous scrolls," I said, "like the riddle about the many branches of one tree. I see they're not five or six separate ideas, but many ideas from the same idea, like the many reflections of a perfect gem, each with its own beauty, but part of the whole."

"Very good, Bassam," he said. "You're beginning to understand. Let me ask, what is this singular tree, this singular life that these scrolls point to? Do you see it yet?"

"I think I'm getting close, but, I don't dare share it yet."

"And why is that, my boy?"

"Because it touches on something very tender, something that's so close to me I'm hesitant."

"That's fine," Zafir said. "That tells me more than you know."

ب هبصه 78 محبوب

THE SIXTH SCROLL

"This bag," Zafir said, "was my father's when he was a boy. It was new then but it shows wear today. I may have to replace it."

I watched with quiet respect as the familiar lines unfolded for the sixth time. Zafir's countenance was relaxed and warm. He spoke the lines as if hearing them from his own father—gentle, assuring, stirring with loving memories of a distant past when the patrons at this night's recital stood reversed, when he was the boy seated at the feet of his own father.

I noticed the scroll sack showed worn creases and a frayed drawstring—a lot of tell-tale wear that had come largely from this very journey. It suddenly struck me that perhaps a new sack might actually be in order before our journey was out.

Reaching inside Zafir produced a long bundled scroll with six leather tassels dangling from the top.

"Most men," he began, "hope to find in these scrolls some ancient and lost guide to riches ...."

I wondered about my turn at some future day, delivering these scrolls to another, would my life be prosperous because of their lessons, prosperous in the way the scrolls teach? Could I know how to govern myself, be humble, have charity, judge well, be a good student of the five teachers and the wisdom they taught?

"... I think your heart is ready, Bassam. Do you understand?"

"Yes, I do," I said.

"Then let us begin."

The beautifully penned characters stood out crisp and clean, the same as before. "You will do the reading, Bassam, and I will listen. If you have a question, you may ask me. But some things I will not tell, it is part of the test."

I nodded and began: "The Song of the Teacher...."

> "To the prosperous, prosperity is not the possession of things, but in the knowledge of their utility. From the earth come the gifts for all, placed there by the Great Beginning, to nourish and prosper

his creations. Only those who receive such gifts with humility will gain the knowledge to properly use such gifts. For what benefit is the gift with no knowledge to use it? The foolish will squander and consume it. The earth is full, and enough to spare for prince and pauper alike. But lacking knowledge is the great equalizer for all creations. And on this principle, the prosperity that endures must also have with it Teacher…."

The words knitted themselves into a beautifully woven fabric of ideas, direction, and counsel—a way of living that stood on its own, the whole cloth of a man's well-spent life.

The scroll spelled out human nature as part of the perfection in which peace and joy are found, a way past the failings of mortality. But men are not excused from the experiences. They are ordained to go through them, as a garment in a furnace, to grow, to be taught, to learn from the fire first hand, without proxy or shortcut.

I paused on an amazing thought I hadn't considered—that perfection is not an ending place, but a pathway of constant improvement—with Teacher as the guide.

"Herein lies true immortality. Not in prolonging your earthly life but in prolonging the virtues you have lived. Each day each man may start his life anew, but when the night comes, therein can no man do his works, for it is night. And happy is he who embraces the words of Teacher—who makes of the stations in his life lessons learned, lessons accumulated, lessons applied and lessons understood—the foresight to live the deliberate life."

I could see the interlocking relationship of self governance, humility, charity, judgment and wisdom. The other scrolls were coming together in the sixth.

It was through the power of *teaching* that the great virtues of wealth are accumulated from one generation to the next. Teaching the virtues become guide posts to the young explorer whose foot first sets upon the paths of his own life. Not simply because he might be learning such virtues for the first time, but because he is *living them*. And therein lies all the difference—*living them* is different than learning them.

"The Teacher extends his hand to help the student along the pathway of life, for it's a pathway the Teacher has passed before."

This is what Zafir does for me now, passing along these scrolls to fulfill the promise passed to him from his fathers, the promise to be Teacher.

"You have read much, Bassam," Zafir said. "Are there questions?"

"Only to ask, who was your greatest teacher, Zafir?"

The old man smiled and closed his eyes, remembering. "It was my father and mother, as you probably guessed—they were my teachers through life. Said my mother to me once at the close of her life as I helped her one day to return to her place, 'I remember when I used to help you to the doorway of our home, and now you're helping me,' and she hugged my arm tighter as we walked so slowly that day, a beautiful day."

"Did your mother read the scrolls?"

"Oh yes, but I don't mean to say my mother and father's teachings were from the scrolls alone. Father took me on many journeys to strengthen me, to put me in the way of experiences. He showed me how to make assorted tools to trap food, to build shelters, to negotiate a bargain, to find my way across vast stretches of wilderness, to live, to survive, to feel the buffeting of life. My mother taught me to see and feel things beyond the power of my own senses, to realize the impact of my life on the peace and well-being of others around me. She gave me a heart to pacify the power of my will. And therein was she *Teacher* to me also."

Mother and father, I thought. The one teaching me to enter the world and wield my strength to protect myself and my family, and the other to teach me that mercy is equally important as justice, and love more powerful than hate. It was a beautiful balance, and I liked it.

"I'm at the riddle," I said.

"Please proceed."

The cold night made me pull my coat tight. I cleared my throat.

"A virtue of wealth is this for thee, One branch one limb on the self same tree; The coin and palace all men may gain But woe is life when spent in vain. For joy that lasts and doth not cease, Embrace the virtues thou Prince of Peace. One branch one limb on the self same tree, A virtue of wealth can be for thee.

"Oh wisdom, behold now the Song of the Teacher—

"Two mirrors faced each other, reflecting their lack, Forever exchanging from this glass to that. Endless their passing, through time did they pass, Till finally came dark to stop them at last. A brush that caught fire, but soon burned away, gave light to them all, their ignorance did slay.

"What meaneth this the song of the Teacher?"

"You have some questions?" Zafir asked.

"The mirrors," I said. "I've stood between two reflections, my image in one mirror forever reflecting in the other, like Teacher."

"Why would that be Teacher?" he asked.

"I suppose the reflections are like the passing along of knowledge back and forth for a thousand generations."

"Do the mirrors reflect knowledge or something else?"

He was right, the riddle said they reflected their *lack*. There is no teacher in this. I shook my head. "I suppose if the image is of another mirror, then there is nothing to see and nothing to reflect. Nothing at all," I said. And then, a new image formed in my mind.

"Mountain lakes are like the mirror," I said, "reflecting the sky and the green and the trees, and we say, 'my, what a beautiful lake.'"

"Indeed," said Zafir.

"But in the dark it reflects nothing, so we don't see it as beautiful. And mirrors reflecting another reflection is just the same."

Zafir nodded. "With nothing to reflect, that ability to reflect serves no purpose."

"What has this to do with Teacher?" I asked.

He pointed to the riddle. "Read the second part."

"A brush that caught fire, but soon burned away, gave light to them all, their ignorance it did slay."

"What happens when a brush catches fire?" Zafir asked.

"It burns hot—and fast," I said. "One time my friends and I were ... well, never mind. But a big one crackles at night and sends great plumes of glowing ashes flying about like stars, it's exciting!"

"Is it a secret?" Zafir asked.

"Oh no! Everybody sees it!" I said. "They all come running to watch, and that was, well, that *could be* all the fun."

"But more than that," Zafir said.

"More than what?"

"How does this slay the dark of ignorance?" he asked.

"Well, I suppose by brightening the dark places …."

"Do you see Teacher in this?"

Could this be another metaphor for the man? That after a long life of growing, at his end, that man's last great duty is to slay ignorance in others?

"He's a light," I said, "is that Teacher?"

Zafir smiled. "I will help you on this, it's abstract but I think you know it already," he said. "Each person spends a lifetime looking to others for validation, evidence, proof of what they are. They want feedback that they are good, of value, loved. We all take that from each other for years and years, like mirrors facing each other. But if one will be Teacher and be a light instead of a reflection, suddenly truth shines on all things. Everyone can see better, understand better, no more vain validation, no more vanity. Only light can shed truth, mirrors cannot perform this."

"So ... the burning brush is Teacher," I said. "It casts light on ignorance. And by burning, the brush dies meaning the best teaching comes at the end of a good and full life. Is that it?"

Zafir nodded. "The virtue of wealth of the sixth scroll," Zafir said, "is to pass along knowledge, to let it accumulate in you all of your life. That means living the deliberate life, and not squandering it lest you have nothing to share at the end of it. And then you, being full in old age, you can impart your knowledge and shed light as the burning brush."

I let the words sink and take hold. "It's a virtue that doesn't come lightly, does it?"

"Over an entire lifetime," Zafir said. "Can you be Teacher if you haven't lived the lessons or endured the hardships?"

I thought for a moment of all the things people lectured me on but didn't live themselves. It was a true saying.

"Never forget this," Zafir said. "You can't teach something you don't live yourself. That's the giving of light, the burning, the consumption of your life in wholesome pursuits of wisdom. That's the action that gives forth the light. You must be what you teach, so be what is good and wholesome, and that is what you teach at the end of your life—even after you've become ashes."

It was a wonderful thought. A man of virtue is virtuous, and therefore is qualified to teach virtue. No counterfeit could suffice. Many limbs of virtue on the self-same tree ... or brush?

"My closing thought, Bassam, is that you work hard to see in yourself what other men refuse to see—that life is always about giving, not taking. Most men fear their endings and become greedy in their last years. They become takers. This is like a long-lived brush that simply shrivels away, consuming what last drops of moisture it can suck from the ground and then dies having never given back. If a man doesn't pick up this one last duty to teach what life has taught him, he has wasted himself. The lessons he learned are lost when his body is laid low. So much precious knowledge and goodness that is gained too often becomes forgotten in the grave. It happens all the time, it is a tragedy."

"This darkness that stops the mirrors," I asked. "Is that death?"

Zafir stood to his feet, shaking the wrinkles from his robes and extended his hand to help me up. "Yes," he said. "Don't you let this ending come to you, Bassam. These deserts are filled with the bones of dead men. But those men who live after death, who gained eternal life—immortality—are the same who taught their experiences and virtues to the rising generations. That is how we advance ourselves in all things. It's no more difficult than the simple act of kindness that the sixth scroll speaks about—that we must all learn through life not to simply reflect endlessly a self image discovered in the flattery from others, but to become, at last, the source of light, of knowledge, of teaching. Is that not the great lesson that Father Moses learned on the mountain when he removed his sandals to step within a circle of sacred light? How many mirrors were silenced that day and how much ignorance was slain in the light of *that* burning brush? It was, alas, the greatest of them all—it was Teacher."

BASSAM

ب هبعه 79 محبوب

AMBUSH!

Along the western shores of the large freshwater lake of Bositeng ("Bowz-e-tang"), which sat half a day's ride before Yanqi, there stretched a vast plain of hardened-soil flatland. Ammar told me this is where the lake's waters had once washed. For reasons known only to nature, the lake had been receding these many years. Perhaps the rivers feeding her had withdrawn their strength—no one knew.

Zafir moved our train along these ancient shores where we and the animals could find drink and refresh ourselves. It was a welcomed stop after the arduous detour around the many difficult passes and climbs from Kurla.

Today was a cold day, the wind blew steady and each of us was wrapped for the duration. A massive wall of dark clouds ahead hung heavy at the near horizon with sheets of rain blowing across the plain. If such a storm dropped her rains on us, we could certainly mire in the mud or be in danger from sudden flooding.

A consultation with Ammar and the men of Modu concluded that we should detour west, to the caravan's left. They elected to go around and approach Yanqi from the higher foothills lest we be caught in a sudden downpour.

Two hours later as we approached that higher ground, we found in the parched landscape a new challenge. It was rippled with thousands of channels cut by runoff from the plateau. Stepping through the etchings of twisting mazes and stony troughs upset the animals. I heard snorting and grumbling as we climbed and descended the rocky terrain, slipping over the tailings of nature's ancient excavations. And then my own bakra started up with her sour attitude.

"Oh hush, old woman," I scolded, scratching behind her ears to calm her. I steered her to the front of the line and took interest in the navigation that was being negotiated with Zafir and the elders.

"We are almost there, old friend," I told her. "You don't want to be caught in the floods that cut these channels do you?"

The ominous storm clouds had turned grey to black and were starting to sink to the horizon. The occasional sprinkle of icy rain started, stinging at my face—I drew my hem for protection.

"This could get ugly," I whispered to Bakra.

The pass we were approaching was still an hour ahead of us, but even from here it loomed high on the horizon as we neared.

And then directly ahead I spotted two horses galloping wildly in our direction, their riders flailing at their beasts with extreme haste.

I sat tall in my saddle. "What is this?" I called out.

More eyes turned to the distant pair whose robes fluttered in panic and their bodies hunched tall over their mounts.

Seeing them coming in a race of wind-whipped dust, Zafir raised his stick to stop the caravan. An eruption of barking shouts slowly brought the great group of 600 to a stop.

The pair of Xiongnu warriors rushed up to the lead and stopped in a cloud of foaming panic.

A tangled mass of frenzied words poured from their mouths and Modu translated for the rest. I could hardly hear for the whine of the wind but I did catch a few—"camel army," "horse soldiers," "bandits," "*ambush*."

Zafir immediately turned his camel about and pointing with his stick due south, shouted his orders.

The captains of 100 and of 50 whipped around and galloped their camels toward the rear, cutting through the baying and snorting, shouting orders to the men. In moments the mighty train slowly rolled about on itself, turned to the direction Zafir had ordered, and as quickly as we could, our animals picked up speed until we could break out into a gallop toward the river valley we had just worked so long to avoid all that morning.

Sofian came up panting next of me. "Zafir's orders, you follow me, now!" he shouted, and pulled his camel out of the thick line to the left. I followed in full gallop, escaping the great dust cloud kicked up from the hundreds of hooves clamoring over the stony landscape.

My bakra snorted loud but took the strikes of my stick in stride. She leapt over the broken ground and closed in behind Sofian's thundering beast. I clung to Bakra's shaggy coat and stole a glance behind. Stretching off for a thousand paces, the great caravan was spread out far to the back, and lost in a thick cloud of rising dust whipped about by wild winds.

But what is this? I caught sight of the top of the plateau as we galloped past and to my horror I saw lining the ridge many hundreds of brown and black horsemen and camels standing, watching, leaning shoulder to shoulder at the edge, looking down and estimating Zafir's fleeing men as does a vulture his easy prey.

At that moment, as if by some unseen release, the expansive army of man and beast suddenly started over the ridge and down the sides of the slopes. Their leads struggled through the loose gravel for sure footing as the horde hurried to secure the firmness of the foothills below.

A boom of thunder clapped just at the river and I quickly looked front again. The black storms began falling on us at last, heavy drops of icy rain pelted us with fury as we raced against the panic. It came suddenly, in wind-whipped cascades of blurring gray, stinging our faces and bare hands, bathing us in soaking darkness and smothering our vision with pelting droplets and blowing sand. Surrounding me were hundreds of riders, spreading out left and right as I followed Sofian. Had it not been for his distinct saddle covering pulling away in the front, I might have lost him in the chaos. But what of Zafir? And then came his words, *If there is trouble, and no other rises to lead, then you must follow a captain.*

I took great handfuls of Bakra's thick fur on her neck and clung tightly, squinting past the painful spray and shouted her forward.

THE LONG RUN

For the better part of a quarter hour, the roaring storm drowned out the pounding hooves of Zafir's caravan as we raced for the river pass through the mountains that led directly to Kurla. I saw nearby to my right a camel stumble and fall, throwing its rider into the dirt. Other camels leapt over, but the rider didn't move before he was lost to view in the wind-whipped clouds of dust and dark.

Galloping ahead, the shadowy mountains opened up into a wide V-shaped gateway, the river pass that pointed toward safety. The lead riders led us directly toward it and we raced past the foothills, finding a smooth passage winding south. Kurla was visible before the river emptied into the plain beyond, but for the choking haze of windy sand, its discovery remained masked by weather. The cold wind blew hard in our faces.

Racing through the relative safety of the river bottoms, the captains signaled us to govern our panic and bring our beasts to a half gallop. Already some of the camels smelled water at the river and fought their masters for a drink, while others growled and whined to the beatings as the men pressed them onwards. As the river basin narrowed, they formed us up three-abreast to follow the contours of the snaking passage.

For half an hour longer we continued the hurried march, sitting astride our mounts, soaked to the skin in the cold and wet, trusting in our beasts that foamed white and glistened in sweat.

The rain abated a few moments, giving us a chance to catch our breath, and then fell again in sheets. It stopped several times more, each long enough for the chilly wind to blow us cold, and then started pouring again.

Sofian chose a bend in the river to give the men a brief respite.

"Water your animals quickly, and fall into line, we can't delay," he ordered. "The robbers don't rest, neither will we." The beasts spread their front legs to reach and gulped water with growls and pushing. As soon as a camel lifted her head to look, the rider snapped his stick, "hut hut!" and fell in with the trotting band that continued past.

I really struggled to keep up with Sofian who lunged ahead to direct the fleeing train. Catching up finally, we could hardly exchange words before Sofian shouted orders, circled around to urge the stragglers onward. I kicked my bakra to keep up.

Where the river emptied from the mountains to meet the farmlands on the northern outskirts of Kurla, a series of stair-stepping hills guarded either side. Sofian eyed these suspiciously narrow passes carefully, signaling Tou to his side. I heard nothing over the rumbling of hooves and the wailing wind—but their gestures told me enough. Sofian raised his stick and motioned full gallop forward. In seconds the mighty column of beasts went thundering through the last mountainous gateway toward Kurla.

At that very juncture, as if so conspired from the start, there suddenly blossomed on the smooth slope of an overlooking hillside another cloud of dust, a second army of bandits shouting and galloping toward us. Some

200 killers waved their swords in the rain and the wind, chasing down the slope and across the plain to attack our flank.

The roar of retreat and the fury of the wind drowned their cursings, but I discerned their intent immediately. They wanted to cut off our retreat to the city. I was sure we could reach the city walls if we hurried, but there suddenly appeared yet a third band of men, maybe only a hundred, but enough to challenge our escape. They stood atop the last elevated slope and raised their swords as if challenging Sofian to engage them in real battle.

Sofian reacted immediately to the flanking maneuver and turned the column to our left toward the eastern foothills. We galloped to the higher grounds while Al Murrah and Xiongnu split off to engage the attackers. I leaned backward to see the swords collide but the charge disappeared too quickly into the black swirls to do anything more than focus on the blind flight ahead.

The train raced through the heavy, cold drops toward the eastern mountains for half an hour longer until pure fatigue forced us to an impatient walk of panting exhaustion.

Twilight with the pouring rain and moaning winds became true allies in the cause of hiding our retreat, but now had become our greatest threat as exposure and the chilly night could reign total disaster if the train couldn't find some place of security for the night.

We stumbled along in the pouring storm, using as our only guide the black mountains eastward contrasting against the darkened sky, a vaguely discernible but looming invitation toward an unknown destiny.

I clung to my bakra, soaked and shivering, my hands numbed, knuckles burning, the water running down my neck and dripping off my headdress, soaking my legs that ached from the cold wet.

I couldn't stop working over the cleverness of those schemers and their carefully planned ambush. They had funneled Zafir's treasure to points south by cutting off every retreat to safety. Such a conspiracy could involve many hundreds of men, men who understood exactly how such a group would respond to danger. It was a brilliant plan, and if Xiongnu and Al Murrah had been successful in delaying or stopping the bandits' pursuit, then our survival would have a greater chance of success.

Sofian drove hard, leading the men over the slippery dangers of the mud and wash, at last finding some higher ground in the shadow of the mountains. The rounded, barren hillsides were packed with pebbles and small rocks, and even in the dark, this natural depository from old runoff gave the caravan more sure footing than through the slippery mud on the flats.

81

STONE CANYON NIGHT

With the night almost upon us, the rains at last abated to a light and sporadic sprinkle. A slight parting in the clouds allowed just enough starlight to give us a sense of direction, and thus to the east we were guided toward one of the steep canyon enclosures along the base of a high plateau.

Finding ourselves among rocky piles of boulders and shallow canyons, we came to an alcove securely surrounded on all sides but a narrow opening, by high walls of stone.

Sofian decided it would have to do.

He led us through the narrow entrance and dispatched a few to search out as best they could in the darkness the boundaries of the enclosure for safety. It was found suitable, and fortunately for us, the rain stopped about this same time and the air went still.

The camels were exhausted and almost too weary to properly dispose of their burdens.

I knelt my bakra and stepped off for the first time that entire day onto wobbly legs sapped of their strength. My wet, cold clothes clung to me uncomfortably, but I had a change in my back pack. Peeling quickly the cloth from my body in the frosty blackness of that canyon cold was the worst moment of pained freezing I'd had in my entire life. With dry clothes pulled over me, the feeling of warmth came quickly.

My first order of business was a fire. My hands were so stiff from gripping the reins for so many hours, I could hardly open them. I rubbed them and shook them, trying to limber so I could use my bow drill—we had to make fire.

While the others were unburdening their camels and mingling about, I felt among my writing supplies and produced a dry sheet of papyrus.

With some dead twigs and dry grass I found beneath an overhang I managed my bow-drill and started a small fire.

The light was a cheerful beacon to others who came with makeshift torches to light their own. Manure sheltered by rocks was dry enough to fuel other fires, and before long, the yellow warmth of 20 fires brought life back to our camp. Men found dead shrubs and roots, and the heat began to dry out the labors of that cold and wet escape.

It didn't take long for a degree of peace to begin thawing among the men. The licking flames cast dancing shadowy forms on the rock walls of the canyon enclosure. Tired and broken bodies warmed themselves with hot tea, some foodstuffs and dry clothes. Coats and shawls, headdresses and blankets were propped by the fires, releasing vaporous clouds as they dried. They cast enormous dancing shadows on the cliff walls around us.

After a couple of hours of rest, eating, and reflection, we started to recover. A pair of Al Murrah left the enclosure at Sofian's command to check that our fires were not illuminating the mountain sides, revealing our secret whereabouts. After an hour, they returned with a good report that we were well sheltered and hidden from spies hunting in the night.

Sofian went about instructing the men to assess their property, their supplies, and to seek out their companions. He wanted an accounting of those who were missing. Each man represented a responsibility, and Sofian would measure our strength from the scattered reports.

With the necessities of life distributed for the security of all, a calm descended slowly, granting gifts of rest to some, and nightmares of remembering to others. By the end of first watch, many were asleep.

I laid on my mat, wrapped in dry blankets, watching straight above into the night-strewn sky. The storm clouds thinned after a while, letting a few stars shine. The temperature dropped and it didn't take long for a sheen of frost to cover everything. Puddles that were formed by the many hoof prints finally fogged over—early proof that by dawn all of them would be frozen.

I wanted to sleep but my brain was too full of questions and thoughts. None of my close friends remained in this group. I wondered what happened to them, were they killed? Did they escape in another direction? Word around camp was that at least a third of our group had split off with Zafir. I hoped that's what happened. The bandits had planned their attack well and did a good job of splintering us into smaller groups.

I decided to spend the restless time with my journals, and lit my lamp—a familiar ritual to ease my mind.

I propped myself against my saddle and wrote about the terrible ambush and the fighting that clashed beyond my view in the darkness of a freezing storm. I described our frantic escape and the many raiders who worked so hard to chase down our blood.

I recognized a certain cunning and complexity to the bandit's contrivance. It needed to be recorded and remembered—how each counter-move was cleverly anticipated by placement of two additional armies. I also gave in detail an accounting of the impact the wintry storm played on our survival.

"Had it not been for the storm we couldn't have escaped," I wrote. "The handiwork of God's benevolence in all our efforts is undeniably real, and something I won't speak about openly, but I'll remember it as a testimony always."

I didn't know how to report the outcome of the missing part of the caravan and expressed my worry for the others. Had they suffered the ultimate loss or had they escaped with their lives? Knowing the experience of the men that should have escaped with Zafir, and the power they represented, I knew Zafir should be all right. He was probably worrying more about me, wondering if I was safe.

With that comforting thought to sleep on, I pulled another blanket from the sticks by the fire, wrapping in penetrating warmth My coat would need more warmth, it had become soaked. My sleeping mat was already dry, so I laid down to watch the flickering flames lap at the cold air. Normally I might choose to rest near my bakra for warmth, but not tonight. She sat kneeling not far from me, eyes half shut, watching me closely in case I offered her something to eat.

"You sleep on your own tonight," I said. "You stink."

82

FROZEN DAWN

By first light we saw a thick frost covered everything. The men struggled to stoke their fires and for some a few hot coals remained to simplify that task. I had retrieved my coat earlier and slept soundly, wrapped in its dry warmth.

Some men managed to get water boiling and that made for good tea, but the convenience was short lived as the sky grew brighter. Sofian didn't want smoke signaling our enemies where we had spent the night.

A scouting party returned with a report that no bandits were in sight, but counseled against any attempt to regain Kurla. The lands northward were just too dangerous, they said, especially with our depleted numbers.

While this was going on, I remained curled up hoping to have a few more moments of undisturbed rest. I had shut the noise from my worries and remained snug in my blankets, testing with slight movements the muscular aches and pains that burned from head to foot. I opened my eyes to see men organizing their belongings, setting aside food and water, and checking with their captains to inventory their treasures and labors.

I finally roused myself and looked about for any fire that could warm a tea or something that could help me start the day. The ground was frosted hard and my breath clouded in the biting, brisk air.

Just then, Sofian strode into my camp.

"Get up, Bassam. We are leaving shortly."

"What of Zafir? I don't see Fawzi or Ammar, or …"

"They're not with this group, Bassam," Sofian said. "We don't know where they went. Some Xiongnu warriors said a large group broke off before the river basin and turned east. If Zafir was among those, perhaps it was a rouse to divert the bandits from the main body. No one seems to know."

"Is there a new plan?"

"We are working that out right now. We'll need to make some important choices. Get your things ready, we have far to travel."

With at least 200 men missing, the main body was without some of its strongest swords. Sofian speculated that the Xiongnu warriors had stayed with Zafir, splitting off to the east, right at the approach to the river basin.

"Zafir knows the direction we last left him," Sofian told the elders. "We'll continue south to the river and there should be little traffic this time of year. It should offer somewhere a good place to wait at a village or stopping place for Zafir to catch up with us. We must make in one day what normally takes us two, and I can assure you, Zafir is doing the same."

It took a few moments longer and the men climbed on their animals and started filing out of the rock enclosure. By then I was up and putting my things together in my back packs.

As we emerged from the cliffs to the open plains, I scanned the sky to see the grey canopy of yet another covering of heavy, dark clouds swirling around as they had the day before. The wind was choppy. Cold gusts of sand pelted us in waves. I groaned inside. I had become accustomed to the sand a long time ago—it was the icy rain I could do without.

With a wary eye to the northern horizon, Sofian elected a fast walking pace immediately south. Al Murrah rode ahead and sent horse-mounted warriors to scout the lands to the front and others west for signs of followers. We remained on highest alert, prepared to chase down any spy we found. Sofian maintained the pace south, hugging the foothills, until we were well clear of the region around Kurla and the passes leading to it. Our new destination remained a full day's ride away to the ancient river Thaum ("Thou-oom").

A HINT OF RIVER

At midday we paused for a water stop at a little creek. It was good for all of us to stretch our knotted muscles, look for food, and examine the changing territory.

I stepped off my camel and went straight for the hard ground. I laid flat on my back and pressed my shoulders to loosen my spine. A few pops later and the burning stopped. Never had a camel ride drawn so much strength from my posture. The cold was making my muscles tense. Or was it a strange feeling that we were being followed?

The local villagers we passed gave assurance that the little creek that supplied us with water was one of many tributaries of the Thaum. "It lays directly in your path, straight south," they said. The news brought hope that an end to our escape was only half a day's ride away. If the locals were correct, we should arrive there just after dark.

I watered my bakra and let her feed on the sweet grasses as I filled two skins and hung them from her saddle. Wanting to put more distance between themselves and the bandits, Sofian didn't let us tarry long. Half an hour later and we were back on the road.

Our steady advance took us beyond small mountains and foothills. By mid-afternoon, the landscape unfolded in a vast flat of uncharted expanses of blowing green grasses that were interrupted every few hundred paces by an island of large rocks taller than a man. This lumpy, green flatness reached to the horizons in all directions.

With no hills or mountains to interfere, a view of the landscape gave some sense of security that no other traveler could hide their pursuit—we could easily spot any movement coming toward us. In fact, we all were feeling better as the day wore on, that the growing distance between us and our attackers north was putting safety back into our pursuits.

A welcomed bonus today was the cooperation of the weather. Thinning clouds allowed long rays of sun to reach us, although this warmth also stirred the wind.

By early evening, a haze of blowing dust suddenly rose up, filling the vast plain with obscurity, growing stronger as the sun neared the horizon. At least there was no rain. I felt protected from the elements in my yak coat and decided right there that Fawzi was wrong—it will never leave me, the extra weight was worth it. Fawzi could throw out his if he chose, but *this coat,* I decided—this coat that Tou helped me buy will always stay with me.

Sofian drove us past small villages, the bleating of crowded sheep camps, and the pleadings of traders and sellers who offered foods and wares as we hurried by. It was a temptation to trade a few of my coins for a little bread or cheese or a few wilted greens, but there was no pause allowed. We had to beat the setting sun.

By dusk we had forged at least a dozen small streams and stammered down and up at least twice that number of dry stream beds. I was puzzled at the strange sight—Once again, plenty of water flowing across this flat land yet no orchards and farms or lush fields. I wondered if the best soils were long ago washed away, or was it the lack of industry in the people? I decided to ask Ammar the next time we met.

We did not reach the river before dark set in and Sofian was forced to stop short and camp down the men. It was too dangerous to proceed, especially along ground that was not a proven trail. We were back on a landscape of sand, and spread ourselves out in a large clearing.

By all estimations, the river was no more than a three hour ride. It could be our guide, leading us south to the company of the larger villages or whomever we might find. And there we could wait for Zafir.

I built my little camp, secured my things in the saddle, and laid down with my blanket pulled over my head to let the sand blow past, hushing by me in rhythmic crescendos of the living desert. Soon enough, fatigue overcame my anxieties and I was lulled safely into a deep sleep of vivid dreams.

WHITE-OUT

I was dreaming about running from a lion chasing me through a black stream of mud when suddenly I awoke to a blinding bright haze. Someone was shaking me fiercely.

"Wake up, Bassam, wake up, they're coming!"

"What? What do you say?" and immediately my eyes burned with the sting of blowing dust and sand. I slammed them shut again and pulled my mantle around my face. Looking with narrow slits, all I could see was boiling dust swallowing me up, swirling walls of light so thick and brilliant that no horizon or direction could be made. The wind roared in my ears and the eerie light that seemed to come from everywhere obscured everything with such intensity I could discern no directions at all.

"Get up, someone has followed, we must leave this place now!" the voice said. "Leave your things, the camp has emptied out but for you! *Now*!"

What? Gone?

I leapt from my sleep and almost fainted for standing too quickly. My head suddenly buzzed in a dizzy vertigo as I grabbed the blankets and mat in a bunch, holding my hem around my face.

The stinging sand rushed at me no matter what direction I faced. I could see nothing through the hazy swirl that was beyond my bakra and the lone figure in front of me with his beast. Covering over and tightening my headdress around my nose and mouth, I realized just then that in the blinding haze I had lost all sense of direction—there was not a thing to be seen beyond five paces in any direction.

I licked my dry lips under the protection of the mask and felt the moisture immediately sucked away by the cold blaze.

"Where is that goat fat," I wondered aloud as I mounted my ride.

Seeing the stranger on his camel stepping away into the white-out, I quickly ordered my bakra up and held my things in my lap. I slapped the riding stick to Bakra's shoulders, hurrying her toward the stranger. The man in front wasted no time waiting for me.

I shouted to be heard, "Where are we going?" But the wind smothered my words. "Hey! You! Where are we going?"

The man made a hurried motion to follow and turned forward to ride into the blowing blaze. I could see only that single rider ahead, a fading form in the stinging blast—all others were lost to view and lost to voice. I could hear nothing but the loud wailing of the blasting wind.

I chased after the stranger who galloped away a camel's length ahead of me, and tried to keep up. I was still awakening from my badly needed rest, and was feeling confused and disoriented. The confusion swirling in my head was no less chaotic than the blizzard of sand through which I charged.

For several long minutes we pressed ahead, pushing without pause or relief into the roaring blast of blinding white. So many questions piled up in my mind—more than I had answers.

Who are we running from, I wondered, and how did *they* find us in the night? Who was it who woke me? Am I following Sofian, did he go this way? Where are the others?

I looked down at my things bunched up on my lap and decided lest they fall to the ground I should stow them away. I managed to sloppily roll the blanket and sleeping mat into an uneven wad and reached around to stash them beneath a rope tied about the saddle. Looking forward again, my eyes widened in shock—the man in front of me had completely disappeared.

ب هبصه 85 محبوب

BLINDED BY DAY

I kicked the sides of my bakra and hurried her forward, calling aloud. "Hello? Hello?" but the roar of the winds simply carried my plea away into the emptiness of the blinding billows.

Stronger gusts rose and fell, pummeling sheets of sand into my face. My bakra bucked at the assault, but I dug in my heels and smacked her shoulder with the stick. "Not now, old girl," I shouted. "Hut, hut! We'll find shelter from this difficulty, but now is not the time to be stubborn."

She consented although the wind had chanced and began spitting its fury directly into our faces, blinding both me and camel. The rage worked the particles through the fabric of my headdress and into my nose and mouth, the creases of my ears, through my hair and down my neck. I could hardly breathe and held up my arm against the stinging onslaught hoping to see the ground with enough detail to discover what path lay before me.

I thought I saw the depressions of hoof prints in liquid-like sand but these were filled in with brown silt almost as quickly as I spotted them, then new depressions were just as quickly carved open.

"What trick is this?" I asked, trying to hide a fearful realization that the wind's devious ways might be leading me the wrong way.

Looking about through squinting eyes I could not discern from the light above me or to any side, and certainly not by any shadow, what direction I might be going. There remained no option other than to make my best guess at a straight line and follow it. I gripped the reins tighter and kicked my beast again, bolting her headfirst into the washed-out wall of gritty resistance.

After what felt like a good hour of relentless struggle against the terrific pounding, my bakra grunted and growled and slowed to a dead stop, standing straight and standing still. The sand and haze whipped all around us, tugging at her fur, her eyes mere slits.

I leaned down, squinting into her face.

"Are you done, old girl?"

I tried striking her on the shoulder, but she only turned her head and showed her teeth.

"This is not good, Bakra," I mumbled, and ordered her to kneel.

Leaping off, I pulled her reins in front and ordered her to her feet again. With a lighter load she consented to continue, but growled at me just the same. I pulled hard and stepped through the soft sands forward into the blinding bright.

It was hard. I couldn't even keep my eyes opened, and to gain any bearings whatsoever, I had to raise an arm to shield my face. Each time I thought to check my surroundings, I looked at my feet but the shifting sands blew into oblivion any shape or sense or depression.

I couldn't figure it out. Shouldn't a band of 400 men leave a trail, some kind of marking of traffic in the sands? Especially if we're all fleeing from whatever army or an unknown danger was after us? I thought about simply stopping and sheltering myself behind Bakra to let the storm pass by.

No, I decided. Not smart. If an enemy found us, if that enemy was so determined to follow my footsteps this far already, they wouldn't let the prey slip through their snares simply because of the inconvenience of a cold rainstorm or the darkness of night or *this*, a truly blinding sand storm that obliterated my every footstep. But perhaps, that too is a blessing, I thought.

I continued forward, recalling a similar escape many months earlier when I was also alone. But on that frightening night it was warm and dark, and the stars above guided my path directly and with amazing precision.

And then I remembered.

"Oh my, oh my—Bakra! Of course!" I scolded both myself and her aloud. "Oh Bassam, how could you be so stupid? *You should have reminded me, Bakra.*"

I ordered the camel to kneel and pulled her around with the reins so she could create a buffer between me and the sandy blast.

Huddling on the leeward side, I tried to hunch myself over to create as strong a windbreak as possible. And then, fishing around in the side pockets of my yak coat, I produced my small, folded heaven-board and the miniature south pointing ladle.

"This better work," I said to Bakra, "or you will be walking a lot longer than either of us can afford!"

I opened the heaven-board and laid it out flat on the ground, then rubbed the bowl of the ladle clean on my shirt and then set it on the board. In vain I opened my coat to block the wind, hovering over the device as best I could.

But there was no miracle help. The wind immediately tugged at its tail and refused to let the magic unfold, blowing it off its correct course and coating the board with a fine layer of powdery sand.

"This will not work, Bakra!" I shouted toward her ears.

The camel just blinked with condescending disinterest.

I decided I had to do it right, so I pulled down my sleeping blanket from the saddle bag. The wind caught it immediately and I had to fight its flapping corners long enough to tuck the short side a little way under the saddle.

Lying on my stomach, I crawled underneath and wrapped the two opposite corners beneath me and pulled it tight. This created a tight, enclosed canopy so I could try again. I blew the sand from the board and re-set the ladle.

Giving the device a little push with my free hand, the air settled long enough that the handle turned in its usual fashion. It came to rest pointing at least 20 isba to the right of the track that I had been following. I tested its accuracy twice more and got the same readings. "I've been going too far east," I said.

I estimated the general direction and poked my head out of the covering to get oriented and immediately got another face full of stinging sand. I coughed it from my throat and nostrils and wrapped my head again, spitting sand and blinking it out of my mouth and eyes.

With a good idea of what direction to go, I gathered up my supplies and squinted as best I could into the haze to estimate a more accurate direction south. I ordered Bakra to her feet and patted her on her neck.

She was still being a bad camel, allowing me to lead her, but that was all. I had to pull for the balance of the light that remained.

It was the most difficult work I had ever done. Pulling the reins against my beast, and leaning forward into the jaws of an enemy throwing half the desert into my way was almost too much for the both of us.

When the fall of dusk came, the strangest sense of vulnerability shivered up my spine. Though it was dark, the wind did not abate, nor the sand in my face. It was no use.

I wondered about ending my journey—lost as to where and how to camp myself—worried that at first light I might find myself waking up in the middle of discovery by my pursuers.

But the forward journey had to stop.

Slowing my pace to consider the ground, I took inventory of my situation. I had no idea where we were, only that we were heading south. There was no sign, no signal, no track or noise hinting to me that I was anywhere near anyone else.

For all I knew I was perhaps a day, maybe two, or maybe more away from where I was supposed to be. It was the first time I seriously worried that I could actually die in this lonely, deserted place. But there was a river ahead, a large river to guide me to safety. I had hope in that. I knew I had to keep myself calm and be deliberate, and not let panic get the best of me.

Deciding on a patch of sand beneath, I stopped and knelt my camel.

With the light swallowed up into inky black, the wind was kind enough to quiet herself at about the same time. But not completely—she was determined to keep that haze in the air and hide the stars and any hint of truth about my situation.

I felt about like a blind man, kneading through my things as I knelt in the dark, thinking by feel to be well in the wind shadow of my bakra's large bulk. I found my mat and blanket and covered up as best I could and let the sand blow over me.

Lying there I felt my stomach growl, making me think about food and water. I had not stopped to eat the entire day. Reaching to my bag again, I took the water skin, and then remembered some dried dates I had purchased a few days before. Digging around in the bag, I pulled out three. I thought about the risk of running out of food and decided not to eat very much, just in case.

Settling back to my sleeping mat, I pulled the blanket over my head, and sent my thoughts to the little girl whose offering of the dates I couldn't resist.

She was so kind, perhaps not any older than five or six years of age, and no doubt sent by her father to tempt from the men of Zafir a little of their gold or silver—an offering of compassion for the young one.

I smiled at the joy that shined in the little girl's sparkling eyes after I gave her an eighth of silver for her two fistfuls of dates. She took my coin, clutching it in hand, and raced back to her father's awning, shouting something glorious in a little girl's way. They were foreign words that no doubt expressed the success of her first sale, but her face and actions needed no translation.

The memory made me smile as I rested my eyes—the memory that I gave someone so young a wonderful experience as a merchant, something that warmed her heart, perhaps gave her courage, and might have changed her life forever. And with such happy thoughts crowding out the heavy worries and fears, I finally fell asleep. All around me the rhythmic whispers of the wind blew across the sands and gently tugged at the blanket that covered me.

NIGHT PHANTOMS

Morning woke me suddenly and I sat upright. The sand was still blowing and I had to cover my face again. The weather had not changed, I could hardly see more than three or four camels away in any direction, and certainly no horizon or sky.

I guessed from the brightness that it was early, maybe an hour or so after sunrise. I fought the usual demons of loneliness and fear, knowing that it will always take courage to face the elements. I was determined to press on. There had been too many pains on this trip already, I couldn't shrink now.

And that river—*it had to be close*, even if my measurements were off by a little or a lot. That river—one of the great rivers of the east—was somewhere to my south. I had to come to it soon.

I drank a little water for breakfast and chewed two more dates. I took another reading under my blanket and established a direction due south.

"Up you go, hut, hut!" I said to Bakra. "No time for lazy sleeping, we have work to do. A river awaits us, plenty of drink for you and maybe yak milk over honey and rice for me, we'll see. But *you* Bakra, you must earn your keep today, you stinky camel."

She obeyed and stood with a growl. We began the same plod that had hurried us all of yesterday.

The blasting torment grew more fierce as the morning wore on, but I kept the pace at a good fast walk despite the blinding obscurity. With relative confidence in the direction I had calculated, my thoughts drifted to random conversations with Ammar.

"Three important rules in the desert," Ammar said. "First, never get caught alone."

I bravely smiled to myself. "Oh Ammar, what would you say if you saw me now?" I never felt so alone—no companion but this camel, no direction except south, and no knowledge about what awaited us if we were to turn around. I was lost, I was alone, and I was breaking rule number one.

"The second rule is," Ammar said, "you must always carry water for twice the duration of your trek."

"Why twice?" I remembered asking.

"Twice because you will always have enough to go halfway and if you change your mind, you will have enough to go back." And then he and Fawzi laughed at me as if it was a big joke. What was the joke? I still didn't understand it.

The third rule was a serious matter that Ammar discussed at length.

"You must know about the dunes and how they can trap you," he said. "There are the old dunes of heavy sands, and the light sands that always move. I'll teach you to know the difference."

He explained that the unique properties of every desert lay in the sands that accumulate there. "Walk a beach and beneath your feet is a mixture of tiny pieces of coral and broken shells. Walk the Nafud and find a fine, powdery sand that is easily stirred. Walk the Gobi and find heavy sands, slow to move, full of pebbles, resistant to the breeze."

The heavy sands of the ancient deserts did not move much, he said—only in the strongest storms. And that's why they remain loath to encroach. But across their peaks a dusting of finer sands could always be on the move, flowing at the behest of whatever stirring tormented them. They could cover tracks, blur the path ahead, hide traps, fill drop-offs between dunes and make the quicksand.

"Quicksand in the desert?" I asked. It didn't make sense. "Are you talking of an oasis or hidden springs among the dunes?"

"No, it is much more dangerous than that," Ammar said. "In wet quicksand, you can stand or float. But in the desert? It won't hold you at all. The dust of fine sand can pile up in the fork of two branching dunes. The sand is not compacted, it is full of air between the grains, in pockets, in caverns below. The wind blows them into the great creases and fills them until a traveler is tricked into thinking there is no fork where one dune branches away from another. The traveler thinks the smoothness is a road between dunes, a broad plain, a good place to cross. But don't be fooled, Bassam. Stepping off the heavy sands into the finer sand will not hold you, especially if it is newly laid there, and you will sink into it like a rock in water. You won't stop until you come to the heavy sands again."

"And how deep can such traps be?" I asked.

"The old dunes can be as solid as stony ground," Ammar said. "But like islands in the sea, they're the caps of great sand mountains. To either side when they fork away, a canyon is formed that can be as deep as a man is tall, or a hundred times more. I once found a skeleton at the bottom of a dune that towered over me more than 200 cubits. And do you know why such bones stood intact, as if the man had simply stopped there to rest in the shade? It's because the lighter sands accumulated in a storm. He found them by accident, by stepping off the proven path. He slipped down the collapsing hole and disappeared in an instant. The sand closed in about him to hide the evidence. Just that fast."

I shuddered. The feeling of crushing suffocation was too horrible to imagine.

"No one knows how long it takes the sands to pull a man to the bottom, but it was fast enough when he first stepped in. And then later, months or years or hundreds of years, what man could say? When the winds moved the sands to another place, his bones were freed. That day I found him he was a desert mummy, standing half pressed into the base of the giant dune, his leathery face caught in mid-scream, and his arm stiff, reaching out for something to grab hold of—anything, a rope, a friend, his bakra. But in the end, all that he caught was futility. No one knows how many years he was buried there. And now, for those who happen upon him, they pass by in fear or reverence or in disgust. Such dead men and animals have been the seed for many legends and tall tales, some of them true, most of them not. You must respect the sandy deserts, Bassam. These dunes, they're never as forgiving as the wind. The wind will sooner leave her traps and tricks than take them back. But the man who doesn't watch his step will quickly discover that God did not make him to endure such a long stretch of time in the belly of a dune."

I had remembered the vivid image etched into my memory —an image of the poor lost soul and his last act in life cast forever in the grizzly form that now stands alone in some far away desert.

"Don't men put those bones to rest when they find them?" I asked.

"Oh no," Ammar had told me. "Like you, all merchants are traveling to a destination and haven't time or wherewithal to do it. And besides, the sands will come again and cover him over."

"How will I know to recognize the traps—these loose sands that stand so kindly among the real dunes?"

"Their caps, that's how," Ammar said. "The old dune ridges will always stand above those the wind moves about. The ridges are not easily moved. Follow the ridges through a desert and you will be safe. Stay away from the sloping flatlands, especially after a storm. Some of these are traps."

I had seen my fair share of desert storms, but I had never seen a white-out. Ammar was so talkative that day, sharing his experiences, his knowledge—almost emptying his brain of its hard earned memories as if he was off-loading a burden that he, at long last, could finally share.

"Those white-outs, they are the finer sands," he said. "They're light, more easily held in the air. They can be caught in updrafts for a long time and climb high to mask the sun, the stars, the moon, even a man's sense of direction. And that's how you become lost, Bassam. The white-out plays tricks. You can't see with the sand blowing in your face, and you can't see your path because the sand fills your footsteps as you walk. It comes at you from all sides. What you see for shadow or direction is wrong. In such storms it's better to stay in one place and wait for the winds to stop."

Ammar's answer had unwound into an odd and tense lecture, almost angry, making me wonder if my friend had been caught in such a white-out. Perhaps the blowing sand had once confused him, sent him wandering into a trap. I decided that the next time I met up with Ammar to ask him about his trips and the sands and their tricks—and why he spoke of it so.

I listened to my memories many times over to pass the hours as I leaned into the whiteness ahead of us. I made two more stops to check directions, climbing beneath my blanket each time to work the south pointer—and went sparingly with each of my water drinks.

Toward the day's end there was still no river. I wondered what I could be doing wrong to have missed it. The map I had seen was clear in my mind and I remembered seeing the river drawn distinctly, with large branching tributaries. It skirted around the northern edge of the Taklamakan desert going east where it turned south and cut the great desert in two. If the map or my memory was wrong, supplies would be precious for the next few days no matter what happened.

Inside my saddle bag were some morsels of dry breads and a few pieces of jerked goat meat, crumbs of hard cheese. I had one full skin of water, another half full. It will have to do.

And then, as before, the blinding haze gradually turned grey, signaling the setting of the sun and the approach of night.

I found myself having come to a flat spot and put Bakra down for the night. I was grateful for the calming winds of that evening, although there were no stars to be seen and only pitch blackness in every direction. When the last of the day's light extinguished, it was the darkest I had ever seen. Putting my hand directly in front of my face and even closer showed no contrast of shape or shadow.

"I might as well be blind," I said to Bakra, but she wasn't listening.

Spreading out my sleeping mat next to her, I pulled out my blanket as before to cover my head from the sand that continued to blow.

Then my imagination began to work.

My creativity was vivid enough, but on a night like this, it became my vice. Camped alone in the pitch with the haunting whine from the wind and the shush of the sand across my blanket sent my mind into a spiral of wicked tricks.

At first I was sure I heard crunching footsteps that stopped just cubits from my camp. I froze, wondering if I was discovered. Long tense moments crept by and then? Nothing more. Did they move on, did someone remain there waiting, or were those really footsteps?

A long while later I heard my name being called—far off, quietly behind the wind and the sand. Twice I heard it, distant and weak. I was tempted to call back, but stopped. *What if it was a trap*? Could that expose my place to some short knives? More moments passed—long and empty. And there was nothing more.

A while later I caught myself staring into black nothingness and thought I saw something move past me, something large and close, a great blackness that towered over me. It made me jump—but fighting my mind again, I chose to lay there as if asleep, willing the shape to move on. More long moments and no apparition appeared, no rescuing friends with torches, no empty calls for dinner—just the blackness and the wind and the moving sands.

I huddled close to my bakra. I scratched her shaggy course of fur and felt the throbbing of a big heart beating steady and calm. She was warm and the night was cold. I spoke to her calmly, assuring, wondering if the darkness was bothersome to her as well. And then, as an afterthought, I remembered Khan, and took one of Bakra's reins and tied an end about my ankle lest she wander in the night and leave me helpless and alone. I wrapped up in my blankets and pulled them tight.

I knew the night would lapse quickly if I could silence the sirens that tempted my quick imaginations. I turned to flooding my mind with deliberate thoughts of the scrolls, my friends, my home, my dear Rasha, their voices and laughter, and the promise of the refreshments at the great river I could hunt down at first light. With such thoughts I let my eyes close, my ears ignore, and soon enough, the badly needed sleep was upon me.

CLARITY

I lay snug in my blankets, wrapped in my yak coat, when the rising sun tried to awaken me—warming my cheek, enticing me gently from restful dreams. Bakra snorted and shook her head, tugging the rein tied about my ankle. I squinted at her through one eye.

Above me a canopy of deep blue gave hope for a good day with no storm or clouds, no more freezing rain or chase. I inhaled through my nostrils the cold morning air and its earthy perfumes, and sat up yawning and scratching my head. I tested the bad taste in my mouth and frowned. *At least no blowing storm*, I thought with relief.

Next to me, Bakra remained kneeling, blocking the cold breeze that made me shiver. I pulled my yak coat tighter and looked at her with blurry eyes still milky from the night's slumber.

"I see you slept well, old girl," I said, and suddenly stopped in mid-sentence. It was just then that I saw for the first time that *there*, there beyond her shaggy humped back, coming into slow focus and perception, a tall, looming far-distant rounded shape rising from the near horizon.

"What is this?" I said wondering. I hurried to stand, dropping my bedding to my feet.

"What is … Oh, NO," I gasped aloud. My eyes could not open wide enough.

From the very exact spot where I stood—spreading out in every direction—*everywhere,* an enormous sea of giant frozen waves of massive rolling sand dunes that crowded in tight around me—thousands of them, flowing peaks in layer after layer, ridge after ridge, rising then falling, curving high, falling low, sculpted summits with gentle slopes and steep slopes and rippled slopes, billowing away in stubborn resilience all the way to the horizons beyond. Mountains, hills, slopes and slides—of sand. I was surrounded, I was caught.

From the tops of the highest dunes, silky vaporous trains of wind-blown dust streamed with glistening freedom along waves of breeze, settling into crisscrossing canyons of shadow and mystery, rhythmically whispering a gentle, prolonged hiss, then an ending hush.

My heart sank—a cold, hard fist swelled in my chest as the scene changed from stunning surprise to shock, then denial and finally, panic. *Am I dreaming*?

I turned about in a slow circle to see for the first time the prison in which I stood, flooding my memory at once with everything I had heard—its very name warning *all away*, warning of death, warning of suffering—and warning to me.

Somehow, some way, some time in the dark or lost in the haze, rushing in the confusion of flight, I had managed to put myself into the worst possible way, the worst possible trap, the worst pit of depressing desolation on earth—I was locked in the timeless grip of the great *Taklamakan Desert.*

ب ﻫﺒﻌﻪ 88 محبوب

DECISIONS

I raised my hands in front of me as if to beg an answer from no one in particular. Maybe I expected the desert itself to reveal the mystery.

Where was my path through the darkness from the previous night? *Where* were the hoof marks of my bakra stirring about before sleep? *Where* were the trails of 400 men fleeing south from an unknown enemy? And where were the palms and the oasis and the squatters living at the banks of the *Thaum,* the river they promised me stands as a barrier between villages and the dunes of the Taklamakan?

There was nothing. All of it gone, or all of it never there. Nothing.

With broom-swept neatness the winds of the desert had erased the footstep disturbances from the night before—she had completed her eternal chore to banish the intruder, tidy up after the trespass, and make everything clean again.

I closed my eyes and tried to solve the puzzle. *What did I do wrong in the travel?*

Was I not following the path according to the maps and my south pointer? I tried to orient myself, pointing one arm east, the other south—*there* was the sun, *there* was south, did my south pointer betray me?

What possibly had I done to land myself in this place, the very place of death that every caravan since the first worked so hard to avoid?

"Old girl, we found no river and I think I know why," I told her. "We must have passed over it in the storm. You should have smelled it, my selfish friend. Where was your nose for water *last* night?" She remained kneeling, disinterested in the whole affair. She blinked her eyes and looked away.

"Since you're my only companion today, you will be my listener and hear me out, is it a bargain?" An ear flicked and she sighed.

"That is well, then," I said. "We are in a bad place, Bakra. We must have somehow … we must have come upon the river when it was running low. Remember that Sofian told us so? It must have gone underground for some distance, or maybe it didn't have enough strength this time of year to cast itself across so great a desert as this."

But could so large a river hide itself that completely? If so, how far back did I need to travel to find it again, if finding was possible? Or, were the maps wrong? Did the river lay yet a day's travel in front of me?

I tried to remember what day it was, and started counting back. It could be important for me to calculate my place on the map, if I had such a map.

"We were in the cold canyon walls the first night of our escape from the bandits, and then ... and then we spent two nights on the trail, or was it three? Bakra? Are you listening to me?"

She wasn't.

"How many day's travel have we since Kurla?" I asked. She flicked her tail once and looked away again. "All right, I take that as a vote for two days and two nights, I agree. And two more nights directly south when I practically had to carry you most of the way through the haze, that brings us to the start of the fifth day. That should put us at about 600 stadia into the desert, maybe more, if we advanced at our usual pace, and if our true direction was south."

Six hundred stadia, I sighed to myself. That's a long way into a place whose name warns men to stay away.

"Do you know what that means, girl?"

She twitched her other ear.

"That means we have another 1,500 stadia to travel if we continue south. What is that in Roman miles? If you want to trade with the Romans, my bakra, you must learn to speak in their terms. But never mind to you, I'll figure it myself. "

I calculated that by traveling at least 200 stadia a day there was a full week of desert in front of us. And *this* with barely enough water for four days? Could I last another three, maybe four with no water? We wouldn't make it—it could be death to think it.

I slipped on my sandals and walked from the camp to test the sands. They were heavy, grainy, and took my weight with no give. My bakra's foot spread nicely in such sand, as if she was born for that terrain.

To the distance my eye followed an imaginary path southward. It could not be a straight line. It wound about like a frustrated snake, left and right, up and down, across and repeat. But the slope of the dunes' ridges gave me hope that I couldn't be forced to cross between them often. To the north, if I were to return in that direction to find the river if that's where it hid, the path was just the same—twisting, turning dunes that seemed to grow shallow as they crowded up against the dark blue of the distant horizon.

"We must think this through, Bakra," I said. "We can return north to whatever fate was chasing us, or take this chance going south that we'll make it out one way or the other, and risk running out of food and water. What will it be? How long can you travel with no supply?"

The cold wind blew at my face, and I thought about the magnificent army of bandits that was so well organized. Could such a band still be searching for the stragglers? And finding none, would they dare chase their hopes into this great desert if there was no trail to follow, no sign or tease that men had come this far? If they had come searching the dunes, what chance could I have against one or two, or many more before finding the strength of my company?

With my supplies stowed I climbed onto the saddle and tapped Bakra's shoulder, "Hut hut old girl." She stood to firm footing and awaited direction from the riding stick. "Since we can't decide between us what direction to go, we will let good common sense dictate our decision."

And with that, I steered my beast toward the smooth, winding ridge of the nearest dune and headed toward the nightly spinning of the sacred constellations on a path pointed directly south.

NO MAN RETURNS

Plodding along at a good camel's pace, I nudged her to stay on the tops of dunes, taking the slope up and the ride down again—an eternal quest of balance and pace to keep astride the ridges.

Each crest was a path—clean, smooth, gently finished like an ever-changing work of art. The curving path led up and across, peaking for a pace before slowly dropping down a long downhill stretch.

Stepping along nature's contours, I steered my bakra to follow the most direct line south while maintaining good footing atop the firmer sands. My advance was almost imperceptible as one dune rose up to replace another, all of them looking identical—cousins, brothers, friends. I just shook my head at the immensity of it all and complained to my bakra, "Is there no end to this place?"

No sound nor flying thing interrupted the vast emptiness around our little patch of life that crawled through the Taklamakan except the sound of my breathing, Bakra's usual murmuring, and the soft breeze that tugged at the dunes with a soft moan and a hush.

As moments turned to minutes and then hours, my mind began racing with impatience and worry. I watched the blowing sands kicked up by Bakra's steps fall silently down smooth slopes, the precipice of perhaps a terrifying sandy slide to the bottom of these mountains should my bakra miss a place and stumble. I wearied of the fear and finally stopped working her so much, putting trust in her instincts for a secure path forward. I turned my mind to other things.

"There are many legends about this place," Ammar told me during that night by the fire at Zafir's ruins. "Some say the ghosts of men killed in the heat will rise when the wind blows and in great armies they go roaming, seeking vengeance for their failed opportunity. They go marching with an oath to slay the trespasser who dares walk where they could not."

My imagination was set afire by Ammar's tales and I wondered if any man had ever seen such a host. Was the woman I saw a drift of sand, a strange dream, or perhaps, one killed gone roaming?

"Only those who have become lost among the dunes," he said. "Only they have seen the host that rises up after them—when the winds blow, hunting them out to make them unwilling conscripts into their ranks."

Such ghost tales were as varied as the great desert itself. And who could doubt such tales, this being such a vast and mysterious detour for all who traveled in these lands.

Ammar explained that the length of the Taklamakan was measured a thousand times and each journey ended the same—seven full weeks to the day by light camel train from the rim of the great basin to the great river in the east—that same river I somehow missed. And were I to travel farther east, Ammar spoke of another desert that lay beyond, the gravel plains of the great Gobi.

The original plan was to drop south from the Xiongnu lands and lead the caravan between the two great deserts, following the banks of the Thaum River for survival. The river could drop us directly south. Eventually, the path was supposed to intersect with the southern caravan route from Chang'an. Turning east, it was a direct path to the great trade center itself.

I mapped it in my mind what might await me if we continued our trek south, cutting through the Taklamakan's width. Other rivers watered the southern rim of the desert and these supplied some villages as well. Perhaps we could stumble upon the old trade towns of Qarkilik ("Quark-ee-leak") and Miran ("Mirror-on"). And if I was measuring too far to the east in my calculations, maybe we could run into Lop Nor, that legendary lake that *wanders*. And if a mighty river was swallowed up in the sands in this winter cold, could finding a lake be any easier?

"Tell me about the lake, Ammar," I asked long ago. "Why do they say it wanders?"

"The two great rivers that travel around the Taklamakan flow into Lop Nor. They fill the lake each spring. But the strength of the rivers is never the same, at least not for a long time. It always changes. The lake will grow and shrink and find its lowest level in one place or its highest in another. Some men say it thus wanders the land."

"And does it wander?" I asked.

"That lake has stayed in the same place each time I've visited," Ammar said, "although it's in a great plain that could let it wander should conditions change."

"And just how far does one follow the river to find this lake?"

Ammar explained the lake is centered about halfway down the east edge of the Taklamakan, some twelve days by camel out of Kurla. A caravan leaving Kurla heads southeast for much of that journey.

"It is not a well known place because few men have traveled it," Ammar said. "The caravans do not drive for Lop Nor. Instead, they point themselves eastward and travel for Dunhaung where there is safety and rest and much business. We guess at the distance to Lop Nor by studying our maps, Bassam. As poor as our maps are of this entire region, that is the distance to Lop Nor—twelve days by camel."

I let the memory of Ammar's words take form, especially the cautionary end that "few men have traveled it." I knew we were headed into an unknown as well, no matter who had measured the distance.

"What do you think old girl?" I said to my camel. "The desert is twelve day's across at its greatest middle, it is twelve day's from Kurla to the lake, and we are toward the desert's eastern end. It tapers here, it is not as wide

Kashgar

Tumushuk

TAKL

Yarkand

DE

Hotan

Ker

Turpan
Yanqi
Kurla
AKAN
Loulan (A)
Lop Nor
Loulan (K)
Lake
Qarkilik
Charklik
RT
Qarqan
ya

as in the middle. At this end it shouldn't take as long to cross it going south. How many days to cross it here, what do you think?"

With Bakra otherwise preoccupied with the journey, I filled in the rest of the exchange and gave voice to both sides of the conversation.

"Why, Master Bassam, is it not clear that at this far end we have less distance to travel if we go directly south?"

"Oh my lazy Bakra, it is less travel only if we find the southern river or the villages there. Otherwise, we could wander everywhere not knowing if we were out of the desert or not."

"We must risk it, then, Master Bassam."

"Oh my ugly Bakra, you suggest a life and death decision! How could I know if that is wise or not? I've never been here. And Ammar's maps, I don't have them with me, but .... *What*?"

Suddenly, I remembered.

"The map on my arm? Very good, Bakra! You have earned your keep today. Now that you speak of it, I'll do just that. Tonight if there are stars I'll see if I can tell you where we are, at least one place on the map that might help. Will that make you happy, Bakra? Could that make you stop bothering me with so many questions?"

She turned her ears back.

"You're a poor listener, Bakra," I said.

I decided to ration my water carefully. On each of our two stops that day I took a full ration according to the counsels of those who often traveled the deserts. As for food, I could survive on less.

I counted out the sweet dates—eleven remaining. Four heavy bread crusts, and two small servings of jerked meat. I estimated there was enough food for maybe three days, water for four, and nothing for my bakra. I had already stretched the water supply, there was none to spare.

Trying to pass the long, lonely hours caught me staring at the mechanics of the amazing plodding beast beneath me. Her head glanced left to right as if something might change, but it never did. The look on her face was complete boredom. Two feet moved in unison, first left, then right. She sighed every dozen strides or so, probably wondering when the end might come. She was steady, ever moving, never seeming to tire. Bakra was a good and faithful friend.

When the sun started to sink in the west, I felt refreshed from the clean weather that accompanied us for so many hours. The wind continued to blow cold as if readying for a coming winter, but there was no cloudy sky or hint of blowing sand to bother us.

I steered for the top of a ridge to set camp. Finding a sheltered side of a dune, I knelt my camel and removed her burdens.

With nothing to burn, I thought briefly to look to some empty sheets of my writing papyrus, but decided I could go without. I fumbled around for a little nourishment as the sun's lingering light quickly gathered itself to the west.

"You old girl, you must do this last hard trip without my help," I said, scratching her head. And then her jaw moved as if chewing. "Hey wait a moment, what is this? What did you find in your mouth?"

I looked down and found my bakra was chewing! "Have you been stealing from my bag?"

I squatted down by her head and pulled back her lips and made a startling discovery. She had a cud! She hissed and turned at the annoyance, but not before I spied it there between her teeth, a green foul-smelling chew.

"So! You have been holding out on me like everyone else, Bakra! Where did you find this cud of yours?"

Giving the question a little more consideration, I decided I didn't want to know where that cud came from. Camels have their way, several ways in fact. It suddenly occurred to me that it wasn't worth considering any further—I might not like what I discovered.

The sky above was beautiful orange, deepening into a rich red that was swallowing up the remnants of that day's work. To the east the stars began to shine as the twilight faded. I spread the mat and sat wrapped in my yak coat. It didn't take long for the jewels above to remove their cloaks and show their beauty. I stretched back my neck and traced the beautiful lacy covering that forever marked a place among the stars. Rising on the horizon appeared the important stars, one after the other as the night descended in totality.

Hanging there in its usual place, the pole star shined steadily like a familiar old friend.

I listened in the darkness to the soft breeze that touched the sand here and there. With stars above I could at least detect some contrast against the desert and the horizon, but all before me was flat black and devoid of texture.

I pulled off my coat and rolled the sleeve on my left arm. Raising it to my cheek, I pointed to the horizon and sighted down my arm while sliding two fingers toward me. When they touched both the horizon and the pole star, I felt for the place on my arm where my fingers stopped.

"Oh Bakra!" I said, "Why don't you think of these things yourself? How am I supposed to see the dots on my arm with no lamp here by me?"

The camel didn't even turn.

I decided this was too important to risk with just my memory, so I fumbled around for my ink pot and a pen. Finding the exact spot once more, I drew a line on my arm. In the morning I would discover where I had found myself.

LINES AND MAPS

Before sunrise I was already seated cross-legged on my sleeping mat. My coat lay around my waist and my sleeve was rolled to the shoulder. In the pre-dawn cold I found the line from the night before, just below my shoulder muscle and just above the third dot.

"Let me remember," I said, recalling the names Ammar made me memorize. "The first dot was Leuke Kome, the second, Al Jawf, the third, An-Najaf," and kept counting and reciting until I remembered Kurla, Loutan, and the next ...

My camel looked at me, waiting.

"Don't look at me, Bakra," I said. "You should have been paying attention yourself."

She turned away, flattening her ears.

"Ah ha! I remember! It's Dunhaung," I said. "That's it, of course, Dunhaung, number 12."

With the riding stick I went to a smooth sweep of sand to draw a map of the desert region. I made a wide oval going left to right.

"You must pay attention to this map, Bakra. It will get you out of this place."

To the left of the oval, the west side, I poked with my stick. “This is Mouru, do you remember it? Do you remember Najeeb’s, and the best white fish ever? And a girl named Kalila? … well—that part, *never mind.* No, you couldn’t remember, you didn’t even come into town. Serves you right, Bakra.”

I traced the stick along the upper part of the oval, retracing the route the caravan had traveled. When I came across two-thirds of the way, I stabbed the sand.

“This is Kurla. Have you forgotten the long race through the sand and rain? No, you haven’t, I can see that you’re still angry. But you did well, old girl. That was a very long run, a very hard run. I’m proud of you.”

Next, I drew a line from Kurla straight down, cutting through the oval of my desert map from top to bottom.

“I should have copied those maps when Ammar wasn’t leaning over my shoulder,” I said. “This could be much easier.”

The placement of Dunhaung was outside of the oval, to the far right side—east of the desert.

“Dunhaung is an oasis city, the place we were supposed to visit after our stop in Turpan. Do you see it, Bakra? Pay attention, I won’t repeat this, any of it.”

She shut her eyes a moment, growled in her throat, and flicked her tail twice.

I thought hard. If Dunhaung was the middle point going south, and I was working my way directly south through the desert, then …. I scratched the stick from Dunhaung, all across to my left and intersected the other line down from Kurla. The lines met at my approximate location on the desert.

“It’s not halfway, but almost,” I said aloud. Halfway in or halfway out? Either way, the shortest trip was south, out of the desert, and not east to find Dunhaung.

I put on my yak coat and looked down at my map. *Almost a half.* There was still a long way to go, and with scant supplies. Did I choose wisely to go this way? Back north was a known danger, but could this be any better?

I stood and stretched my back. Looking across the desert toward the south I could see very tall, mountainous dunes standing beyond the horizon, above the rest. The elegant slopes curved upwards with a steepness that could be difficult—it meant some climbing sometime tomorrow, unless I could find a better route. Climbing those ridges—did I have enough energy and supplies to go beyond those great sand barriers for at least another seven days, or should I try to go around among the lesser dunes and take more time?

I knew in my heart I had reached the point of no return. I shouldn't pretend my way into a foolish fatal finale, nor should I abandon my courage. The decision was made already, and second guessing—I decided at once—was just a waste of time.

I climbed aboard Bakra and ordered her to the dunes. She complained, but snorted with more strength in her lungs, and that was good.

The action of a camel's foot on the sand is amazing. Each hoof closes as it is lifted forward and spreads out again, automatically, over the sand with the weight causing the action. This distributes the weight across more surface making her more stable on the loose sands. It was the perfect desert transportation.

I gave the neck of my bakra a gentle pat. "This is more like it," I said aloud. "Here we are in the middle of this vast and terrible desert, it's cold, we awake with frost each morning, nothing alive, not even in the sky, the sand is forever moving, and you my friend, you keep walking forward with no food but the storage in your hump. I can feel it is growing soft and tender, Bakra. If you become sore—I will walk."

My camel never showed expression except discontent. Yes, she had long eyelashes, and yes, she had a smooth gait, even in gallop, but if discontent was a root word for camel, it fit perfectly.

For most of the sixth day we loped along at a good pace, a caravan pace that I tried to push beyond 200 stadia by day's end. I estimated we passed the half-way point through the width of the great desert sometime today, leaving less than a thousand stadia, maybe five days travel left to go. However, I was down to three day's water.

"We will make our supplies last, Bakra," I told her. "You have your hump and I have my supplies. Perhaps we both can last longer if we are careful. And that morning frost, if we must, perhaps there is a way to capture it for water, we will see."

The dunes passed beneath us in hypnotic repetition, one after the other, climbing, descending, putting the same color sand behind us as that which yawned out before. Nothing grew or lived in the dunes, no birds or grasses, not even the flies that kept me company for so much of the trip. But the most frustrating of all was losing track of time. Losing time meant losing distance because all measurement depended on a day's travel. Ammar had warned me of such tricks.

"It comes to a man in many forms," Ammar said. "You have heard of the visions of water on distant sands that are never there, the awake dreams that people or animals are near but are not. These are the signs of a mind parched for water. You must know these signs and look for them or they will find you looking. I've seen it many times, rational men leaping off their camels and running into the sands tearing off their clothing, falling into the sand, writhing about until dead, or worse. You must not allow the desert to play that trick, my friend. And it will if you don't obey the three rules of the desert."

I thought back to the caution. I guessed that time and place could come in a few more days when my water ran out. Could I contain myself for the duration, even if it was three more days after?

"The time and direction also plays tricks," Ammar told me. "If you're following a path according to the sun and you don't stop to check your direction, you will wander from your straight line many times and add distance to your trek, and stop many days shy of your destination. Use the night to travel if you can, the stars will guide you directly while the moving sun will fool you. But the distance is measured in days. You should write them as you go, Bassam. If you begin to lose your way and your mind, a record of the days will save you if you know what you're doing."

Good idea, good advice, I thought. And with that, I reached around behind the saddle and drew out my writing kit. I dipped the pen and checking for the rhythmic rocking motion of Bakra's steady foot-fall, I wrote about the passage of time thus far, beginning with the retreat from Kurla until today. It was difficult to highlight any singular event because the days were beginning to blend into one—the night, the morning, the evening, the camps, the midday stops, the water breaks. The diminished focus bothered me.

What day is it, anyway?

ب هبعه 91 محبو ب

GHOST LIGHT

At the end of my fourth day, I circled about a place to settle down for the night.

I had discovered a secret of the dunes—that the highest dunes caught the highest winds and though safer, they were colder than those below. But, camping below, on the wrong side of the winds, could bind me half buried by blowing sand before morning. At least such places could let me rest warmer.

Finding a place suitable for stargazing and sheltered from the winds on the leeward side of a low dune, I knelt Bakra and removed her saddle for the night.

So, when did I last eat? I wondered.

I had the date that morning … or was that yesterday? I couldn't remember and the very doubt triggered a surge of sudden concern. Did not the dunes look the same and the days look the same? Each night at camp my stomach cramped for food but my thirst begged the loudest. I was tempted to take more of my water but decided I could wait just a little longer.

Kneeling down in the cold sand, I put out my things and tied the leather rein to my ankle again. I thought back to that terrible time of my kidnapping and remembered how Khan had tied his slave rope to my wrist and how I tricked him on the fourth night. Perhaps my bakra had a similar plan, and with that, I tightened the knot that much more.

The cold was settling in. I pulled the blankets to my chin and bunched another into a wad for a pillow. Lying on my side I watched the sliver of a moon setting in the west. In a few more days it should be higher in the sky to guide our journey farther after sundown. I needed to add more distance to the day, more stadia each time I climbed aboard Bakra. Perhaps the moon was the answer.

The moonlight on the Taklamakan was breathtaking. The silver light splashed over the land and painted the dunes gracefully with stark shades of bright grey and long, black shadows, and my eyes grew heavy just enjoying the scene. I stared into the emptiness, anxious at the slow pace I was forced to travel for lack of water. What I would give for just one clay jug, one discarded skin, even a helping of that nasty cistern water—the dry of my mouth was chapped and sticky.

And then, just then, something caught my attention. There to the north, what was it? I *thought* I saw something, something off in the darkness. *Is my mind starting the tricks so soon?*

Suddenly—there it was again—some kind of distant movement. It wasn't something near, was it sand blowing from the tall dunes, catching the last of the moonlight? It wasn't man or beast, it was ….

I threw off the blankets and stood up for a better look.

Far to the north I could see something ... flickering—bright and dim, shadows on the tops of large dunes, shadows some long distance away. *What is that*, I wondered aloud and looked hard to see if it was real or not.

And then it happened again, changing shadows and light. It couldn't be the moon—was it my imagination?

Finding the distant place among the many shapes of the dunes, I began to realize what it was—a faint glow, so faint I could hardly discern it except for its dancing on the top of a far-away slope. The glow moved around in light and shadow, like a breeze-bothered fire, shifting, hiding, flaring to life again, casting new shapes on the tops of black shadowed dunes.

Whispering to Bakra as if someone might hear, I lowered my voice. "I see something that doesn't belong, Bakra. I see the glow of something among the dunes over there in the blackness—it must be fire. I have to go see if someone is camping by us. Am I being tracked, or is this a traveler prepared with supplies to cross these sands? Maybe they'll have water for us, you watch the camp, I will go see."

I slipped the rein off my ankle and tied it to the saddle that rested on the ground.

"You stay here, Bakra. I'll be right back."

Slipping on my sandals, I mapped a route. I decided to count my steps across the seven switchback dunes that stood between here and there in case I had to return in the black of night. I hoped to hurry back before the moon set, and if I overshot the camp, that could be a fatal mistake.

Taking Suoud's sword and checking for my knife, I stepped cautiously away from Bakra, shushing her the whole time to keep still.

Alone atop the ridges of the dunes, I hurried along in the long shadows—running low, wondering if any eyes were already busy in my direction. I found sure footing and crossed the first three dunes easily enough, and then feeling winded, I stopped to catch my breath. The glow *had* to be a fire. It was brighter as I came nearer and I could plainly see its light flickering against the tops of the higher dunes that I saw from my camp.

Running then stopping, I felt the fatigue of too little food and water beginning to cramp my stomach and legs. I suddenly wondered if I could make it all the way back, even in the daylight.

Coming upon the seventh and last dune, I slowed with caution and approached its back, the dark side. Slipping off my sandals for better footing, I climbed quietly up the shadow of its mighty slope. It was exhausting work, especially with my heart pounding and my lungs heaving for breath.

Nearing the top, I knew caution was important so I fell to my hands and knees and slowed my climb.

It was clear that if this was an enemy, they could easily spill my blood and go looking for my camp. I had to be careful, and crept quietly. Reaching the top, I suddenly stopped and realized—*the wind!* Surely their beasts were camped with them. Was I upwind or down of them? They could certainly smell me out before any human could.

Wetting my finger I found the breeze blew toward me, softly.

The sand was cold and gave way stiffly on the backside of the dune, and stuck to my knees and palms.

Before peering over the top, I removed my headdress and carefully eased my head slowly upward, up into the cast of the warm light until the fire's yellow glow was on me at last.

There below, just an easy stone's throw down the slope in a little clearing between two dunes, a small cook-fire twitched in the breeze, casting moving shadows. Two men hunched about it, preparing their tea, and behind them six camels knelt, their loads rested on the ground beside them. I could see that they carried feed for the camels, water, large satchels, and even a bundle of sticks for fuel.

Is this the supply train that men carry for a trip through the Taklamakan, I wondered. *Or was this the haphazard gatherings of a hoped-for surplus to survive a hurried trek without much foresight or planning?*

From this height, I could not make out the faces of the men nor hear their words. But I spotted another dune around to the right that was closer and cast just as large a shadow.

Backing down into the darkness, I skirted around the camp and climbed my way again.

Stealing a quick glance to the west, I saw that the moon was touching the horizon and sinking fast—I had no more time.

Nearing the top of the dune, I suddenly heard their voices.

I froze, thinking they might have heard me. But no, they were in casual conversation.

Not just any conversation—they were speaking in my own tongue, using the correct accent. My heart quickened in anticipation that perhaps I had stumbled upon men from my own caravan, men I might recognize, old friends, maybe? Men sent on a search to find me?

"South, all the way," the one voice said. "I don't understand."

"They know the way, or travel as if they do," said the other.

"But to come this far? No, I don't believe it."

"Aye, but I expect another day or two. I sense we are nearly upon them."

"And if not? What then?"

"If not, we'll return, no harm done."

"Return? Can we be that sure?"

"The storms are coming, it won't matter."

"Even so …."

"Even so I don't intend on dying in this Godforsaken place."

"And you think they will?"

"Probably. We'll give it two more days."

"You should have ordered more men here."

"No, I told you, it's a waste. They're scattered, but we'll try it two more days. More coffee?"

I shrunk behind the ridge. *The trail*? Who knows of tracking trails in these wind-swept dunes? It is impossible. I had to see who these men were, these men who spoke of tracking in this desolation. It sounded like a rescue operation, perhaps they were sent by Sofian to find *me*, perhaps it is help at last!

Slowly peering over the top, the yellow light was on me again. I spied one man standing with his back to me, retrieving something from a saddle while the other had his head turned away, speaking something.

I held my breath and studied their robes, their sandals and coats, the saddles they leaned against. I smiled in hopeful anticipation—everything was definitely western.

These have to be friends, I thought, and was just starting to stand and call out to them when something inside told me to restrain, to hold fast and wait—to wait and first see their faces. At that instant the standing man turned to sit and reveal himself just as a passing gust blew the flickering flames to darkness, and then stopped just as quickly and the flames leapt to life casting bright yellow light on the faces of …?

My pounding heart suddenly froze and my jaw fell open in horrified disbelief. There at the fire sat Khan and Habib.

INTO THE DARK

I gasped and ducked out of sight, curling up as small as I could and slid down the back side of the dune—holding my breath, trying not to be heard. I tried to shrink into the shadows, making as little noise as I knew how.

Finding my footing at the base of the dune, I ran around its back toward the seven-dune route back to camp. I couldn't hurry fast enough, plying through the sand, spreading my toes till they hurt, back to the tops of the ridges and running as fast as I could back toward camp. I felt white panic burn across my face like dry fire and my eyes wide in pure terror as I ran through the darkness. I slipped over cold sands with abandon, hunting out the tops of the dunes

"How did this happen, *how did this happen*?" I gasped to myself. "How did those wretched butchers find me? Did they hear me?"

My lungs ached, my feet burned against the push, slipping again. I clutched my sandals with one hand and held the sword out of the way with the other, and kept up this way until the last dune was ahead of me.

The pieces suddenly fit together in my mind, the great conspiracy behind the ugliness that bewailed the caravan and my friends.

The ambush near Yanqi—yes, it was making sense. Only Al Murrah, only a traitor to his honor could have known what defenses Zafir would use in an escape. It must have been Habib and Khan who hurried ahead to work a plan that enlisted Xiongnu rebels into one mob of killers. How else does one defeat Zafir's 600 swords in the land of the Xiongnu? *With more Xiongnu.*

And what of the stranger who ushered me out of my sleep and into the white-out without the protection of Sofian? Did he lead me into a trap, or was he truly rounding up the last stragglers before the bandits could fall upon us?

It had to be, it must be the work of these traitors, I decided. That's why every move was so well anticipated, followed, preempted, and countered. Only Al Murrah. Only Al Murrah could track as they did. Only Al Murrah could follow an unidentified prize so far into the terrible Taklamakan. And if they knew who it was they had been tracking these six days, they wouldn't be sleeping this night. Or perhaps they did know, and it was only a matter of time before they caught up?

My panic kept me running past my ability.

Arriving back to my bakra in a breathless heap, I fell down at my things and fumbled around in the dark for the straps of the saddle. I threw it atop Bakra and swept up my belongings and bunched them under a rope and ordered her to stand.

Pulling Bakra by the reins, I took a sighting according to the stars and with the contrast of black peaks against the jeweled sky to guide me, I hurried into the moonless night.

LOOKOUT DUNE

I stepped briskly for an hour, pulling my bakra by her reins. It was especially difficult in the night, to feel my way along through the black as best I could. My only guide was sighting dark shadows of dunes against the stars, hoping to stay atop them according to plan.

Such a rush taxed me terribly and I slowed to conserve strength. My fatigue and weakness was taking a heavy toll, breathing hard, wondering if there was a better way. Should I stay the night somewhere and travel on Bakra by day? The knowledge of two swords behind me, with supplies to outlast my flight, and tracks in the sand to lead them to any hiding place, urged me to flee.

I pulled the reins hard, catching a misstep here, an almost tumble there. The black velvet sky rolled overhead, raising up from the eastern horizon the important stars that stared at me as if asking what urgency pushed me on this long walk. With no moon to light my way, I was forced to continue until strength gave out.

But what of the morrow? Should I stop to sleep to have energy enough to out-pace my trackers come first light? Or were they already upon the trail, having heard my escape and were at this moment on the heels of my chaotic retreat? It was fear that drove me on through the night.

When the night dissolved into shades of morning grey, I paused to secure my position. Behind me, nothing that I could see moved along my track. Ahead of me, large dunes were erupting sheets of loose grey that sifted from their tops in long rippling streamers. The wind chilled my damp clothing.

"It's time, old girl," I said, bringing her to a kneeling stop. I wrapped my headdress before climbing into the saddle.

Tapping her shoulder with my riding stick, I ordered her forward.

"You can make it old girl," I said. "We haven't the luxury to worry about this desert any longer. Our old enemy wants both our lives and he's here to steal treasures from Zafir. If I'm that treasure then we must hurry. I will not be taken again."

I reached behind the saddle for my water skin and squeezed out the final drops, an act of finality that strengthened my resolve to fight to the last.

The sun's hazy return sent long shadows rolling over the dunes on this seventh day out of Kurla. The warmth was energizing despite hunger and thirst. With no sign of trackers I mapped a path ahead through the lower dunes. I had to stay off the horizon lest I be seen. I had to keep the taller dunes between me and them, if at all possible.

Turning west around the highest of the dunes, I forged a snaking path until midday. It was the usual stopping time, but could I afford it or should I continue?

My bakra argued with me and then stopped in her tracks, breathing heavy.

"It's difficult, Bakra, it's difficult." And then I looked down at her, pulling the reins to turn her head. There was no more cud, but she started to foam around her mouth.

"You've carried me far on this journey, Bakra. It's been a good adventure together," and realizing I was at the end of my flight, at least for a while, I ordered her to kneel.

She did so painfully, groaning and sighing, and I stepped off to lead her on foot. "We can make good time if I hurry and you rest without me adding to your burden," I said.

My legs were almost too stiff to move. Knots froze their movement and I rubbed them to keep going.

I drove on for two hours until, finally, I had to stop.

My shoulders were burning from leaning forward with the reins, and my throat was parched for even just a little moisture. It made me cough.

Cracked and bleeding lips were worse in this cold and dry. I had to shake my head at the physical erosion that was tearing away at both of us. This place, I thought, if it didn't starve or thirst you to death, it could mummify you on your feet.

"Where is that goat fat?" I asked aloud, half expecting my camel to offer it up like a street beggar for my silvers. There was none of course, but still, where was it?

With our forward motion dragging ever slower, I knew we had to stop for a rest. What I wanted was a flat place below the ridges, somewhere in the shadows and out of sight.

Off the side of our path, where two massive dunes intersected, I saw a flat place where others dunes below us collided in silence. It was overlooked by a tall, rounded dune rising 50 cubits like a lookout place that could give me a perfect view to spy on those who might be following.

"There it is, old girl," I said. "That's the protection we need, a shelter from the sun and wind, a hiding place should others be looking."

Steep slopes of sand climbed above on three sides—perfect for a moment of rest. I walked her down the incline and knelt her in the shadows and removed her saddle. She stretched out her neck and rested her head on the sand, closing her eyes to mere slits.

"Aren't these dunes the test of us, Bakra?" I said briskly, rubbing the back of her neck, then rubbing my own.

"I don't know that we've touched any solid soil for a week. So much sand, we must be standing atop hundreds of cubits, a land of wind-blown sand, building mountains with no rock to hold them. How deep do you suppose this sand is piled? This must be God's storage place, his supply for when the seashore runs low, do you believe it?"

My bakra sighed deeply with a new rattling noise in her throat. I knelt next to her to soak in the quiet of this place. Her hump was limp, her ribs showed, and that shaggy excuse for fur hung like a moth-chewed blanket.

I looked her over, examining the beating she had taken on this long trek, and I couldn't hide my expression of pained regret. "When we're home again, life will be delicious for you, Bakra. Your family, your pasture, and no more treks. Your days will be healthy and full."

She just looked on, her eyes clouded and empty, a long stream of white saliva dripping from her jowls.

"Okay, then I'll tell you the great secret of our long journey because I think you have wondered this yourself—unless you have known it all along, have you Bakra?" I asked. "Then I'll tell you since you wouldn't help me figure this before, I'll tell you that in the Roman measure we have traveled 5,500 Roman miles since we left Rekeem. Can you believe it? Forty-thousand stadia! And you did this by yourself—except when I had to carry you like a baby through that sandstorm!"

She let out a long sigh and closed her eyes again.

Seeing this I worried I might have pushed us both too hard—no more travel for now, we had to rest.

"I will check to see if we are followed," I said. "This place I will name Lookout Dune, a mound of sand that took a hundred years to grow just so you could have shade, and I could watch for enemies. It's the marker for our little alcove."

She flicked her tail and grew quiet.

With Suoud's sword in hand, I climbed the side of Lookout Dune for a good view northward. For a long while I watched, thinking that if Khan and Habib had found our trail, they would have to follow it in full view for at least part of the way. Any other route could waste too much time, and how might anyone hide six camels in the middle of nowhere? Anything less than riding the ridges and they could be caught in the impossible maze of confusion and danger that twisted around the sandy canyons below.

The rolling shapes of the Taklamakan shimmered in the long shadows of the cold morning. Frosts melted from the sunlit side of the dunes, but in their shadows they hugged the sands in thin molted blankets of grey.

Is it time to attempt gathering such frosts for water, I wondered. Perhaps I could try—it was a puzzle I might be forced to solve.

The sands that sprayed from the dunes gave motion to the scenes north, the only movement that I could see across the vast stillness. If the traitors were looking for me from behind some large dune, they were hidden well because I could see nothing moving, nothing but the blowing sand.

Looking the other direction I plotted a less formidable path south with fewer climbs, following with my eye a route that could take us the rest of that day. I had to take another reading. With Bakra at the end of her ability to carry a load, I knew the remaining four days might be double that—and with no water.

Sliding down the dune, I slowed myself on the loose sand, pushing a gentle slide that rolled innocently to the bottom in a puff. Stepping around to the depression of my camp, I suddenly stopped in shocked surprise.

My camel was gone.

THE REINS

"Bakra?" I called hesitatingly, not sure if someone had crept behind me and stolen her.

Was this another trick? Her saddle was there, my sandals, everything as I left them, except my bakra. She had to be near. If she had wandered I should have seen her from my perch.

Hurrying the rest of the incline to my camp I quickly found the disturbed sand bearing the depressions of her prints and followed them directly toward a slight rise. I scurried up the slope, cautious but worried, quickly reaching its top—and then I heard her cry.

"Bakra!" I shouted. "Where are you?"

It was a desperate, wheezing cry.

I followed the noise around a tall mound that sloughed off from the higher dune, and there, between the tops of two dunes just below where a drift had piled between the ridges, there she was caught in a broad, sloping pool of sand, and struggling to gain her footing. Her kicking and thrashing about had caused her to sink into the loose sands.

My heart froze. The sand from above was flowing into the pit, as if filling a void beneath her, drawing her slowly down at the same time. She was already buried to her mid-section.

"Bakra! Hold still!"

Her eyes were white with panic, and she kept kicking her legs. Each movement made more sand flow in around her.

"Don't move! Don't move! Stay there Bakra, I'm coming!"

I quickly circled around directly opposite her, staying safe enough to avoid sliding into the same slippery trap. I found a solid bank of old sand upon which I could take a stand.

"I'm here, I'm here, just hold still."

She kicked more, working her legs to climb and her hind quarters sank beneath the surface, making her snort.

I drew out Suoud's sword and thrust it deeply into the compacted sand next to me. Hanging to it with one hand I reached down with the other, stretching as far as I could toward her. Scratching at the end of her reins, I caught one with my fingernail and took it into my hand. Pulling it to me, I took a firm grip.

"I've got you Bakra! I've got you! Don't worry."

She stared past me, blankly and wide eyed. Feeling the pull on her reins she started kicking.

"NO! Don't! Stop!" I said, forcing my voice to calm, and almost whispering. "Please, Bakra, please, just wait, just be still. Your kicking makes you sink, you must stop."

I wrapped the reins twice around my hand and braced with my legs to pull her toward me.

"Gently raise your front leg, that's all you need to do Bakra, just one foot, you can do it," I said. "Reach for the solid sand here, right here beneath my feet. I know you can find it, and you can climb out."

I stole a quick glance at the steep slope of the two dunes. They fell off at least a hundred cubits down—this was no shallow bog she struggled in.

More sand sloughed from the sides, and the weight began to compress her breathing. Only her neck and hump were showing. She still wore the blanket mother had laid on her before our trip, a gift to ease the load.

"You can do it old friend," I urged. "Just let me think of … how to get you … just, please, don't move." The strain on the reins was heavy, burning into my hand, strangling it with a pinching tightness. I didn't know how much longer I could hold.

She was sinking fast now, her hump slipped under and only her head showed—pulled awkwardly toward me by the reins.

"Steady now, use your neck, I'll pull you and you pull against me. Together we'll get you free."

She opened her mouth for breath but the sands were smothering, frightening her to kick again.

"I won't let you go, Bakra! I won't let you go!"

One last time her legs churned the mire, then without warning the sands beneath her collapsed and the mouth of a dark cavern opened up, swallowing in gulping torrents a great cascade of flowing sands. I pulled hard as Bakra kicked and clawed at the sides but those too gave way and she was swept helplessly into a crushing blackness that immediately slammed shut with a thunderous clap of smoke and dust. The reins wrenched violently, pulling me toward the same suffocation. I braced with my legs and groaned for strength but the leathers tore from my hand—one loop, then two, then slipped from my grip like a snake to its hole.

I looked at my empty hand in horror and screamed, thrusting into the loose slough, pushing hard, deep, frantically feeling for the reins, her head, anything. Then—*what is this?* My fingers touched something, I pulled it quickly.

My heart sank—It was her blanket.

I clutched it to me and fell backwards onto the slope—numb, horrified, blinded to the rivulets of sand that slipped from the sides to fill the void, to reset the empty stage, to reload this deadly trap she had triggered so innocently.

My eyes burned with panic, my body heaved with overspent fatigue. *No, No, NO!* I wailed, and reached out with empty hands, begging, petitioning, pleading to undo this horror—to act, to rescue, to *something.*

Where is my bakra? I could only stare in panting disbelief as an ugly new silence started screaming at me with such deafening ferocity that I could not block it from my ears, my mind, my worst imaginations. Could it be? Did I just see it, *here* at arm's length, a horrifying raw reality unfold with such brutality it could steal away my dear friend, my companion, my last link to life—and there was not a single thing I could do to redeem it?

"Bakra?" I whispered.

Silence.

I sat frozen to my place and felt the last slivers of hope dissolve into the leaden gloom of incomprehensible despair.

Bakra was gone.

SACRED PLACE

The setting winter sun spread warmth over the massive dunes of the endless desert wastelands of the unforgiving Taklamakan. Following its undeviating cycle of rising and sinking, the bright orb finished its day and dipped as usual toward the short end of the sky, nudging growing shadows to cast a gentle comfort across a crumpled form sobbing in the sands.

I laid there on the slope of the dune next to my sword, bawling like a young boy for his pet, my face buried in her blanket clutched tightly to me. *Oh my bakra, my bakra.*

I prayed a miracle, thinking it might, but no—this place, was no miracle, this deceptively innocent spread of taunting beauty in these shifting, evil sands was nothing from goodness.

This is no sculpted handiwork of God in these dunes, this is the devil's work—a great wickedness looking to snare the innocent, to destroy, to kill.

I felt that much a dead man—no camel, no water, no food, no friend, the loneliness had never felt so smothering. In my anger I decided I should be in the pit with Bakra—neck deep in the death grip of the Taklamakan—for what was left of me now? I was as buried as she—each breath a stark reminder that those, too, were now numbered.

"This evil work, this evil work is the work of Habib," I said aloud. "Habib and his murderous men!" I shouted in rage to no one there.

The tears were dry stains in the dust of my face, and my heart pounded with true pain—pain for Bakra, my only living link to home, my companion for such distances and difficulties, faithfully present in all things—the truest of friends.

I finally forced myself to my feet to climb from the depression of my struggle. With grunting strain I pulled my sword from its place and dragged it behind forlornly around the sandy crypt. I shuddered at the crushing death that now embraced Bakra. I followed the tracks she had made a short time before, temporary monuments to my long friendship that soon would be swept neat and invisible by the evening breeze.

Finding my way back to my little oasis, the shadows had crept across it as a shroud. I slumped to the ground and blinked through tears to pick aimlessly among my belongings.

Her saddle I had no use for, but her back packs, yes. Those I could carry.

I laid out my journal supplies, the sticks and fabric of my muyuan, some black rocks and black rice, a few collected spices, and my blankets. Some of these I might need, the others I could leave.

The sword of Suoud should stay at my side, also my knife. The sheath? Oh, yes, Suoud's sheath, back at the pit, I must not leave it. In my pockets I made sure I carried the south pointer and the small message of love from my Rasha. It had been some time since I had opened it. I should read it again.

I was on my hands and knees, directly over the bag, sorting the supplies, trying so hard to be thoughtful about what to take or to leave, wondering aloud at the futility of packing or not, when suddenly from above, a voice called out—"Well, well, if it isn't our old friend *Bassam*."

DUEL

My heart froze. Looking up, there came Habib and Khan sliding down the large dune toward me with grins of predator for cornered prey smeared across their faces. Khan was the first to step off the dune, kicking sand from his sandals. There was angry revenge furrowed in his eyes and he strode like the victor in a gladiator's fight directly toward me, placing hand to sword.

"I took a beating for you, you vomitus spit! And now the revenge that I swore!" and drew his sword from the sheath that hung to his front.

My entire soul ignited with rage as my executioner stood up before me, and I quickly looked about to see what escape might be near—then I saw Suoud's sword lying in the sand just within reach.

"Don't even think it," Khan warned with angry bravado.

I gritted my teeth and took a fast breath into my lungs. I was in no mind for a taunting braggart—not now, not any more. *If this be my end* I vowed from the deepest core of my eternal existence, *I will end it on* my *terms.*

With resolute abandon I reached for my sword just as Khan closed the distance.

The little man's angry face shouted as he raised his weapon high in the air to strike. I remained on my knees when I felt my sword's grip tighten in my grasp, then heaved its blade from the sand, swinging it quickly toward Khan in one continuous and smooth circular arc, twisting my body hard, adding my other hand to focus all my strength into the hit.

Khan saw the blade sweeping at him and quickly dropped his sword directly in front to block the blow. But it was too little and very much too late.

A thunderous clang of steel meeting steel sent Khan's sword breaking in two and my blade continuing its swipe, slicing deeply across his abdomen to empty him cleanly before he could even take another step. The kidnapper's knees buckled and with an open-mouth shock of surprise he slumped forward into a heap on the ground.

I ended the sweeping circle of my strike and scampered to my feet, shocked at the speed of what had just transpired.

Pulling my sword close for a quick glance, I saw neither smear nor chip had dulled its glinting edge. And there at my feet lay Khan, his body quivering, his face planted in the sand, his fingers still clutching the hilt of his broken sword, twitching spasmodically, and then going slack as the remainder of his life drained into the cold sands beneath him.

I stepped around the body to the sandy flat and faced Habib at ten paces. He stood in place, silent, but watching with a smirk on his face, his sword drawn, but not raised for an attack.

He shrugged as if Khan meant nothing. “So, you kill a little man and think you’re a great hero?” he said in a bluster of arrogance.

“It is no hero who takes another’s life,” I said, “but now the numbers are even and the fight fair. One killer lies dead, soon there will be two.”

“Your talk is mighty big for such a stupid boy,” Habib sputtered. “Now you can fight a real man and feel my cold steel reach into your spine, then I’ll throw your body into the pit—with your beast—where you can ride her there forever.” He raised his sword to an attack position and stepped toward me.

I took my stance and the two of us circled about in cautious maneuvering. Undoing the belt of my coat, I shrugged it off to free my movement.

Habib grinned behind his black shiny beard. “So much for your armor,” he said. “I could use a good coat. I’ll be thinking of you when I wear it to make my fire tonight.”

I ignored the idle threats and glanced at the steps in the sand as Habib feigned a thrust and backed off smiling to circle again. With swords in offensive posture, we taunted like circling desert cats.

“You should know before you die my young friend, that your captain is dead and his treasure is captured.”

“You lie,” I said.

“No, it’s true. Else why did I and my recently deceased friend have the time to come hunting for you?”

“You aren’t hunting for me,” I told him. “And you’re no match for Zafir, neither you nor your bandits. You’re here because your army was defeated and you ran because that’s what cowards do. You were compelled to come hiding in the only place you could. And then you followed me here.”

“We didn’t follow you Bassam. In truth we didn’t know you were here until you spied on us last night.”

“I saw your fire from across the desert. Al Murrah knows better than to call an enemy to his fireside like that. You broke your oath and the integrity has left you, Habib.”

Habib’s face spread wide in a condescending grin. “You worship heroes who don’t exist, boy, Al Murrah is a myth. The hired thugs Zafir uses are only there to intimidate for a good trade, that’s the fraud you believe in.”

“Not the Al Murrah I know. And you’re not one of them. You won a place of trust in Zafir’s heart but your greed has cost you everything. *Everything*, Habib.”

"Ha! I *have* everything, you ignorant boy," he smirked, "including your head."

"Without integrity, you have nothing," I said. "You are nothing—nothing to me, nothing to Zafir, and God will not prosper you for your evil."

"God? You invoke the name of your great savior in As-Samawah?"

My eyes widened at the mockery.

"Oh yes," Habib said." I heard about your knife and your great heroic killing of the monster Moluck. Did you know you are a hero to the people of As-Samawah? Oh yes, they discovered your murder in their alleyway, and when word spread, your name was praised on the lips of all. You're their hero, Bassam. *Bassam the Hero*."

"I defended my life against a man about to kill me, and when I learned he was the murderer of Suoud, I knew that one day I would meet the others to finish it, and I had to be ready."

"Be ready to meet the edge of my sword, boy. You're overdue."

I was watching the movement of Habib's footing through the prolonged moments of our verbal fencing. I saw Habib's feet placed in a defensive posture and then exchange smoothly to a power position, one foot behind the other, balance forward. Habib was good with the sword though no strike was tried. I could see that my chance would come when Habib brought his left foot down directly to the side of his right, presenting his full body front before turning to the protected stance.

"I see that you no longer carry the sheath of Al Murrah," I said. "What happened, Habib, are you ashamed of your fathers who died valiant heroes in the service?"

Habib's face clouded. "Don't you speak of my fathers, you ignorant wretch. You don't know the ways of men and the shortness of life? You're nothing but a bastard child—*kin of Zafir*."

"Your legacy of honor ended when you betrayed Zafir and conspired against Suoud."

"Oh, stop with this honor *excrement*. It is *an honor* to me that you die on my sword this day. That's a legacy I'll brag about to my grandchildren."

"Grandchildren? And what woman had the likes for you? Who is it that trusts your promises, Habib, or did you buy her also?"

The words triggered something in Habib's rage and he growled like an attacking dog and came at me with a mighty thrust of his sword. I twisted and the sword missed, singing through the air. Habib turned about to face me again.

"Tricks, boy? Tricks? I'll show you tricks." And he swung madly at my torso, catching my shirt and putting a long flesh wound diagonally across my chest that began to bleed. I slouched my shoulders against the burning and winced at the pain.

"That's the target, Bassam," Habib smiled. "Let me finish the X and that's where I'll put the tip of my sword."

It was not very deep but grew into a ragged red ribbon across my shirt. I backed away and met the next thrust with my sword. Steel clanged against steel.

Habib backed off and thrust again, in the same sweeping manner that felled Khan, but missed. Then bringing down his left foot to his right, he was just pulling his sword into position when I saw my opening. Habib's eyes suddenly widened to their whites, realizing instantly his mistake, but I was too fast. With raised elbow for power I stepped forward with my sword pointed directly at the right chest of Habib and thrust it with all my might, pushing it into him and all the way through.

The traitor's face broke open in anger and he let out a howl of rage, crumpling against my sword, dropping his own beside him.

I quickly pulled out in a downward motion and Habib slunk to his knees and fell backwards, locked in grimacing pain. His face quickly paled and he clutched feebly at the wound.

I stood over him putting my foot squarely on his chest. "Habib, you are a *dead* man," I panted, gasping for composure. The exertion drained energies from me that already waned with weakness. "This day I am three," I whispered, "—the victim, the judge and the executioner."

"You're the coward," Habib groaned hoarsely. "You hide behind ... another man's glory... You will never earn your own ... You will never gain the *honor* ... You are the weakling ... I spit on you."

I looked down at him, shaking my head. "You don't understand it, do you?" I said. "The honor was never yours, Habib. It has always been Zafir's. All you had to do was be worthy of his trust."

"You fool ... and your tricks ... you wretched fool ...." He coughed blood from his mouth and then weakly pulled his outstretched left arm across the sand toward his side. Bending it at his elbow he raised a trembling fist of defiance at me.

My eyes darted from Habib's to the man's quivering hand, suddenly seeing for the first time a small freckle or blemish—dark blue, almost black—neatly inked below the third knuckle, centered. *The blue ring! The eye of the Owl! The Order of the Crescent!*

My eyes widened in anger, and Habib let his arm fall back to the ground, grinning that he'd won some sort of small victory.

My jaw tightened. "*You.* You are a *son of Ka*!"

Habib smiled with red teeth, blinking his eyes slowly, and groaned from his gut in a weakened brag. "It was there ... all the time ... the sign, for anyone ... to see," he gasped. "You are ... such a stupid boy ... There are more ... of us ... hiding."

"No Habib. Today *there is one less.*"

Putting the tip of my sword to Habib's throat I pressed my foot heavy onto his chest making the man struggle for breath. I locked eyes and breathed carefully the words I had vowed to pronounce should God grant me this very opportunity.

"In the name of Suoud who you murdered for gain, in the name of Zafir whose good men died at your hand, in the name of my faithful friend who became another of your victims this very day, in the name of all those whose blood cries from the earth for vengeance because of you, I strike you down. May God find a place for what you might have been, Habib. You failed Him here—*don't fail Him there*."

Habib opened his mouth as if to utter a cursing but his words only gurgled in his mouth and his eyes widened in fear. I took a step back and raised my sword high over my head, gripping the hilt tightly, and with all of my strength I swept the blade downwards in a great arc. The sand beneath Habib's neck absorbed the cold steel as it shushed to a stop, finishing quickly that sword's most important and final work.

At that very moment, all across the vast continental paths of caravan trade and defense, the honorable sons of Al Murrah could amend their annals of history, their sacred scrolls of valiance, their pillars of monument erected to honor the legacy of greatness among their ranks, to exclude from their numbers, now and forever, the name and memory of a promising but traitorous warrior once proudly known as *Abu Habib al-Majid*.

BASSAM

ب هبعه 97 محبوب

THE PHOENIX

I stood over the body many long minutes—panting, weak, my heart still pounding, my head swimming, crowded thoughts still reeling from the shock of the few moments that suddenly swept past me with unbelievable dispatch.

I was unable to take my eyes off these enemies who had so tormented me, whose hands were bloodied by the innocence of an untold number whose bones lay scattered from Leuke Kome all the way to the desolation of the Taklamakan.

Habib's left arm lay lifeless at his side. I reached over with the tip of my sword and pushed back his third finger. There at the base, hidden in the folds of the flesh, I could see the tell-tale blue crescent. It was darkened with age, inked partway around, hidden to all except to those to whom he might present a palm stretched flat, and even then, slight enough to miss the attention of the casual observer—the sign of a murderous band of traitors.

How many such marks might be hidden beneath clothing, headdresses or even just a head of hair to signal betrayal within the corps of Zafir's trusted associates and all of Abdali-ud-din? I shook my head in disbelief. No doubt the old chief knew of the conspiracy but did not share it openly.

Confident that the traitors were indeed slain and this was no nightmare from which I might awaken, I stood back to decide my next action.

And then— all at once and quite by surprise— a gentle thought of comforting awareness seemed to blossom in my deepest feelings. I quietly realized something profound had just taken place. The sword of Suoud that had been wrested on that dark night of his murder back in Leuke Kome had found in a most unusual and miraculous manner its own path to vengeance. And justice. As if led to this time and place by forces unseen for reasons unresolved.

The thought made me smile—smile for the first time in many weeks. I looked into the deepening blue above me and let the entrancement linger a moment more. "For you, Suoud," I whispered.

I wiped the blade on the garment of Habib, then carried the weapon with me to the top of the Look-Out dune. I knew Habib's camels couldn't be far, and spotted them patiently kneeling on the pass, parked out of view from my camping place some 50 paces away where their growling could be hidden when Habib and Khan came for me.

From that vantage point I could see the path the camels followed to find me. Their footsteps were step for step on the exact path I recklessly pounded out with Bakra the night before—now trampled and smothered by my pursuers.

Habib knew how to track in the sands—he had learned the skills well, he was *Al Murrah*. But the winds did not do their job that morning and I scolded myself for forcing my bakra to make our hideaway so simple to discover.

I approached the camels with caution, displaying with my raised hand superiority and demand. They growled but remained kneeling as I rummaged for water among their supplies. Finding a skin, I brought it trembling to my lips for the first time in so many days, or was it weeks? I gulped it down to my great relief. Never before had anything tasted so sweet, so delicious.

I tore open my shirt and splashed a little water on my wound, wiping at the cut, and grimaced at the momentary sting. Finding an old garment, I pressed it against the long, clean slice and found no fresh blood. I was satisfied it could heal quickly.

Digging deeper into their supplies, I also discovered wood for fire, straw for cud, knives, ropes, three pouches of gold and silver coins, clothing, and to my great relief, not four but eight more skins of water—and some dried fruit and meat. I quickly chewed on some dates and cheese, feeling strength and encouragement gradually return for the work that remained.

Leading a camel to my camping place, I went about disposing of the dead. First, I tied the men's ankles with their own ropes to a saddle, and dragged them three hundred paces, well out of sight beyond my little camp, to the dropping slope of a steep dune.

"These will not desecrate the place of my bakra," I said, and then unceremoniously cut the bodies loose, letting them roll to the sandy gorge below. They piled up like so much discarded refuse, castoffs that these two had proven themselves to be.

"Here, let this be your payment for the trespass," I said to the distant dunes, tossing the rest of Habib into the heap with as much ceremony as a mere afterthought. "Payment in full," I said, letting go, finally, of the knot in my gut and at long last able to turn my back on the men for the very last time. As for their bodies, I knew the desert sands would do the rest—washing over with forgetfulness the unmarked grave of these who did so wickedly.

With two hours of light remaining, I decided the best use of my time was to pack up and get back on the path south. I still wasn't sure how much time was in front of me to escape this wretched place, even with the new hope these supplies and camels brought to me. *Has God once again answered someone's prayer in my behalf? My Rasha's? My own? Am I truly being watched over?* The answer was so clear that I needn't even ask the question, and I gave thanks from the depths of my heart as I hurried about my chore.

Taking a few minutes to create a memorial for my bakra, I turned my efforts to organizing the camels and supplies. Tying them together into my own little caravan, I stowed my gear on the lead camel and climbed onto the saddle. Seeing that everything had been left exactly as I wanted it, I ordered her to her feet.

"Hut hut hut!" and she dutifully rose, stirring the other five to their feet. Following the commands of my riding stick, I set out with my little train across the ridges of dunes that led south.

It took more than an hour of riding for my head to clear and my emotions to check. By then, my little group had wound across two dozen large sculpted dunes that reared their backs for many minutes each.

The day was finally spent and the lengthening shadows quietly called to the early stars, with the sun slowly sinking in the horizon.

At that very moment, I pulled the camels to a stop and stretched back my neck to watch the sky erupt in beautiful orange and yellows, brilliant in the sun's halo, sweeping upwards in ever changing hues of shimmering gold streamers that ignited the long slivers of clouds stretching across the heavens above. I smiled at the scene, a spectacular display that must have been held back just for this very time. And then I felt the usual evening breeze stirring—just as it had every night during my travails through the desert.

I stopped the train and turned in my saddle to peer northward. Searching the horizon, I focused on the distant place I had just left—and there I watched and waited.

The orange sky above slowly dissolved into warming reds, and the desert shadows grew longer across the expanse, changing their elongated shapes according to the slender curves of the dunes that made them.

Watching the distant scene a few moments more, I saw exactly what I wanted, and a broad smile spread across my face. I pondered quietly at the display I had prepared that was now making itself visible for any traveler to see. For several minutes more I looked and nodded in satisfaction.

I mouthed a silent farewell to my friend, my bakra, and turned again to ride a little longer, leaving the anguish of my travail behind me forever.

"Day 338—Dear Rasha, At some future day, if a man stumbles upon the sacred ground of my Bakra, he might be puzzled by what lay there. First he will discover at the place where two dunes butt together, a broken sword of ancient design pushed into the heavy sands, and a brown weathered twine tied to its hilt and stretching away. If the stranger is patient for the evening breeze that comes blowing from the east just as the sun sets, he will see the twine perform magic. He will think it is coming to life. Hanging on the far side of Lookout Dune, out of his sight, a beautiful red silken bird rests on the steep slope of the sand. When the evening breeze begins to blow, the bird will take wing. And by itself it will be lifted in the arms of the gentle wind and rise. It will climb into the sky like a phoenix, tethered to the earth by the twine, marking a place of tears. It will hang above, not fleeing or hiding, but fluttering in wonder and glory as the sky above it fades from pink to orange to dusk. And when the last light of the sun disappears and the wind dies, the bird will gently float back to the dune, disappearing from view as before, to rest for a season, until it rises again.—Bassam"

End of Book 1

The Saga continues in Book 2 "Zafir and the Seventh Scroll"

Watching the distant place a few moments more, I saw the evening breeze lift the silken bird into the sky like a phoenix, tethered to the earth by the twine, marking a place of tears. I whispered a silent farewell to my friend and turned away to ride a little longer.

ABOUT THE AUTHOR

As a young child Paul B. Skousen grew up mesmerized by a faded Asian carpet that hung high in the main hallway of his family's home. It depicted desert nomads seated on a rug spread over sand, camped between palm trees, their camels pastured nearby. A couple of hunting dogs stood anxious, awaiting their meal, and in the background, rose the rolling desert sea of nondescript dunes, forever undulating toward the horizon, frozen in time. It was an era and destination he longed to see for himself—and over the years that followed, he did.

Skousen enjoys visiting the Middle East for archeology digs or just renewing friendships. He is a journalist by trade, finished graduate school at Georgetown University, worked as an analyst at the CIA, and was assigned to the Situation Room as an intelligence officer in the White House. He is a professor of communications at a local university and college. He's a married father of ten, grandfather to 32 at last count, and is the author of the three-volume Bassam series and several non-fiction books on politics and history.

www.ingramcontent.com/pod-product-compliance
Lightning Source LLC
Chambersburg PA
CBHW050734030726
47505CB00002B/261

9781630728991